LUNA KAYNE
STEP DARKLY

*To those who found me
on the Radish Fiction app.*

*Thank you for reading along
as I wrote this story.*

CHAPTER 1
JOSHUA

I remember the first day I saw her like it was yesterday.

Little Emilia Connor.

She had medium-length dirty-blonde hair tied into two high pigtails, a Band-Aid covering a skinned knee, and glasses. She was wearing a light pink sundress.

She stood in the first row of her third grade class as they sang a song for our school's spring assembly.

I had just transferred to her school because my mother was secretly dating her boss—who happened to be Emilia's father—and it was getting serious. We moved so they could be closer together. I was at the end of eighth grade, and I'd left my friends and a decent life behind so my mother could follow her dream of living the high life.

At thirteen, I was old enough to have been told about their plans to move in together, but my mother and Emilia's father considered her too young to know what was happening until it was permanent. There were many times I envied her ignorance.

Sitting with my new class and watching hers sing their little hearts out, I heard her voice above all of them.

She beamed her bright smile at anyone who would look at her as she animatedly hit all of the notes and stupidly grinned into the audience without a care in the world.

I hated her instantly.

Things have changed a lot in those fifteen years, but what hasn't changed is our disdain for each other and our rivalry.

I always felt as though I were never enough around her. I was the kid from the slums who didn't fit in. I knew the value of working hard. My old man died at forty-five because of an aneurysm. He worked too hard for other people and never hard enough on himself.

I never asked to be pulled out of that life, and being near Emilia always made me feel like I didn't belong in this one.

There was something about her I never saw in any of the other girls. Her hair was always in place, and she wore the simplest yet prettiest dresses. If you didn't come from these parts, you would never have been able to tell from looking at her that her father was one of the most successful businessmen in the city.

As much as she got under my skin, once we matured, her laugh always triggered something inside of me. It became difficult to be close to her with so many conflicting feelings waging war with each other.

Everything about her life was perfect.

Everything but me.

I know she tried to be nice, but it was an act, I felt it in my bones.

I was never enough.

Then, in my graduating year, her gloves came off. Playing a caring daughter and a kind human being must have been too difficult for her, because she just stopped trying.

By then, my mother had already married and divorced her father, but Emilia's dad never stopped showing interest in my life.

But she did.

She stopped speaking to me altogether during my senior year. Even though I moved out with my mom during the divorce, Adam still had me over for the occasional dinner, and Emilia would breeze into the room, acknowledge Adam with her smiles and kisses, and leave just as quickly.

I became a ghost in her presence.

Emilia's dad offered a few of the guys from my graduating class entry-level positions at Connor Realty, and most of us jumped at the chance since no one else was interested in hiring kids right out of high school.

Then Adam began to mentor me, causing Emilia to distance herself from her own father.

When she graduated, she took a nice little trust fund and went to college as far away as she could. She's been home for one holiday in the last five.

And now she's on her way here.

Adam didn't deserve a daughter like Emilia.

Thumbing my fingers across Adam's last will, a charge builds inside of me, and a smile creeps across my face. My little Emilia tried so hard to run away from her own life, but that's the thing about destiny: eventually, all roads will lead you back to the path you're meant for. And I've been waiting for her to stumble back onto hers for a long time now.

As I sit quietly and wait for her to arrive, I realize my first instincts all of those years ago were right.

I hate her.

I remember riding this same train into work with my dad for Take Your Kid to Work Day. That must have been over fifteen years ago. It's like a whole lifetime has passed since then.

Nothing looks the same now. Everything has changed. It's darker, and, although it's raining, that has nothing to do with the Chicago weather.

The happy little girl who made lunch beside her dad in the morning and sat on his lap on the train, looking out at the lively city as we rushed through it, is gone. I see everything differently—or maybe it's more clearly. I guess that's what happens when we grow up.

Everything looks gray now. It's almost as if the rain is washing away the vibrancy and exposing this city for what it really is. Or it could be because I hate this place now.

When I left for school five years ago, I vowed never to return.

And look at me, returning.

And on top of that, I need to face my demons. One in

particular. In about ten minutes, I'll be in a room with the one person I never wanted to see again.

Joshua Darkly, my dad's protégé and, once, a long time ago, my stepbrother. I thank everything that ended quickly.

Dad's second wife wasn't a kind person when my dad was absent, barking orders at staff and putting me down. Every time I tried to talk to my father about, I was met with the same speech about giving our new family a chance and learning to be a part of a larger team. It was never about me not accepting them, but he wouldn't listen because she played the respectable adult and loving wife so well. That woman should have been an actress.

Then, within one year, the cheating started. With one of dad's business buddies, a real slimy guy.

I walked in on them one night, and she tried to explain it away. Then she backpedaled and told me it was a one-time thing and blamed my father for working so hard. She was always the victim, even when she'd been caught holding the metaphorical knife.

When I refused to listen to her sad excuses, she dropped all pretense and threatened me. She said she could destroy Dad's real estate empire and take all of his money if she wanted to. I didn't know any better at the time, so I stayed quiet.

When Dad finally caught wind of her affair, she took him to the cleaners anyway. His business suffered a huge setback, and he had to lay off a lot of his employees just to stay afloat and start rebuilding.

She was finally gone, and that was a silver lining, but I couldn't get rid of Joshua. My dad had a soft spot for him. He hired him as an intern right out of high school, and he slowly weaseled his way in and up the ladder to eventually work directly under my dad.

But that changes today.

Looking out the window once more, I remember the smell of my dad's cologne. It was never overpowering; I only caught it in fleeting moments, and now I'll never catch it again.

The news of his heart attack crushed me; dead at fifty-three. I always thought we had more time. I was always going to make amends and make up for everything.

There was supposed to be more time.

Now, all of my father's accounts have been frozen. I should have opened my own account when I got my first job, then my second, but I just never had time. Between work and school and trying to go out with friends, I never stopped moving.

Now I'm paying for it. Actually, I'm not. My funds have all been frozen. *I'm not paying for anything.* I sourly huff to myself at the ridiculous thought.

I've been self-sufficient for years. Dad set up a little trust fund for me to help me out, but I barely touched it after my second year of college. For once, I wanted to do something for myself. I didn't want to be owned by anyone. So I picked up a job at the university library, then another one at a club just off campus. My grades are a little lower than I'd like, but I'm not going to fail.

However, once the banks are notified of a death, everything gets frozen, even my own money I put into the account. I learned that the hard way.

It doesn't matter now. Once the will is sorted, I'll take control of Dad's real estate company. I'm confident I can convince the board to hire a new lead manager to carry on the company the way my father would have wanted.

And I'll get everything started right after I fire Mr. Darkly.

He will be the only casualty in this.

I've wanted to do this for years.

He's been as horrible as his junkie mother. He's no

different, and Dad was too good of a human being to notice that Joshua is just as much of a leech as she was.

I fell for all of it once. Never again. I tried to be a good stepsister. I tried to include him when I found out he was joining our family, but he did everything he could to ignore me.

Every good deed was met with disappointment. Then he turned his back on me in his senior year of high school, when I needed him the most, and I was done.

He would never look out for me like I'd always imagined a big brother would. He had his heart set on hating me.

Every chance he could, he pushed his way into my dad's business. I had planned to go to school here and work my way up to learn all about the business my father built. But every time I was around, Joshua made everything difficult.

His snide remarks, his speaking down to me. And it didn't help that Dad looked at it like a sibling rivalry.

Joshua was not my sibling.

Whenever he was around, I could do nothing right, and he could do nothing wrong.

In my senior year, I applied to the farthest university I could find, and as soon as I graduated, I was gone. I came home during my first year to visit for the holidays, excited to see my father and spend some time alone together. To my own surprise, Joshua had been invited into our house to celebrate like he was still family.

He was never my family.

After that disaster, I made excuses and never visited during Christmas again. Year after year, I spent the holidays alone, trying to build up the strength to return, but I was never strong enough.

And now I regret everything I missed out on.

All because of Joshua Darkly.

I can't wait to fire him today.

"How many minutes late is she now?" My impatience is boiling.

I've always been able to maintain my composure, but there's something about Emilia that makes me want to snap. She hasn't stepped one foot into the room yet, and already I feel the cracks threatening to break.

"T-ten minutes, s-sir," my newest assistant stammers, and I roll my eyes. I need more backbone in here. These fresh-out-of-school kids haven't had enough life experience to be working in such a high-stress job.

I know the reputation I've built for myself around here: I demand everyone's best. For some, it is too much to handle. Such is the case for the newest member of my administration team here. I'll have to talk to my secretary about finding her something lower down. I can't have her getting all emotional in some of our more difficult meetings.

Just as I'm about to apologize to the lawyers for the late start, my secretary pops her head in. "Just heard from security. She's checked in and is on her way up."

At this information, the men in the room shift in their seats, and my stomach tenses. The anxious feeling settling into my gut is new for me. I embrace control, and I've always been able to restrain my emotions—except when she is present. What is it that decimates my self-discipline around her?

Her.

Emilia Connor, my old stepsister. How she is Adam's daughter, I will never know.

Adam was always hardworking and fair, but not her.

Emilia has done nothing but live off of her daddy's money. The last I heard, her grades are dropping, and she's spending most of her nights at a club with friends, partying it up on Adam's hard-earned money.

She's always hated my mother and me. When the divorce was finalized, my mother told me she barely got a dime because of Emilia, who went running to her dad with lies about infidelities. I've been sending my mother money to help her out now that she's on her own. It doesn't matter; I can more than afford to support her now.

And Emilia didn't stop there. She went out of her way to punish Adam, skipping holidays and always providing the weakest excuses.

I've never understood how easily she took her privilege for granted. I never fit in with the rich kids, even when I became one myself. I found my friends among the boys whose parents worked for my stepdad.

After the divorce, Emilia's true colors came out. Her disdain for me cut into me every time I saw her. I didn't deserve it.

I never asked to be added to her family, and I never asked to be removed from it.

I worked hard to get good grades through school, and I even managed to pick up a scholarship to a local college. As I studied, I worked at Connor Realty and learned about everything from the mailroom to where I'm sitting now: in my own office, one step under Adam.

Adam was my mentor. Even after the divorce, he still took me under his wing and helped me learn everything I needed to know. He offered the same to Emilia, but she shunned him.

Instead, she punished him by moving to the opposite side of the country. She was all too happy to take his money, and she gave nothing back to him.

Her whole life, she's been nothing but a spoiled brat. Adam was too kind to her, and it is going to stop now.

Now she's stepping into a world I control.

She doesn't realize it yet, but when she left for college, she also left unfinished business with me behind, and I've waited patiently to see her again.

As my office door slowly opens a second time, a surge of satisfaction builds in my chest.

She's never treated me as family, and that is just fine by me. She's been running up a tab with me since that school assembly, and it's time to pay up.

Now I know something she doesn't, and I can't wait to put her where she belongs.

CHAPTER 4
EMILIA

"**G**ET OUT OF HIS CHAIR!" My words burst out before I can control myself, and I take brief satisfaction in watching Joshua's face fall as everyone around my father's desk jolts in their seats.

No one speaks to Joshua Darkly like this, and the look on his face confirms it.

How could I ever expect he would give my father the respect he deserves? He hasn't even been buried yet, and Joshua is already sitting at his desk, in his chair.

"Ms. Connor. So good of you to join us—fifteen minutes late, as usual." The men around the desk stand as Joshua tries to keep his voice steady, but a quick glance at his clenched fists tells me I've already begun to provoke him.

Good. I'm just getting started.

"What are you doing in his chair?" I control my anger and demand again.

"I'll take it by your tone, Ms. Connor, you did not see the name on the office door when you walked in. This is my office now. We expanded into the floor above us, and Adam took a bigger office upstairs. He gave me his old space so I could be closer to the teams I manage. You would know this if you had kept in touch with your father." As his last words come out, I feel sick to my stomach and drop my eyes to the ground.

I spoke with my father every couple of weeks on the phone, but I always asked that he not talk about work or talk about me with Joshua. I knew who my dad was dating. We talked about his brother and sisters and about my cousins. I kept conversations about me light and vague. I talked about what I was learning. I told him I had a job at the library, but I didn't tell him I was working at the bar. I didn't want him to worry about me. We just didn't talk about work or anything involving Joshua.

But this comment is a new low, even for him, and as I look back up I see the realization on his face. He knows he went too far.

Before he can save face and once again look like the calm, reasonable person he has always tried to project, I cut him off. "I see you're the same as always. Let's get this over with. Gentlemen, which one of you reads the will?"

My patience is wearing thin. There is nothing left here for me. I want to be done with this and on a plane home by the end of the week so I can process everything and grieve in peace.

"That would be me, Ms. Connor. I'm Mr. Mathers. I'm so sorry for your loss. Your father was a great man." I reach out, shake his hand, and nod my head in thanks, then I move to sit at a table off to the side.

Folding my jacket across my lap, I look up to see a meek assistant coming my way. This seems like Joshua's type: agreeable, quiet, and feeble.

"Can I get you something to drink?" Her voice is barely above a whisper. On closer inspection, the poor creature looks like she wants to be in this room less than I do, and I offer her a smile.

"Just a glass of water. Thank you." The men look at me, and I drop my expression into indifference and nod for them to continue.

Mr. Mathers starts with some kind words about my dad, and the other men in the room all nod knowingly. He was a great guy, and judging by the smiles of the men, they were all his friends—all except for one.

When he moves into the legal jargon, I struggle to listen. At times, I fight to keep my tears down. I sat at this table as a child, coloring while my father worked, and I almost expect him to walk through the door. My memories collide with Mr. Mathers's words, and I snap back to the conversation as he reads one particular section of the will, and Joshua's eyes shoot in my direction.

"What?" I instantly feel sick. "What does that mean?"

As I ask the question, Joshua doesn't move. He doesn't offer an answer. Instead, he sits still and waits for his attorney to explain it to me. As he stares me down, my heart beats hard into my throat.

"It means that Joshua Darkly is the sole owner of Connor Realty for the period of one year. Once you have successfully completed a mentorship program under him, you may take over half of the company as a partner. During this—probationary—time, you will be granted an allowance, which will be managed by Mr. Darkly." Mr. Mathers lets his words linger and waits, a little paler than before, for my response.

There is silence as I process the words of my dad's will. As that silence continues, I notice the men becoming a little less confident—all except for one.

Joshua hasn't moved. The air between us is becoming

heavier by the second. He knew this was in the will. He probably suggested it.

"This is ridiculous. I'm in school. I can't be mentored here —with him." I can't even look at Joshua now. I just jab my finger in his direction as I continue to talk to the lawyer, and he shifts his stare between me and Joshua, hoping he'll back him up.

And he does.

"On the contrary, Ms. Connor. You can, and you will if you wish to see any part of your father's business in your inexperienced little hands." Joshua's condescending tone carves into my brain, and my hands shake uncontrollably. I clasp them tight under my jacket as he continues. "Besides, I've taken the liberty to contact your school. Your grades will be transferred to the university here. They have all of the same classes you were enrolled in. It makes one wonder why you went all the way across the country to go to school."

My body seizes at his suggestion, then I jump up to speak.

"You can't do this. This is my dad's business. You can't control my life. I'm not a child. Let's just settle the business then. He buys me out, and no one will ever hear from me again. He can't control me." Tears threaten to flow down my face, but I breathe my panic away.

"I'm sorry, Ms. Connor," the attorney cuts in. "Your father's will stipulates that nothing can be done with the company for the period of one year, until you finish your mentorship and Mr. Darkly signs off on completion."

"HIM? What if I don't agree to it?" There has to be something in here that will set me free from this nightmare sitting at my father's old desk.

"You are well within your rights to forfeit your part of his estate, but this is ironclad. Relinquishing this requirement will mean giving up everything, including your school tuition and any monies in your trust fund. When the year is over, if you have not completed what your father asked, everything will be turned over to Mr. Darkly." Mr. Mathers drops the will onto the desk, then looks at me directly. "Emilia, you meant the world to Adam. I trust this was written with your best interest at heart. He has faith, as do we all, that this is merely a small hurdle for you."

All eyes are on me as I glance around to each person. My fate has been handed over to the man who took my dad away from me. I won't be returning home, to my school, to my friends.

I'm to remain here, in the hell I tried so hard to leave, and holding the keys to my cage is the devil himself.

CHAPTER 5
JOSHUA

"**G**entlemen, thank you. I'd like to speak to Ms. Connor alone to discuss a few things." I stand while buttoning my jacket and reach across the table to shake each hand with a nod.

The reading went as well as I had hoped, but for some reason I don't feel as much satisfaction as I thought I would.

As the men file out of the room, I catch my soon-to-be old assistant's attention.

"Have my secretary reschedule the rest of this afternoon." What's-her-name nods and quickly scurries out behind our lawyers.

I need to get more initiative in here. People who walk with purpose and demand respect when they speak.

People like Emilia.

The thought surprises me as I turn to watch her. Standing without a sound, she turns and walks to the full-length window. She carries herself with both strength and grace. I see it even now, when she's down and we're ready to tear each other apart.

Just watching how she made the lawyers nervous ignited a spark in me. I don't get to see much of that around here.

As she gazes out over the city, I take the pause to steal a look at her. She's just as stunningly fierce as she was the day she left for college. Everything about her falls into place. Her hair is slightly tousled, but it looks like it was styled that way.

The curve of her hips catches me off guard. Her body is firm under her fitted skirt, and my body reacts at the sight of her. Her hair is darker, and she is no longer wearing her glasses, so she either had surgery or is wearing contacts. She's grown a lot in four years, and—

"I bet you're really enjoying this." Her words pull me out of my thoughts.

"Pardon?" I'm not sure if I heard her right since she's still facing the window.

Slowly, she turns on her heels. Her indifferent face is now red, and tears threaten to roll down her face. Instantly, I'm thrown back into our present situation.

"You. You're just like your mother. How is that piece of trash these days?"

I know she's backed into a corner. She has no way out of this, and she knows it. All of her accounts were shared with her father. They are all in my control now, and there is nothing she can do about it but lash out.

She's under my control now. The thought punches me in the chest.

"Apologize." My words growl out of me before I realize where I'm going with this.

"What?" A tear rolls down her cheek, and I watch her hand begin to tremble. I can sense her anxiety from here. This is a side of her I've never seen, and it sparks a protective nerve in me.

But I'm not ready to entertain that yet.

"You heard me, Emilia. I won't tolerate any rude behavior from you." I stand my ground, waiting for her challenge.

I know it's coming. Something deep inside of me has been waiting for this for years, and I'm eager to begin.

"Or what? You'll take me away from my friends? Oh wait." She huffs out her resentment and lets it hang around us, and a pang of exhilaration builds inside of me.

There's a lot of suppressed anger in her we need to deal with.

"Oh, Emilia. I'm just getting started." I sneer back at her as I continue, "One can read that will many ways. But in the end, you need me to sign off, or you get nothing. I was going to set you up with a room on campus, but I've changed my mind. I'll meet with your new instructors this week to discuss your curriculum. You will live in your father's home with me." As I continue, the cracks on her solemn face begin to widen. "In addition to your studies, which you will excel at, you will learn the company. Since I'll be handling both my workload and your father's responsibilities, you'll be learning everything along with me—as my new assistant." My words shock me as much as they do her.

I probably should have thought this through, but something about her makes me react.

I need to control myself better.

Watching her world crumble around her is giving me a twisted pleasure I've never felt before. My little Emilia was on the wrong path. Although she doesn't see it right now, these new rules will be the best thing for her, and pushing her beyond her limits is lighting me up from the inside out.

"And, Ms. Connor, I'll remind you that, while you will receive an allowance, it is at my discretion as to how much you will get. Keep this in mind as you ponder what your next words will be." I'm not above forcing her hand now.

She will fall in line because I hold this over her. But I'll work on her. I'll tear down her hate for my mother and me. We'll deal with her anger, and I'll uncover everything she tries so hard to hide from the world. Then I'll guide her. I'll teach her, and then she'll fall in line because she needs to. Eventually, she'll surrender because it will bring her joy.

I will provide her joy.

Again my thoughts surprise me. I expect everyone's best, but I've never wanted to take responsibility over anyone as much as I want to with Emilia right now. My need to take complete control with her is something I need to process.

"I..." Her soft voice startles me. I failed to notice she's turned back to the window. She's speaking over her shoulder, but she won't look me in the eye. "I apologize. Saying that out loud was rude."

I'll take it, for now.

"Thank you. Gather your belongings. I'm taking you home." The day has suddenly drained me, and I want to remove Emilia from the office to try to settle her mind. This unexpected turn of events is beginning to consume her, and I'd rather we be away from the office in case of any more outbursts.

"It's not my home anymore," she mutters under her breath as she folds her jacket over her arms and walks out of my office in front of me.

I stop briefly to schedule a phone call with my secretary for the end of the day. We'll need to discuss replacing that assistant with Emilia. As I finish telling her I'll be unreachable until then, an excited voice catches my attention.

"Emi? Is that you? Girl, it's been forever!" I recognize the perky voice as one of the women on our sales team, and I glance to Emilia as her face relaxes a little.

"Rosie? Wow. It's been forever." Her friend isn't slowing down, so Emilia opens her arms for a hug.

"I'm so, so sorry about your dad, Ems."

"Thank you." My heart tightens as I watch her face fall again.

I cut in. "Rosalyn, Ms. Connor and I were just leaving for the day. She'll be back next week. You can show her around then." It's not a question. She understands further conversation isn't welcome right now.

"Yes, I'd love to. I'll find you—on Monday?" I meet her response with a nod and place my hand on the small of Emilia's back to lead her out.

As I make contact, her back straightens. Looking down to make sure she's all right, I notice her breathing has become deeper, more labored, and I'm suddenly left wondering if she feels some of the things I'll be thinking about later.

For now, the only thing I want is to have her settled into the house with me. Once I have her there, we'll discuss her rules and my expectations.

CHAPTER 6
EMILIA

As the driver turns into my old neighborhood, I sense Joshua's eyes on me, although I can't bring myself to look directly at him. Neither of us has said a word since we left the office.

The details of the last hour are beginning to overwhelm me, and my arms rest heavily in my lap, numb with helplessness.

With each landmark we passed, my heart dropped a little more. Our old high school was a difficult building to drive by. To an outsider, I'm sure it seemed like I had it easy there, and I did for a time. But then Joshua came, and he and his mother ruined everything.

I lost so much of myself because of them.

I was supposed to be putting all of this behind me. I was supposed to be freeing myself from the shackles that held me here and suffocated me.

But I'm not. Instead, I'm doing a one-year sentence. I'm twenty-three years old, and I'm Joshua's ward.

Maybe I should have come clean and told my father everything. Maybe things would be different. I had always planned to tell him when I felt stronger. Now I'll never get the chance.

And after everything, he believed the lies Joshua filled his head with. He believed I was too irresponsible to take over his company. He thought I was a spoiled little rich girl.

The thought punches me in the stomach, and I fail to notice we are parked in front of my old house and Joshua has already stepped out of the car.

I suddenly feel ill. I'm not prepared to walk through those doors and not see my dad. Tears well up in my eyes, and my hands begin to shake.

Not now. Just wait a little longer until you're alone, I tell myself.

I don't want Joshua to see he is winning all over again, but it's too late.

My grief hits me hard. As I try to push it back down, Joshua impatiently leans into the car.

"Don't make me carry you out of—"

Before he can enjoy my pain, I turn my head away and cut him off. "Just give me a minute. Please," I choke on my plea, and at least he has the sense to stand up and wait for me.

I take the time to glance out over the yard. It's just as I remember it, and I wonder if the old tree fort I built with my dad is still out back.

The day is beginning to take its toll. I'm getting tired. I tell myself I'll simply get into the house and go to sleep early. I'll feel better in the morning, and I'll try to figure something out then.

As we walk through the front doors, I'm instantly regretting the trust I placed in my surroundings. I trusted I had time, and I trusted I would have the money I made. I shouldn't have tried to pay my trust fund back these last few years. I should have opened my own account and saved my own money instead. But I wanted to show my dad I could do it.

Now none of it matters. If I don't do what Joshua requires, I have no money, no home, and my education stops immediately.

When we enter the foyer, Joshua places his hand on my lower back a second time. I wasn't ready for this contact either, and I freeze. My nerves are eating me up from the inside out. His touch is affecting me, and I don't know why.

I take a large step away from him, forcing him to drop his hand, and when I turn to look at him, he's staring at me again.

"I'm tired. I think I'd like to skip dinner and go to sleep." I've lost my fight for the night, and I don't want to lose any more privileges today.

"When did you last eat, Emilia?" My name sounds odd coming from his lips, and although his voice is stern his face shows concern. It catches me off guard.

"Just before I got to the office. That's why I was late," I lie. I haven't eaten yet today, but I'm not about to sit down to dinner with him like we are a big, happy family. I have no family here.

"Very well. I'll ask the cook to bring a light meal to your room later. Come." Without checking to see if I'm following, he leads me up the stairs of my own father's house, and a spark of anger flickers inside of me. This isn't his home; he can't lead me through it.

When we reach the top of the stairs, he walks past the spare bedrooms, then stops in front of my old room. My words are out before I can control myself.

"Let me guess, you've taken my father's room." I know it wasn't called for. But I feel like I have nothing left, and I need to get a reaction out of him. I want him to feel the anger I feel.

Dropping his cool facade, he steps into me. I can't help the gasp of breath I take as I back into the closed door behind me, and he doesn't stop.

When he's flush against my front he lifts his forearm, bracing it on the wall beside my head, and my stomach tightens.

I don't know what he's going to do.

I gather the courage to look up at him, towering over me, and that's when I see something in his eyes—a confidence, maybe. A primal confidence as his lips twitch at the corners, and as he leans into me more, I feel like I'm shrinking.

"No, Emilia." The way he says my name is thick, almost hypnotizing, and I hold my breath, waiting for him to continue. "I've taken the second master. I'm down the hall from you."

I swallow hard as I glance down the hall, and my brain starts to imagine what his room must look like.

What am I doing?

My body begins to tremble. I need to move away from him and be by myself. Grabbing the handle behind me, I let the door fall open as I step into my old room.

The blood drains from my face as I look around what was once my room. It's exactly the same as I left it. Nothing has changed; nothing was taken away.

"I can't stay in here," I blurt out. My panic is doing the talking for me.

I was sure my dad would have changed this room after I left, but he didn't. Everything is the same. My bedspread, teddy bears, even my dresser and little vanity. This is a teenager's room, and it holds so many bad memories for me.

"Making demands already? We're just getting started." His tone is laced with frustration, and I don't deserve any of it.

"I'll stay in one of the other rooms," I offer as I try to step into the hall, but Joshua doesn't move to let me pass.

"You'll stay in this room tonight. None of the other rooms are made up. So you'll sleep in here...." He closes the distance between us in one step as he lowers his voice. "Or you'll sleep with me."

I step back at his suggestion.

Concern claws through my conscience. I'm not worried about his comment though—I'm troubled by my body's reaction to it.

I'm too close to everything right now.

As if catching himself, Joshua takes a half step back and changes his tone. "My apologies, Emilia. I will see about making up another room for the night. I skipped lunch for our meeting, and I'm hungry. I'm going to eat some dinner. I'll be back up to see you later." He offers me a nod, then steps out of my room and closes the door behind him, shutting me in like I'm a child.

I'm left with my defiance, and it settles into me. Joshua Darkly is not my owner, and I am not a child. I won't stay here in my room, waiting for him to check in on me.

I've worked too damn hard to separate myself from that little girl to just welcome her back.

Grabbing my phone, I open my Facebook app. I haven't been on this thing in forever. Scanning through my old friends list, I click on the name I'm looking for and send off a message.

> Hey, it was so good to see you at the office today. Are you around for some catching up?

I place the phone on the bed and open my bag to look for some more comfortable clothes. I haven't gotten the first item out when my phone pings a response:

ROSIE

> I was just telling Vicky and Marta you were back. We're having drinks at The Hole. Why don't you come down? We'll be here all night. We missed you.

I'll be there in 20. I'm calling a car.

I still have a couple hundred dollars left to my name, and I'm going to enjoy myself on it.

Trading my stuffy office outfit in for a pair of jeans and a low-cut top, I skip into the bathroom to fix my makeup, then make my way out and down the hall, careful to avoid any staff or Joshua himself.

I'm not the same girl who left here five years ago. I've grown up, and I refuse to be treated like a charge.

Tomorrow, I'll begin my year, and I'll make Joshua regret every second of it.

But not tonight.

Tonight is mine.

CHAPTER 7
JOSHUA

When I half suggested Emilia share my room with me tonight, I felt an invisible punch to my gut. Why now, after all of this time and all of her lies and games? Her defiant nature speaks to the part of me I keep well-hidden—a part that really wants to rise to the challenge and rein her in.

She hasn't even spent a whole night in this house, and she's already dictating which room will be hers.

I almost denied her request, but there was something about her expression when she asked for a different room. It was unsettling, and I can't put my finger on why. I will allow her this one thing, but this is where it ends.

Tomorrow we'll have a discussion about rules, and she will obey them. I don't care if she likes them. She will live by them for the next year, and she will quickly learn who makes the decisions around here, or she will face the consequences.

That doesn't answer the lingering questions I have for myself though.

I react to her; I always have. But why?

She lit me up like napalm when she challenged me in my office, and she softened my frustration when I saw her tears in front of her father's old house. My entire body is on alert around her, my emotions swing like a pendulum in her presence.

And now she's up in her room, and I'm down here eating by myself. In the silence of the dining room, I suddenly become aware of my heart. It's beating a little too fast.

This is what she does to me. She pushes and she challenges, and one day someone is going to push back.

That day is today, and that someone is me, I think to myself as I chew on my rice.

A throat clears beside me.

"How is she settling in?" Ms. Billings asks as she refills my water.

"Sylvia, I told you I can get my own water. Thank you," I softly remind Adam's housekeeper.

"Oh, I know. I don't mind. There isn't too much left to do tonight," she answers as she places the pitcher on the table.

I smile. Sylvia has worked for the Connors for as long as I've been here. This place is as much hers as it is mine.

"Why don't you join me? There's too much food here for just me." I smile, and she considers my words as she shuffles in place. I continue, "I know you used to join Adam for dinner some nights. I'd like to continue that. Please?" I finish, pointing to Emilia's unused plate and cutlery.

She takes another second, then she smiles and nods as she pulls out the chair and reaches across the table for the spoon to serve herself.

"How is Emilia? I haven't had a chance to see her yet," she asks cautiously.

"Lively as ever," I answer.

Sylvia has seen our past. She knows we have a rocky

history, and she has always been neutral territory. She's like a mother to Emilia, and she has always been very kind to me, even after the divorce.

Then I remember Emilia's room.

"Oh, Sylvia. Before you go tonight, can you take a small meal up to Emilia, then make up the spare room beside mine?" I ask.

Sylvia's expression is curious. Her mouth is open, and it looks as though she's trying to form a thought so I ask, "What's wrong?"

"Well, it's just that I can't take Emilia a meal because she isn't here," she responds. I'm momentarily confused and wondering if she's beginning to lose her mind.

"Of course she is. I just left her in her room," I answer.

Sylvia places her fork on her plate. "No, I mean I saw her leave about ten minutes ago. A car picked her up."

Blood rushes to my head at her words, and I try to keep a composed expression on my face. "Did she say where she was going?" I ask evenly as I look down to cut a piece of chicken.

"Oh, I didn't speak to her. I saw her through the kitchen window." She pauses and looks at her plate for a moment, then continues, "Maybe I'll go make up that spare room right now."

"No. Leave it. It's getting late. She'll sleep in her own bedroom tonight. If you'll excuse me, I have some things I need to take care of." I rise, and Sylvia stands with me.

I quickly thank her for the lovely meal then waste no time making my way to Emilia's bedroom. Almost everything is exactly where it was—except the skirt and top she wore earlier, which are lying on the bed.

Great. She changed, and I don't even know what she's wearing.

Glancing into the top of her bag, I'm confident she hasn't

decided to fly anywhere. She left most of her personal belongings.

Although I didn't explicitly say to stay in the house, I know she knows it was implied, and she's chosen to disobey me.

My skin suddenly feels too tight for my body, and I stretch the muscles in my shoulders.

She has no idea who she is up against now.

I will find her and bring her home if I have to physically drag her back here myself.

If she had just done as I expected, she'd be getting settled into a new room and we would be off to an acceptable start. Now she's going to have to earn my trust and work for her rewards.

I won't let her walk all over me the way she did with Adam.

Her free ride is going to crash and burn tonight.

There are easy ways to learn lessons, and there are hard ways.

My heart pounds in delight that Emilia has chosen the hard way.

CHAPTER 8
EMILIA

I know I wasn't supposed to leave the house tonight, but as each drink went down, I cared less and less.

I missed my friends, and seeing Rosie, Vicky, and Marta tonight reminded me how much. After all of the hugs and group selfies died down, it felt as though no time had passed between us.

I've also always wanted to see the inside of The Hole. When I left for college, I was too young to get in.

So much has changed.

Looking around the bar, I recognize some old friends of Joshua's off in a corner. They're getting louder and louder as the night goes on, and I slump a little more in my seat, hoping no one recognizes me—one of them in particular.

"So when do you leave?" Marta's question startles me out of my spying as she plunks a round of creamy shots down on the table.

"Well, that's the thing; I don't," I answer to smiles around the table.

Rosie takes her shot and pauses for a minute. I know what she's thinking.

She was my closest friend all through high school. I told her everything. She knows why I left, and that knowledge is written all over her face. She's the only one who knows my secrets.

"Not that I'm complaining, but why are you staying, Ems? I mean, don't you have school?" As Rosie asks her question, her eyes widen. I know this isn't what she wants to ask, but our friends don't know my whole story.

"I'm transferring here for my last year. I'm going to stick around and learn the company. Dad would have wanted that." Vicky and Marta nod in solemn understanding, and I flash Rosie a quick wink. I'll tell her everything later.

"Okay, bathroom?" I stand, and suddenly the last two hours of drinks catch up to me. I'm wobbly on my feet.

I rarely drank at school. I took the job at the club to make more money, so I could pay my trust fund back faster and see my friends on the weekends. I thought I was killing two birds with one stone.

All hands point toward the back of the bar, and I glance over to the group in the back corner. Everyone seems preoccupied, and I nod to the table as I work my way toward the bathroom.

A couple of faces look familiar, but for the most part I'm a stranger in this place now. I prefer it this way.

With only two women in line in front of me, I pull out my phone. My stomach knots as I scroll down my lock screen. I have a text from my roommate, one missed call from Kyle, along with a text saying good night—and a long list of missed calls and texts from Joshua.

Shit.

My stomach heaves at the thought of tomorrow. I haven't even been here one day, and he's already controlling me.

As I jam the phone back into my pocket, a stall opens up, and I step in quickly. I suddenly feel a small tinge of guilt. Not because I missed Kyle's call, but because I missed Joshua's.

Stepping to the sink, I wash my hands and take a look at myself in the mirror.

I'm definitely tipsy. My face is relaxed, and my hair has flattened a bit, but I don't care.

A rumble in my stomach reminds me I haven't eaten since yesterday.

Double shit.

This is easily fixable. I reach into my purse to double-check how much money I have left, and it's enough for some food for the table.

I'm walking toward the bar when a body steps in front of me, blocking my path.

"Oh, I'm sorry," I mumble. Without looking up, I move to the side to let them pass, but they move with me, blocking my way again.

As I look up, my heart suddenly becomes heavy.

"I heard you were back in town, Emilia." Sean's slimy voice slithers straight into my stomach, where all I have is two hours' worth of shots and drinks.

"Excuse me." I firm my voice and straighten my back, trying to make myself look taller than I am. I take another step to the side, only to blocked by him a third time.

"What? No smiles for your old school buddy?" As he speaks, he leans closer, placing a hand on my arm. The smell of whiskey and beer on his breath doesn't mix well with what I've had to drink, and I swallow my disgust.

"We were never buddies," I answer, brushing his hand off. I take a step backward to put some air between us, but he doesn't allow me the distance. He steps into me, and the room begins to spin from lack of oxygen.

"Well, word has it you are working with us now, so we're going to be buddies. Real close buddies, *Feelya*." I swallow hard at the nickname some of the boys gave me in high school.

Feelya Emilia.

Triple shit.

As if my next year couldn't get any worse.

"You work for my dad?" How did I not know this? I should have paid more attention to my father's business.

"Yeah. Joshua got me the job shortly after you left." Then I realize my year could actually get worse. "He got all of us jobs. You know, all of your—*buddies*." He punctuates his last word with a sneer.

I know exactly what he's trying to tell me.

On Monday morning, I'll be a little sheep walking into a lion's den.

My face heats up. I'm not sure if it's from the shots or the present company, and I make one last attempt to pull myself away.

"Hey, Sean. You okay? The guys are waiting for their drinks," a deep voice says from behind him, and for the first time Sean backs up and gives me my space.

"Yeah. I just got distracted. Saying hi to an old friend here," Sean answers, and I glance over his shoulder to see who he is speaking to.

Noah offers me a nod, and I return it, but I can't bring myself to smile. Joshua and Noah have been best friends for as long as I've known them. He always seemed nice, but I never really got to know him.

Right now, I just want him to remove this nightmare from my path.

"Well, come on. I'll help you carry them." He pauses,

waiting for Sean to go with him, and I'm thankful he isn't leaving without his friend.

Sean shoots a revolting sneer at me and turns toward the bar.

There go my plans to order food.

When I make my way back to the table, Vicky and Marta are having a conversation, but Rosie's eyes are locked on me.

My backside hasn't even hit the seat before she's talking. "I didn't even see him in here."

"He was in the back corner. It's okay." I grab the bottle of water I ordered at the beginning of the night. I really shouldn't be drunk for this.

"Do you want to leave? We can go somewhere else," Rosie offers and everyone at the table perks up.

"Sure. I haven't eaten yet today, so maybe we can go for food?" I offer, and everyone nods in agreement.

As we stand, someone taps my shoulder.

"Hey, Emilia. I'm not sure if you remember me. I was wondering if you'd like to dance. Just one song?" Noah offers me a smile, and I look at the girls, who have already sat back down to wait for me.

"Um, sure. Thank you, Noah," I answer.

He smiles at his name. "You do remember." His blue eyes light up as he holds out his hand, and I take it, allowing him to lead me to the dance floor.

As we make our way through the couples swaying slowly to the music, I catch sight of Sean out of the corner of my eye, standing with his group. His eyes are locked on me, and a cold shiver shoots up my spine.

"It looks like you are celebrating," I say. Noah looks confused, so I tilt my head toward his group.

"Oh, it's a farewell for one of our team members. They're moving on from Connor Realty."

His answer surprises me. "You work there, too?"

"I was hired on with Joshua right out of high school. I manage a team under him," he answers, and suddenly I feel out of place.

Noah always seemed so laid back. He was nice to me, but he works with Sean and his friends, and they work right under Joshua. Come Monday, I won't be able to trust any of these guys.

My only ally at Connor Realty is Rosalyn.

The music dies down, and I step back to say thanks, but his arms tighten around me.

"How about one more dance?" He smiles down at me. I must look confused, because he keeps talking. "Look, Sean is drunk, and it looks like he's either going to ask you to dance or harass you again, and I don't want a fight to break out."

I giggle at his suggestion that I could even handle myself in a fight with Sean.

"I'm not going to fight him," I reply, realizing this is the first time I've smiled in about twenty minutes.

"I'm not talking about you, Sweets. I'm talking about Joshua."

CHAPTER 9
EMILIA

*S*hit, *shit, shit, shit.*

As Noah says Joshua's name, I stop dancing and look up to meet his stare, but he's not looking at me.

My heart slowly tightens as I follow Noah's eyes past our table and toward the entrance to the bar.

Standing at the front door and staring right at me, Joshua's body is the only thing I see, and I instantly feel a pinch of guilt and a pull in his direction.

"You asked me to dance to keep me here? For him?" I look at Noah. He has slowed his steps, but he keeps his arms wrapped around me.

"I think you owe it to yourself to give this year a chance, Emilia." The serious expression on his face carries a hint of kindness, and I huff out a laugh.

I'm being treated like a child from all sides now.

"He told you?" I ask incredulously. How many people at my dad's work know I'm there under Joshua's authority for the year?

"Joshua is my closest friend, and I work alongside him now. I'm the only one he confided in. No one else knows about your...situation. It's not what you think. He would never—"

I cut him off. I don't have the patience for anyone else telling me what is best for me tonight. "It's exactly what I think it is." I attempt to step back, but he spins us in a half circle and doubles down on his grip.

"Trust me, Emilia. There are hills worth dying on; this is not one of them. Make this easy on yourself and leave with Joshua." He lowers his voice and continues, "You know he won't offer you any other option, right?" His words linger between us, and my fight drains out of me.

Noah is right. I can leave quietly with Joshua, or I can cause any number of scenes—and all of them will end in me leaving with Joshua.

I've had too many drinks, and I'm wobbly on my feet. Come Monday, the rumor of my drunken rampage would be going around the office before I even started my shift, and I don't want this version of me to be the one everyone is talking about.

I won't do that to my father.

There's something primal in Noah's words. He's made me feel like property, like I'm being collected, and for a brief moment, I'm at peace with the sensation, which worries me.

Sucking in a deep breath, I release my grip on Noah's arms and sigh out a reluctant, "Fine."

Looking in Joshua's direction, Noah nods once, then loosens his hold on me. He thanks me for the dance as he leads me back to my friends.

Before they stand, I flash them a big smile and stifle our plans. "Hey, guys. I need to get going. I'm suddenly really tired from the day. Here." I fish the last bills out of my pocket and drop them on the table, then I grab my jacket and purse.

"Appies are on me this time. Thanks for having me out. Let's do this again, okay?"

"Well, at least stay for the food. You said you haven't eaten since yesterday," Rosie states, watching me curiously as someone steps behind me.

I know who it is without looking.

"Yesterday? You told me you ate earlier today." Joshua's deep voice sinks into me as his breath tickles along my neck.

"Oh, I got confused. It's been a long day," I answer feebly. I turn to look at Joshua, and my nerves tingle when our eyes meet.

He knows I'm lying. It's written in his intense stare. He sent at least twenty texts, and I chose not to answer a single one.

Suddenly, regret fills me. I've disappointed him. I shouldn't feel like this. I should be thrilled I was able to get under his skin once more, but I'm not. Instead, I want to be alone in my room, away from his harsh gaze.

I look back at my friends. Vicky and Marta have already begun to look over the food menu, but Rosie is sitting still, watching Joshua and me. I shrug. "I'll see you in the office on Monday." I wave, then I turn and lead the way to the door with Joshua close behind me.

His car is parked in front of the entrance. He never planned on staying. He only came to collect me.

Without another word, Joshua opens the passenger door for me. As I settle into my seat, he slams it shut beside me, rattling my nerves.

I draw in a deep breath as he rounds the front of his sports car, settles into the driver's seat, and starts the engine.

As we drive, he leaves me to sit in silence. After a few minutes, my defiance rises. I refuse to let him control the situation.

"I was just out with friends." I don't look at him when I say the words.

He continues to drive like there is no one else in the car with him.

My face heats with anger. "I didn't do anything wrong."

More silence.

My impatience claws away at my composure, and my voice rises with my next words. "I don't deserve any of this."

Joshua slams on the brakes at my declaration, and the seat belt burns a strip into my skin as my body lurches forward.

I quickly glance around only now aware of my surroundings. I recognize the back roads that lead to my dad's house, and when I meet Joshua's glare, I realize it would have been better to enjoy the silence on the drive back.

"You don't deserve this? Ha. That's the funniest thing I've heard all day." His chuckle holds no humor, and the blood drains out of my head as he continues, "Poor Emilia never does anything wrong. Let me ask you something: did you understand you were not to leave the house tonight?" He lets his question linger.

"I—you never told me I couldn't."

"Was it implied? Was it understood you were not to leave the house, Emilia? Answer the question," he demands and waits again, his eyes fixed on mine.

"I—" I consider lying, but we'd both know I was, and I don't want to make this worse. "Yes. I understood I was not to leave the house. But I'm not a—"

"And at some point before I arrived at the bar, did you see my messages and choose not to respond to them?"

I realize how this looks from his point of view. "Yes, I—"

"And did you blatantly lie to me when you told me you ate earlier?"

I start to sink under the weight of my mistakes.

Resigned, I answer, "Yes. I lied, but—"

"But nothing, Emilia. You've taken every chance you could today to defy me. Your father's last wishes are all written down in that will, and you are taking every opportunity to disappoint him—*again*."

My stomach knots, and a wave of nausea rolls through me. He's bringing the memory of my father into this, and I can't handle his accusations.

"You know what? I don't need this shit!"

Joshua doubles down on his expression, and I don't have it in me to fight about my dad. I whip off my seat belt and open the door before he can lock me in. "I'll walk the rest of the way back."

I'm thankful for the fresh air as I take a couple tipsy steps forward. Before I make it away from the car, a strong grip on my arm spins me, and I'm face-to-face with Joshua. His eyes are bright, and I step back to give myself some space.

The scent of his cologne hits me, and his proximity overwhelms me. All of this contact today is piling on, and I need some space to breathe.

Without warning, my body moves on its own. First to the car as my thighs press up against the side; then I'm bent over the hood as Joshua shifts my jacket up my back.

"What are you doing?" I squeal as I brace my palms against the hood. I'm trying to right myself, but his hand on my back holds me in place.

"What I should have done this afternoon, Emilia. Remember, your choices brought this on." His tone is eerily calm as I struggle under his weight.

Nothing happens for a moment, and I stop squirming to look over my shoulder at him when a sharp pain lands on my ass through my jeans. My stomach lurches at the sensation.

"Wh-what are you doing?" I yell the same question again

and try to push myself up, but his hand only holds me down. "You can't—"

My panic is cut short as a second smack hits harder than the first, and I lean my entire body forward into the car, as though it'll give way for me, but it doesn't.

"Oh, I can, and I will, Emilia. You're lucky you are still wearing your pants." My heart thuds into my chest at his threat.

When he pulls his hand back, I panic. I'm still lying across the hood and looking horizontally down the road, and the scenery begins to spin.

"S-stop," I blubber.

I've started crying. I've never cried in front of Joshua. I would never let him see me down, but my tears are here for the third time today, and I breathe deep trying to stop them. "Please, stop." My breathing has turned into short, restricted gasps, and my body tenses in panic.

"Take a deep breath, Emilia." Joshua's hand comes down, but there is no contact. Instead, he rests it on the curve of my bottom, and I suck in as much air as I can.

"Good."

I'm elated at his pleasure with me, then instantly confused by my reaction.

Why do I care if he's happy with me?

I don't have time to consider the answer. He continues, "Emilia, you have a choice. You can make this year as easy or as difficult as you wish. You lied to me, you left the house when you knew you shouldn't, and you didn't answer my texts. I won't tolerate any disobedience. But you have the chance to settle this right now."

I have conflicting feelings. I worked so hard to get away from everything here, and I'm living the worst possible version of my life right now.

"Your punishment for lying to me and not answering my messages is this." As he speaks, he taps his hand along my ass. Then he asks me a question I never in my life thought he would:

"Do you accept your punishment, Emilia?"

When I woke up this morning, I did not think that I'd be standing on the side of the road tonight with Emilia bent over the hood of my car.

For more than an hour after I found out she was gone, I left message after message. As the minutes ticked away, panic began to build. I was worried about Emilia.

What is happening to me?

If it wasn't for Noah's text telling me he saw Emilia at The Hole, I'd still be looking for her.

Since the moment she walked through my office door today, she's done nothing but fight me. I know I shouldn't have made the comment about her disappointing her father, but I need to push back as much as I'm being pushed.

If we're going to move forward, she needs to confront her anger, and there's only one way I know to get her talking: by jabbing at her buttons until she snaps. Now here we are, and there is only one question left to ask.

I'm no longer running on anger. Seeing her safe in the bar

with Noah calmed my ire, and all that remained was her initial defiance. And that must be atoned for.

Once I hit below the belt, she punched back, and I was ready for her. I could tell by her sluggish movements when she jumped out of the car that she'd had some drinks. Her senses were dulled.

She moved easily across the hood of my car, and I was momentarily grateful Noah was at the club tonight. The image of someone else taking advantage of Emilia in this state sparked my protective side.

Running on instinct, I lifted her jacket and pulled my hand back. My desire to clear our slate overrode my restraint.

Her body jolted to life at my first spank, and it shattered my composure.

She can't hide how she responds to my control. I'm guessing that beneath her anger and her shame at being spanked lies a woman who, deep down, wants to balance the scales between us.

And now here we are.

I maintain connection with her as I rest my palm on her bottom, and hold her to my car as I tell her about her punishment.

Then I pause to take a deep breath and ask the question that needs an answer to confirm both her consent and my suspicions:

"Do you accept your punishment, Emilia?"

The chill of the evening air settles on me as I wait for her to consider my words. The hint of a smile tugs at the corner of my mouth as her back rises and falls. She's listening to my instruction to breathe deeply.

I allow a full minute of silence to go by. Then I move my palm along the curve of her ass, and she clears her throat.

"I..."

My body is heavy with anticipation. I know what she wants to say, but I can tell by her hesitation she is afraid to say it. I won't move until she decides one way or the other.

"Yes." It's barely a whisper. She sinks her body onto the hood of my car, and I allow her a few more seconds before I begin.

"You can tell me to stop if you need, but I strongly urge you to experience this, Emilia." Again a silence lingers between us, then she nods her head in hesitant understanding.

In appreciation for her honesty and her bravery in accepting this—and from me, no less—I offer her some information I probably wouldn't have shared otherwise.

"When I couldn't find you, I began to worry, Emilia. We've always stood on opposite sides, but I hope this year will change things for you. I truly hope you will grow into the woman your father thought you were. I intend to be here fully for you, and I ask the same from you. There are consequences for disobedience."

When I lift my hand, she sucks in a sob, and I bring my palm down on her butt once more. This isn't something I want to draw out right now. Every part of me wants to get this over with as much as she does, so we can move on with balanced scales.

I deliver two more swift smacks, then she takes a deep breath.

"I'm sorry," Emilia gasps. I think her apology shocks her more than it does me.

It is done. Releasing my hand from her back, I step to the side and allow her to stand.

Slowly, she raises herself off the hood, leaving a small trail of tears sparkling in the glow of the streetlight.

The silence between us caries so much emotion. This is a

side of Emilia I've never seen before, but, if I'm being honest, she's also never seen this side of me—almost no one has.

She continues to stare at me, frozen, unsure of herself. Her hair is messy and wet from her tears, and her makeup is smeared across her delicate features as her lower lip trembles.

Then she sucks in a deep breath of air, and I notice she looks a little paler than she did before.

"Emilia?" I whisper softly, trying to get her to do something so I can act accordingly.

"Um...I'm...I think I'm gonna be sick." She doubles over the side of the road and takes two deep breaths before she vomits all over the pavement.

My instincts take over, and I move to her side, pulling her hair back and wrapping my arm around her waist.

Her body heaves, and my heart hurts for her. I can't say I wouldn't be in the same spot if the tables were reversed. If I was given this many restrictions in one day, I would be testing my boundaries and pushing back too.

The only difference is, I don't think I would have been strong enough to acknowledge my defiance and accept my punishment. As the thought hits me, I feel a little admiration for Emilia creep in.

She's hurt, and she's alone right now. She has no family left, and her closest friends here haven't seen her in years. She has no one here, and the one person she doesn't want in her life is holding her hair out of her face as she vomits.

I don't want this to foreshadow the year ahead. There is something about Emilia that draws me to her. As much as she fights me, I feel a connection to her, and it is something I need to explore.

"I want to go to the house." Her words are quiet as she stands beside me, pulling a tissue from her pocket and wiping her mouth.

I'm hurt that she doesn't call it her home.

She won't look directly at me as she pushes out of my grip and moves to the passenger seat.

I open the door, let her into my car a second time, and close it behind her a little more gently than I did before. Then I walk around to my side and get back in.

Without a word, I put the car into drive, and we ride home in silence.

We still have one part of her punishment to deal with when we get back, and she's not going to like it.

CHAPTER 11
EMILIA

My head was filled with one thought for the rest of the silent drive home:

What is happening to me?

Everything I worked so hard to accomplish over the last five years is unraveling piece by pathetic piece.

I can't allow myself to become unguarded; I can't put myself into positions like this. Drinking excessively was a poor choice, and I'm paying for it.

This house is empty without my father in it. Everything has changed. Everything but me, it seems.

I tried for five years to put everything behind me, and it all fell apart in less than a day. I'm still the same little girl on the inside.

Feelya Emilia.

Dammit. I thought I had dealt with everything. I thought I was stronger than this.

Lying across the hood of Joshua's car was surreal. I've dealt with nothing. In fact, I'm going in a direction I never knew existed.

In that little moment, I welcomed his punishment. I needed it. When his first spank landed, something opened. I felt like I had somewhere to put all of my anger. A floodgate appeared, and I felt lighter.

But this is Joshua. I can't allow whatever this is. Not with him.

I'll never make it through a year in this house.

I wish Kyle were here. He is always so easy to talk to. How am I going to tell him I won't be back? His psychology classes have provided a great deal of insight into some things I was dealing with.

This day has become too much to fight, and I fall in line behind Joshua as he unlocks the front door and walks quietly up the stairs.

He opens the door to my room. Then he steps back to let me enter, and as I pass him I catch the scent of citrus in his cologne.

"You'll sleep in your old room tonight. Your punishment for leaving without asking me." His voice sounds loud in the quiet house. This is the first time he's spoken to me since the roadside, and memories of his spanking flood into me, humbling me, and I can't meet his eyes.

I'm too embarrassed. I asked for it.

I turn once more to look around my room. I really don't want to be in here tonight, but maybe I'm tired enough that I'll sleep until morning. Then I'll request new accommodations when I'm better-rested.

"We have the weekend to get used to this arrangement, Emilia. Go to sleep. I'm just down the hall, and Ms. Billings is still on staff. She's in her quarters. We will speak tomorrow." He looks exhausted as he steps into the hall, and I waste no time shutting the door between us.

I don't like being so close to him.

My bags are where I left them. I shuffle over to my old bed as my phone buzzes in my pocket. My roommate, Kelly.

KELLY

Just got off work. What's going on? Sandra said some guys came in earlier with a school admin and boxed your stuff up. They said you aren't coming back.

Yeah. My plans changed. I just found out. I'm here for a while. Problem with the estate. I'll message when I know more.

As long as you're okay. Kyle was by asking about you. Word is going around that you're leaving for good.

I'm okay. Thanks. I'll text later.

I turn the phone off and drop it on the bed. I need some silence to process everything.

I have no idea what I'm going to tell Kyle. I met him a year ago, at a campus party, and we had just decided to start seeing each other. Now I'm here, and I don't know where this leaves us.

As I unpack, I remember I only brought my tiny baby doll nightie to sleep in. I was supposed to be by myself in a hotel room right now.

I move to my dresser, and sure enough, the clothes I left behind are all still here. My heart breaks at the thought that Dad held on to everything, waiting for me to return. And now it's too late.

An ugly cry bursts out of me as my favorite memories of him come back. Life was supposed to be so different—my father was supposed to be in it, and Joshua was supposed to be gone.

And I still haven't eaten.

As the thought hits me, I remember I tossed a granola bar in my bag when I left this morning. I dive my hand into the bottom of the bag, find my treasure, and pull it out, tearing off the wrapper and chewing it down quickly between my tears.

Then I catch my breath and pull out my old pajamas from my dresser, which I know are no longer going to fit me.

Baby doll it is, I think to myself as I pull everything onto the floor and get changed.

The granola bar will have to do. I'm not sure I can stomach anything else anyway.

I just want today to be over.

Old pictures of me cover my dresser, and used notebooks still sit on my desk in a neat pile. I worked so hard to get away from here, and all my hard work only brought me back.

Today wasn't supposed to end like this. I need to sort out a plan to stay sane until I find my way out.

For now, I don't want to look at these reminders. I pull the sheets off the bed and cover as much of the room as I can.

Climbing onto the bed I never thought I'd sleep in again, I close my eyes and pray that when I wake up, it will all just be a dream.

It's only one night.

What's the worst that could happen?

CHAPTER 12
JOSHUA

All of these conflicting feelings refuse to quiet in my head. It is now two in the morning, and I'm still awake, processing the events from yesterday.

I worked hard under Adam, and I pride myself on maintaining a controlled level of indifference around everyone. It's what makes me great at what I do.

But then there's Emilia.

No matter what she does, it eats at me. She gets under my skin whether she's happy, sad, angry, or defiant. She pushes buttons I didn't even know I had. But the one button she pushed tonight is the one I can't get out of my head.

My mind won't stop replaying the sound of her sweet voice asking to atone for her actions. I'm even more surprised at myself for pushing for it.

My control was gone, replaced by instinct and a need to clear the slate. She felt it too. I know she did.

But now I'm relinquishing some of my own power. By taking control over her, I hadn't realized I'd be giving up some of my own. Now I'm here, in the middle of the night, with a brain that won't stop processing everything over and over again.

Lying in bed staring at the ceiling isn't going to get me to sleep any faster, so I head to the kitchen to find something that might help.

Walking barefoot down the hall in the dark, I instantly perk up at the sound of muffled sobs. As I step closer to Emilia's room, they get louder. She must be crying hard; these doors are solid wood.

I stalk up to her door and place my ear as close as I can to listen.

Has she been up all night crying?

I decide to leave her to her own fate, and I turn to step away when a wail jolts me out of the still of the night.

Without another thought, I spin back to the door. I open it to try to help, and I'm faced with...nothing.

Her bedsheets are draped over her little vanity, and her comforter is over her desk. It almost looks like she's tried to cover up her past.

And there she lies, asleep, on top of a sheetless bed, wrapped around one of her pillows. Her face is buried in it, and she's crying.

She's dreaming.

As I round the bed to sit beside her, she mutters "no" and "stop" over and over again. She reminds me of her younger self for a moment.

This is no dream; it's a nightmare.

I lean in a little closer to give her arm a shake, and her eyes shoot open as she gasps for air. The moonlight sparkles against the tears covering her face, and she takes a few short breaths before she leans into me.

The force of her weight against me almost sends me

backward off the bed. Then she wraps her arms around my midsection and pushes her face into my chest.

Impulsively, I pull her closer, into a deep embrace. My heart pounds in my chest. I'm confused that she is allowing me this close to her.

Her wet cheeks snuggle against my bare skin, and I take a few moments to chastise myself for wearing only my pajama pants outside of my room. She's trembling in my arms, and her skin is cold. It's just then I realize she is wearing barely anything, and I follow the light of the moon over her curves.

Her little nightie is sheer white, and there is just enough light in the room that I can see through the thin fabric.

What feels like long minutes pass between us. Then her arms begin to loosen around me, and her breathing evens out.

"I can't stay here..." She drifts back to sleep.

Looking around her disheveled room, I have to agree.

I stand and pick her up with me. Cradling her tired body in my arms, I walk into the hall, unsure of where to go. Only two other rooms have beds that are made: her father's old room and my own.

I think, under the circumstances, waking up in her father's bed might be more damaging to her emotional state, so I turn into my room and walk over to my bed.

When I place her down on the mattress, she rolls over onto her side, facing me, and I lift the covers over her scantily clad body. I catch a small glimpse of her nipples through the transparent material, and I quickly look away, pulling the covers up and tucking them around her neck.

It's hard to imagine the room around me is quiet, because the sounds inside of me are screaming out. My heart is pounding into my ears, and I'm not sure having her this close to me for the next year is such a good idea after all.

I shouldn't want anything to do with her.

But I do.

I want to be her shoulder to cry on. I want to dole out her punishment. I want to help her overcome her nightmares and everything else holding her back from being the person I know she is.

And I want her to want things. Things I sense I could pull out of her if the circumstances were different.

What is happening to me?

I can't process all of this on a lack of sleep.

I grab an extra pillow out of the closet, close the door to my room behind me, and make my way into the office. I'll sleep on the couch in there for the rest of the night.

Our year together hasn't even started, and I already know it will be a series of challenges as well as a turning point for us both. I just need to figure out what direction I'm going.

CHAPTER 13
EMILIA

The pounding in my head hits me before I open my eyes. I roll over to reach for my phone, but my hand falls short, only finding more bed.

This isn't my bed. The thought confuses me before I remember I'm not on the little twin bed in my dorm room anymore.

Dread sets in as I open my eyes to face my old room, and I bolt up, disoriented, but my stomach is left behind on the bed.

The night slowly trickles back. I recall Rosie and the girls, then Sean and Noah, and finally Joshua.

Oh damn. Joshua. This isn't good.

I went to sleep in my old bed last night, and I don't remember anything, but I'm extremely tired still.

And I had a dream.

A wave of disappointment washes over me. I spent five years away, and on my first night back, my nightmares returned. And, judging by the lived-in state of this room, I'm in Joshua's bed.

I swing my legs over the side of the bed and smell the cup on the nightstand before I see it.

It's sitting on a piece of paper with a note scribbled across it. I would recognize Sylvia's handwriting anywhere.

Glad to have you back home. Drink this.

Lifting the glass to my nose, as if holding it closer will make it smell better, I take a sniff of the contents.

Phew! I'd know that smell anywhere. I've had this drink once before Rosie stayed over one night in high school, and we broke into the liquor cabinet. We were both so sick the next day, and Sylvia made us drink this creation. It worked in minutes. I was always too afraid to ask her what was in it. It smells like dirty socks and grass with a hint of apple.

Holding my breath, I knock it back. Then I breathe out of my mouth and decide to get out of the room before Joshua returns.

As I near my own room, I hear shuffling coming from inside. I'm not ready to face him yet. Spinning on my feet, I jog down the hall and into the bathroom for a shower instead.

I release a sigh of relief as I open the door and rush through. Then I close it quickly and drop my forehead against the cool wood. I'm momentarily thankful I've avoided him when a voice freezes me in place.

"You really should knock. Someone could be naked in here." Joshua's tone sounds entertained as I spin around and take in the sight of his muscular body.

Then I realize he is right. Someone could be naked in here. And that someone is Joshua Darkly.

I try to maintain eye contact, but I can't. His confidence is doing something to my sanity, and as my eyes take in his sculpted chest, I understand how the guy has no shame.

This is the kind of body you see in magazines. His chest

flows deliciously into his rock-hard abs, which drop into a perfectly angled V, pointing right at his thick—

"See anything you want, Emilia?" he asks, and my brain instantly screams, *Everything!* Then I remember who I'm talking to, and I straighten in place.

I shouldn't want anything from Joshua—other than my father's company.

"Cover yourself up," I demand, meeting his eyes as his own drop down my body.

"I should tell you the same thing, but I'm rather enjoying myself." As I look down, I suddenly remember my see-through nightie.

Dammit. I forgot I only had this to sleep in. I can see my chest right through the thin material, and my nipples are pointing right at Joshua; he can see them too.

My confidence fades fast. I step to the side and pull a towel off the rack, clutching it in front of me. Then I offer a defiant shrug. I won't be clawing back any of my pride in here.

I've amused him. Joshua lets out a quiet chuckle at my expense, catching me off guard. I haven't heard him laugh in a long time.

Picking up a towel of his own, he secures it around his hips, and his face returns to the calm, composed expression I'm used to.

"Where were we? Oh, yes. I was about to get in the shower, and you were..." He lets his sentence linger as he waits for me to make up an excuse. I've got nothing.

Even wrapped in a towel, I'm drawn to him, and I'm instantly irritated because my brain is obviously not connecting properly with the rest of my body.

"I thought I heard you in my room," I offer meekly, and he takes a second to consider me before responding.

"I've asked Sylvia to begin making up the other room. She's probably collecting your belongings." He doesn't offer anything more.

"Oh. Thank you," I answer quietly, and I suddenly begin to feel bad.

I thought I'd have to fight to get out of my old room after my behavior last night.

"But you thought it was me, and you ran in here to, what? Avoid me?" His voice drops as he asks his question.

"Well, I—" I start. I try to gather my strength as he takes a slow step toward me.

"And why, Emilia, would you feel the need to avoid me?" I know what he's suggesting, and I push myself back against the door.

"I—" My heart beats harder against my chest.

Matching me with another step of his own, he continues, "Are you feeling particularly bad about anything that happened between us, Emilia?"

With every step into me, the air becomes hot and heavy. I take another step back to give myself some space, but he doesn't allow my retreat.

"N-no. I..." There are no words I can think of right now to get myself out of this, and I'm not sure I want to.

"Or maybe you're feeling good about it. Do you think we might have some unresolved *business* we should explore together?" His words sing inside my head as I push myself into the door as hard as I can.

A smile grows across his lips. Taking his last step into me, his body becomes flush with mine, and he leans into me, knowing I have nowhere to go.

Slowly, reaching up in between us, he takes the towel from my hands and removes it, exposing my barely covered body to him.

"Tell you what. Why don't you take this little thing off, get in the shower with me, and I'll clean last night off of your body...my Emilia." His arrogance sends goosebumps across my exposed skin as he whispers into my ear while his fingers twirl a strand of my hair.

Emilia's hair is as soft as it looks. It slides through my fingers like fine threads of silk, urging me to grab more of it.

It's a good thing she didn't hop into the bathroom a few minutes later than she did. Images from last night have refused to leave my mind, and I was almost ready to do something on my own about it.

Now I have her here, and she's still wearing that little piece of see-through fabric.

This is too much.

A spark shoots through my veins as I hear the little bump she makes against the wall behind her. There's nowhere left for her to go.

Her breathing has already deepened. I can't deny there is something between us. For two people who have hated each other for so long, something has been causing this intense charge since I first saw her in my office yesterday.

She should never have left for those five years. She accomplished nothing by running away. She only built up this energy like a dam, and her confusion about why her body is shivering under my touch is almost breaking my composure.

My eyes drop down her face, pulled in as though hypnotized by her biting her full lower lip. The wet from her tongue catches the light, and I slowly start to take over.

The only thing I want right now is Emilia pressed up against the tile of the shower while I explore everything underneath that thin layer of material. Everything else has been shoved out of my brain.

I decide to push her. Placing my hand over hers, I pull away the towel she is holding. To my complete delight, she releases her hold on it with a soft gasp, and it drops to the floor.

"Tell you what. Why don't you take this little thing off, get in the shower with me, and I'll clean last night off of your body...my Emilia."

My Emilia. The thought tears through me. I know I'm not talking about my guardianship or her father's last wishes.

I've got her. I know it.

As her shoulders slump, her eyes gaze up at me. She's waiting for my lead, and I drop my head down to—

A sharp knock at the door jolts me out of my pursuit, and Emilia jumps under me.

"Excuse me, Mr. Darkly. I've moved everything into the new room, and breakfast is ready. Shall I wake Ms. Connor?" Sylvia asks through the door. Emilia takes a deep breath.

I raise my hand to cover her puffy lips, and her body settles for me as it betrays her defiance. She has no idea how easily she answers to me, but she will.

"No. Thank you, Sylvia. I'll wake her and let her know. We'll see you downstairs shortly. I'm sure she can't wait to see you." I drop my gaze down to meet Emilia's dark blue eyes once more as we listen to the housekeeper's footsteps patter along the hall and down the steps.

I know my moment has passed. Her eyes are wide, and her body is as stiff as a board against mine. I can't contain the smile spreading across my lips as she tries to hide behind her cool facade.

She can run. She can move a whole country away from me, but she can't hide. And now she knows it. She looks worried, and I don't think her fear is because of me. I think she's afraid of herself. She's terrified that she gives her power to me so easily.

"Where were we?" I ask, but I know it's futile.

"I was just leaving." Emilia hardens herself against me. She places her palms on my bare chest, sending a shiver into me as she continues, "Which room is mine?"

"You're in the only one left." I turn away from her and smile to myself as I drop my towel and start the water in the shower. "It's the one beside mine. If you forgot how to get to it, you can go through the adjoining door in my bedroom." I sneer to myself as I keep my face toward the shower. I haven't had this much fun in a long time.

"Of course it is," she mumbles as she rattles the doorknob. The cool air from the hall rushes in, and I turn to see her hesitate before she glances down the hall for Sylvia.

The curve of her ass in that nightie is almost ending me. Thoughts of spanking her the night before charge into my psyche once again. I now regret not removing her pants when I punished her. Then I'd be staring at some marks.

Before I decide to act on my impulse to pull her back into the bathroom and try again, she steps out of the room.

One day soon, there won't be a distraction or an escape for Emilia. I feel her in my bones. It's all just a matter of time.

But for now, I need to finish this shower and get down to breakfast before she can think of another reason to run off.

We have some things to discuss.

"Are you still having nightmares then?" I hear Sylvia's voice from the open dining room doors, and I'm disappointed I've missed some of their words.

But I'm not one to eavesdrop, so I keep moving into the room.

"Nightmares?" I inject myself into the conversation as I walk over to pour myself a coffee. I know if I don't keep this topic going, it would end on my arrival, and I want to know more about these *bad dreams*.

"Oh, good morning, Mr. Darkly. I have a plate ready for you. I trust you slept well?" Sylvia moves off to the side, and I step between her and Emilia, flashing as bold of a smile as I can. I keep my eyes glued to Emilia, and, to my satisfaction, she breaks our stare first.

"Good morning, Sylvia. I slept as well as I could on the couch in the office," I respond. I see by the look on Emilia's face that she'd been wondering whether she slept alone last night. "What were you saying about nightmares?" I look directly at our housekeeper.

I know Emilia won't answer my question.

As Sylvia slowly opens her mouth, her eyes nervously dance between the two of us, and before she can answer, Emilia jumps in.

"Sylvia was just asking me if I had a nightmare last night. I think it was just a long day. The flight and—everything." She picks up her fork and shrugs.

Sylvia takes her cue like a pro. She nods in agreement, then silently excuses herself from the room.

"Really? Because when I came upon you in the middle of

the night, it sure looked like you were having a nightmare." I say it directly to her. I'm tired of dancing around.

"What were you doing in my room?" she challenges without looking at me. She keeps her eyes on her plate, moving her food around like she isn't interested in a response, but I know she is.

"I heard you crying from the hall." I wait for her to give me what I want.

"And what were you doing in the hall outside of my room?" she bounces back, and I realize we are, in fact, now dancing around.

Sitting back in my chair, I pause and wait for her to look up. After a quiet minute she does, and I'm not impressed, but I've got bigger things to discuss.

"We will continue the topic of your...*nightmares* another time." Then, leaning toward her, I continue, "And Emilia? We will discuss them another time." I can tell by the defiant little smirk on her face that she thinks I'll let it go, but I won't. "For now, we have some things we need to discuss." I wait for a moment to gauge her reaction.

She knows what the will says: she is bound to me for the next year. So much has already happened between us in the last twenty-four hours. As I pause, I watch her for signs of acceptance.

She sits quietly, finishing her breakfast. Her eyes are burning a hole through my head. I know what she wants to do. She wants to scream at me. She wants to tell me exactly what I can do with my rules, and she wants to run away.

But my little girl can't do any of that.

She takes a sip of her coffee, then places the cup down and leans back in her seat.

Her expression is firm. She's a fortress, and I love seeing her like this because it's no fun breaking into anything that isn't heavily guarded.

She's being as defiant as she can without earning herself any more punishments.

"Go ahead then. Do your best." She challenges me again, and I instantly want to throw her onto the table and turn her into my breakfast.

My entire being warms at her words. But now isn't the time to entertain my carnal desires, so I sit back and offer her a smile before I begin.

"I know this arrangement isn't ideal, Emilia. I know you had other plans. And, yes, I knew about the guardianship caveat in your father's will. He asked me if I would be okay with it. Granted, none of us knew what would happen." I pause as I remember my conversation with Adam about his daughter.

In truth, I miss Adam. He'd been like a father to me for the last fifteen years, always offering advice and checking up on me.

"But it did happen. And you seem more than eager to run my life without knowing anything about me." Emilia's cold voice snaps my attention to her, and I notice the tears threatening to run down her face. She's hurting, too.

I cut back in quickly. The last thing I want is for this to turn into a petty fight. "You're right," I start, and she waits for me to finish. "It did happen, and I wish it hadn't. But we need to work our way through the next year together. I intend to honor your father's wishes." I stop there and look at her. I'm not willing to explain myself any further. This is my challenge to her: keep yelling at me like the spoiled little rich girl she is, or to grow up and accept her circumstances.

I brace for an onslaught of profanities, but none come. Instead, she leans forward to take another sip of her coffee and places it back down, never taking her icy stare off me, and I continue.

"You will live in this house with me, and Sylvia is here as well. I've arranged to meet with your professors to discuss your situation. In the meantime, they've agreed to a modified schedule while you get settled into your new life. You will have a driver take you to school in the morning, and in the afternoons you will work with my administrative team while you learn the company. You are in your last year of school, so consider it an internship. You will not hold a job outside of Connor Realty; you'll find there is more than enough to keep you busy here." I pull a piece of paper out of my pocket and take a long look at it.

The numbers on the sheet don't make sense to me. "I need to contact the bank again. We've asked them to send back the remaining funds in your trust, but I think they've made a mistake." Before I can tell her it looks like they've sent over the beginning balance, her soft voice cuts me off.

"It's no mistake," she says, leaving the mystery wide open.

"I don't understand. You were away for five years, and you worked a few hours a week at the library—that's barely enough to buy groceries. You still had rent and everything else. Where did you get the money?" As I ask, I'm not entirely sure I want the answer.

"I didn't just work at the library. I worked weekends at a local club. I got to share tips; we raked in a lot of money. I was— um, trying to pay my trust fund back." She doesn't offer anything further, and I sit in silence.

I know I'm gawking at her. Adam couldn't have known she worked at a club all of this time. He said he was concerned she was going out a lot on the weekends. He never knew she was working. And for what? She had a trust fund.

"Why did you—"

"Look, I don't drink much. I thought that was evident by me vomiting all over the side of the road last night. I wanted to see my friends, and one of the first nights they took me out to the bar, I found out they needed staff. Most of the students didn't want the job because they wanted to drink and party. I just wanted to see my friends and watch out for them. It was good money. And I wanted to pay... I wanted to..."

Her words trail off, and in an instant I feel like shit. She wasn't living off of Daddy's dime. She was trying to prove to herself and everyone else that she didn't need anyone. She wanted to make her father proud of her.

It was the bar and the partying that sealed Emilia's fate for the next year. I remember the conversation. Adam was so worried she was heading down the wrong path, and I did nothing to take her side or give her the benefit of the doubt. If Adam had known this bit of information, his last will would have read very differently.

I don't have the heart to share this with Emilia. Not now, when tensions are still so high.

"Anyway, it doesn't matter now. The fund is frozen. I have nothing to show for it." She stops her sentence there, but, judging by her glare, I'm sure it is followed with an unspoken, *You win.*

Willingly or not, we are at odds with each other, and this next year is going to be a stroll through a minefield. But that is another topic I'm going to need to shelve for another time.

"That particular account is frozen until the mentorship is done. I am sorry, but there is an allowance," I try to offer, and she chuckles. I know I'd have the same reaction if the tables were turned. "I have some house rules I'd like to start with." I try to change the topic, and she leans back in her chair and crosses her arms.

This isn't going to be easy.

"First, you are not to leave the house without telling me where you are going. You'll find I can be very accommodating, but there may come a time when I do not allow you to go out. This is at my discretion, and it will not be disputed or ignored. Do you understand me?" I look to her with no emotion.

Although I thoroughly enjoyed the outcome of last night, I won't tolerate any further disobedience, and she needs to know her punishments can become more severe.

Without a word, she nods. No doubt she's too embarrassed to challenge me on this point.

"Second, you will respect my position in this house. I know we have our differences, but I am charged with being your guardian, and you will act accordingly at all times. You may question me—respectfully—in private, but when anyone else is present, I expect nothing but the grace you are known for."

Another nod, and I continue, "And third, when we are in the house together, you will eat all meals with me. Not by yourself, not in your room, unless you are studying for exams. You will eat here with me and tell me about how you are doing. Those are the only three rules to start. Do you understand all of them?"

I threw in the last rule at the end. The truth is, I know she won't want to eat with me, and I'm going to try my best to bridge the chasm she is intent on keeping between us.

"I understand." Her expressionless face stares me down, and I feel a weight lift as we come to our agreement and cease fire. At least for now.

"Do you have any questions for me?"

As she straightens in her seat, the sound of Sylvia clearing her throat at the door catches my attention.

"Apologies, Mr. Darkly, but it seems Emilia has a visitor." Sylvia steps into the room followed by a thin kid who looks to be around Emilia's age.

His eyes land on me. I don't recognize him from her high

school friends, but his face lights up as he continues past me to Emilia.

Emilia jumps up from her seat and rushes over to the plainly dressed boy, wrapping her arms around his neck.

"Emilia! I thought I'd surprise you. I know you need the extra support this week, with the funeral coming up. I missed you."

I don't like this.

Standing slowly, I clear my throat, and Emilia releases the guy standing between us.

"Oh, sorry. Um—Joshua, this is...um—"

The new guy doesn't allow her to finish. Extending his hand, he steps toward me and finishes for her: "Hey. I'm Kyle. Emilia's boyfriend."

"Hey. I'm Kyle. Emilia's *boyfriend*." My stomach knots at the word. I shouldn't feel bad about being his girlfriend, but for some reason I do.

"Joshua Darkly." They shake hands, and Joshua looks at me over Kyle's shoulder. I know he has some new questions now, and a lump forms in my throat.

A jolt of my old self surges through me as Kyle moves back to my side. I have someone here from my school, from my current life, and I feel a little stronger than I did five minutes ago.

"Why don't you join us? We were just having breakfast." Joshua steps back to offer Kyle a seat at the table, but he stands still.

"No, thank you. I ate on the flight. I was hoping to get in some time with Emilia here." He squeezes me against his side, and I'm thankful he's asked for time on our own.

"Where are you staying?" I ask.

"Well, I was hoping to stay here, with you. You know how it is, living on a student's salary," Kyle answers.

I tense up at his response.

"I'm afraid that isn't possible," Joshua answers for me as my stomach drops.

"Why not? This is your house, is it not?" Kyle looks at me, and I instantly feel like a child all over again.

I wait for Joshua to answer, but he doesn't. He's hanging me out to dry.

"The house belongs to the estate, and it isn't settled yet." My face heats up as I answer.

"Oh, I see. Well, I'm only staying until after the funeral, then we can fly back together," he responds with an innocent smile, and my anxiety builds just thinking about the conversation we need to have.

I pause, trying to think of how I'm going to explain my situation. I don't want to do this here, with Joshua standing over me, watching me accept my defeat. I don't want to tell Kyle he'll be getting on the plane home alone.

My nose starts to tingle as tears seep into my eyes. I take a deep breath and prepare to start talking when I hear a throat clear. Looking up, Joshua's eyes are on me, but I can't make out his expression.

He's not smiling, He's not happy. If I didn't know him, I would think it was a look of concern.

"It's an easy mistake. Why don't I call in a reservation for you at The Plaza? It's not far, and your stay will be covered. Emilia is lucky to have someone here to support her in saying goodbye to her father."

Joshua's words shock me. He sounds sincere, and he looks at me and continues, "I'm sure you will want to get him settled and talk, Emilia. I'll see you back here for dinner at five. Kyle, you are welcome to join us. I'd like to get to know you better."

I can't think of a single thing to say.

This is it. Today, I'll be cutting my ties with my former life. Today, I'll be saying goodbye.

"Thank you, Mr. Darkly," Kyle answers, and I swallow hard as I will my tears to retreat.

"Please, call me Joshua," he responds, then turns to me. "I have another guest coming tonight, Emilia." His tone is flat, and my heart tightens. Was Joshua just toying with me earlier? Does he have someone in his life? *Why do I care?*

"Oh?" I question.

"I wanted to give you a little notice; my mother will be joining us." As his words register, my throat restricts, and I suddenly find it hard to get air into my lungs.

"Oh" is all I manage.

That woman is the last person I want to see, and now I have to deal with her while her son is holding my leash. How quickly I'd almost forgot about them working together. But if I'm going to survive this year, I need to focus. I can't allow myself to become distracted by anything.

"Kyle, I trust you'll have Emilia back in time for dinner." It's not lost on me that this isn't a question, and Kyle shifts his stare between the two of us.

I know he's confused. When I left, I told him I'd be back within a week. I told him I was my father's only immediate family. So much has changed.

"Uh, sure, Joshua. We'll see you at five?" His question is meant for me, and I nod as he says to Joshua, "Thank you again."

"I need to get my things," I mumble. I no longer feel like I'm a part of the conversation—just the topic. I need to get away from the house so I can breathe. I need to prepare myself before I come face-to-face with that horrible woman.

"While Emilia gathers her belongings, I'll get your information for the hotel," Joshua offers, and I turn to leave.

I run up the stairs, burst into my room, and grab my luggage. I don't want to be here today if I can help it, so I'll shower at the hotel.

Dragging everything I still own down the stairs, I look up to see Joshua and Kyle waiting for me at the front door.

"Emilia, you look like you're running away," Joshua says as Kyle lets out a laugh beside him.

"If only it were that easy," I grumble. Kyle continues to smile, unaware of how much truth is in my words.

Joshua knows it though. He shifts his weight as his smile fades.

"I've asked Niko, our driver, to take you to the hotel, then anywhere else you need to go today." Joshua reaches behind Kyle to open the door, and the sunny day pours into the foyer. "See you both at five then."

Walking between both men, I take a direct path to the parked car and meet Niko at the trunk to stuff my belongings in.

"So, that's Joshua," Kyle states as he walks to his side of the car and opens the door.

I shift my eyes between him and our driver. I'm not sure how much to say in front of this guy. Niko replaced our old driver after I left, and I don't know him well enough to trust him.

"Kyle. I have a lot to tell you—at the hotel," I respond slowly, hoping he'll take the hint, and he does.

As the car begins down the driveway, I glance out the back window at the house I once called home. Standing in the open doorway, motionless, is Joshua.

I'm Kyle. Emilia's boyfriend.

His voice has been grating in my head since they left this morning.

She isn't his to claim.

She isn't yours either.

The incessant voices in my head are in top form today, and I take another sip of my drink in hopes of shutting them up before everyone gets here.

I replay his arrival in my mind and take comfort in my suspicion they haven't been together long. There was no instant affection or intimate connection when she first saw him. Rather, Emilia looked—uncomfortable.

I can't help the smile crossing my lips as I wonder if her discomfort is because of our earlier connection. Maybe it was guilt.

I'm more concerned about my own reactions right now. I've felt disconnected from her since the car drove away. It didn't feel right, letting her go with him. I have incredible control over everything in my life except my feelings for Emilia.

We've always been at odds with each other. None of this makes sense. She insults my family every chance she gets. She punished her own father and essentially ran away from home as soon as she could; she ran away from me. She challenges me on everything. Yet I still feel like there is something out of place. There is something wrong about all of this.

"There you are, Joshua." My mother's voice pulls me out of my thoughts as she enters the dining room.

I walk over to greet her with a hug and a kiss on her cheek, and she leans into me. I don't get to see her as often as I would like now that she lives a few hours away, but I am happy she's seeing someone and staying busy.

"Thank you for coming back for the funeral, Mom. I appreciate you being here for me. Can I get you something to drink?" I ask. Sylvia enters the room and makes her way to the liquor cabinet as she listens for her response.

"I'll have a glass of red wine," she answers. Then, craning her neck to look around me, she speaks to Sylvia directly. "But none of that cheap table wine Adam used to keep on hand." When she meets my disapproving gaze, she pretends to be offended. "What?"

"I'm sure she wasn't going to get you any of the table wine."

Sylvia mutters under her breath behind me, "Not anymore."

I stifle a smile as memories come back. These two never really did get along. I know my mother always thought it was because of Emilia.

As she enters my thoughts again, the front door opens and voices drift into the room. Sylvia hands the wine to my mother and excuses herself to tend to our guests.

"I guess that's her then." My mother takes a deep breath in and breathes out steadily.

"Her and her boyfriend. Please give them a chance, Mother."

She pauses, thinking about my request. I know Emilia made it difficult for my mother while she lived under this roof, and I know I'm asking a lot. But Adam was an important part of my life, and I need to fulfill his last requests. I owe everything to him.

"I'm doing this for you. Only you," she answers, taking a sip of her wine.

"I know. Thank you." I nod as Emilia and Kyle enter.

As soon as I catch the scent of ginger, my skin prickles. That's what Emilia smells like. Sweet ginger. I first caught it in my office, but I didn't recognize it as her smell until we were in the car together last night.

"Can I get you two something to drink?" Sylvia follows the pair into the dining room and makes her way back to the bar.

"I'll have a white wine, please, Sylvia," Emilia says softly.

"I'll have whatever he's having." Kyle points to the glass in my hand. Sylvia makes sure he wants a Rusty Nail, and he nods. I'm pretty sure the guy has no idea what goes into it, and I raise my glass in cheers.

"Kyle, I'd like to introduce you to my mother, Cordelia Connor."

When I say her name, Emilia drops her head and takes a deep breath. I remember walking in on an argument between Emilia and Adam one day after the divorce because my mother hadn't changed it back to her maiden name.

Emilia wouldn't listen to reason. My mother had already established a life under her married name, and she didn't want to go through the hassle of changing it again. Everyone understood this. Except for Emilia.

I stay still, watching Emilia as Kyle reaches out for my mother's hand and shakes it.

Then he steps back to Emilia's side. They take their drinks from Sylvia, and I notice only Emilia says thank you. As Sylvia excuses herself once again, Kyle looks between my mother and me.

"You are not a Connor?" he asks me, and I immediately feel defensive with no idea why.

"No. My mother and Emilia's father separated before they could pursue any adoption avenues," I answer flatly, hoping to end the line of questioning, but he keeps it going.

"I'm sorry for your loss." He offers his condolences as Emilia and my mother look to the floor. I keep my eyes on him. His expression doesn't match his sorrow, and I become uneasy with his tone.

"Thank you," I answer cautiously, then wait for what he's getting at, and he doesn't disappoint me.

"It's bittersweet moments like this that reconnect you with family. You must have missed *your sister*, with her being away at school for so long." His concern is empty. I try to work out what his plan is, then I see it written all over Emilia's face.

Shame.

He recognized me as competition the second he saw me today. The only way he can cut me down to his level is to reduce me to brother, to something she would consider taboo. But I was never her brother, and something tells me he knows it. The way he examines me as he speaks tells me she's already told him about our past.

Before I open my mouth to regain my standing with Emilia, my mother bursts out laughing, catching us all off guard.

"Oh, dear. Emilia hasn't told you anything about this *family*, has she?" She uses air quotes around "family." I take a drink and let my mother continue since it looks like her answer is going to help me.

She points between Emilia and me and chuckles. "These

two hated each other. I'm sure underneath it all, they still do. After all, Emilia disliked anything that got between her and her father. I should know."

I sense Emilia tense up at her insinuation, and I prepare to cut in when Sylvia opens the door from the kitchen and announces dinner.

I breathe out a deep sigh and look at my mother, who shrugs her shoulders in feigned innocence.

I should have known this wasn't going to be easy.

Stepping back, I allow Emilia to pass, and I'm not surprised she instinctively takes her old chair. Then I lead my mother around to the other side of the table, facing Emilia and Kyle. I decide to take the seat across from Emilia and help my mother into her chair beside me.

I had four dinner settings placed, leaving the head of the table empty. That has always been Adam's chair, and I can't bring myself to sit in it yet.

As we settle into our seats, Sylvia wheels out a cart from the kitchen with four bowls of soup. She serves the women first, and Emilia straightens when her bowl is placed in front of her. Then, smiling up at Sylvia, she's met with a sneaky wink from our housekeeper.

The chef's cream of mushroom soup was always her favorite growing up. As she leans over to take in the smell, my mother groans quietly beside me. She isn't a fan of mushrooms in any form. Sylvia knows this, and the two ladies exchange a smile at my mother's expense.

I'm proud of my mother for recovering quickly. She asks Kyle about his studies, and he starts to tell her all about his psychology courses. As he speaks, he makes a point of touching Emilia. A quick squeeze of her hand, or his hand on her shoulder. I watch her as it happens, and her reaction feels off.

When I put my hand on Emilia's back the first day, I saw

her calm down. I felt her settle. Their touches look tense to me, but it's lost on everyone else at the table.

Kyle does most of the talking during our first course, and I notice he's speaking directly to the women. I can't quite tell if my mother is interested in what he is saying, but I assume it is a better option for her then talking with Emilia, so I sit and observe.

While I don't look directly at Emilia, I've been watching her constantly out of the corner of my eye. I know she's taken a number of opportunities to look my way, which excites me on a dark level.

Just before our plates are cleared, I catch her watching me, and she shies away quickly, setting off my primal side. I feel the need to chase her and make her look at me like that again.

As Kyle continues talking about his future work prospects, I watch as she attempts to focus on the last spoonfuls of her soup. Try as she might, she can't hide from me, and her face slowly reddens as I refuse to look away.

Our bowls are quickly cleared, and dinner is served. Everyone looks happy with the grilled steak and shrimp, and utensils begin to clang on plates. When Sylvia places mine in front of me, I ask if she'd like to join us, and she politely declines, making her way back into the kitchen.

"That's my boy." My mother beams, speaking across the table to Kyle because Emilia hasn't looked at her since we sat down. "He's so philanthropic."

I pause at her choice of word. Then it registers as Emilia snaps her head up.

"Sylvia is not a charity case, Cordelia." Her words are clipped, and I grip my knife and fork a little tighter, bracing for an outburst from Emilia.

But instead, it is my mother who surprises me. Dropping

her fork onto her plate, she sits back and crosses her arms with a gleeful grin stretching across her lips.

"No, dear. I'm not talking about Sylvia—I only see one charity case here. Tell me, Emilia, how does it feel to be completely broke?"

The events of the last two days have sunk me into a deep haze. Absolutely nothing has gone the way I hoped it would, and I feel helpless to dig my way out of the hole I'm sinking further into.

I feel like a little sheep being herded along, and I have no choice but to put one foot in front of the other and follow. My decisions are no longer my own. I have rules, and they're set by the one person who should be packing their things and leaving Connor Realty for good.

But no. I'm having dinner with him instead. And not only him. I have to sit at my father's table and be kind to Joshua's horrible mother—the wretched person who tried to bankrupt my dad.

The one good thing about today has been Kyle.

I didn't realize how much I needed him until the moment he walked through the door. He's the only thing keeping me above water.

It crushed me when I told him I had to stay here and I was

transferring schools, but he took it well. He even offered to help me get out of this mess.

He gave me the pep talk I needed to set foot back into this house for dinner, telling me everything in life is temporary until we find those things worth making permanent.

I almost hit my breaking point early on, when Joshua used my father's name to introduce his mother. Hearing it feels like nails on a chalkboard.

I know full well she only kept his name for the prestige. It makes it easier to stay on A-lists. Everything that woman does is to further herself, and Joshua seems more than happy to follow along.

Thankfully, Kyle was there to squeeze my hand, reminding me I'm not alone. I have an anchor, and I can do this. I can survive this year.

I'm also grateful there is plenty of food I can stuff in my face to avoid conversation. *I'm going to be eating a lot over the next year.* I snicker to myself at the thought as I glance over to Joshua.

He's been uncharacteristically quiet, and I feel anxious as my favorite soup is served. When I look up at Sylvia, she gives me a little wink, just like she used to, to remind me I have her support as well. I smile back. I missed her so much.

After my mother passed away, Sylvia slowly became the woman I went to for advice and support. She's become very much like my second mom.

When I look back to Joshua, he's listening to the conversation between Kyle and his mother while he eats his soup, and I'm suddenly uncomfortable.

Just this morning, he had me pinned in the bathroom. He's never spoken to me like that, and now here he sits, slurping his soup down like nothing happened. Was it all just a joke? Am I the fool, again?

My heart and mind wage an internal war when I'm near him.

My thoughts dissolve as Kyle's hand squeezes my knee, reminding me to stay strong, and I take a deep breath. I steal one last moment to look over at Joshua, and his eyes burrow back into mine. Caught in my stare, his smirk breaks me, and I shove my eyes back to my food.

My retreat feels so awkward; I'm stuck knowing Joshua knows I was looking at him. With nothing else to do, I gulp down the last of my soup as Sylvia comes back out to take the bowls away. She replaces them with dinner, and I take a deep breath knowing I have something to do for the next ten minutes.

Joshua asks Sylvia if she'd like to join us, and she declines as she carries our bowls out of the room.

"That's my boy. He's so philanthropic." Cordelia's voice scratches along my eardrums, causing me to shiver. As her words register, I'm suddenly protective. Sylvia has been a valued member of our family for years.

"Sylvia is not a charity case, Cordelia." I speak up and look her directly in the eyes for the first time.

They can say what they want about me for the next three hundred and sixty-five days, but I won't allow them to behave poorly to Sylvia.

Joshua's mother drops her fork onto her plate and glares at me with a horrible look on her face. It was the same expression I remember when she would order our staff around years ago and I'm ready for her. She will not insult my family while I'm in the same room and Sylvia is more my family than she ever was.

"No, dear. I'm not talking about Sylvia—I only see one charity case here. Tell me, Emilia, how does it feel to be completely broke?"

For a moment, her words confuse me, then my brain plays catch-up.

She knows.

But how does she know? Noah said he was the only one who was told outside of the lawyers.

Joshua.

I shift my eyes to settle on him, and he's looking at his mother, stunned.

Of course he told his mother. They're in this together, the voice in my head reminds me. He's obviously shocked she's sharing their little secret.

As his eyes shift back to mine, my body burns hot with anger. I know my cheeks are flushing red from the inside out.

"What is she talking about, Ems?" Kyle's voice beside me is the only thing grounding me right now. I didn't tell him everything today. I didn't tell him I could lose everything, that at the moment I am utterly poor and relying on the mercy of the one man who has always been out to take everything I hold dear.

I didn't tell him about what has been happening between Joshua and me. I can't manage to bring that to my surface right now.

I've been a fool to let my guard down around him.

I sit still, looking at Kyle as he waits for my response, but I don't want to answer him. Not here, in front of *them.*

"Well, there's a little thing in her father's—" Cordelia is taking too much pleasure in answering for me, but she doesn't get far.

Joshua cuts her off. "Mother, enough."

And that is exactly what I've had—enough.

"Kyle, I'd like to leave now, please." I'm shaking so hard, and my voice is barely above a whiny whisper. It is taking every ounce of strength I have left not to yell and scream at the two monsters sitting across from me.

"You're not going anywhere." Joshua's calm voice draws my attention, and I can't hide my emotions as I swivel my head to glare at him.

He's talking about his stupid rules? Now? I'm ready to tell him where he can shove his rules.

Instead, I grit my teeth and remind him of his first rule. "I'm telling you where I am going—with Kyle, to his hotel room, to spend the night." The utensils shake out of my hand as I stand slowly.

Kyle rises with me. Joshua and his mother stay seated, and I notice Sylvia at the door out of the corner of my eye. Her face looks sad for me. If I don't get out of here soon my anger is going to turn into sobs.

This isn't the way anything was supposed to go. This was my father's house. It should be my house, yet I'm the one who has to leave tonight, and that vile woman gets to sit at his table and eat his food.

I take Joshua's silence for acceptance, and I turn to leave as his chair slides back along the floor behind me.

"While I appreciate that, I have decided you will stay here tonight." Joshua's words freeze me in place.

I force myself to turn around. Tears fill my eyes. One blink, and they'll trail down my face.

"Don't," I start. It's my attempt at firing off a warning shot.

As I wait for his response, his mother watches everything unfold. The horrid smile on her face tells me she is taking a disgusting level of pleasure from my pain. It's the same look she had when she took my father for most of his money.

There's my line.

I feel it in my bones.

This isn't going to end well for me.

Joshua controls everything right now. If I fight, I'll leave here penniless.

As everything begins to cave in on me, my hands shake uncontrollably at my sides.

This is not the hill you want to die on. Noah's words from last night play into my head.

"Emilia, I—" Joshua starts, and I make one last attempt.

"Please." I suck in some air before my sobs escape.

I'm silently pleading for his mercy in front of everyone, asking for a kindness I'm no longer sure lives inside of him. A leniency I know I don't deserve in his eyes. I'm throwing myself at his feet and asking for permission to run away again. I need to be in a safe space, and that is no longer in this house I once called home.

The air around us grows thick as he continues to stare at me.

Everyone remains still as statues as Joshua weighs my words before dropping his napkin onto his plate. Then, finally, with a deep breath, he answers.

CHAPTER 18

JOSHUA

"What the hell was that about, Mother?" I ask as I stomp back into the dining room.

Watching Emilia's face fall when she realized the insult was aimed at her almost crushed me, but it was nothing compared to the glare on her face when I tried to stop her from leaving.

Any progress I made with her over the last day is gone.

Cordelia washed it all away with one sentence. And now we're back to square one. Actually, I need to work to get us back to square one.

When she announced she was leaving, I panicked. I told her in front of everyone that I wouldn't allow it, and that was a poor decision, but I instantly felt dread. The fear she might not return to me painfully clawed into my bones.

After all of this, she's going to walk out of here with Kyle. He'll have her to himself, alone for a night to convince her of all of the reasons she shouldn't open herself up to me.

I decided to keep her here, but in a second everything

changed. Her soft plea screamed into my soul, and my heart clenched tight at her pain.

Watching her try to fight back tears, I realized I wasn't doing what was best for her. I was treating her like my possession, and I was catering to my own fear rather than focusing on hers.

It's no secret how much she hates my mother. Yet there she stood, humbling herself in front of everyone, asking me to protect her, and I couldn't even get that right.

Letting her leave with Kyle was the right decision. The history she shares with my mother cuts deeper than I thought it did. I didn't realize how hard she had taken the divorce, even after all of this time.

As soon as I nodded to release her for the evening, she turned and left, only waving meekly to Sylvia.

I followed them into the front hall and waited for Kyle to leave. Then I asked her to message me in the morning and be home before Sunday dinner. I promised we would eat alone to discuss the upcoming week and her father's funeral.

I watched her move cautiously down the stairs and into the car, and I instantly felt regret. I should have known she and my mother would fight. I should have kept them separate until much later. I need to help Emilia overcome her childhood grudge against my mother, but now wasn't the time, and Cordelia did nothing to help the situation.

"What? You know that one has had it in for me since the day I first walked into this house." My mother takes the last sip of her wine.

"Emilia is mourning the loss of her father. This is not the time to air your grievances," I chastise her as I walk back to my seat and grab my glass. As I take a generous gulp, I realize I forgot to ask: "How did you know about the contents of the will?"

Crossing her arms, she leans back in her seat to answer. "Adam and I shared a piece of property when we were married. He turned it over to me when he passed. As a beneficiary, I can request a full copy of the will."

Her answer catches me off guard—I forgot about the small mention of her in the will.

I wanted a chance to better explain Adam's final wishes regarding Emilia. And now not only does my mother have the wrong idea about Emilia's misfortune, but Emilia must think I've been sharing everything about her with my mother behind her back.

I know deep down my mother is hurt by Emilia's refusal to ever accept her as family. Over the years, her disdain has only grown.

"Listen, what you read in the will is—" I start, but she cuts me off.

"It's fantastic, Joshua. Adam left everything to you. I knew he saw through that girl's lies. I knew it." Years of resentment billow out with her words. I have the feeling I don't know the whole story, but now isn't the time to dig up the past.

"No, Mother. It's not what you think. Emilia is here for the year to learn the business. Then she will take over half the company. It's my responsibility to see she is fully prepared for her role," I answer, sitting down in Kyle's vacant seat.

There's no point in bringing my plate over; I've lost my appetite.

"Yes, but I also read the part about you needing to sign off. If you can prove she isn't fit after the year, or if she decides to leave, it's all yours." I see the hope in her eyes, and I'm sad that she isn't thinking about Emilia right now.

Even with half the estate, there is more than enough money for many lifetimes of secured futures. I know my mom still feels left out with the small settlement she received, and this is somewhat of a judgment day for her.

"Mother, what Adam has willed to Emilia is rightfully hers. At the end of this year, I will sign off on her commitment, and I do hope she stays the year." I try to keep my cool as I respond. I don't want to discuss the feelings I have for Emilia with my mother, and I don't know how to make myself more clear.

Tonight has shown me how alone Emilia is—I won't leave her in her solitude. We have one year to undo all of those years of pain, and in that moment when she pleaded with me to leave, I decided I would do everything in my power to make her mine.

"Well, it's been one day, and she already left," she says matter-of-factly, but I don't have it in me to discuss Emilia any further.

"It's getting late, and I have some arrangements to make tomorrow for the funeral." I stand, and Sylvia clears her throat at the door. She's holding my mother's coat. I have a feeling she's been waiting with her jacket for a while.

My mother circles the table and stops in front of me with her arms outstretched, and I return her hug, then say good night. I'm too tired to escort her to the door.

I pour myself one last drink for the night, then I pull out Emilia's chair and sit down. The smell of sweet ginger still lingers at her seat.

I wish I did so many things differently tonight.

Letting Emilia walk out of here with Kyle in the state she was in took more composure than I thought I was capable of. Every inch of me wants to go to the hotel and drag her back home—to *her* home—and take care of her.

This is where she belongs. I know she knows that.

Instead, I let her go. I gave her permission to remove herself from something she felt was unsafe.

She felt I was unsafe for her.

"Mind if I join you?" Sylvia asks from the door, startling me back to the room.

"I'm not sure I'm good company right now," I answer, silently hoping she doesn't leave me here to play out all of the scenarios of what Emilia is doing with Kyle right now.

But I hear liquid filling a glass, and Sylvia pulls out the chair I sat in earlier. "You both have such a history," she starts, and I chuckle.

"Of course. She's my mother," I answer.

"I'm talking about you and Emilia. As much as you both try to run away from each other, you always end up back in the same place." Sylvia takes a sip of wine, then laughs to herself. "Ugh, this table wine is the cheap stuff, isn't it?"

I smile along with her. Adam knew his expensive drinks. He stocked the best, but when it came to the cheap stuff, he was awful.

"I never ran away from Emilia." I speak my thoughts out loud.

"Oh, yes, you did. And more than once. Do you remember the night of Emilia's thirteenth birthday?" she asks, then takes another sip, waiting for me to recall the memory.

"No. I don't remember it," I finally answer.

"That's because you weren't there." Sylvia smiles at me, and I already know I'm not going to like this story. "Adam had an important meeting out of town, and they were going to celebrate when he got back. Emilia decided she'd have a little birthday dinner anyway, and she asked if I would invite you. I did, and you said you'd be there. Emilia spent all day trying on different dresses and doing her hair. I bought her a little makeup kit with lip glosses, and she tried every one of them on. She was so excited."

As she tells the story, my heart sinks a little.

Now I remember her telling me about the dinner. I'd been mad at Emilia for knocking a picture of me and my dad off the table earlier that day. She was always so clumsy. I was trying to get back at her for breaking the frame I'd made specially for it in shop class.

I handled hurt feelings poorly back then.

Just as I begin to feel awful, Sylvia continues, "Then dinner came, and she sat in her seat and waited. I found out you'd left a note that you were going out for a while. When I told Emilia, she said you were probably just out getting a gift."

I'm close to asking her not to finish, but I need to start knowing the real Emilia. "Then she showed me a shoebox and told me that she got you something too. She still had hopes you were coming back. After two hours passed, I came back in to convince her you weren't coming, and she wasn't there. I finally found her in the tree fort she built with her dad. She'd pulled out her pillow and a blanket and she sat there cuddled up and clutching her little shoebox. I asked her if I could sit with her for a bit, and she said she would wait for you by herself. She only wanted to spend time with you. I finally had the chef carry her sleeping body in before he left for the night. After that day, I don't think she ever went out to her fort again."

Sylvia takes a long pause, followed by a deep sigh. "My point is, both of you have run away at different times. I know Emilia better than anyone here, and I still see how much she needs you, even if she doesn't realize it yet." She stands with her glass and walks toward the kitchen door. "Give her time. I've got to get some things done. It's getting late."

"Wait, Sylvia." I call her back before she disappears behind the door. As she peeks her head back in the room, I ask, "What was in the shoebox?"

"I never looked in it. As a matter of fact, I think it's still out there. I saw it a couple of years ago, when I remembered the fort and went out to check on it. There was a shoebox in one corner. It was closed though. For all I know, it could be empty." Sylvia stays in the doorway, waiting for my next question. She knows me too well.

"Where's this fort?"

"Can we talk about what happened?" Kyle asks cautiously as I enter from the bathroom, tying the complimentary robe around me to hide my flimsy sleeping attire.

"Are you asking as my boyfriend or my therapist?" I answer as I sit on the couch he's relaxing on.

"You're deflecting. That's your therapist speaking. I'll bill you later," he says with a smile, and relax a bit.

Kyle and I were friends for a few months before we started dating. I met him at the bar during one of my shifts. My roommate Kelly was in one of his psychology courses, and the class met up to celebrate the end of finals.

After a long few hours of toasts, dancing, and shots, he made his way over to me to ask me out, saying my roomie thought we would be good together. Of course, she remembered nothing in the morning.

I ended up giving him my number, but I made it clear I was only interested in being friends. I know I'm not what most of these guys want. My daydreams tend to lean to a darker place, and I didn't feel comfortable exposing myself to a friend of my roommate's.

But he accepted my friendship, and we ended up spending a lot of time together. We had a long break at the same time during the day, and we'd meet up around campus to study together.

We shared none of the same interests in school, but I enjoyed his company.

It turned out he didn't know my roommate very well after all, and our friendship slowly became more closed from the rest of my friends, so I felt a little more secure sharing some parts of me I didn't normally talk about.

It was during the holidays last year, when Kyle asked me why I wasn't going home, that I decided to open up, and he became a bit of a confidant for me, offering advice and some coping techniques to help me in times of high stress and anxiety.

I told him about my family, and about Joshua and his mother, and he's always been there to lend an ear whenever I need it.

Our romantic relationship is still new. He knows I have hesitations, but I haven't told him all of the reasons why yet. I thought we would have more time to talk about all of that, and now we're about to say goodbye.

The last time we spoke about my home was just before I left. I told him I was coming here to take everything back, and that I'd only be gone a week or so, then I would be back to finish school. We are both in our final year, so after that we would both be free to go wherever we wanted.

It was going to work out perfectly.

Except it's far from perfect.

"That is my life for the next year, Kyle. I don't know if I can make it," I start, and he leans over to slide a cup of tea in my direction.

"Speaking of which, why did your stepmother say you were broke?" he asks, reminding me I failed to tell him everything earlier.

"Because I am. My father's last wishes were that I learn the company under Joshua's guidance. I guess since I left to go to school, Joshua has been working his way into my father's head, and he left him in charge of everything—including me, for one year," I answer, then take a sip of the berry-flavored tea.

"But what about your own money?" he asks, sipping from his mug too.

"I was using the trust fund as my account. It all got frozen when the bank was notified...." I bobble my head to finish the sentence. I haven't talked to anyone yet about my father's passing. I'm just not ready.

"Oh, wow...." His words trail off as he begins to process what I've been trying to accept over the last two days.

I shift in my seat and take another sip as I let the silence float around us. This is the first minute of real peace I've felt since I landed in this city.

I need more time with my own thoughts. Tomorrow, I'll be back at my father's house, and the chaos inside of me will begin to grow all over again. Then I have to visit this new school, get settled at work, and prepare for my father's funeral on Thursday.

After that, I need to say goodbye to Kyle and the life I won't be returning to.

"What are you thinking about?" Kyle's question startles me, and I take a second to look at him before responding.

He's been the closest thing I've had to family since I left home. He knows the most about me.

"I can't come home with you." I choke on my answer. He already knows this, but saying it again, out loud, is more for my own realization than to remind him.

"I know. Come here." Leaning forward, he sets his tea down. Then he opens his arms to offer me comfort, and I crawl across the cushion in between us into his embrace.

"I don't know if I'm strong enough to be here for a year without my father, Kyle. I don't know if I can play their game." Tears follow my words as I bury my face into his chest.

His soft shushes soothe my hurting heart as he rocks gently and runs his fingers through my hair.

"I've been thinking about that, Emilia," he begins, then pauses as if unsure of himself. Then, after a silent minute, he continues, "You said Joshua transferred you to this school easily enough. Maybe I can talk to my instructors about transferring out here to be with you."

My body stiffens.

"Are you okay? You feel tense."

"I-I..." I stutter out the start of a sentence I have no intention of finishing. I'm just trying to buy some time to compose myself. "I'm surprised, is all."

My first thought was about Joshua and how that would upset him. But the thought of Joshua upset didn't make me happy like it should.

I felt guilt. But for what? Outside of my father's will, I am not Joshua's. His first loyalty will always be to his mother and himself. They are probably sitting around my dad's table right now discussing how long it will take to get rid of me.

"I know it's a lot to take in, but I'm starting to think this is something we should talk about. Joshua and his mother did nothing to comfort you tonight. You have no one here who is truly concerned for your well-being. Now I'm talking as your boyfriend. Do you want me to stay?"

Just as I'm about to answer him, my phone vibrates in my pocket. Pulling it out, I check the lock screen.

It's Joshua.

CHAPTER 20
JOSHUA

Please accept my apology for tonight. I would like the chance to talk to you about it on Sunday. Sleep well. Message in the morning.

I stare at the unsent message on my phone, my fingers tracing lazily over the worn shoebox I found in Emilia's fort. Sylvia wasn't kidding when she said it was run-down, but I could tell instantly that Adam and Emilia worked long and hard to build it together.

Their names are still written in permanent black marker on the wall inside. I never knew about this place. In all of my time living here and later visiting Adam, it was their secret. That fort was something special she shared with her father.

Instantly, I felt like I did in high school. Like an outsider, never quite fitting in. But this time it's different. That feeling I had back then wasn't me being left out, it was the desire to fit in. And not with anyone—with Emilia. I wanted to be the one who had these secrets with her.

How did I not see this sooner?

Lying in the corner was the shoebox. It wasn't wrapped, but faded pencil crayon drawings all over the surface show that Emilia took the time to decorate it in her own way, just for me.

Picking it up, I could feel something was still inside, but for all I know now, a small animal could have crawled in it and died.

I haven't brought myself to open it yet.

Sprawled out across my bed, I can't stop thinking about Emilia. I wish things had gone differently tonight. I wish she was sleeping safely in the room beside mine.

I wish she was lying in this bed with me.

And I wish I could go back to this day. The day I left her alone on her first teen birthday.

Unconsciously, my fingers begin picking at a corner of the box.

She had turned thirteen when this box was last open. Our parents were divorcing, and my mother had moved out. I ended up staying with Adam at first; they agreed it would be less disruptive for me. I was starting my final year of high school, and I had all of my friends around me.

Sylvia was right. I didn't give Emilia much thought back then. I was filled with a lot of anger at her for telling Adam lies and making their separation difficult. She seemed to always be around when things were going wrong for me, and it always felt like she tried to make them worse.

This was the last birthday she ever asked me to celebrate with her. Then after she graduated, she was gone. There was no goodbye.

It wasn't until she left that I felt the loss. I even asked Adam if I could join him over Christmas when I heard she was coming home for a visit. I had hoped some distance had settled her anger as well, but it didn't. I will never forget the disappointed look on her face when she walked into the house, gifts in hand, only to find me, the one person she obviously didn't want to see.

The sound of a dull rip catches my attention as I realize I've begun opening the corner of the box.

If there is a dead animal in here, I don't want it in my room, I tell myself as my fingers begin to curiously travel along the lid.

Chances that it's the gift she got me are slim. If I was treated as badly as I treated her on her own birthday, I would have destroyed it a long time ago.

The cardboard has become soft over the years, and the box opens without effort. Pink tissue lines the inside, and it almost looks like it was wrapped yesterday.

My breath catches in my throat, then suddenly my heart skips a beat. Staring back at me is my favorite photo of me and my dad, the one she knocked over the day I left her alone on her birthday.

I remember everything so clearly now. I was so mad. I yelled at her and wouldn't give her a chance to speak. I left everything there on the floor when I stormed out. Later, when I returned, the photo was gone, and everything had been cleaned up. I thought it was thrown out with the day's trash. Not taking the photo with me was always a regret of mine, because I thought it was gone for good.

But the photo isn't what is pulling at my heart—the frame I made for it in shop class is here too. Emilia must have taken the pieces and spent some of her own birthday trying to fix it for me. I can tell she did it herself because of the pink sparkly glue along the lines where the frame broke.

I would have been furious with her for doing this back then. I would have seen it as her trying to make my special photo hers with these sparkles.

Now I just see how bad she must have felt. I didn't have much left of my life with my dad, and she must have felt horrible for breaking one of my only memories. And she sat there alone on her birthday, trying to fix it for me.

And now the tables have turned. She's coming home to a place that feels foreign, and she only has her memories of her father now.

It was my mother's turn to smash her pretty picture in front of Kyle and me, and I'm not the one who is fixing her with sparkly glue right now.

Right now, she is with Kyle, and everything is wrong. My soul feels like it has just put its pants on backwards.

He isn't right for her, and it's best he is leaving after the funeral. Emilia needs to immerse herself in a healthy routine. She'll be more focused on herself and her father's wishes.

And she'll be more focused on me.

The selfish thought overpowers me. I can't deny my needs. I can't act on them right now, but I can't lie to myself.

I know deep down I want her here for the year. I wanted it the moment Adam asked me my thoughts on his will, and if I'm being completely honest, in the end, I want her for myself. But it isn't a greedy need I feel. I want her for myself because I know, deep down, I am what she needs.

I want to correct our past and bury all of the hatchets that keep distracting us. Emilia is her father's daughter—she's proven that by paying back all but $8.36 to the trust fund that should have been all hers to use up.

She did this all by herself and only for herself. No one here knew what she was doing, not even Adam. She didn't do it for praise. Anyone else would have taken the money, put it into their own account, and never looked back.

She has a rare strength. I'm drawn to her fire like a moth to a flame; I can't help but gravitate to her.

There is no one better to run Adam's company with. But for now, our focus will be on Adam. I'll make the last-minute arrangements for his celebration of life, and we'll say our final goodbyes to one of the greatest men I've ever known. This week will devastate Emilia, but I'll do everything I can to make sure she has what she needs.

Then Kyle will leave. Once he's gone, I'll begin to work on earning her trust.

I pick my phone up and open the message I had typed out to Emilia. I know I asked her to message me in the morning, but I can't leave tonight as it is.

I press send, then I turn off my phone and place it on the nightstand. Whether she does or doesn't respond will keep me up, and I need to get some sleep.

I'll check my phone in the morning.

Then, placing Emilia's gift beside my phone, I slide under my covers and take a long look at the photo. But it isn't the lost image of my dad and me that holds my attention. Before I close my eyes to sleep, the last thing I see are the pink sparkles in the cracks of my frame.

Every time I open the doors to this house, it feels less and less like my home. My heels clack against the marble in the foyer as I close the large door behind me and turn to face my unwelcoming space.

A door near the back of the house shuts, and footsteps head my direction. I stop still for a moment, hoping it isn't Joshua.

Sylvia's face lights up as she enters the front hall.

"There you are, my dear. I was worried about you. Mr. Darkly told me you texted him this morning to say you were fine, but I still worry." She circles me to help with my jacket and gives my arms a little squeeze.

I know she heard everything last night. She knows where I stand right now. Hell, I'm not even standing. It's more like I'm sitting...cowering, maybe.

"I'm fine, Sylvia. I just needed to get away from *her*," I answer quietly, and she nods in understanding.

"No need for low voices. Joshua is in the office, making some funeral arrangements," she offers, and I'm instantly sad he didn't come down to greet me.

What the hell is wrong with me?

"Oh." Everything to honor my father has been planned without me. I'm merely a guest at Joshua's event. Nothing is mine anymore.

My anger begins to boil. I'm being excluded from everything. No one knows my father like I did—certainly not Joshua.

"Oh, dear. I know this must be hard on you. I miss your father every day. He was the kindest man I ever worked for." Sylvia's words pull me out of my downward spiral.

It took Kyle all of last night and most of today to build me up to coming back here. I haven't even seen Joshua yet, and I already want to tear him a new one.

"He was great, and I know you do, Sylvia. He considered you so much more than an employee. So do I." I stop talking as I notice tears well in her eyes.

Sylvia is my family, and this is my home. The thought surprises me as the realization sinks in.

My father set this in motion because he was worried about me, and because I never told him everything I should have. Instead, I ran away. My situation is all my fault. Cordelia can call me whatever she wants—I'm no victim, and it's time I show Joshua just what he's up against.

"Excuse me for a bit, Sylvia. I'm going to speak with Joshua." The look of shock on her face matches how I feel inside, but I need to start on better footing. This whole weekend has been a giant shit show, and I'm done playing the role of the doormat.

Dropping my bag by the door, I kick off my shoes and head toward my father's old office in the back of the house.

As I get closer, a combination of laughter and voices comes from inside. My instinct tells me to turn and leave. I'm not in the frame of mind to be ridiculed in front of anyone else right now.

The fire I first felt has died, and I turn to retreat as I hear a voice speak up inside the room.

"Come in, Emilia." Joshua's words are direct. It isn't a request.

The voices inside sound masculine, but Cordelia could still be in there. Bracing myself for that possibility, I take a deep breath and open the door.

"Good morning. How did you know it was me?" I ask as I stretch my neck through the door to—thankfully—only see Joshua and Noah.

"Sylvia is the only other person in the house, and she doesn't hover outside of doors. She knocks." I instantly feel like a child at his tone. I didn't mean to eavesdrop.

"I was just going to give you some privacy, I can come back," I offer, and both men stand at my words.

"Nonsense. Please join us. This pertains to you," Joshua answers.

"Hi, Emilia. It's nice to see you again." Noah takes a step toward me and shakes my hand. Then he returns to his spot, tucking his wavy blonde hair behind his ear.

"Hi, Noah. It's nice to see you too." I smile, then shift my attention to Joshua. "Sylvia tells me you were making plans for my father's funeral." I know my words are direct. I'm making a point with the words "my father," and I pause to let them linger.

"Yes, I was just asking Noah if he would join me in being a pallbearer. I know it would mean a lot to Adam," he says, then offers me the same pause.

"And you were laughing?" I ask.

"Oh, no. I just reminded Joshua about the time Adam caught one of the admin staff in the filing room with one of our delivery guys. Adam had to talk to HR about what he saw, and we've never seen his face so red," Noah offers, coming to his friend's defense.

"I see." I'm not in a laughing mood, so I change the subject. "And who else are the pallbearers?" I decide to start slow.

"Wilson and Manny were Adam's closest friends outside of work, and Benny, his old driver, has asked if he could do the honor. So we have five. I thought—"

Before he finishes, I interject. "What about Kyle?"

Both men stiffen as they exchange a glance.

"What about Kyle?" Joshua repeats my question through gritted teeth, and I already know he isn't happy with my suggestion.

"Have you considered asking Kyle to be a pallbearer?"

In all honesty, I have no idea why I'm suggesting Kyle. I wish I could just carry my dad myself.

"Emilia, your father never knew Kyle, and—"

I cut him off a second time. "But I know him. He is representing me."

"All of the pallbearers are representing you, Emilia. I was thinking of asking Adam's nephew. I thought you would want Kyle to be with you." His tone sounds sad, and my stomach twists. I don't want to entertain my loss in front of these two.

"He can still sit with me. If you don't have a sixth, I would like it to be him."

Joshua stands still. A heavy silence weighs down the room, and Noah isn't excusing himself, which tells me he knows more about everything than I think he does.

"I will consider it, Emilia, but you need to be realistic. After the funeral, Kyle will be leaving. Things might not work out, with you being apart from each other for a whole year. We should have a pallbearer who knew Adam and would be honored to—"

Joshua is trying to manage my decision, and my defiance rises again. "I've told Kyle all about my dad. He's not leaving me. He's decided to move here to be with me," I blurt out in an effort to balance some of my control.

It's the middle of a bright sunny day, and we're standing in a well-lit room, but I feel like I've been plunged into darkness, and I'm rattled to my core with one word, growled out by Joshua:

"WHAT?"

CHAPTER 22
JOSHUA

After my failed dinner with Emilia last night, this visit with Noah is just what I need. We were instant best friends when he started at my school in ninth grade, and we grew almost inseparable because of our similarities and our differences.

Noah was always so calm; barely anything fazed him. I had a lot of anger after my dad's death. Then, later, I became angry at Emilia for hurting my mother. Noah has been here for me through everything, and he always has a different perspective for me to consider.

At work, he's my guy. His charming personality smooths out my rough edges, and he gets things done. He's the only one left I trust entirely.

I spend the first twenty minutes catching him up on everything that's happened since Emilia walked through my office door, and I spent the next ten minutes defending my choice to let her walk out of here last night with another man.

Of course, I left out Emilia's punishment. There are just some things you don't talk about when it concerns someone you care about, but Noah is completely aware of my interests and capabilities.

Asking Noah to be a pallbearer was an easy decision. Adam included Noah in so many things both business and personal, and I know my friend admired him as much as I did.

Then Noah started in on the office stories. Working at Connor Realty never felt like a job. I loved working with Adam and Noah, and most of our management team are the best at what they do. Besides that, it's a great place to be, and I can't help but laugh at Noah's recollection of Adam's discussion with HR over one of our secretaries.

As his laughter dies down, the floor outside of the office creaks.

I know those footsteps can only belong to one person.

I call Emilia in and watch as she looks around the room. Her features soften at the sight of both of us.

Her eyes look heavy. I hope her lack of sleep is because she and Kyle were up talking all night and nothing more.

It's only when Emilia asks me directly who the other pallbearers are that I realize I've been daydreaming. I'm just about to suggest Adam's nephew when she cuts me off.

What about Kyle?

My entire body prickles at the suggestion. I take a quick look at Noah to confirm my apprehension, but he shows no change in his expression as he glances back—a reminder that I should hold my composure as well.

I decide on a cautious approach. Kyle is not a good option. He didn't know Adam personally, and I still have a bad feeling about him. I want to put my foot down and tell her no. She's irrational, and she'll come to regret this decision.

But that isn't how I wanted to start off my day with Emilia, so I decide to tell her I will consider it. But when she cuts me off for a second time, my patience wears thin.

"I've told Kyle all about my dad. He's not leaving me. He's decided to move here to be with me."

Emilia's words shock me to my core.

I'd just finished telling Noah about Kyle leaving after the funeral. He was going back to school, and she was going to get on with the life she was meant for. This unexpected information slams into me, and my ears ring as my control breaks.

"WHAT?" My question roars out of me. I no longer have time for her misguided interest in Kyle.

I should have never allowed her to leave last night. I should have excused everyone at dinner but her and dealt with her then, in the dining room. Now Kyle has had the whole night to make these inane plans, and she's had no one there to look out for what's best for her.

"W-well, I mean, we talked about it, and you said you transferred my classes over so easily. He said he would look at doing the same thing." Her voice sounds more unsure than it did a minute ago.

Good.

A silence lingers between us as I make plans for Kyle in my head. One wrong word could send Emilia running right back to him, and I won't allow her to gamble her inheritance on him.

"That's really thoughtful of him, Emilia. To consider moving here." Noah speaks purposefully, breaking the tension. It pulls her attention off of me long enough for me to get my head back in the game.

More than ever, I'm thankful for my friend. I don't know how this would go if he wasn't here.

"It is," she answers slowly, then looks back to me and continues, "We're going to discuss it more after the funeral. We were thinking we could get a place together close by. Students don't make much, and I thought my allowance could go to our rent."

I've gathered myself, and my facade is back. "I think it's great that he wants to support you, Emilia, but the terms are set. You will live under this roof for the year. We can discuss your allowance going toward his accommodations after the funeral though. Why don't you have him over for dinner on Wednesday? We'll discuss his being a pallbearer then. Noah, would you like to join us?"

Noah knows me well enough to know this isn't a question. He instantly nods as I continue, "And Emilia, you could invite Rosalyn as well."

Emilia's full lips part. I know she was expecting a battle. But she doesn't realize I've already won the war.

"Okay. Thank you. I'd like that." Her smile returns, and I take the opportunity to change the subject.

"I'd like to order some flowers for the service. What do you think your father would have liked?" As I ask my question, I move around the desk and take a seat. Then I grab a piece of paper and begin to write some notes, but they aren't for Adam's funeral.

Sitting down is an invitation for Emilia to join us or excuse herself, and I already know what her choice will be by her body language.

"He always loved lemon balm. I know it's not a flower, but he used to ask Sylvia to plant it outside his office window and along the deck every summer. For flowers, he wasn't picky, but my mother's favorite were forget-me-nots and tulips."

I forgot how Emilia's face softens every time she speaks about her mother.

"Thank you. That is what I'll order," I answer, swallowing hard, as my mouth has suddenly become dry.

"You want to join us?" Noah asks as he takes his seat in

front of the desk. I notice she places one foot behind her, and I'm suddenly happy that I can finally read her better.

"No, thank you, Noah. I've got to put my things away. I'll see you at dinner, Joshua."

I nod and let her go.

As the door closes, I allow my smile to leave with her.

When I look over to Noah, I'm suddenly irritated by his smirk.

"What?" I bark out at his chuckle.

"Man, that one has really got you, doesn't she? I mean...I've never seen anyone get under your skin so easily. It's not often I get to watch my best friend lose his shit. And she has no idea, does she?" he asks.

I have bigger fish to fry.

"Shut up," I retort, ignoring his chortles. "I want you to do something for me," I say a little quieter.

He leans forward, grabbing a mint from the bowl on the desk. "You want me to look into the kid?" he asks, though he already knows the answer.

I nod as I slide the paper I was writing on across the desk. "This is everything I know about him. I'll text you the picture of his driver's license I took for his hotel booking," I finish as he reaches across the desk for the paper.

"I'll start making some calls." He pockets my note. Then, leaning back in his chair, he takes a second to consider his next words, and I wait for him to continue. "Can I give you some advice?"

I breathe deep at his question. Noah's advice is never sugarcoated, and he's almost always right. I don't respond, which is his cue to proceed.

"From everything you've told me and everything I've seen, Emilia is a strong woman, but I sense she doesn't feel strong right now. She most likely feels lost and very much alone.

People in those situations tend to cling to any support they can find. You two have this volatile history, and there is a metric ton of angst between you. If you want to be the one who helps her find her way back home, you need to unlearn some of your own lessons and let go of some of your perceptions. What I'm trying to say is, over this next year, you're going to need to do just as much work as she will if you want to be that one person for her."

I sit in silence as his words soak in. I know he's right. My own year isn't going to be easy, and I need to start by accepting that Kyle is probably a great guy who is becoming closer to a woman who barely tolerates me right now.

We need to undo years of assumptions, and I need to start by pulling apart our roots and repairing our foundation.

While Emilia learns the company, I will learn her.

Then I will earn her.

"Now, all that's left to talk about before we break for lunch is the annual corporate dinner."

Joshua has been all business since we got to the office this morning.

After arriving at the house yesterday to find him and Noah discussing the funeral, I spent the afternoon unpacking and sitting outside in the yard by myself. Joshua gave me some space, and our dinner was fairly quiet, with only a few general questions from Joshua about my time at school.

The morning on campus was uneventful. It turns out my course load will be lighter than the one I had back home. Joshua was able to negotiate my internship in exchange for a large chunk of the remaining credits I need, so I'm doing two classes in the morning, and the rest is hands-on experience.

After a quick tour of the office, including the new floor expansion, we got to work. While the tech team set up my clearance and passwords, Joshua shared the company's latest news and growth projections. We reviewed an outline of my responsibilities, and I have to say, my workload is disappointingly light, but Joshua explained I'll have more duties before I know it. Right now, our priorities are my dad's funeral and getting settled into my classes.

"When is the dinner?" I ask, now aware of how much I don't know about my father's company.

"Two weeks from now; the last Friday of the month. In light of our current situation, would you like to look at rescheduling?" he asks as he keeps his eyes on the paper resting on the desk in front of him.

A part of me wants to reschedule, and another part of me doesn't want to have it at all. This was my father's favorite work event. He used to talk about it for months leading up to it. Recognizing his coworkers for their achievements meant everything to him, and I don't know if I can get through something so important without him.

But this isn't about me. I know my dad would want the night to go on.

"No. The date is fine. Thank you," I answer and Joshua sits back in his chair, examining my face for a moment before returning to his original position.

"Very well. If you are up to it, I would like you to present the staff awards this year on Adam's behalf."

Joshua's request catches me off guard.

I haven't been an employee at my father's company for a day, yet he is asking me to do this for him.

"Yes, I'd like to do that for you...I mean, for my father," I answer eagerly, then wince at my misspoken words.

My stomach knots in excitement, and I suddenly guard myself.

I am not doing this for Joshua; I am doing this for my father. I need to get my thoughts together and focus.

"Wonderful." If Joshua heard me correctly, he didn't show it, and I breathe a deep sigh of relief as he writes some notes down in his little book. As his pen moves across the paper, the edge of his mouth curves up into a subtle smile, and I'm instantly happy with myself for making him happy.

"Mr. Darkly. There's a gentleman here for Ms. Connor. He says they have a date for lunch." The secretary's voice speaks through the phone, and Joshua looks up to me for confirmation.

"That must be Kyle. I told him to wait downstairs. Sorry." I mumble my apology, and Joshua presses the intercom to respond.

"We're just wrapping up. Send him in." Then, releasing the button, he speaks under his breath. "He's not good at following orders, is he?"

I shrug and rise to gather my things as the door opens.

"So this is where you work. Hello, honey." Kyle, all smiles, makes his way across to me and leans in for a kiss. Shifting my head to the side, I silently hope he'll just kiss my cheek, and he does.

At the company I plan on owning one day, I need to keep up a professional appearance, and making out with my boyfriend doesn't fit my new narrative.

"Hello, Joshua. This is a nice office." Kyle breaks away and reaches his hand out to greet Joshua.

I notice the smallest hesitation in Joshua, no doubt because our meeting ended a little sooner than he'd planned, but he stands and extends his hand. "Kyle. It's nice to see you again."

I place my hand on Kyle's arm, hoping to pull him to the door.

"Thanks. Did Emilia tell you the good news?" Kyle beams, and I jump in before Joshua can ask what he's talking about.

"Um, not yet. We've been busy at work, and I haven't had the time." I offer my lame excuse.

I'd like to convince myself that the reason I haven't told

Joshua the news yet is because we were so busy with work, but I know that is a lie.

I received Kyle's text a little over an hour ago, when we were driving back to the office. Joshua and I were both sitting quietly in the back seat. I had every chance to say something. And I didn't.

I don't know why I didn't.

When we left campus, I felt a little weird. I became overwhelmed with the thought of starting over at a new school and the loss of my dad, and Joshua took over for me. He asked all of the right questions—questions I would never have thought to ask. Questions that only benefitted me.

For a while, I felt as though he was taking care of me. It felt like he was looking out for me. And it felt great.

As we drove back to the office, I was just about to thank him for his help when my phone buzzed. It was Kyle with his good news.

Only receiving it didn't feel so good, and I said nothing. Instead, I sat quietly, staring at the screen of my phone long after it went black.

"Well, we have some time now. What is this good news?" Joshua asks, glancing between the two of us, and I suddenly don't want to be the one to answer him.

"I was able to transfer my credits to be with Emilia," Kyle responds as I stand quietly between them.

I watch Joshua process Kyle's words. His demeanor is different than yesterday. Today, he seems more collected. I can't tell what he's thinking.

In a different world, these two would never be friends. I am the only thing they have in common. They are complete opposites in everything from their physical appearance to their business choices and their personality.

Kyle has always catered to me. He listened to me when I

spoke. My last year before I went off to college was a struggle. I couldn't talk to Sylvia about what was going on because I knew she'd make me tell my father, and I knew it would crush him. I tried one night to talk to Joshua about it, but that ended badly, and after that I knew I could never trust him with anything. So Rosalyn heard it all. She sat with me between all of the tears, and she promised to keep all of my secrets.

Sharing with Kyle was different. He listened. I never told him everything, but I knew if I needed, he would just let me speak, and I would be heard. It's probably all of his psychology courses.

Joshua's muscular physique looks more prominent beside Kyle's lithe frame. His posture is more purposeful, where Kyle always looks a little more aloof and casual.

"Interesting. You must have some friends in high places to be transferred so quickly. It took a lot of groundwork for us to get Emilia registered over halfway through the school year," Joshua responds slowly, and I shift my stare back to Kyle.

In all truth, I hadn't realized how difficult it must have been to get me into classes that were probably full and already half done. Suddenly, I become aware of just how hard Joshua worked to pull me back here.

As I prepared to come back and settle my father's estate, he was already working to keep me here. It was never going to work out the way I imagined it would, and Joshua knew that from the start.

"More luck, really. The psychology department here is down a couple of TA's, and I had my instructor make a call. It's too bad we can't be at the same university, but we are together, and that is what matters. Right, Emilia?" Kyle hangs his arm over my shoulder and squeezes me into him, and the embrace feels momentarily possessive.

At his question, Joshua's eyes travel back to me, and it feels like he's challenging me to answer. So I do.

"Right." I smile at Kyle, then drop my gaze to the floor.

Why do I feel like I've done something wrong?

"I'm just excited we can be together after all. Isn't it wonderful, Joshua?" Kyle's question feels awkward, and I suddenly sense he's overstayed his welcome in this office.

The air feels almost unbreathable, and Joshua's stare is beginning to weigh me down.

Before he answers, I break away and pull Kyle to the door. "I'm hungry. Let's get lunch. I'll tell you all about the city over a sandwich."

I reach out for the door when I hear Joshua clear his throat.

"Dinner on Wednesday, Emilia?" Joshua reminds me, and I keep moving out of the office.

"Right, I'll ask them and let you know," I answer loud enough that he can hear me from his office.

I drop my notebook onto my new desk, then I pull open the drawer and grab my bag as Kyle stops beside me with one hand on my arm.

Kyle normally isn't publicly affectionate, and his touch feels awkward. I glance back to the office to see Joshua standing in the open doorway, watching us. All of a sudden, this PDA feels more like it is meant for Joshua's benefit rather than my own.

"What about dinner?" Kyle asks. He draws a line down my arm, sending a strange shiver up my spine.

"Joshua wants to have you over for dinner on Wednesday. Just a thing with friends," I answer, checking to make sure I have enough money for lunch.

"Really?" His voice is odd, and it draws my attention to him as he grins in Joshua's direction. "Tell him I wouldn't miss it for the world."

"Tell me you have something on the guy." I can hear my desperation in my voice, and I hope Noah can't detect it through the phone.

"Your first day in the office with her going that well?" He chuckles through the receiver, telling me he heard me loud and clear.

"Not now, Noah." That's my signal to ease off.

To say it's been a day is an understatement. My emotions have been swinging like a pendulum since I woke up this morning, and I walked into the dining room to find her sitting patiently at the table, waiting for me so we could eat together.

I want every morning to be like that.

Seeing her smile as I joined her surprised me, and I haven't been able to get the image out of my head all day.

As we sat together talking to the department heads about Emilia's transfer, I had a moment when something felt wrong. The smallest of hitches in her voice as she spoke about the rest of the year alerted me. No one else in the room caught it, but it hit me hard. I turned my head to take her in as she began to falter. It was almost undetectable, but I felt she was calling out for help, and without thinking, I answered her call.

I waited for her to finish, then I asked some questions of my own. As I spoke, I noticed she began to relax as the attention moved off of her. Her body offered the smallest of cues to continue speaking for her, and I was more than glad to take care of her. She leaned back in her seat and let me take over the conversation, and it felt amazing to support her.

Everything dropped out from under me when Kyle showed up for a lunch date. We were getting on well in the office, and I had hoped to order lunch in and keep going, only to be derailed by this kid.

He isn't the same person I met on Saturday at the house. There is an inflated sense of confidence behind his smile now. Watching him put his scrawny arm around Emilia set me off inside, but I kept my composure. Showing my dislike toward him will only distance Emilia from me further. Instead, I let them leave together. Again.

"Got it," Noah answers, and I hear him shuffle some papers on his desk. "We need to meet quickly before you leave tonight. There is some kind of organized protest going on about one of the properties we plan to tear down."

It takes me a second to respond, and I realize I need to get my head in the game. I'm the head of a multimillion-dollar company, and my first thought is about Emilia.

"Sure, I'll drop by in an hour on my way out. Is there anything else?" I ask, feeling a little foolish.

"Yeah, I'm fucking with you. You do need to drop by though. I wanted to let you know I am looking into everything. I don't have much, but, since I'm fully aware you have no patience, I wanted to touch base." Noah laughs into the phone.

"What do you have?" I ask a little too quickly, and more papers are shuffled around.

"You texted earlier and said Kyle was transferring because of a shortage of TA's in their psychology department. I checked with a friend in sociology, and he told me there is no shortage in either department. He checked the TA list for Kyle's name, but there is no mention of him. It might not be anything though because the transfer hasn't happened yet, but I wanted to let you know. I'm still waiting on everything else, but I expect I won't hear until tomorrow."

I find relief in knowing there is a chance he isn't completely clean.

As I weigh the information, there's a soft knock at the door. My secretary must have stepped away for a moment.

"Thank you, I'll drop by in a bit. I've got to go." Ending the call, I address the person behind the door. "It's unlocked, come in."

Emilia pokes her head into the office. "Faye isn't at her desk, and I was hoping to talk to you before I leave."

"Of course. Come in." I stand to greet her and gesture to the chair in front of my desk.

Sometimes taking control is not leading. The voice in my head urges me to stay quiet and give Emilia the chance to speak first.

"Thank you." She smiles as she walks in and pulls out the chair, and I sit back into my seat. "I just wanted to say thank you for your help at the university, and for helping me here." Her tone is quiet, and it isn't lost on me how difficult this must have been for her to say.

Not even a week ago, she was planning a very different future for herself. Now she's sitting in my office, working under me and thanking me for my help. I don't know if I would have the strength to be gracious if I were in her position.

But Emilia stands apart from the rest of us. Her determination is an inspiration to me.

"You're welcome. How was your first day?" I decide to offer her a small mercy and change the topic.

"It was fine. I was mostly reading at my desk. Going over our corporate plans." She smiles with her response.

"Dry stuff, I know. I wrote a lot of it, and you couldn't pay me to read it." I chuckle, and her smile turns into a laugh, sending me into another emotional tailspin.

I could sit here all night and listen to her laugh, but it's gone as quickly as it started, and her guard is up again.

I feel a flash of anger. She is taking herself away from me. I want to enjoy her smile, and she is back to speaking cautiously. This is a bad habit I will need to break her of.

"I was wondering if I could go out with Rosalyn tonight. I don't have anything nice enough to wear to my father's...um, to his..." Her words trail off, and her throat tightens as she tries to swallow her sadness.

"Of course." I open the drawer to my desk, retrieve my wallet, and pull out my credit card. "Here. Your payments haven't been worked out yet. Please, take my card. If you need anything else for work or school, feel free to get it."

She reaches out to accept the card. Her cool fingers gently brush along my warm skin, sending signals straight to my cock, and it reacts to such an innocent connection.

"Thank you," she responds, and I can't help myself. In one primal moment of thinking with the wrong head, I push.

"And if you need anything new to sleep in, remember my favorite color is see-through." I put my intention out there with a hungry smile. Considering what my brain wants to say, this is tame.

I know where she stands with Kyle, but I won't sit back and let him write her story.

When I get through with Emilia, Kyle will be lucky to even have a footnote in her book.

"Um...okay," she mumbles.

I sit still, enjoying the flush taking over her face.

The tension is palpable. It ebbs and flows between us as she shifts awkwardly in her seat. The pull is intoxicating, and I wonder if she feels it too.

"Wh-what time do you want me at the house by?"

Her question delights me. Following my rules is easy for her, and my brain immediately lists five new rules I would love to have her obey right now.

"How about nine o'clock? You start classes tomorrow. After you are done shopping, why don't you and Rosalyn go out for dinner. On me." I decide to reward her, and I point to the card as I watch her smile return to her soft lips.

"Thank you." She stands, no doubt trying to get out the door before I change my mind. "Rosie has a car. I'll be home before nine."

As she leaves, I already know her fate. It doesn't matter what I find out about Kyle. Emilia is not his, and she never will be.

In my darkest depths, I've known it ever since I first saw her, even before I knew certain things about myself. I can try to fight it, but every road I take leads to her. Under her graceful exterior lies a storm, and it rages for me. She has a darkness about her, and I can't look away. I gravitate to her, and my ache to control her is intense.

Emilia will be mine; she was always meant to be.

CHAPTER 25
EMILIA

"I still can't believe this restaurant is where your old house used to be," I say, picking up a spoon and leaning over the table for my first bite of the triple-chocolate cake we decided to share.

"Isn't it crazy? By my best guess, I'd say this table is where my bedroom used to be. Remember all of the sleepovers we used to have, like, right here?" Rosie smiles at me and continues as she reaches for her own spoon, "My parents are happy though. Everyone on the block got more than market value, and it was enough for them to retire early."

"It's amazing how some things change so fast," I say as I moan down my second bite of the decadent dessert.

"And how some things stay the same," she responds quickly, catching my attention. I am suddenly curious where she is going with this.

"Are you kidding? What has possibly stayed the same since I left home?" I ask as I place my spoon on the table and reach for my water. I'm both nervous about and interested in her response.

Rosie was my best friend all through high school. I'd say she still is, but we did lose touch while I was away. Letting go of almost everything back home helped me move on from some things. At least I thought it did.

Rosie was a lot like my father. She knew some things bothered me about this place, but, unlike my dad, Rosalyn knew exactly what those things were.

When I compare five years ago to now, I don't see any similarities. "As a matter of fact, nothing is the same outside of our friendship."

Rosalyn smiles then reaches her hand across the table, and I don't hesitate to reach my own out to meet hers. "I feel the same way. But I meant you and Joshua."

At his name, I reflexively pull my hand back, and Rosie continues, "See? Even now, just hearing his name sets you off."

Have I become so easy to read that my own body betrays the mask I wear? Indifference is what I have always aimed for in his presence, but the more aloof I tried to be, the more he always pushed my buttons.

"I'm just trying to get through my dad's funeral, and everything is so—" I pause to think of the right word, then offer a sly smile as I complete my sentence. "Different. Nothing is the same anymore, and there are some things I never wanted to face that I am going to need to."

"Just because you chose not to face them doesn't mean they've gone away." My eyes meet Rosie's, and I instantly know what she's talking about. "Maybe you should have the talk you wanted to have with your dad, but with Joshua. Maybe that part of him has changed."

Rosie's words take me back to the night I tried to talk to Joshua about some of the boys in my class. He verbally backed me into a corner. I tried to defend myself and tell him some truths about some of his friends, but he shut me down before I could even get my words out.

That was the night he told me what he really thought of me. I'd heard it all from his friends, but coming from him, it crushed me. After that, I never tried to confide in him again. I never defended myself. His opinion of me would never change.

"No."

"No?"

"No, I won't be having that talk with Joshua." My answer lingers between us for a long minute as I turn my attention to the cake on the table between us.

"Tell me about Kyle." Rosie's change in topic confuses me for a moment, but I'm thankful to not be talking about Joshua any longer.

"Oh. We met at school. He's nice." As I speak, I immediately feel defeated again as Rosie stiffens.

"Nice? Really, Ems? *Nice* is an aunt who sends you a card on your birthday. *Nice* was never your type." She snickers at me, and I can't help but laugh.

"You don't even know my type, Rosie. I never had a type in high school."

"I think we need one more glass of wine before we get the bill." Rosie speaks directly to the waiter as he saunters up to the table. Then, turning her attention back to me, she continues, "Fair enough. Neither of us dated enough to have a type in high school, but I know you better than anyone. *Nice* would never have been it. What's Kyle like, you know, when you're alone? And if you say nice again, you're walking home." She giggles.

As her laughter dies down, I shrug. "Honestly, it wasn't everything I imagined it would be." I drop my voice and answer quietly as the waiter returns with our wine.

"Wait." Rosie pauses as the waiter circles around beside her and leaves us with our drinks. Matching my lowered tone, she asks as she leans into the table, "Are you saying Kyle was your first?"

"He was. You know I don't like to be—touched. Most guys in college won't wait around long enough for a 'frigid bitch to thaw out.'" I actually quote one of my previous boyfriends.

"Oh, Emi. I'm so sorry you put up with that garbage. I wish I was there for you," she starts, and the last thing I want is for her to feel sorry for me.

"Hey, it's fine," I lie. "It was a great way to weed out the losers. Kyle was actually my friend first. He knows a little about our high school years. He was fine with being friends for the longest time."

"He sounds like a great guy. I can't wait to meet him on Wednesday." She smiles at me, then flashes a mischievous grin. "Now, back to when you're alone. What wasn't like you imagined?" she asks. Then she takes a gulp of her wine and waits for my response.

I want to say he was gentle, hesitant, and caring, because he was. But that was also what was wrong about it. It was nothing I wanted, and it made the entire experience feel awkward. I had reasoned that my first time was bound to feel odd, but the second time was a lot of the same, and I began to wonder what was wrong with me.

I'm a walking oxymoron. I don't trust anyone quickly, and I don't like to be touched, but the thoughts I have tell a different story.

Am I incapable of having a caring relationship when my fantasies drift toward dark rooms and being bound? The gentleness of Kyle's touch was lost on me. As I closed my eyes, I imagined being taken by rough control, only to be met with shame when I opened my eyes to find Kyle staring at me lovingly.

Instead, I breeze past Rosie's question with a shrug. "Probably just first-time jitters."

"Hm. Or he's *nice* but not your type. I still think you need someone stronger than you are. And you, my darling, are mighty strong." She smiles and raises her glass in cheers. I lift my own glass, and we take a sip before she says, "Speaking of which, how is everything going with Joshua?"

"What do you mean?" I ask as nonchalantly as I can manage.

"Well, two strong-willed individuals under the same roof. It's only a matter of time before you both burn that house down. You know that, right?" She looks over the rim of her glass as she takes her last sip, then places it on the table.

The look on her face tells me she wants to say more, so I wait. "Speaking of things that haven't changed, how about your feelings for Joshua? Have those changed? Or just festered?" she asks, and now it's her turn to sit in silence.

"I don't know what you're talking about." I huff out a half laugh.

"Ems, I was always with you. I know you had a crush on him in junior high. You took everything he said and did to heart because you liked him so much."

"Everything does change after all then." I avoid answering with my observation.

Reaching across the table for the bill, I drop Joshua's card on top of the little piece of paper and grab my purse, hoping Rosie will get the hint that I'm ready to leave.

My hopes are dashed when she crosses her arms across her chest and tries again. "Fine. One last question. That sexy little nightie you picked up tonight. Were you thinking about Kyle or Joshua when you bought it?"

You know it's time to call it a night when the words on your laptop screen stop making sense. It's almost eleven o'clock, and I suddenly feel exhaustion creeping in.

I had Sylvia bring my dinner up, and I've been sitting here since I came home from work, trying to tie up some loose ends before they turn into a knot. It doesn't help that we are down the most important person in the company.

Adam was not the type of owner to assign everything to those under him and go golfing. He had his hands in everything. He mentored everyone, and he led by example. This made for a lot of strong employees, but it also means he left behind a lot of responsibilities that need to be reassigned and managed.

I was briefly interrupted by a commotion and some laughter in the hall just before nine. Emilia has only been here for a couple of days, but the house felt too empty without her tonight.

Hearing her move around her room and laugh with her

friend settled me, and I found an odd comfort in working while she was nearby.

I turn off the office light and walk down the hall toward the sound of two distinct voices. Emilia must have invited Rosalyn over.

As I knock on her door, the room goes quiet.

"Um, come in," Emilia calls out, and I open the door to find the two friends sitting on the bed with various pieces of clothing draped around the room.

"It looks like you both had fun," I state as I curiously glance over her items for any sign of more revealing pieces.

"We did. Thank you so much for dinner." Rosalyn stands as she speaks, and I get the feeling she understands it's time to go. "I need to get home. Work tomorrow." She shrugs knowingly.

"You're welcome, Rosalyn. I'm glad you enjoyed yourselves."

"And thank you for the dinner invitation. I'll see you on Wednesday, um...Mr...."

"Joshua. Outside of work, it's Joshua," I confirm, and her smile returns as she grabs her jacket.

Swinging her purse over her shoulder, she knocks one of Emilia's small bags off the dresser. When I lean over to pick it up, my fingers touch the soft fabric of the item that spilled out, drawing my full attention to the little item I'm now holding.

Emilia gasps from the bed, then jumps up and walks toward me, and I'm suddenly more awake than I've been all day.

"Oops. Sorry, Ems." Rosalyn laughs nervously as she continues, "I know my way out. I'll see you tomorrow." Both women wave as she leaves the room, shutting the door behind her.

Her friend's hasty retreat makes me wonder about their

conversation tonight. I can't help but run my fingers over the silky piece of cloth. I'm mesmerized by the way my skin glides effortlessly across it. I want to hold it up so I can get a full view, but I know Emilia is about to try to take it back.

"I'll just—" She reaches out and grabs the part dangling over my fist. As she tugs, I hold firm, gauging her reaction.

Her gaze shoots up to meet mine. I sense panic behind her wide eyes, and I can't stop the grin from spreading across my face.

"What have we here?" My question sounds more forward than I would have liked it to. I know I'll scare her off if I come on too strong.

"It's just...I saw it when I was getting some things to sleep in, and I liked it. It wasn't necessary. I'll pay you back when the allowance comes through." She tugs once more in a second failed attempt to retrieve her item.

"No need," I respond and loosen my hold so she can take it back. "What is it?" I ask, trying my best to sound ignorant. I know exactly what it is; I just can't see it in its entirety...yet.

The lace and straps along the top are a dead giveaway for a nightgown, and, judging by the lack of fabric, I would say it is short. I can't decide if it's blue or green, but I know it is see-through, and the light in the room shimmers off of it.

"Oh, um...it-it's just a thing t-to sleep in," she stutters.

I've decided I enjoy Emilia like this. She's lost in my questions, and she's not analyzing our conversation. Her brain isn't shutting down her heart. I know because I'm still standing in her room.

"Show it to me." I drop my voice lower as I stay where I am. It's not lost on me that she hasn't stepped away from me yet.

Lowering her attention to the material in her hands, her breathing deepens.

If only she'd let me take control of her here like she let me at her school.

My cock hardens at the thought of telling her what to do, and my own breathing has almost come to a complete stop as I wait for her decision.

As if the war in her head has concluded, she gives herself a little shrug and opens the fabric, holding it in front of her sheepishly. She's no longer making eye contact.

The lingerie looks fluid in her hands, and I instantly find myself fighting the urge to tell her to put it on.

"I, um...thought maybe Kyle..." Her words sound empty to me. I wonder if she believes herself.

But she's right. As much as I want to see her body fill out this little thing then remove it from her, the circumstances need to be different.

"Shame," I whisper.

"P-pardon?" I know she heard me; she's just looking for more to go on, and I decide to give it to her.

"I said it's a shame that something so..." As I speak, I reach out to run my fingers over the fabric, and her lips part as she takes in every word. "*Inviting* will be wasted on someone who may not appreciate everything it offers."

The air in the room around us feels galvanic as everything fades away. Continuing to play with the material she's holding, I enjoy the silence between us.

This is the side of Emilia I want to explore.

My sanity comes close to crumbling as I watch her tongue jut out and lick along her lips. Her eyes focus on mine, but I maintain my resolve.

I won't take what's mine while she's attached to someone else, even if I don't believe for a second he is the right choice for her.

I expect more from Emilia. She needs to leave Kyle and come to me on her own, and now is not the time.

As much as I want to continue nudging Emilia in my direction, I need to back off a bit. The doe-eyed look on her face is becoming torturous.

"It's getting late," I offer, and she blinks a few times before straightening in her place.

I know I had her. For a moment, I had her here with me. Her brain checked out, and I had the real her. I keep my face frozen in indifference, but on the inside, I want to smile.

"Oh. Yes, it is." She clutches her lingerie to her chest. Then she turns, picks up the bag it fell out of, and faces me. "I'll see you at breakfast?"

The fact that it was a question is not lost on me, and I nod and smile as I reach for the door handle.

"Um, Joshua?" I turn to give her my attention, and she continues, "Thank you for helping me get something to wear for the funeral—and for dinner. I left your card by your keys in the front hall."

"You're welcome, Emilia. Have a good sleep." We exchange a smile at my good night.

As I walk to my own room, visions of Emilia holding out her nightie in front of me taunt me. I want to turn around and give in to my needs, but I keep moving farther away from her room.

It's all a matter of time now, and I can be a patient man if it means finally getting what is mine.

CHAPTER 27
EMILIA

My first couple of days at my dad's company seemed to go by quickly. I spent most of my time learning my key contacts and my new responsibilities, and I haven't run into Sean or any of his buddies from high school yet, but I think it's just a matter of time.

Joshua spent most of Tuesday out of the office. I spent the day learning his secretary's responsibilities so I could cover for her when she had to run an errand or take some personal time like she is right now.

When Joshua returned from his last meeting, he asked if I was up to speed enough to handle Faye's work while she ran some errands for him. The truth is, I was more than up to speed, and I was excited to show him what I could do, so I jumped at the chance.

Faye is the definition of organized. As she taught me what I needed to know today, she took her own notes along with me, so I had two detailed instructions to go on.

Opening Joshua's calendar, I scanned the rest of his day for visitors. To my disappointment, it would be just me.

"You look a little lonely." I snap my head up to see Noah walking toward my desk with a folder full of papers. "Is Mr. Darkly available?"

I glance at the phone on my desk. "It looks like he's on a call. I can message him to tell him you're here if it's important."

"It is important, unfortunately." He offers me an apologetic smile as he taps his file, and I open the message app on Faye's computer to tell Joshua Noah is here to see him and it's urgent.

The response comes back almost immediately.

"He says to wait for a few minutes. He's just wrapping up a business call."

Noah pulls up a chair and sits in front of me. "Thanks. You don't mind if I hang here with you for a bit, do you?" He flashes me a little wink, and I offer a flattered smile back.

"I don't mind," I answer, then pause. I don't know what else to say.

Thankfully, Noah fills the silence. "So tell me, how are your first couple of days?"

"They've been a little dry, but I'm learning a lot," I answer, and he nods.

"It must be difficult to be uprooted in the middle of your last year."

"It wasn't easy, but it hasn't been too hard. Now that Kyle is moving out to be with me, I won't feel too alone."

Noah leans back in his seat, considering his next words. "Right." His pause feels awkward. "Look, if you need anything, someone to talk to, I want to let you know I'm here for you. I know you don't know me well, but I want to see you and Joshua succeed."

My breath catches in my throat at his words.

Does he know everything?

"What do you mean?" I ask, silently praying he doesn't know what I think he knows.

He takes a moment too long to respond; he quietly watches me before finally settling my curiosity. "The company. I want to see you both successful together as the owners of Connor Realty. I think if you have patience and give some things time, you'll find your...*arrangement* will benefit you both, together."

I feel like he is only partially speaking about my dad's company.

"Oh. Thank you. I appreciate that," I answer as a click in the phone tells me Joshua is calling through.

"Tell Noah to come in. Thank you."

At his name, Noah stands and slides his chair back to its original position. Nodding with a smile, he turns to the door and lets himself into Joshua's office, leaving me alone with my thoughts once again.

I use the downtime to go through some details for our company dinner. Winners of the staff awards have still not been finalized, but the details of the event are already decided. The dinner and ceremony will be held at The Plaza, where Kyle is currently staying. They have a wonderful catering and event-planning team there.

When I check out the tentative seating arrangements, I notice some eraser marks around my table. It looks like revisions have been made since my father's passing, and I am sitting in the seat my father was going to sit in. Beside my name is a +1 with a question mark, and I notice Joshua has the same beside his name as well.

Taking a pencil, I erase my own question mark and write in Kyle's name, then I close the file and leave it for Faye. That took all of five minutes of my time, so I return to silently looking around for something to do.

As the hour drags on, nostalgia gets the better of me, and I search through my dad's calendar to see what he would have been doing now. It looks like he scheduled this hour each day to catch up on emails and paperwork.

My heart feels heavy, and I look to the ceiling, imagining him still sitting upstairs in his office. So near, yet so far away. Just as I feel the sting of fresh tears, I hear a throat clear in front of my desk.

"I'm sorry, I was just—" I try to stammer out a greeting, but the woman hovering over me cuts me off.

"I saw what you were *just doing*. Really, Joshua needs to hire better staff. His last secretary...what was her name? Faith? She was always so rude to me. I'm glad he replaced her, but you don't seem much better." The woman flips her blonde hair and looks around as if she owns the place, and I get the impression only one of us knows she doesn't.

"You mean Faye? She's running an errand. I'm filling in for her. I don't recall seeing anything in Mr. Darkly's schedule about a visitor this afternoon. You are?" I plaster my best smile across my face and wait for her answer.

She's looking at me as though I have two heads. She feigns shock that I, someone who has never met her before, don't know who she is.

"Well then, I guess Faye didn't tell you everything, did she? Very well. I'm Tawny Davenfield. Joshua will want to see me." Her confidence creeps under my skin, and my patience begins to waver.

"And why will he want to see you?" I ask one last time, hoping to get an idea of who I'm dealing with before I send this lady packing.

"I'm Joshua's fiancée."

Noah wastes no time dropping his file on my desk and pulling out a seat to get comfortable.

"Is this everything you have on Kyle Hollis?" I ask as I slide the file around to face me.

"No.. There's nothing about Kyle Hollis in there," Noah answers.

"What?" I ask incredulously. I've waited for two days for more information about the guy, and I still have nothing.

"I found nothing on Kyle Hollis because Kyle Hollis doesn't exist." Noah leans back in his seat and continues, "This is everything I have on Kyle Gershaw."

As the realization that Kyle is using a fake name sinks in, I slowly open the file to the first piece of paper inside. Staring back at me is an older version of the man who is pretending to be Emilia's support.

Impatience races through me like a speedboat, and I try to look at the next paper underneath, but Noah's hand blocks my attempt.

"Before you read this, I need you to promise me we will talk about all of this. You won't make any rash decisions, and you won't show it to Emilia yet."

My anger surges at my friend's request. "Why? She needs to know if something is wrong. If he's hurting her, I'll tear him apart." I bark, my urge to protect her immediately rising to my surface.

Noah pulls the file back into his possession and speaks slowly. His concern for Emilia is evident, and it alerts me to my own impulsiveness. "Joshua, I've seen everything in this file, remember? It's not good, but you need to think only about Emilia right now. This is a really bad time for her. Her father's funeral is in two days. She's lost everything. She's a strong woman, but even she can only take so much." Leaning back and tapping the folder, he continues, "The information in this file will anger you, but it will devastate her regardless of how she feels about him. You don't want to be the one who does that to her. Just promise me, when you are done looking through everything, we will sit here and talk about it until we figure out a plan." Noah clutches the file and waits for my response.

"After I read the file, we will talk about it. If Emilia is in danger, though, I reserve the right to handle things as I see fit." I slide my own little demand in there and wait.

Noah nods, accepting my terms. Then he slides the file back over to me.

I hastily open it and read over the first page. Kyle's real driver's license was issued three states over from his fake one, and it turns out he is my age—five years older than Emilia. He looks older with a beard in the photo staring back at me.

As I turn each page, Noah gives me the rundown. "At first I was getting nowhere. I checked all of the psychology classes at Emilia's university, and he wasn't listed anywhere. Then I expanded my search to all of the class records over the last three years. I still got nothing." As he speaks, his voice speeds up. I think he missed his calling—he would make a great detective. "So, I called a guy."

"You know a guy?" I'm almost more interested in Noah's story than I am in the file now.

"Shut up. I know a guy," he answers with a chuckle. "Anyway, he has access to software that will run photos against DMV databases. By pure luck, Arizona's database was connected, and out popped his real identification. After that, I was able to pull up all of this information."

Noah opens his mouth to continue, then closes it, and I turn the pages, looking through his history.

I know I hoped to find something on this guy, but my heart sinks further with every page I turn. Emilia was nothing more than a target. Prior complaints from other universities under a couple other fake names show a history of settling in at a large university and choosing victims to pursue, usually women from wealthy backgrounds. The large campuses make it easier for him to blend in and lie without being discovered quickly. Anyone can walk in off the street and sit in on a lecture. He cons his way in and lives off their dime for as long as he can.

"The guy's a gold digger," I say to myself and Noah mumbles his agreement.

"It looks like he chose psychology because Emilia's roommate was taking a psychology class. He wouldn't be able to get too close to Emilia's classes because she'd figure it out. He must have thought he hit the jackpot when her father passed away," Noah says, and the blood rushes to my face.

"Fine," I say, closing the file folder.

"Fine?" Noah echoes.

"Yes. Fine. I've read everything, and Emilia's life isn't in danger. I can't say as much for Kyle, but I agreed we would talk about it first. So, talk."

Noah reaches across the desk to take back his file, but it's my turn to claim it.

This file isn't leaving my office.

"Okay, look. You know I'm all for being honest. You both have a lot of things to talk about, but I don't think this is one of them right now. I think—"

I cut Noah off. "How can I not say something? Kyle is going to take all of her money. If he—"

Now it's Noah's turn to cut me off. But he lowers his voice, reminding me Emilia may hear us arguing. "What money?"

It stops me cold as Emilia's situation sinks in.

Emilia has no money—not right now, anyway. Kyle is hanging around, waiting for an outcome before he decides what to do.

"You're right."

"If we share more of Emilia's dire situation, or offer him an out, maybe everything will resolve itself. If you're asking for my opinion, I say we wait until after the funeral. Emilia is extremely vulnerable right now. You said you gave her rules— she sleeps in her own bed each night from now on no matter what until we can deal with Kyle. He 'gives her the support she needs' to get through the day, then we make our move, on our terms. Can you do that?" he asks, and for a moment I'm not sure.

Back in high school, I couldn't be bothered to spend any of my time on Emilia. I let her down until she stopped relying on me at all, and look where it got her.

I won't let her down again.

"I can do that."

"Good. One last thing. Try not to be alone with the guy. He has a habit of pushing your buttons, and I wouldn't want him to focus on your money instead." Noah says as he stands, and I rise and follow him to the door.

I open it just in time to see a shocked Emilia sitting at Faye's desk as Tawny hovers over her, announcing she is my fiancée. I glance over and see the "you're fucked" look on Noah's face as he quickly leaves me in my own hell.

"Ms. Davenfield. It's a pleasure to see you. I didn't think we had an appointment today," My smile isn't warm.

In all honesty, I used to allow Tawny's advances in front of Faye—it was no one's business who was or was not mine. But things are different now that Emilia is sitting in that chair.

I care very much that she knows this is a lie.

"Oh, I just wanted to stop in and say hello. I heard about Adam, darling, and I'm here to offer my condolences in person. I ran into your mother, and she told me you weren't doing well with the news." She feigns altruism, and I catch Emilia rolling her eyes.

"I'm sorry; I should introduce you—" I start, and Tawny cuts me off.

"Oh, it's not necessary." She says it as though she has no need to learn the names of those she deems less than her.

"Oh, I think it is. Tawny, this is Emilia Connor, Adam's daughter. Emilia, Tawny's father owns the new arena; we recently acquired it for them." I watch as two distinct personalities meet.

Emilia graciously stands, setting aside any first impressions. She extends her hand to welcome Tawny, who she currently thinks is my fiancée. I can't help but be proud of her for holding it together. She is her father's daughter.

Then there's Tawny, who technically doesn't own anything and truly does live off of her father's money. She's staring down her nose, clearly threatened by my temporary secretary.

The two shake hands, and I'm ready to cut this surprise visit short.

The truth is, I always forgot about Tawny as soon as she left my sight, but now I need to draw some lines.

"I think I interrupted something. You were saying?" I direct my question to Tawny, but I know she won't answer, so I look at Emilia, who helps me out.

"Ms. Davenfield was just telling me she's your fiancée." I catch a hint of sadness in her tone. It sets me on fire.

"Tawny, is this true?" I pretend to be more shocked than I am.

"I—well, you know, it's just a matter of time really. I mean..." She falls over her words, and I think Emilia gets the point, so I change the subject. My day has already been too long.

"I'm sorry, Ms. Davenfield. I have a conference call about to start. Can I ask the reason for your visit today?" I ask curtly.

"Well, your mother reminded me about your employee dinner at the end of the month. She said you were going to ask me. You know, as a representative from my family's company."

I can't believe the nerve of my mother.

I'm just about to say no when Emilia clears her throat, drawing my attention to a file she has open on the desk.

"I just added Kyle as my plus-one on the seating arrangements. Do you want me to change yours as well?"

The question stuns me for a moment, and it's just the amount of time Tawny needs to wedge herself in.

"Sure, put me down. I'm looking forward to it. Joshua, I'll be in touch." Tawny spins on her heels, no doubt trying to make a quick exit before I come to my senses.

As my momentary fog clears, I look over to see Emilia erasing the +1 and adding in that crazy woman's name, and I'm reminded all over again how much worse this is going to get before it gets better.

I know another thing Emilia doesn't know, and this secret sucks.

Strip away all of our history, and I see a lost girl who has innocently chosen to trust a user. I want to make everything better for her, but I know when she looks at me, she doesn't see her hero. At least, not yet.

"Emilia, I'm giving you the rest of the week off," She straightens up in disagreement. "Thank you for coming in this week. I know how difficult this is for you. You will attend classes tomorrow morning, and I've already advised your instructors you have a funeral and will be out Thursday and Friday. They will give you your work for the week at the end of classes tomorrow. I heard from Sylvia; your boxes from your dorm arrived. You can spend some time getting settled, and we have dinner tomorrow night. I'll be available if you need anything, and I'll see you at home for dinner."

Suddenly, I am tired. This new information about Kyle has worn me out, and the effort I'm using to keep from hurting him is draining me. Top that off with Tawny, and I'm done. I need to be in this office alone tomorrow. I need to compose myself before I invite Kyle back into our home for dinner, and I need to work out a few other details.

Emilia stares at me for a moment before nodding, and I see her exhaustion as well. Jumping into a new life is taking its toll on her.

"Thank you, Joshua. I appreciate you trying to help," she answers, and I feel guilty.

Am I trying to help her, or am I trying to help myself?

Or are they both the same thing?

CHAPTER 29
EMILIA

"I love that blue-gray color on you, Ems. It highlights your eyes." Rosalyn rifles through my jewelry box, looking for a necklace to borrow.

This reminds me of high school. Rosalyn and I shared so many pieces of clothes and jewelry that I'm sure she still has a bunch of my things in her closet.

"Here's my old necklace. I forgot about it." Rosalyn laughs as she holds it up between us.

"It would go great with your dress. Want me to help you put it on?"

She hands me the dainty silver thread and spins around, lifting her curly auburn hair out of the way for me.

As I release the clasp, Rosalyn turns back to me and takes a deep breath.

"Are you okay?" she asks, and I suddenly feel exhausted.

"Honestly, I'm not sure. I barely got through class today. Everything is starting to sink in. I feel like I've been running around for a solid week, and I haven't had time to really think about tomorrow. Sometimes it feels like he's not gone. But he is, and tomorrow is coming, and I need to deal with it. I'm thankful Joshua told me to stay home for the rest of this week, and I don't know what I would do without you or Kyle here."

She pulls me into a big hug before we both start crying.

The sound of the doorbell catches our attention, and we break apart, taking deep breaths to compose ourselves.

"This should be the guy you've told me all about," she says with a smile. I check my hair in the mirror, then usher Rosalyn out of my room and down the hall.

As we hit the top of the stairs, Kyle smiles up at us. A wave of sadness hits me with each step I take down the staircase. This is the beginning of my public mourning. The next couple of days will be filled with the stuff you do when you lose someone you love.

I still remember my mother's funeral. It felt like my tears flowed forever. There was a dinner, a viewing, a funeral, a luncheon, and an endless sea of *I'm so sorry* and *My condolences*.

I don't want to do this again, but I have no choice.

As the memory of my mother's passing hits me, my throat begins to close, and I look to the ground and cough to hide my sob. Rosalyn jumps around from my side and takes over the conversation, and I'm once again happy I have her with me . She stayed by my side for all of my mom's funeral, and she knows me well.

"You must be Kyle. Emilia has told me all about you. I'm Rosalyn." She extends her hand, and he shakes it.

"I am. I hope it's all good things." He smiles at her and continues, "Emi has told me a lot about you too." He withdraws his hand from hers and circles my waist, pulling me into him for a kiss as the door to the dining room opens.

As we break away, I sense eyes weighing heavy on the two of us. Rosalyn has a sly smile on her face, and Joshua and Noah watch quietly from across the room. Then I remember I'm missing an introduction.

"I'm sorry. Noah, this is Kyle. Noah is a close friend of the family." I stop short. I suddenly feel exposed in front of everyone. I haven't enjoyed being the center of attention for a long time now.

Noah takes my cue and walks across the room for a handshake. I keep my eyes focused on the two speaking in front of me, but a nagging voice in the back of my mind tells me Joshua is still looking at me. I'm too nervous to look over at him.

"Mr. Darkly, I have all six place settings ready. Would you like to wait for our last guest, or shall I seat you now?" a woman announces from the doorway. I swivel my head at our group, counting to myself. There are five of us.

"We'll sit and have our drinks. Our last guest will be along shortly." I watch Joshua as he answers, and my stomach knots at the thought of who it could be. I'm not sure I can handle his mother or his friend Tawny tonight.

Without hesitating, Joshua turns to meet my eyes. "I've asked Sylvia to join us as our guest." My heart flutters at his announcement. I'm so happy he thought to include her. She is our family too. "Ladies, after you." Joshua steps back and allows Rosie and me to follow our hostess, and the boys fall in behind us as we are seated.

I notice again that both heads of the table are empty. Six of the eight seats at the table have place settings, three on each side. I sit in the middle, Rosie is seated to my left, and Sylvia will be seated to my right.

Kyle sits down across from me and Noah takes his seat across from Rosie, leaving Joshua sitting opposite Sylvia. As I watch the two men exchange glances, I'm struck by the thought that Joshua requested the seating arrangements—Kyle looks a little uncomfortable sitting between the two friends.

"I hope I'm not late." Sylvia enters from the kitchen, and the men stand. "I had to talk to Chef for a moment." Joshua silently chastises her for working off the clock, but she cuts him off with a stern smile. "Oh, don't give me that look."

Everyone around the table chuckles as Sylvia circles the room, and I stand to give her a hug before we all sit down.

The conversation flows smoothly between everyone except Joshua and Kyle. During the three courses, neither has so much as looked at the other, and I think I'm the only one who's noticed.

As dessert is served, Kyle and Rosalyn start talking about our neighborhood as the rest of us listen. Rosalyn is offering information on the best places to rent that will place him close to me and his new school.

Each time Kyle speaks, I notice Joshua and Noah exchange glances. They're suddenly making me feel uncomfortable, and I'm not sure why.

As Kyle continues on about his plans to move here, I'm struck that neither Joshua nor Noah are offering him any advice on real estate, and this is the business they are in. Instead, they listen quietly as he continues to share his plans.

At a brief lull in the conversation, Joshua lets out a long sigh. He looks as though something is weighing on his mind. Though I'm thankful he's taking on most of the funeral arrangements for my father, he looks extremely tired.

He reaches for his glass, takes the last gulp of his drink, and slides his cup back into its place. Then he looks at Kyle for the first time since we started eating.

"You know, I think there are some properties over on Gershaw Avenue that might be a good fit for you," he offers.

I search my memory for the street name. "Gershaw Avenue?" Kyle looks confused as I continue, "I don't remember that street. Is it new?" I look around the table, and Rosie shrugs. I don't think she's aware of it either.

"It's part of a new district near the university Kyle said he was attending," Joshua answers.

Kyle nods. "I'll have to check that out," he says quietly.

"Yes, Gershaw Avenue is worth looking into," Joshua answers confidently. Then he leans back in his seat and changes the subject. "Anyway. It's getting rather late, and Emilia told me you've agreed to honor her father by being a pallbearer tomorrow. We have a few things to go over. Why don't the three of us go to the office and leave the ladies here to catch up over a final drink of their own?" The three men stand to leave together, and I smile at Kyle as he walks out behind the other two.

A little voice in the back of my mind nags at me to ask to go along, but Noah is with them, and Rosie has already grabbed the bottle of wine and is refilling our glasses, so I decide to stay.

They're just making arrangements for tomorrow.

What's the worst that can happen?

JOSHUA

Nodding to the women, I turn to lead the guys out of the dining room.

I catch the hesitant look on Noah's face.

I know I agreed to wait, but I can't sit here and allow Kyle to continue to deceive Emilia. This is a bad time for her, but the alternative is to let her be preyed upon and lied to.

The walk to the office is quiet. I'm sure Kyle is using the time to try to work out a plan. I'm sure he's wondering just how much I know, and if Noah is aware as well.

"Anyone want a drink?" I walk over to the liquor cabinet and pour myself a brandy. "Help yourselves."

Noah gestures for Kyle to go first. He shoots me a glare behind his back, and I shrug in return.

When Kyle turns his back to pour himself a brandy, I take the time to turn on the recording device. Adam showed me how it worked years ago. He used to record his conference calls and some meetings so he could go back over any information he needed to.

The recording device is in his bedroom, so there's no chance Kyle will see it.

"Have a seat...*Kyle.*" I point to a chair in front of the desk. He pauses to consider his situation, then takes the seat. Noah pulls up a chair next to him.

If I'm being honest with myself, I knew I would be doing this tonight. I can act like the thought just came to me, but it didn't. It's been festering since yesterday. Since the moment I found out Kyle was a liar. In that moment, I knew I'd be calling him out tonight.

I'm surprised I held out this long. Last night after work, I drove around the block of his hotel at least ten times before I decided against going in. The only thing that held me back was knowing Emilia was in the house by herself, and I wanted to be near her.

"Emilia tells me you're happy to support her by being a pallbearer tomorrow," I start, then pause, taking a long sip of my drink before I continue, "Adam and Emilia are very important to us. Adam was a good man who deserves to be put to rest by those who loved him, and Emilia deserves to be surrounded by those who want what's best for her."

Kyle looks between Noah and me while I speak. He's still unsure. This can go one of two ways for him. If Noah doesn't know, he can play along and take the warning that will be coming next. If Noah does know, then his con is up. I almost see the wheels turning in his mind as he gulps down his drink.

Then, going all in, he gives up and just asks, "Does he know?" He tilts his head in Noah's direction.

I pause a moment longer. I'm not giving him the satisfaction of a quick answer. Now that he's seated before me, I take a good, long look at him.

I see a different person than I did even a few minutes ago.

There's no competition. To challenge me, he needs to want the same thing I do. He wants money. I want Emilia.

"If you're asking if he knows Kyle Hollis doesn't exist and that you're lying to Emilia to con her out of her inheritance—yes, he knows," I answer and Noah nods in solemn agreement, his expression indifferent.

"I see." Kyle places his glass on the desk and cautiously leans back in his seat. He still has a sense of confidence about him, but I know it is misplaced.

He will leave here having won something tonight, but it won't be Emilia.

"You haven't told Emilia?" he asks. There is no love in his voice. This is all one giant business transaction to him.

"Not yet," I answer, waiting to see where he'll go with this.

"And I'm guessing you won't. I know she doesn't trust you. She won't believe you are telling the truth." He tries to fill in the blanks, and I notice the stunned look on Noah's face.

"You're probably right. But I am within my legal rights to give her just enough money for her lunches for the next year, and you'll have to pay your own way. Do you think you can keep up your lie for a whole year?" I ask.

I know guys like him. He won't put in the effort. He knows I'll find a way to prove his lies about transferring. I'll have a whole year to get the information to Emilia without implicating myself.

"What are you offering?" His words are to the point, and Noah shifts in his seat.

I know my friend is nervous. I haven't shared my plans with him because I knew he'd talk me out of it, and I want this done.

"You stay for the funeral. You support Emilia like she deserves. Then, the day after, you tell her your assistantship fell through and you need to go home. I'll pay for a flight anywhere you want, and you never contact her again." I wait for him to ask the question I know he wants to ask, and he doesn't leave me hanging.

"And what's in it for me?" Noah shifts in his seat again, trying to get my attention.

He knows where this is going. He gave me the idea himself yesterday when he warned me to be careful about Kyle going after my money.

"Two hundred and fifty thousand dollars," I say coldly. Noah leans back in his chair; I imagine he's having a silent aneurysm.

Kyle looks like he's desperately trying to hide his excitement. He thinks he's won, but it's just money to me.

Emilia is the real treasure.

As a greedy smile crosses his lips, red-hot anger rises in my stomach. To reduce Emilia to a dollar amount is making me feel ill. The truth is, she's priceless.

"Three hundred and fifty thousand," Kyle demands like she's a bargaining chip, and I'm ready to beat the guy to death with my own hands when the door to the office bursts open, and in storms Emilia with tears pouring down her face.

"Ems." Kyle switches on his lie as all three of us jump out of our seats and wait for her to say something.

Her face is red, and her hands are shaking. She's clutching something that I can't quite make out. Deep sobs flow from her as she looks between Kyle and me.

He takes a step toward her, and she raises her hand.

"Don't. Don't you ever touch me again," she yells, and he freezes, dropping the loving boyfriend persona.

"What's wrong, Emilia?" I ask softly. I didn't hear the creak outside the door this time, so I wonder for a moment if she found out something on her own.

"I heard everything."

"Before I forget and tomorrow gets busy, I've asked Joshua to make sure you are both sitting with Kyle and me at the service. So tell them you are with the family when you arrive," I say. Rosie smiles and nods, and Sylvia grabs my hand like she used to when I was upset.

"Of course, dear," Sylvia answers as Rosalyn pours all of us a glass of wine.

My eyes sting as I become emotional.

"Kyle seems nice," Rosie says with a wink, reminding me of our earlier conversation, and I release my tension with a smile.

I can always trust Rosie to come to my rescue by changing the subject when I need it most.

"He is. Speaking of which, I never asked if you're seeing anyone, Rosie." I shift the attention onto her.

"Not at the moment. The most sexual tension I get is when Maynard calls me up to yell at me for taking another sale from his company. We're kind of rivals—I just pretend it's sexual tension. He's usually pretty pissed." She shrugs, then says, "Hey, I'll take what I can get."

Sylvia and I burst out laughing, and she joins in.

"Maynard? That's not a very sexy name," I chuckle.

"I know. I thought maybe it could be shortened," Rosie says.

"May?" I suggest.

"Nard?" Sylvia backs me up, and we all start giggling.

"Okay, stop it! I'm not going to be able to have a serious conversation with the guy the next time." Rosie wipes a tear from her eye as she begs us to let it go, but I have one last question.

"Does he look like a Maynard? Or is he hot?" As I ask, Sylvia stops laughing and listens intently for her response.

"Let me tell you: the guy is crazy hot. The first few times, we spoke on the phone I was all cocky. Then I was introduced to him in person at a city event, and it knocked me down a level —or eight. Now I just try to keep our conversations on the phone. I can't look at him and talk to him at the same time." She pretends to fan herself.

"What about Kyle? Is he marriage material?" Rosie asks, putting the attention back on me.

"Oh, that reminds me. I wanted to wear my mom's promise ring to the funeral. My dad asked a friend to help him make it for her when they were dating because he couldn't afford to buy a real ring at the time. I know I'm going to forget it when tomorrow gets going. Can I give it to you to bring with you?" I ask Rosie, and she nods.

"Absolutely. I've gotta see this ring. Can you get it now, so we don't forget?" she asks, and I look at Sylvia.

"It should still be upstairs in your mother's keepsake box in their closet," she answers me. I stand and quietly go up the back stairs so I don't interrupt the guys' conversation.

Opening the door to my dad's room is bittersweet.

Everything feels lost. It's all still there in its place, but the love and the meaning behind it isn't here anymore.

Making my way to the closet, I pick up the little box of my mom's favorite things. Small mementos my dad kept close by after she passed away. The scent of her perfume welcomes me as I remove the lid. Sitting on top is her ring, neatly stored in its own little box. I pull it out and palm it, then I close everything else back up.

I'm about to sneak back downstairs when I notice a red light blinking from the side of my father's room. His recording device is working, which means someone in the office turned it on.

The only one who would know about that would be Joshua, and I wonder for a moment why he would feel the need to record their conversation. A tinge of frustration builds inside of me. I know he doesn't like Kyle, but I'm instantly upset he would secretly record him.

I pick up the headphones attached to the recorder and decide to listen before I march in there and tell Joshua how I feel.

At first, I think the headphones are no longer working. There is a silence, then I hear Kyle ask, "Does he know?" and everything begins to crumble around me as Joshua answers, "If you're asking if he knows Kyle Hollis doesn't exist and that you're lying to Emilia to con her out of her inheritance—yes, he knows."

Word by word, the person I thought I knew falls away. It's Kyle's voice I hear, but he isn't the Kyle I knew.

He spent so much time with me. How could I not know?

I told him all about Joshua and his mother. I told him about my dad and his company. My heart feels heavy as I realize he was just fishing for information.

I asked him to help carry my father to his final resting place. How could I have been so stupid?

Kyle's cold voice brings me back to the conversation in the office, and I realize my anger silenced their voices. I missed part of their conversation.

"And what's in it for me?" Kyle asks.

I can't believe what I'm hearing.

That is all I was to him. A dollar figure. Kyle was never my friend; I was a target. I am dollars and cents to every man around me now. My value is only in my monetary net worth. For such a sought-after commodity, I feel less than worthless.

Both of my arms are numb, and my face is hot as I listen to Joshua's response.

"Two hundred and fifty thousand dollars." His voice is calm. There's no emotion in it.

I'm a dollar amount, a transaction. He'll pay Kyle off, then spend the next year moving me out.

I won't let that happen. I quickly look around my father's room, but there isn't anything here for me. Where Joshua and Kyle throw money at everything, I would give every cent, every single thing away, just to have my parents back. Just to feel their love again.

I'm not as quiet as I was sneaking into the room. I don't care who hears me now.

I'm done.

I leave my father's old room and walk to the office. My chest tightens as I grab the handle and turn, pushing it open and walking in uninvited.

For a second, I catch a different look on Kyle's face. Then he tries to move toward me.

"Don't. Don't you ever touch me again." I meant to communicate my boundaries calmly, but I can't. I'm too hurt by all of the men in my life right now. So I yell at Kyle, and he instantly backs down.

"What's wrong, Emilia?" Joshua asks innocently. Of course he wants to know how to play me as well.

"I heard everything," I say, raising my voice on the last word. My rage overpowers my control, and I take a deep breath and try to settle down before continuing. I can't handle myself when I become too emotional, and already my hands are shaking at my sides. Composing my thoughts, I lower my voice, but I know I still sound a little unhinged.

Good. That might work in my favor.

"Nifty little recording device my father has in his bedroom, isn't it?" I ask Joshua. The expression on his face falters as I shift my eyes to Kyle. "My dad used to record his meetings and calls so he could refer back to them later."

Kyle shifts nervously at my revelation. Now I see a new side to him. He's still trying to figure out if he's leaving here with anything tonight.

Standing here in front of these three men is beginning to humble me. I have nothing; I'm just a ward. Most children have more freedom than I do. These three men were all in here speaking for me. Deciding what to do with me.

I tried so hard to get away from everything, and I've somehow sunk even deeper into this misery.

"Kyle, get out," I say quietly. "There will be a ticket waiting for you at the airport...under whatever your real name is. You're leaving here with nothing else." I look at Joshua to confirm because, as I've been reminded over and over again, I have no money, which means no power to make my own decisions.

Joshua nods, and I continue. "Get. Out," I say once more. He stands, staring at me, and I can't take it anymore. This decision is mine, and he's second-guessing me. I don't care who hears me yell. I breathe deep and summon all of my anger with a final yell as tears flow down my face. "GO!"

Noah immediately moves to the door and ushers Kyle out of the room before turning to Joshua. "I'll let everyone out," he says softly, and Joshua answers him.

"Thank you. You can go too. I'll see you in the morning."

As the office door clicks shut behind me, I feel lost and so very alone.

"Emilia, I—"

I hold my hand up to stop Joshua from continuing. "Do you have proof?" I ask indifferently.

"Yes. I'm so s—"

"Show it to me."

I stand waiting for him to respond, and he stares back at me for a minute. Then he opens the desk drawer and pulls out a file folder like the ones from the office.

Stepping up to the desk, I open it. I'm met with a photo of a man who could pass for Kyle's older brother. Kyle Gershaw— Gershaw Avenue. Of course.

I turn a few more pages, and I've seen enough when I come across the written accounts of Kyle's method of operation. It's by campus security from a few different universities.

Then I remember I'm still clutching my mother's ring, and my words are out of my mouth before I realize what I'm about to do.

"I'll take his deal," I say somberly.

"What?" Joshua asks, searching my face.

"Two hundred and fifty thousand dollars, and I'll leave you everything else. You'll never see me again."

"**I**'ll take his deal." Emilia finally speaks as she closes Kyle's file, but she keeps her eyes lowered.

Confusion sets in, and I struggle to follow her train of thought. "What?"

Taking a deep breath, she slowly raises her eyes to meet my own. Tears stain her flushed cheeks, but otherwise she looks calm. "Two hundred and fifty thousand dollars, and I'll leave you everything else. You'll never see me again."

Her words cut through me. How can she reduce herself to a few dollars? After everything I've tried to do for her over the last few days, how can she think I would just let her go? I owe it to both her and Adam to help her succeed, and this is what she's bringing to my table?

My anger rings into my ears. I immediately want to show her she has a place here. I desperately want to put her into it.

"No."

"Why? I'll stay for the funeral, then I'll leave. I'll sign all of this over to you." She waves around the room as she continues, "I only want to take my parents' photo albums and our home movies—and this." She opens the little box in her hand to show me a ring that looks like it only carries sentimental value.

As she waits for my answer, I take a long, hard look at her. We've both come a long way since I first saw her in the school assembly, singing with the rest of her class. We've both hurt each other over and over again, whether we meant to or not.

We hurt each other because we were hurting. It was our only release. It was the only way to temporarily stop our own pain. We hurt each other because neither of us recognized that we needed each other on a different level—a darker level.

She still doesn't realize it.

But I do, and I'm not letting her leave.

"That offer isn't on the table for you, Emilia."

"Why not?" Tears roll down her cheeks. "Am I not worth at least that? You're taking everything else of my father's. Please just give me enough to start over."

Her plea gives me pause. Suddenly I feel the pain in her heart as though it's my own.

Noah was right. She is strong, but we all have a breaking point, and this is hers. Her world is crumbling around her, and she thinks I want to take everything.

She's right—to an extent. I want every part of her, but I'm not interested in her money or her share of the company. I have more than enough of my own.

I want to occupy the heart and the mind of the woman who only wants her memories. When faced with choosing a fortune over a photograph, I want this girl standing in front of me, clutching a handmade ring instead of the many diamond rings lying around.

I want to hold the highest place in the heart of the one who values love and loyalty over money.

But that takes time, and it's time I'm willing to spend. But only on Emilia.

Standing before me is the one person who challenges me. She drives me crazy in so many different ways. She doesn't see status or money when she looks at me.

Most days, she doesn't even like me.

But she does need me. I feel it in my bones. I feel it because I need her, and I'm not willing to let her control this conversation any longer.

"Trust me, if I was going to—buy you—for two hundred and fifty thousand dollars, *leaving* isn't what you would be doing for me, Emilia."

My suggestion causes her to step back. Wide-eyed, she takes a deep breath, scanning my face for signs of sarcasm.

I'm not joking.

"Why are you doing this to me?"

"Because I can." I know I'm provoking her, but she needs to refocus. Tonight needs to come to a head, or she won't be able to calm down, and tomorrow will be even worse for her.

She's hurting, and her emotions are consuming her. I need to consume her emotions, so I continue, "Your father granted me guardianship of you. I'm seeing more and more why you need this so badly. You need structure and rules—and consequences." I pause for dramatic effect, and Emilia's breathing deepens.

I'm affecting her like she affects me.

I take a step toward her, and she backs up like she did that morning in the bathroom. Her need to place distance between us is only so she can attempt to build up her walls. What she hasn't figured out is she isn't building her walls to keep me out —she's trying to contain herself because she doesn't understand herself. Yet.

"No, I don't," she bites out defiantly.

"Well, we have a whole year to find out, because that deal is not available to you, Emilia. You are my ward, and you will live under this roof according to the rules I've set. Now, if that is all, go to your room and get some sleep. Tomorrow is an important day." I shut the conversation down to her surprise, and she doesn't move while she processes the fact that I just sent her to her room.

Her dire situation sinks in, and she slumps her shoulders in defeat. When she turns to leave the room, I'm sure she is grateful this part of the evening is over for her.

At least, she thinks it is.

I have a feeling she'll catch her second wind shortly. Then I'll give us both what we need.

As she stomps down the hall toward her room, I turn back to the folder lying closed on my desk.

I sense naivety in Emilia. She hasn't experienced enough to recognize her feelings as frustration, as a fire that needs to be fed and managed, and so she turns it into an emotion she understands: anger. And then her anger controls her.

I need to help her change her perception, and I have a strong feeling I'll begin shortly. The next time she allows her anger to control her, I will control it, and that will be our beginning.

I open the drawer and drop the file in. I have no need to see Kyle's face ever again, but I will hold on to this in case he decides to resurface.

I press the button to stop the recording. Then I sit down at the desk, cradling my face in my hands to process the evening.

While it didn't go the way I wanted it to, it is done. But it left Emilia in a volatile state. I'm sure the Rosie and Sylvia heard everything. Pulling out my phone, I text Noah to ask how everything went after he left. Dots move across the screen as he types his response.

NOAH

Explained to the ladies as best I could. They are both coming here in the morning now, before the funeral, to go with Emilia and support her, so heads up. I'm at the hotel. Kyle is packing, then I'm driving him to the airport. I'll charge his flight on my card. He'll be gone by the time you wake up. She okay?

She will be. Talk later. And thank you.

As I drop the phone on the desk, Emilia's door slams again as footsteps thud down the hall toward the bathroom.

When I step out of the office, the shower turns on, and my need for discipline returns.

I told her to go to sleep.

She knows it wasn't a suggestion.

I imagine she went back to her room to think. Her emotions have gotten the best of her, and she's trying to challenge me in her own way, without directly coming at me, because she knows that won't end well for her.

At this rate, she won't sleep at all tonight, and her father's funeral will be a giant ball of emotions she won't be able to manage.

Slowly I stand. I remove my jacket and leave it on the desk. As I walk down the hall, I listen as she petulantly shoves things around in the bathroom, and I begin rolling up the sleeves of my shirt.

She's about to spin out of control. Tension radiates all around me, and I'm not even in the same room as her yet. It controls her because she doesn't understand it.

As I square myself in front of the door, soft sobs tangle with the sound of the shower spray. This is overwhelming her.

I decide to give her one last chance to listen to my order, and I knock on the door.

"Go away," she barks, and I have to take a long breath to steady myself.

"Emilia, I told you to go to sleep."

"I'm taking a shower."

"You'll take a shower in the morning. Go to your room."

At my order, a choked sob pours out of her. She's at her limit. She'll either turn off the water and go to sleep, or she'll challenge me directly.

I wait.

"No. I'm taking a shower. I said *GO AWAY!*" she shouts, and I can't control the twitch in my lips as I reach for the door handle.

"You'll take a shower in the morning. Go to your room."

Joshua's words rattle around in my head like coins in a tin can. Why can't the guy just ignore me like he used to? Now I'm in pain, and I just want some time to myself, and he's just adding to my stress.

I hold my hand under the shower stream to test the warmth as steam clouds waft around the room. Tears roll down my face and drip into the shower, joining the water as it flows over the tiles and empties down the drain.

I can't trust any of the men here, and Joshua won't let me leave. Two hundred and fifty thousand dollars is nothing to him. I just need enough to finish school. He could have had everything else, but he's not willing to let me leave here with anything, and there is nothing I can do about that.

I thought I knew Kyle. I trusted him, and the person who left here tonight was not my friend. He was nothing like the person I knew, and now I'm mourning two losses: the loss of my dad, and the loss of someone who was never real.

Noah is Joshua's friend. As nice as he pretends to be around me, I have to remember: he was standing in the office tonight. He knew all along, and he told me I could talk to him if I ever needed anything.

I can't do this.

"No. I'm taking a shower. I said *GO AWAY!*" I direct all of my rage at the door separating Joshua from me, and my hands begin to tremble.

The truth is, I can't handle myself when I'm like this. I'm so mad, I feel like my body is going to explode.

For a moment, I hear nothing, and I release a sigh of relief. Then the handle clicks, and my heart jumps into my throat as Joshua enters the small bathroom with a stern look on his face. I'm thankful I'm still wearing my nightie.

"There. Just getting this door out of the way." His tone is calm as he walks in, stopping a few feet away from me. "That's better. It's easy to yell at a door, Emilia. Now do it again to my face."

His confidence knocks me back. I want to run away, but the only exit is right behind Joshua.

"I need to take a shower. P-please give me some privacy." My words are so quiet and weak, I barely hear myself say them.

"No! Go. To. Your. Room." Every word is a challenge, and I want to cry and yell and run away all at once.

"Please," I mumble, barely above a whisper, hoping for the same leniency he granted me the other night at dinner.

"Now, Emilia."

As the air in the room grows thick with steam, I try to find my voice, but it's gone. So I slowly swivel my head from left to right and back again.

Then he smiles, sending a shiver down my spine.

Reaching behind him, he closes the door, then turns back to face me. That little act makes my heart skip a beat. I know everyone has left the house, and Sylvia is probably in her quarters. We're already alone. But closing us in the bathroom feels more personal. It's as though the door to my cage has been shut, and there is nowhere to go. And I chose this.

I could have just turned off the water and left. Why am I pushing this? I silently chastise myself.

"I won't tolerate disobedience from you. I thought I made myself clear on that."

"I just..." I try to explain myself, but suddenly feel light-headed.

"Shh." I find his shush oddly soothing, and I stop speaking as he raises his hand for my attention. "You know my rules, Emilia. I am going to punish you for this. I know it will help you."

As he says the words, my body responds to him. Everything feels out of place. I hurt, and all I am thinking about is how centered I felt after he spanked me on the side of the road. I felt like, for a moment, I belonged somewhere, and it was the craziest feeling.

"I—" I'm trying to buy some time, and he doesn't allow me any.

"Bend over the counter." As he speaks, Joshua doesn't take his eyes off me, and I can't move. Something deep inside of me works against my better judgment. I want to obey him, but I can't.

Instead, I take a step closer to the shower, and he takes a step closer to me.

"Your first reaction isn't to fight me, Emilia. You're fighting yourself. You know you need this. What scares you is that you need this from me."

I can't want this from him.

I don't even like him.

My hardened nipples become sensitive against the soft

fabric of my nightie, and I panic. Taking my last step into the shower, I push myself under the spray, clothes and all. I let the hot water soak through my new nightie as Joshua stays still, watching me.

Water trickles along the seams as the wet fabric clings to my body, and my mind becomes heady. This is what I've thought about. I've fantasized about a need so dark and consuming that my own being would betray me before allowing me to walk away from it.

"Very well, Emilia. Have it your way." His quiet tone pulls me out of my thoughts, and he steps into the shower with me, fully clothed.

His eyes remain on my own as he stands flush against me. "Let me help you. It's just us here. We're alone. Let me give you what you need." His words are soft as he places his hands on my arms and caresses me gently, careful to avoid my more sensitive areas.

He's touching me. He's touching me, and it isn't sending me into a panic. My thought confuses me. I don't usually like to be touched, but this isn't having a negative effect on me.

"Please," I ask with a deep breath, surprising myself.

His breath is hot against my cheek as he leans into me. "Please what?"

"Please help me."

Without another word, he kneels on one knee and moves me effortlessly down and across his lap. Blinking the water out of my eyes, I wriggle across his thigh, trying to stabilize myself, unsure of where I'm going to end up.

I still the instant his fingers graze the back of my thigh. Calm shoots through me as my body bows to his touch.

"Do you feel that, Emilia? You instinctively accept this." His words catch my attention.

His calm control draws me to him. It's a natural

compulsion my body is refusing to fight against.

"Joshua." I have no idea what I want to say, if anything at all.

"I'm here. No one else. Put your hands on the floor to brace yourself." I swallow a hard lump in my throat. There's no backing out now. I've allowed him to take charge, and my body is begging for this.

Reaching down, I place my palms against the warm tile on either side of the drain. The water ripples over my fingers and disappears through the slits in the floor.

"You need to tell me if you want me to stop. Just say 'stop,' and I will. Do you understand?" His tone is stern but soothing, and a need sparks inside of me.

"Yes, Joshua."

Then I melt as his hand peels the flimsy fabric off my bare ass and grabs my cheek, squeezing it tight. The move opens me up to the running water, and drops trickle between the crevice of my ass and down along my labia. Lost to the sensation of his touch and the warm flow of the water, I close my eyes and drop my head as a moan escapes my lips.

Moments blend together, and I'm not sure how long I slipped into his touch when he shifts in place.

My eyes shoot open as a warm sting jolts me. The first impact registers, and my throat tightens in surprise. The light in the room shines bright into my dilated pupils, and the splashing of the water sounds louder as my body tenses under his smack.

"Are you with me?" The concern in his tone tells me he thinks I'm about to panic, but I'm not.

I feel like I'm flying. As though the floodgates of my pain have been opened, and all of my hurt is slowly draining out.

"I, um—yes." I no longer have control over my reactions.

I'm raspy, needy, and bordering on shameless.

I want more.

My entire body feels awake, electric almost.

"I want you to count each hit, then say my name. That was 'One, Joshua.' Do you understand?" My stomach knots with nervous excitement knowing that more of this release is coming.

"Yes, Joshua."

Without another word, his hand lands on my unmarked cheek. The sound of the water echoing off the tile fills me with a fierce excitement as my body zings to life.

"Two, Joshua."

A third smack hits as soon as the words leave my mouth, and I throw my head back as the impact fills my body with new energy.

"Three, Joshua."

To my depraved joy, the next strike carries more force, and I become giddy as the sting flows straight into my bones.

"Four, Joshua."

Another hard hit, and I realize he is alternating sides. My ass heats up under his discipline. I can't help but move my hips around, silently asking for more.

"Five, Joshua."

My clarity slips into a trance of its own as I struggle to process these new feelings. I hear the shower and feel each drop rain down against my skin. I watch the swirls of liquid disappear down the drain. My senses flow together, filled with an overwhelming need to be his. As his hand makes contact a sixth time, I growl out a depraved moan.

"Six, Joshua."

There is a pause, and my body instinctively shifts again. Arching my back, I shamelessly present myself to him. I'm not ready for this to be over. I need to feel his punishment, but I don't know if I should ask for it. Then his calm voice breaks through my frenzy.

"Shh. It's okay, Emilia. I'm not finished with you yet. Just relax." His fingers slide over my heated cheeks. They follow the flow of the water between my legs, and I can't help my reaction as my body goes limp in his grasp.

This touch—rough yet considerate, strong and powerful—is everything I've ever wanted to feel.

I have no more fight left in me tonight. With every fiber of my being, I want to offer myself to him completely. I want more of this.

A trickle of water follows his fingers toward my clit as he explores my body, and my consciousness implodes on itself. I feel nothing but the sensation between my legs. My head is heavy, and my body sings at his touch.

"You're beautiful." His soft voice slides into my psyche, and I moan for him. I open myself further as his finger presses against my pussy, and everything freezes as I wait for him to enter me.

Slowly and easily, he slides inside as his words rattle around my head. "All of you is beautiful, Emilia. And you are mine. Do you understand?"

"Yes, Joshua." My response flows from me freely. I'm not trying to think of the right answer; I know the right answer. My entire being knows the right answer, and there is an intense comfort in my admission.

My body rocks with the thrust of his fingers as a second joins the first, and I roll my hips in time with him.

Just as tension begins to stir inside me, he pulls his fingers out. Before I can move, another shock wave shoots through me as his hand connects with my tender ass.

My back involuntarily bows on impact. I suck in a deep breath, almost unaware that I've left my body to its own devices.

"Count."

His words pull me back to him, and I panic at the thought I might disappoint him.

"Eight, Joshua."

"That was seven. This is eight."

Two consecutive hits come close together, sending my mind reeling into space. My thoughts and actions are no longer my own.

They're his.

"Nine, Joshua."

"Very good."

I let out a heady sigh at his impressed tone, then immediately rock my head forward as his fingers lightly trail over my tender cheeks.

His touch is heightened by the water raining down, and I'm both giddy and dizzy.

Another spank hits the hardest yet, and I lunge forward on his knee as he sets his hand on my back, steadying me.

"Ten, Joshua." I don't even know how I'm still talking.

I'm out of breath and wound so tight that I don't know how I'll release the delirium I'm now swimming in.

"You were so good for me, my Emilia. I want you to come when you're ready." His words confuse me.

How on earth am I just going to come? Oh...

As the thought leaves me, his fingers return to my sensitive clit and begin moving.

At once, I realize the depth with which I crave his touch. Pleasure or pain makes no difference at this point.

I'm beyond aroused. I'm ready to break wide open; I couldn't control myself if I tried. My body follows his lead, and I brazenly shift my hips to open myself further.

A low groan vibrates from behind me, calling for something deep inside to answer, and I lose my balance in his grasp.

Just as I tilt to the side, his strong arm reaches under me, lifting me up and pushing my back against his solid chest. He slides his hand up over my breast and toward my neck, and his fingers grip my throat as he pulls me close.

His heavy breath against my ear lulls me into a trance. He removes his hand from behind me and returns to my core from the front while pushing my reddened ass into his growing erection.

"Who do you belong to?" he growls into my ear, and his tone demands an answer.

"You."

I belong to him. I want to belong to him. With everything I am in this moment, I want to be his.

My realization hits me as hard as my orgasm does.

Without warning, my legs tremble as my body shakes in his tight grip. I move my hands over his arms in an effort to slow the force of my climax, but he doesn't relent. I have no choice but to open myself up to everything he is giving me.

Words flow freely from his lips, but I no longer have any understanding of what is going on outside the waves currently radiating through me. My body reacts to each jolt of pleasure as my orgasm courses through me, and I struggle to suck in air before I pass out.

Seconds become minutes as my body exhausts itself into a heap in his arms.

As soon as the intensity washes through me, Joshua turns me to him and wraps me up in a tight embrace. He's still clothed, and his shirt sticks to my face. The water is still falling down all around us, echoing sharply off the tiled walls.

Then slowly, piece by piece, the entire room comes back into focus. My endorphin high drains from my body, and I am lifeless in his arms.

"You're okay, Emilia. I'm here. You—"

His words float off, and my body is lighter than it ever has as darkness creeps in.

The only thing keeping Emilia awake last night was her anger. Her pain built inside of her until it controlled her, and there was no way she was getting any sleep if it wasn't dealt with.

I can play the martyr all I want and say I did this for her, but I did this as much for myself.

Emilia needs to know she has a place that wants her very much. She needs to know I want all of her, even the darkest parts she tries to hide. I needed to set a course for us. I needed to show her I will help her when she needs, and I will protect her when she is vulnerable.

And I needed to possess her, to rule her, and take care of her.

The intensity with which she responded was a welcome shock. She moved under my hands, letting go of her hesitations and offering herself to me. Watching her body shudder under each smack, then feeling her grip tight around my fingers as she gave me everything with her release, was beyond anything I have ever imagined, with anyone.

But the one thing above all else was her voice. The sound of her voice when she told me she was mine.

She is mine.

And now I sit in my chair, watching her sleep naked in my bed, and I'm filled with peace.

Last night was the release we both needed.

The sun stretches into the room and slowly creeps up to my bed, where she's still sleeping soundly. I could close the curtains and let her sleep as long as she'd like, but today is an important day. It's going to be a challenging one for Emilia, so she should get up soon.

Carrying her out of the bathroom last night, I knew I had the option to take her to her room, but I couldn't leave her on her own. I brought her to my room, carefully removed her wet nightie in the dark, and wrapped her tightly in my blankets.

She slept through everything. Her body and mind were exhausted. I took my place beside her in my bed and quickly fell asleep myself.

Footsteps in the hall catch my attention, and I sit quietly, waiting for them to pass. Then they stop, and a soft knock on Emilia's door causes me to jump out of my seat and hurry to my own.

When I enter the hallway, I see a look of concern on Sylvia's face as she notices me walking toward her.

"Oh, good morning, Joshua. I was just coming to check on Emilia."

"Emilia is not in her room, Sylvia. She's asleep in mine."

Her eyes go wide at my words, and I offer no explanation. "Oh, I see. Is she okay?" she asks slowly, and I smile.

Emilia is lucky to have Sylvia. If she thought for a minute I would harm her, I have no doubt I would hear about it.

"It's a difficult time for her. For all of us. She will be okay," I respond.

"Okay. I'll make breakfast. Her friend will be by shortly," she offers. It's a suggestion for me to get Emilia up and ready, and I nod.

Turning back toward my room, there is rustling inside. I open the door to greet Emilia, only to see the door that joins our rooms close. I glance to the bed; her pajamas are gone too.

I wanted the chance to speak to her, and she's run away from me again. I'll take solace in knowing this time, she can't go far, and it is just a matter of time before we have the chance to talk about it.

For now, I'll give her space, but I won't leave her alone. She is burying her father today. I won't let her do it by herself.

Emilia did a stellar job of avoiding me while we got dressed. I didn't see her for the next half an hour.

When I made my way down to the dining room, I see Rosalyn has already arrived, and the three women are chatting quietly over coffee. Judging by their expressions, Sylvia hasn't said anything about this morning, but it isn't lost on me that Emilia isn't making eye contact.

"Good morning," I greet the table as I grab my own coffee, and everyone answers back. "I thought the four of us could go together in the car, if that's okay with everyone. Emilia can use your support today."

At the mention of her name, she shifts in her seat. "I'd like that. Thank you," she agrees softly.

We eat breakfast quietly, with the occasional comment from Rosalyn or Sylvia. Emilia only responds with nods. The gravity of the day must be sinking in, and last night is probably causing her mind to work overtime.

As I eat, I get a few last-minute texts from the funeral home, as well as one from Noah, telling me Kyle got on a flight to California late last night.

As I process Noah's text, I place my phone on the table and drink my coffee while I watch Emilia pick at her food.

My sense of authority washes over me in waves. I like who I am becoming for her.

"Sylvia, the only thing I'll ask you to do for me today is make sure you've got a couple of bottles of water on hand for Emilia," I say, and two sets of eyes look up at me.

But not Emilia's. Her eyes stay on her food. She knows I'm testing her boundaries. I'm waiting for her to challenge me and tell me she's got her own water. But she doesn't.

Sylvia nods and excuses herself to the kitchen. When she returns with the bottles of water, the four of us slowly head out to the car that's waiting for us outside. I get into the passenger seat, then I gesture to our driver that we're ready to go.

The car ride is quiet, and as I begin to mentally prepare myself to say goodbye to my mentor and friend, my phone vibrates in my pocket.

NOAH

Heads up. Tawny is here, and she's sitting in the section reserved for family.

Well, shit.

"Sir, there is a woman in the family section—a Ms. Davenfield. She says she is with you. Should I send her back with the rest of the family?" the funeral home manager asks nervously as I exit the vehicle.

I'm thankful we gave them a list of family members allowed in the grieving area. Tawny is definitely not on it.

"No. Leave her there. I'll get everyone settled and deal with her myself." I reply before Emilia gets within earshot of our conversation.

Tawny is the last thing anyone needs today, most of all Emilia.

Turning to the women, I let the funeral director lead us into the building through a side door. As the staff offers everyone something to drink, I excuse myself and walk out front. Tawny is sitting alone in the family area, probably feeling very out of place, craning her neck in every direction for sight of me.

As her eyes land on mine, she stands. She's waiting for me

to cross the room to get to her, and my blood heats up with every step I take.

"Ms. Davenfield," I offer through gritted teeth.

"Oh, Joshua. I was worried about you. You never returned my texts last night." She leans in for a hug, but I extend my hand for a shake, and she sheepishly accepts it.

"Some things required my attention. What are you doing here?"

"Of course I'd come, dear. This is a difficult time, and I'm here for you," she answers.

"I mean what are you doing in the family section?" I try to make my expression even more serious than before, but I don't think it's possible.

"Well, I just thought you needed someone here for you." As she responds, her expression changes. She knows she's overstepped.

I need to get back to the woman who matters to me. "I appreciate your support, Tawny. This section is full, but I notice a spot beside my mother in the back. Please join her. She could use a little support as well. It is her ex-husband she is saying goodbye to today."

"Oh, of course, Joshua." Her face lights up. I can only assume she is thankful for the grace I've offered. I could have thrown her out on her ass in front of Adam's distinguished friends.

Checking my watch, I step back and wait for her to gather her purse and jacket. I let her take a few steps toward my mother before I turn toward the family room to gather the women. It is almost time to begin.

With each step I take closer to Emilia, my anger drains out of me. In my mind, there is no one else here but the two of us, and while I know she isn't ready to publicly accept my support, I will stay near her until she goes to sleep tonight.

Rosalyn and Sylvia are talking quietly in one corner, and as I enter they look up, silently shaking their heads. I glance around and see Emilia standing in front of a table full of photos of Adam. Staring back at her are pictures of her past.

As she stands frozen, looking over them, helplessness sinks in. I can never give her the thing she wants the most, but I will do everything in my power to give her everything else.

Defying the women's suggestion, I take a step in Emilia's direction. I normally would grant her this time, but the service will start soon, and there is something I need to give her first.

Without a word, I pull the little box from my pocket, open it, and reach around in front of her to give it to her.

Her tear-stained face silently turns toward my offering. Then she meets my eyes for the first time today.

"Thank you. I-I forgot it. Thank you. It was my mother's." She sobs a little as her fingers caress the box. Then she takes the old ring out and slides it onto her finger.

There are so many things I want to say to her right now, but I grant her a few more minutes to herself, and I walk back to meet the two women.

"Thank you for remembering the ring," Rosalyn says as they both stand to meet me. "She went up last night to get it..." Rosalyn ends mid-sentence, telling me she hasn't had a chance to talk to Emilia about what happened with Kyle.

It's Emilia's story to share if she chooses, so I change the subject. "We have a couple of minutes before we go out front with everyone else. There is a bathroom if you need."

As I speak, I tilt my head in Emilia's direction, silently suggesting they see if she needs to join them, and both women walk across the room to her.

Once they leave the room, I return to where Emilia stood in front of the table.

Her childhood is in most of these photos.

She's smiling with her mom and dad, and then, when she's older, with only her father. I notice a correlation between her age and her happiness here—as each year passed, her smile fell a little more. The last photo was taken at her graduation, and I never noticed the sadness in her eyes until now. Granted, I might have noticed it then, but I chose to skip her big day, and now I hate myself for it.

Adam and Emily were the poster children for perfect parents. Although, knowing Adam, and from what he told me about his late wife, they were too humble to ever accept that title. They provided Emilia with so much love, but they were strict. She had rules. I realize now how mistaken I was about her. I took her reserved nature as being snobbish, but she was only watching the world around her work instead of judging it.

She never made me feel like I didn't fit in. I was projecting my own feelings onto her. I felt I never fit in. I felt I was never good enough. All she was was careful about who she trusted and who she gave her time to.

She used to want to give her time to me, but I rejected it. Now I need to earn it back.

The epiphany hits me hard as Emilia's hand on my shoulder jolts me out of my thoughts, and I turn, startled, to look at her.

Her eyes go wide as she takes me in. I feel a tear escape down my cheek, and I swallow hard, coughing to clear my mind.

Her voice is almost a whisper. "It's time to say goodbye."

CHAPTER 36
EMILIA

I've been moving through today in a trance. It's as though I'm in the middle of a dream. I'm jumping from moment to moment, and as soon as it's over I'm onto the next one. Someone I've never met before offers their condolences. I nod and smile, then as soon as they appeared they are gone, and the moment becomes a blur and repeats itself.

As the funeral continued, I sunk further and further into the background.

Men and women spoke about my father, and I couldn't always make the connection between their words and the man I called Dad. I wasted the last five years of my life being away from him.

Joshua was right; I could have gone to school here. Less than twenty minutes away from my father. I could have been in his life for the last five years, but I wasn't. I was supposed to have time to come back. My dad was always supposed to be here. He was all I had left, and I wasn't here when he needed me.

The rustle of bodies around me alerts me to stand with

everyone else, and I rise. I didn't notice the pallbearers were already in position to carry my father out. Even now, I feel like I can't keep it together enough to say goodbye.

My mind begins to focus on the details of the funeral. It was my father's wish to have a casket for the funeral. But instead of being buried, he will be cremated, his remains released to Joshua and me.

The thought of having a snack while he is being taken to the crematorium steals my breath from me.

As I scan the six men's solemn faces, a hand takes my own, and I look over to see Sylvia, teary-eyed and offering a soft smile. Then there's another hand, and Rosie leans in close.

"How are you doing?" As Rosie whispers, my eyes land on Joshua. He's standing at the front of the casket, and his eyes are on me.

How long has he been watching me?

"Um. I think I'm good. Did I do okay?" I ask. Right now, I don't remember giving the speech I wrote, and I suddenly feel nervous that I let my dad down—again.

"Your words were touching, Ems. Are you ready? We're supposed to walk out before everyone else, remember?"

Suddenly my body turns sluggish, and my feet are glued to the floor. "I can't. Not yet. I'm not ready." I panic. Rosalyn takes a quick glance over to Joshua. He hasn't taken his eyes off me, and he nods. Sylvia sits back down with me, and Joshua catches the funeral director's attention before leading the pallbearers, and my father, out of the room.

"It's okay, Emilia. Take all of the time you need. They will move everyone into the other room for refreshments." I notice Sylvia patting my hand as she speaks, but I don't feel it.

"Thank you. Both of you. Thank you."

Strangers glance solemnly at us as they leave the room, and

Sylvia offers me one of the water bottles Joshua asked her to bring earlier.

Rosie uncaps the bottle, then places it in my free hand, and I take a long drink before handing it back.

I'm so lost. Home is not a building or a location. Home is where the ones you love are.

And I have no home.

"Sylvia, why don't you and Rosalyn go get some coffee and take a seat at the family table?" Joshua's voice catches my attention, but neither woman moves from my side, so he continues, "I'd like to talk to Emilia. I'd like to introduce her to someone. It's okay. We'll join you shortly. Rosalyn, please put together a small plate for Emilia. She should eat something."

He speaks for me again, and my mind and my heart are conflicted. I am an adult, and again I'm being treated like a child. But part of me wants to let go for once. Part of me wants to be taken care of. Part of me can't fight her own battles today.

My friends excuse themselves as Joshua places his hand on my shoulder. I drop my head and collapse inside under his touch. Taking a deep breath, I will myself not to cry. I know there is someone else standing behind me. I take a quick moment to strengthen and prepare myself for yet another stranger's generic sympathies. Then I stand and turn around.

An immaculately dressed woman gently reaches out her hand to shake my own. I gawk at her in surprise as I take her in. Her raven hair is tied back in a sophisticated yet plain bun, and her makeup is perfect. She's dressed in a simple black dress, and she is stunning.

"I—I'm sorry. I apologize," I stammer, reaching out for her hand. I suddenly feel humbled in front of her, and she smiles at my awkwardness.

"Emilia, I'd like to introduce you to Alexandra Loren. She

knew your father." Joshua speaks slowly, causing me to think there is something else he wants to add.

"I'm sorry we met like this, Emilia. Your father told me so much about you over the years." She speaks with a familiarity I can't return.

"My father?" I start, then confusion sets in as both sets of eyes watch me.

How did my father say so much about me but nothing to me? This woman seems to know me on a personal level, and I'm reminded of everything I've lost. Just as I'm about to apologize for not knowing who she is, a name pops into my mouth.

"Lexa?" I ask. Confirmation flashes in her eyes as I sense Joshua's own eyes on me.

"Yes. That's what Adam called me." Her smile widens, and I return her handshake as recognition finally registers.

"My dad always talked about you on our calls." I smile for the first time today.

Standing in front of me is the woman Dad used to go on and on about, and I can see why. She is the definition of grace and confidence. He would never admit how close they had become. He always just left it at "We're taking it slow" when I asked, but I knew she meant a lot to him.

"He always talked about you as well. I feel like I've known you for a while. Your eulogy was so heartfelt, Emilia. Adam was lucky to have such a beautiful soul for a daughter. Your words epitomized the father-daughter bond so many can only hope for."

My mouth drops open at her words. I wish I could remember my speech, and I hope it comes back to me after the shock of today passes.

"Thank you. Would you like to sit with us at the family table for a while?" I ask, hoping she will agree.

She shares a glance with Joshua I can't read, then she declines. "I can't stay today. Some things require my attention. I hope we can talk soon though. Talking to you makes me feel close to Adam again. I miss him."

Then Lexa leaves, and Joshua leads me into the next room. "I didn't know if Adam had told you about her. I wasn't sure how to introduce her."

"How about like I'm an adult who isn't going to break?" I clip, causing him to stop in his tracks. I know he wants to scold me, and I probably would deserve it, but he doesn't. Instead, he nods forward and ushers me into the room, where many more *sympathies* wait for me.

The clanking of dinnerware and buzzing of conversation lulls as we walk in. Then it quickly resumes as we make our way across the room to Sylvia and Rosie. *These women know me well*, I think to myself as I look at the plate of food at my seat. They are making it hard to not want to eat.

I take my seat and attempt a few bites. Meeting Lexa has lifted my spirits a bit. I almost feel like I can make it through the reception.

Almost.

"Sorry I can't stay, son. My flight leaves in a couple of hours." Cordelia's voice grates into my ears. Joshua stands to acknowledge his mother, who ignores everyone else at the table.

"Thank you for coming, Mother. We appreciate it." Joshua speaks for me, and this time I hate him for it.

I don't appreciate anything that woman has ever done. No —that's not true. I appreciate her leaving. She shouldn't be here today. We all said our goodbyes long ago.

"I saw you talking to Alexandra Loren out there. That whore has no business being here today." Cordelia's crass comment has no place in my mourning, and I stand up to yell at her when Joshua rises as well.

"Mother. That is untrue and uncalled for. Now, we thank you for coming. Have a safe flight home." Joshua speaks low so only those at our table can hear, and I stare him down, barely restrained myself.

Sylvia and Rosie sit on either side of me, eating their food like it's popcorn. Cordelia plasters a fake smile on her wretched face.

"Well, I must go. Tawny is getting ready to leave as well. You should say your goodbyes. It was so thoughtful of her to come today, Joshua." Cordelia's words aren't for Joshua. They are purely for me. They are a reminder that there is someone else here for him.

As she makes her version of a graceful exit, which is anything but, I look back at my plate, and my shoulders slump once more.

I've lost my appetite—again.

I haven't been able to get my mind off Emilia all day. I almost wish she was here in the office with me, but I know it's best for her that she take today and the rest of the weekend to herself.

Her eulogy has been haunting me since the words left her mouth. I misread her so many times.

I saw a petulant child instead of someone who just wanted her father's love. I saw a coldhearted woman instead of a person I pushed away until she no longer came back.

Her eulogy gave everyone the closure they needed.

I glance at the message on my phone. This is the third text from Alexandra gushing about Emilia. I know she misses Adam more than almost any of us. Keeping their relationship private had many benefits, but now Alexandra mourns alone. I make a note to include her in more things with Emilia. I think it would benefit both of them.

My next text catches me off guard. It's like she's reading my mind.

> **EMILIA**
>
> I've been thinking about it. I would like to invite Alexandra up to the cabin next weekend.

The gravity of Emilia's request washes over me. I know what she's asking. I wanted to suggest it, but I wasn't sure how it would be received. If Emilia is asking Alexandra along, then she and Adam spoke a lot more than I thought.

Adam's will asked that his ashes be spread at his family cabin. He's had that place since Emilia was a child, and it is where her mother rests as well. The note was specific that only those closest to him attend, per my and Emilia's discretion. No lawyers allowed.

I could have used my authority and just said Alexandra would be there. I had even mentioned it to her, but she declined. She said it was Emilia's time with Adam, and she wouldn't cause her any further pain.

But this—this speaks volumes.

It speaks to Emilia's relationship with her father, and it speaks to her kind heart, the one I saw as cold instead of searching for its place. While I wanted the time alone with Emilia together, to mourn her father and my friend and mentor, having Alexandra join us is the right thing to do.

I tell Emilia I will ask, then I send off a quick message back to Alexandra, telling her Emilia has requested she join us. She responds immediately:

> **ALEXANDRA**
>
> Yes. Just tell me when and where. Thank you, Joshua.

Setting my phone aside, I take a deep breath and grin to myself.

Things are finally falling into a comfortable place.

"Is that smile for me?" Tawny's voice surprises me. "Your secretary is away from her desk; I thought I'd come in since I made an appointment this time."

"Ms. Davenfield. Please, come in. You said you needed to discuss some of your father's business?" Her face falters for a moment at my direct professionalism.

Mr. Davenfield is one of Connor Realty's top clients, and he's been grooming his daughter to continue his legacy. Personally, I think it is a bad move. Tawny is only interested in status; she wants to rub elbows with the city's elite, not sit in on business meetings. I'm convinced she only comes to meet with me because she has her sights set on landing a husband who can take over his company for her.

"Yes, Joshua. As you know, my father is interested in purchasing the old airfield. Between you and me, he has plans to turn it into an entertainment complex, with a casino, concert hall, dance clubs, and a hotel on site."

As she speaks, I nod. Her father would be furious with her for sharing so much insider information when the property isn't even his yet.

"Well, I'm here to let you know he will be accepting bids in a few weeks. He needs an investment and property company to run the project for him." She sits back in her seat, self-satisfied, and I try to keep calm.

In truth, I have no patience for this.

"That is very exciting for your family's company, Ms. Davenfield." I notice her wince at her title—I know she wants to be "Tawny" to me. "But you could have told me this over the phone. I hate to take time out of your busy day."

"Oh, it's no trouble at all. I love spending time with you, Joshua. Besides, I wanted to confirm my attendance at the awards ceremony. I told Daddy all about it, and he said it was a great idea, going together to show how solidified our two companies are."

Shit. That's her play. I had forgotten how she weaseled her way onto the seating plan. Backing out now would be a slap in her face—I wouldn't usually worry about that, but it would be a slight to Mr. Davenfield and his company if I rescinded the invitation I never actually offered in the first place. I have no good reason for not bringing a plus-one to a simple awards dinner.

I take a long moment to consider my response. I'm suddenly feeling more like prey than predator, and I am not enjoying it. Tawny is fully aware that I have no feelings for her, and the awards ceremony is only two weeks away. I can maintain this as a professional relationship until after the dinner, then I will draw more noticeable lines in the sand.

"We are honored to have your company show their support for ours." Before I get the chance to confirm our date will be only in a professional capacity, Tawny jumps out of her seat.

"Oh, look at the time. I have another meeting to get to across town. Joshua, thank you for seeing me on short notice today. I'll be in touch."

In a whirlwind of flowery perfume that makes my eyes water, she grabs her purse and makes a hasty exit. I don't bother to walk her out.

Dealing with her has drained me. I feel like I need a pick-me-up, so I reach for my phone and reread Emilia's text.

And I smile all over again.

On Monday morning, when Faye suggested I become familiar with our business by helping centralize all of the company files into one large, secure room, I groaned. Who wants to sit alone in a room with mountains of paperwork?

Now it's Thursday, and I'm thankful for the solitude. I wasn't quite ready for face-to-face small talk after the funeral, and I'm still not ready to talk to Joshua about the night in the shower. Between hiding away in here during the day and catching up on my schoolwork in the evenings, Joshua has kept his distance.

The files have given me a chance to learn more about the company and its staff, and I realize Sean was right that night in the bar: all four of them have been working for my father's company since they graduated. I look into their personnel files —a couple of them have been reported to HR with unwelcome sexual advances.

I see the complaints have all been signed off as resolved. By Joshua.

As I continue to read, I begin to feel sick. Something isn't adding up, and I wonder if my father trusted too much in Joshua to help him run his company.

I spent the better part of the day making photocopies so I can ask about them when the timing is right.

As I work my way through employee expense claims, the door to the filing room opens, and I call over my shoulder, "We're reorganizing. If you can't find what you're looking for, just let me know and I can help you."

No one answers. I turn my attention back to the folders in my hand as a quiet minute passes. Then footsteps approach.

"Oh, I found what I was looking for. Hello, *Feelya*. Did you miss me? I missed you."

The sound of his voice makes my arms go heavy.

I wasn't ready for this.

I know it isn't Sean; this voice is deeper. In my gut, I know who it belongs to, and I don't want to turn around. If he wasn't blocking the exit, I would run out. Instead, I've filed myself into a corner.

Memories of being cornered near the bleachers by four boys from my grade creep back into my mind. *Feelya Emilia*, they would whisper to me after that day.

My worst nightmare greets me with a sickening sneer. I turn to meet Brent as his eyes rake across my body.

"Hello, Brent. Sean mentioned you worked here. Are you looking for a file?" I'm surprised by my calm tone. I know it won't last for long, so I hope his stay is short.

"I heard Faye telling a staff member you were in here working on a new project, and I thought it would be a good time to stop by and say hi—you know, when we won't be interrupted." His answer sends chills down my spine, and I falter.

"W-well, I'm here, and you g-got to say hi. I should get bback—" My body slumps as the stutter I thought I had overcome long ago makes its return.

Brent's smile widens. "Ah. There it is. Such a sweet st-st-stutter," he mocks, "I always meant to ask. Did I give you that stutter, Emilia?"

"N-no."

Taking one step too close to me, he forces me to take my own step back. The stench of his cheap cologne fills my nostrils. "Hmm. I think I did. I like your stutter, Feelya. You know, Sean wasn't lying when he said you looked good." His eyes travel to my chest as he begins his conversation with my breasts. "Work just got interesting. Anyway, I just wanted to stop by and remind you that we all work here now. There are four of us and one of you."

"Things have changed, Brent. I own this company n-n-n-now." I try to claw back some of my strength, but this small room is quickly suffocating me.

"That's not what I hear. Word around the watercooler is that my buddy Joshua owns it. I hear he owns you too."

"Where did you hear th-that?" No one should know about that. Joshua told me he wouldn't say anything to anyone.

Brent only offers me a hard laugh in response. He takes another step into me, and I push my back up against some files on the shelf behind me.

"Oh, Emilia. The things I would do to you if I owned you...." His disgusting voice trails off as he lifts his hand to brush my hair away from my face. My entire body freezes momentarily, then I drop my files and knock his hand away.

A dark flash of anger sweeps across his face, and I suddenly become fearful when he leans hard into my face, biting out his words. "Things can become very difficult for you around here. You have no idea how far up my reach goes. Don't make me show you what happens when—"

"Ready for lunch, Ems?" The door flies open, and Rosie's big smile instantly drops. She takes a step into the room and squares off with Brent. "What the fuck is going on?"

"Relax. We were just catching up. I was telling Emilia about everyone in our class who works here now." Brent attempts to backpedal. He steps out of my space, giving me a moment to catch my breath.

"That's not what it looks like. It looks like—" I interrupt her. Rosie knows everything about me and everything about our high school years.

"That's what happened, Rosie. We were just ca-catching up." I relax now that she is in the room with me. Brent looks at me, and I nod curtly for him to leave.

The smug asshole actually thinks I'm covering for him. I'm protecting Rosie. Until I know just how far up this goes, I don't want her telling everyone what she knows. I don't want her dragged into this. It could be her job on the line.

As the door closes behind Brent, Rosie turns to me, incredulous. "Ems. Why didn't you let him have it? I'll back you up."

"Just leave it for now. Promise me, Rosie. I need to look into a few things first. Just don't say anything. I found HR files.... I just need some time to figure some things out. Please?" I plead, thankful my stutter left as quickly as Brent did.

The minute she takes to size me up feels like an hour. Then she responds, "Fine. I'll leave it. For now—but only because I'm hungry. Come on, I'm buying. We are celebrating." She beams at me.

"Really? What are we celebrating?"

"I just closed a big deal on a chain of three restaurants, and I'm taking you to Krayve to celebrate." Now she's almost giggling.

"Isn't that really expensive? We can go somewhere else. I'm not a high-maintenance girl, you know," I laugh.

"What? No way. I wouldn't miss this for the world." She leaves me hanging, and I bite.

"Miss what?"

"My client. He has a meeting now with my competitor. You know, the hottie I told you about? Maynard? Anyway, he's telling him he just signed a contract with us, and—"

"And let me guess: they're meeting at Krayve?" I feign ignorance.

"Yes!" Her giddy answer makes me shake my head.

I usher Rosalyn out of the room. As she recounts her meeting, I reach across the wall to turn out the lights, mentally reminding myself to ask Faye for some help for the remainder of the week. I don't need to be in here alone.

Joshua's signature on those pages is a bad sign—for this company and for me. If he is backing his buddies up, if it's true that he knows everything about what happened, he's been playing me. I'll need to tread carefully to get the answers I am looking for before I decide what to do.

For now, I'm happy I thought to ask Alexandra to come along this weekend. I'll be able to learn more about her, and she'll unknowingly act as my buffer with Joshua. The cabin is extremely remote, and I'm still not ready for a repeat of last week—especially now that I've seen his signature on multiple sexual harassment reports.

These are the times I wish I could sit down and talk to my dad.

"Oh. Look at that. We've officially lost cell service. Now you have to talk to me." Lexa waives her phone between us in the front seat before turning it off and dropping it into her purse.

She's been all smiles since we picked her up.

Emilia seemed happy to see her as well. She jumped in the back, offering Lexa the passenger's seat beside me so she could catch up on some sleep on the drive out of town.

"You know I don't mind talking to you. I'm just thinking about some things," I answer.

"I know. A lot has changed." Her response is both hesitant and solemn. "I miss him so much."

"I know."

We drive in silence for a few minutes before she speaks again. "It's bittersweet. I lost Adam but I met Emilia. She's exactly like he described her. She has his patience, although I think in her it's more like a guard. She does a great job of restraining herself, so you can't tell what she's thinking unless you ask. Kind of like someone else I know." She reaches across the seat to touch my arm as she continues, "How has everything been?" Her voice is low, but I don't want to chance Emilia waking up and hearing us talk about her.

"Emilia has been doing well, considering the circumstances."

"That's not what I'm asking."

I've been waiting for her to push me on this subject.

Alexandra has been present when I've voiced my concerns about Emilia's flippant decisions. I was never on her side for anything, and I always played devil's advocate with Adam.

What Lexa doesn't know is that my feelings for Emilia have evolved.

I know she can't reconcile my description with the woman sleeping in the back seat. She can't because I was wrong, and I haven't had a chance to tell her yet.

"Maybe we can talk about that later. I don't want to wake Emilia up until we get there. She needs to rest. This weekend will be tiring for all of us." As I speak, Alexandra looks into the back seat.

"She looks exhausted."

I lower my voice and keep my eyes on the road. Alexandra has the gift of reading people really well, and I'm not ready to talk about some things. "She's been busy. She started this week at top speed. She was up and out the door for school before I woke up, and she's been working every night in her room. She told me she has a project worth most of her grade, and she's starting behind everyone else because the class already had a few weeks to work on it. I've barely seen her at all since Wednesday."

Lexa chuckles to herself. "She has her father's work ethic. She's managing in her new classes then?"

"Yes, I believe she is. I have a meeting next week with her instructors to make sure."

"And how much does she know about your...*other* dealings with Adam?" She cautiously lowers her voice even further.

"She knows nothing." My answer is short, and Alexandra nods.

I trust Alexandra like I trust Noah, and I know she will keep certain things to herself.

I push a couple of buttons on the dashboard, then music flows quietly into the car.

"*Moonlight Sonata*." She recognizes the song instantly. "I didn't realize you liked classical music. You know this was one of—"

"Adam's favorite pieces. I know. He's the one who got me into classical. He took me to my first symphony after I had a particularly bad week at work and lost my shit in his office. He told me real patience and control was sitting quietly in the chaos. He said to let everything else fall away and listen with my heart, mind, and soul to the notes within the madness. That classical was about taking the time to hear the subtleties that everyone else misses. He said if I wasn't moved after listening to this song, I was not in control: my circumstances were. I learned everything from him." I choke up as the notes pitch into sadness, and I realize there will be no further lessons from the man I considered my dearest friend.

As the song ends, Adam's cabin comes into view. I was so lost in my thoughts, I forgot to give Emilia a three-minute warning for our arrival.

I pull in and turn off the engine. Then I turn to the back seat and watch Emilia. She's in a deep sleep, and a few strands of her hair flutter as she breathes out. I reach over to jostle her awake, and when she makes a soft murmur I quickly pull my hand back. I almost don't want to wake her. I feel like I could sit here and watch her for hours.

The sound of a throat clearing reminds me I am not alone

in the car. I look over at Alexandra, who is watching me intently, and I realize I've made a mistake.

She knows something is up.

I don't hesitate a second time to gently shake Emilia's arm and wake her up. At first, she looks at me confused. Then a flash of recognition crosses her face as she shifts her gaze between Alexandra and me and sits up, rubbing her eyes and yawning.

"I slept the whole way?"

"We didn't want to wake you. Joshua wanted you to rest," Alexandra answers awkwardly for me. Then, looking back to me, she quickly shrugs her shoulders in apology.

"Thank you. I guess I needed it." Emilia reaches for her bag and gathers her belongings. Then she stops suddenly, and her eyes travel beyond the two of us in the front seat. Letting out a heavy sigh, tears fill her eyes as she looks over the cabin. "I haven't been here in seven years."

Alexandra reaches into the back seat and places her hand on Emilia's. "Oh, I'm so sorry, Emilia. I know this must be so hard for you. I know we don't know each other well, but I'm here if you want to talk about anything."

Alexandra looks like she's about to start crying as well. I change the tone by holding out the keys for Emilia. I ask if she'd like to take a few minutes on her own before Alexandra and I go in, and she nods and takes them out of my hand.

We both turn to watch her make her way up to the cabin, and the silence in the car makes my ears ring.

Alexandra hasn't moved a muscle since Emilia shut the door. I don't want to look at her, so I keep my attention on Emilia.

Every few steps, she stops and looks in a different direction, no doubt recalling fond memories of her time here with her dad. The old wood creaks as she steps onto the porch, but it welcomes her quickly as she places the key in the lock and the door swings open.

As she disappears into the cabin, I let out a long breath, and then a moment of silence before—

"When were you going to tell me you have feelings for her?"

Everything looks just like we left it seven years ago.

The blankets are folded in the basket near the fireplace, and I'm sure all of the board games we used to play are still stacked in the closet just down the hall.

There's only one thing missing. And it's the most important piece.

A plume of dust puffs up as I drop my bag onto the sofa. Then I make my way across the cabin and open a drawer near the back door. Without skipping a beat, I pull out a flashlight along with a candle and a box of matches as though I left them here yesterday.

I remember the last time my dad asked me to come out to the cabin with him. I told him I was busy with Rosie that weekend, but the truth is, I sat at home alone.

I knew Dad had invited Joshua as well, and I didn't want to be in the same room with him. It was right after things happened at school, and I was struggling with my own secrets.

Now I wish I'd never left home. I made so many mistakes. I

ran away and left my dad on his own. As if it's whispering in my ear, I hear a voice I don't recognize.

You deserve this.

And maybe I do, but my father didn't. He deserved a better daughter. I failed him, and I can't fix it now.

The faint sound of car doors closing tells me Joshua and Alexandra will be inside soon, and I still need to think some things through.

With my minimal supplies in hand, I unlock the back door and push my way through and outside. As I hit the tree line, I look back over my shoulder to see Alexandra watching me from the back door. I offer a quick wave to tell her I'm okay before taking off down the little trail we made to the creek over the years.

There is something I want to do on my own. It won't make a difference anyway, but I need to talk to my dad now. I need to say the things I should have said over five years ago.

As I get closer to my destination, it becomes harder to hold back my tears. I was so afraid back then. I think I still am. I was afraid no one would believe me. I was afraid my dad would be ashamed, and I was afraid Joshua would discount me like he always did.

The trickle of the creek catches my attention and eases my anxiety as I step into our old garden. My father and I designed this place, and we planted everything after my mom passed away. Her ashes were spread here after we were done, and it's where we will be putting my father to rest tomorrow.

Stepping over to the old bench, I run my fingers over the little plaque with my mother's name on it. I'll have to get one made for my father now. I take my seat on the left side of the bench and run my fingers along the empty space beside me. My father always sat on the right.

The garden is a little overgrown, but it's nothing a couple of days pulling weeds can't fix.

The fruit trees and bushes have grown strong without any help. They went on without me, just like everything else around here. I remember planting them because we wanted to see wildlife, and we decided the berries would bring them in. But the bird feeders are bare. I'll need to check the pantry for some leftover seed when I get back to the cabin.

A little iron holder, just big enough for a candle, sits in the center of the garden. The sun has dropped below the trees, and the light is fading. I stand up to brush the old leaves off the holder and place my candle down on it. Then I strike a match and light it on my first try before sitting back in my seat and searching my heart for the words to start with.

A long few minutes pass as I watch the flame flicker. Then I release myself to my pain and let the tears roll down my face.

"I miss you, Dad. I know I wasn't here, and I regret so many things and I can't fix any of them. And now I'm back, but my home is gone, and there is no place for me anymore. I have nothing to show for the last five years. We were supposed to have more time. I was away, trying to become stronger. I was trying to deal with some things, then I was going to come back and tell you everything and ask you to forgive me. And now I'm nothing more than a ward in my own home, living by the rules of the person responsible for everything, and I'm struggling with so many things I don't understand.

"Joshua and his mother are the reason I left. I should have told you what happened to me at school, but I was too ashamed. How could I tell you that those boys cornered me and hurt me because you laid off their dads? I know you were just trying to save your company because that witch took most of your money—you would have blamed yourself."

My cathartic tears continue to fall, and I let them.

"I know you think you were helping me, but now I just want to be released. I don't think I'm strong enough, Dad. I don't think I can do what you're asking of me. I have nothing left in me I can use to fight, and I don't know how I'm going to get through this without you. I need—"

The sound of a branch cracking nearby catches my attention. I glance around, suddenly realizing it is getting dark and I should head back before someone comes looking for me.

I stand and take one last long look at the flame dancing in the middle of the garden before I blow it out. Then, pulling out my flashlight, I decide to let the waiting wildlife get their turn at the berries, and I make my way back to the cabin.

As I step out of the trees, I see Joshua standing on the porch, looking around. He snaps his head in my direction. If I didn't know better, I'd almost think he was concerned.

"I was beginning to worry. It's getting dark, and you two took off as soon as we got here. Where's Alexandra?"

I stop walking in confusion. "I don't know. I went to my parents' spot for a bit. I didn't see—"

"Hey. There you are." Alexandra's voice startles me. She's coming from the path I just walked. "I went down to the lake to watch the sunset. I thought I'd run into you on the way back, but we must have missed each other." She's a bit winded from the hike, and I notice she doesn't look me in the eye as she passes. She looks like she's been crying as well.

"Well, come in and get settled. I'll get the grill going. We haven't eaten since we left, and you both must be hungry."

My stomach growls as I follow Alexandra quietly back into the cabin and grab my bag. As I turn to walk down the hall, I realize she isn't following me, and I stop and look back at her.

Lexa looks a little pale, and I realize I'm not the only one who is getting used to a new life.

"I'm sorry, Alexandra." I watch her eyes go wide in

confusion, and I continue, "I should have asked. Have you been here before?" As I speak, I notice Joshua stops working in the kitchen. He's watching us, but I don't look his way.

"Um, yes. I came here with Adam a couple of times," she answers quietly.

"I would like to sleep in my old room, if possible. It's the—" Alexandra joins me, and we finish my sentence in unison: "One in the back." We both smile at each other.

"Yes," I confirm. "If it's all right with you. You are welcome to either the other spare room or my father's room. Whatever you are comfortable with. I'll be out for dinner in a bit. I'd just like to wash up." Then I turn to Joshua. I momentarily feel as though looking at him equates to asking permission, and he offers me a small, silent nod.

As I turn, I catch Alexandra watching me, but I can't quite make out the look on her face as I head to my room.

"Go ahead. Say what you want to say. I'm surprised you held out this long." I take a long sip of my drink and keep my eyes on the flame burning hot in the fireplace.

"I don't know what you're talking about," Alexandra replies from under a blanket on the couch, and I shake my head.

"I know you, Lexa. You've been dying to talk about what happened in the car since yesterday. You've been watching both of us rather closely all day."

Her feigned ignorance is trying my patience.

We had a productive, emotional, and busy day. Since the sun rises on her side of the cabin, Emilia was up at the crack of dawn. I found her midmorning in the garden, pulling weeds and pruning branches. We quietly returned Adam's ashes to the earth when the sun was highest in the sky. Emilia kept her hands busy for the rest of the day. Now she is sound asleep in her room.

It's a good time to talk, if there is ever going to be one. If I don't control the timing of this conversation, Alexandra will most likely control it for me, so I offer her an ultimatum: "We talk now, or the conversation is off the table."

Alexandra stares at me for a moment. She knows I'm offering her a chance. One I may never offer again.

"Okay. But first, I want to say thank you—again. Being here and helping to spread Adam's ashes today was..." She chokes on her words. Then she swallows hard and continues, "It meant so much to me, Joshua."

"He loved you, Lexa. He talked about you all the time." Alexandra nods at my words. I know she knows how he felt. Those two were meant to find each other.

"And Emilia is wonderful too." She lets her words linger.

It isn't just a statement. It also carries a question.

Alexandra wants to know how I went from being Emilia's worst critic to someone who cares for her.

"Emilia has surprised me; she's proven me wrong on a couple of things. We are both taking this time to get used to our new dynamic," I answer concisely.

"Joshua. I don't know how to dance around this, so I'm just going to say it. I've known you for four years, and I've never seen you look at another woman the way you looked at Emilia while she slept in the car. You were tender with her. Almost protective." I watch her in my peripheral vision as she examines my reactions.

"Of course. She is my ward for the year, and I will do everything I can to see Adam's wishes—"

"You and I both know it isn't just your guardianship, Joshua. Talk to me." The concern in her voice catches my attention, and I return her stare.

I know she's right. How I feel for Emilia deserves to be honored. I won't hide her away like a dirty secret. Especially not from Alexandra.

"Fine. I was wrong—about Emilia. I put her in a box a long

time ago. I gave her a label, and I wouldn't give her the chance to change my mind. I closed her off from me. I pushed her away until she just didn't come back, and I thought I was happy with that, but I wasn't. Then, when she came home, I wanted to punish her. I wanted to punish her for leaving Adam—and me. I knew Adam put that caveat in the will. I justified it because of the label I gave her, and I couldn't wait to make her pay for leaving. Now she's here, forced to live under my rules, and I'm learning how wrong I've been. I want to be happy with her, but I don't know how to get to that point anymore." I stop talking.

This is the most honest I've been with myself about Emilia. I know exactly what I want.

"I don't want this arrangement. I want Emilia to be here because she wants to be. Because she knows it's what is best for her and it will make her happy. I don't want her to be legally bound to me. I want—"

"You want her to freely submit to you." The heavy truth in Alexandra's statement startles me. "Joshua, are you saying you want her to be yours?"

The tension leaves my muscles at her question.

That is exactly what I want, but I don't answer. Lexa has known me long enough to understand that my silence is my answer.

"Oh, Joshua. I'm happy for you. You know I am. You need someone who will challenge you and grow you as much as you'll support them." Alexandra's pause catches my attention, and I look at her furrowed brows as she chooses her next words. "I think this legal arrangement is good—for both of you—right now. Emilia is hurting deeply, and there are some things I don't think you've talked about yet. There is too much history to start fresh and hope that she'll want to stay. I think you need this arrangement so you can begin to build your new foundation. It won't be easy, but it's not impossible. I've been watching

Emilia, and she reacts to you. You don't notice it, and I don't think she does either, but she inherently waits for your cues. She values your praise. I see it in her, but she has her own demons to overcome. I hope you'll be able to help her with that."

"What do you mean demons? Did she say something to you?"

Alexandra composes herself at my question. "No. I just sense her wounds might be deeper than you think they are. I think you should use this time to reintroduce yourselves to each other."

"Maybe you're right. The arrangement has its silver linings. We should get some sleep. We'll head back tomorrow after lunch. That'll give us enough time to get ready for the week."

I move across the room to the table and set my drink down. Alexandra says her good nights and retires to Adam's room. The logs in the fireplace are glowing embers now. I close the glass doors and make my way down the hall to the spare room, stopping to glance between the crack in Emilia's door.

She's been trying hard at work and in school, and she's been so tired. The moonlight through the window catches my attention, and I quietly walk to the curtains and slide one of them shut. Emilia should have a solid sleep, and darkness will allow her to wake when her body feels it's right, not when the sun rises. As I pull the other curtain closed, I look back at her dreaming peacefully. Her mother's ring on her hand catches my attention.

I suddenly understand how Adam was always so proud of her. I just wish I saw what he did a long time ago. I pushed her away because I didn't want to give her the chance to let me down. I made assumptions about her because it was easier than facing my feelings for her. I never gave her the chance to show me who she was; I wrote her story for her.

Her deep breath pulls me out of my thoughts, and I decide to leave before I wake her up.

I could have done so many things differently. Alexandra is right; we need to work on creating a strong foundation, and I'm determined to begin this week.

CHAPTER 42
EMILIA

When we dropped Alexandra off last night, something felt different. I don't know her well enough to say if something was out of place. The hug she left me with felt like there was a huge conversation behind it, but all she said was, "Just hang on, okay?" I didn't understand, but I got the impression there was more she wanted to say to me, and it's been on my mind all morning.

Luckily, school was rather dry this morning, and I had already covered most of the topics in my old classes.

"Are the expense claims filed in the locked cabinet with the personnel files, or should I start a new section for them on the shelf?" The intern's question startles me.

"We'll include them in the cabinet. Put them on the bottom shelf. Thank you."

This filing project is going by faster now. I hope we can have everything put away by midweek, because I'm ready to get back into the office to help Faye with the awards dinner preparations. The event is this Friday, and I'm beginning to get excited.

It was my father's favorite event of the year. He loved spending time with everyone in the company and handing out all of the awards. It coincides with bonuses, so everyone is always in a good mood.

"So, how long have you worked here?" Sandy asks. Her question surprises me; she doesn't know who I am. I stop myself from telling her the truth.

No one here looks at me as a coworker, and I miss not standing out. I thought I did a good job of blending in at my old school. No one fell over themselves to do anything for me. People just did their thing. They didn't act as though I was judging them or sizing them up for a promotion or demotion.

I came, I went, and it didn't matter.

I miss the way this intern is looking at me right now.

"I just started back after some time away," I answer. It isn't a lie, but I don't feel great about the deception.

"Cool. I've been here for a few weeks."

"Do you like it?" I ask, setting my file down to take a break.

"Yeah, I do. The people are all really nice, and it's got a great vibe. It doesn't hurt that the owner is kind of cute." The camaraderie in her smile makes me smile in return. I love being just another face around the watercooler to her. "Hey, maybe we can grab lunch together sometime this week? I usually head down to the street. There are a ton of food trucks, and it's a great place to sit and people watch."

"I'd like that. Thanks." I feel a little giddy inside—I've made my first work friend. Well, outside of Rosie. But she's always been my friend, so that doesn't count.

The door behind Sandy opens, and my mood instantly changes.

As Sean scans the room, my heart beats harder against my ribs. Settling his attention on Sandy, he smiles as he joins our conversation, and I don't even recognize him. He only sneers and lewdly gawks at me so watching him act normal is unsettling.

"Hello." He lets his greeting linger, and it is obvious he's waiting for her name.

"Oh, hi. I'm Sandy." She smiles.

"Hi, Sandy. It's great to meet you. I'm Sean. I work over in sales." My stomach lurches as he reaches out, and she meets his hand in a shake.

"I'm an intern. I kind of work everywhere." She offers a soft laugh as I stand frozen in place.

"Well, I look forward to working with you, Sandy." I get the feeling only I can sense his lecherous tone. "Could you give us a few minutes of privacy with Emilia?" My stomach tightens as Sandy asks the question I don't want to know the answer to.

"Who's us?"

Then Brent walks into the room, answering her question without saying a word.

"We just need to speak to the old boss's daughter for a minute. We won't be long." As Sean speaks, Sandy's expression changes.

"Oh. Yeah, sure. I'm going to get a coffee. It's my break time anyway." She adds the bit about the break for my benefit. I'm no longer the new friend from work—I'm someone who can get her in trouble. I nod at her as she leaves.

A part of me wants to ask her to stay, or if I can tag along, but I know I'm not welcome anymore. I also don't want to risk having my stutter return in front of her.

Brent waits a few seconds before locking the door. Their cordial smiles are gone. It doesn't matter; they weren't genuine anyway. I prefer seeing people for who they really are.

"I think we all got off on the wrong foot, and we wanted to talk to you and clear the air a bit." Brent speaks slowly, and I know his words are hollow.

"I see," I answer. Sean fidgets in place. Tension is vibrating off him, and I step back for a little space.

"I think we can all agree that we were just kids in high school, having fun like kids do. It was a long time ago, and we're adults now." Brent watches me as he speaks. He's measured, and my face heats up.

All of the pain, the nightmares, the stuttering. Everything was just kids having fun. Except I know it wasn't, and so do they. They were eighteen when it all ended, and it ended because I left for school on the other side of the country. They didn't end it because they became mature adults; I ended it when I ran away.

"It was only five years ag-go." My stutter returns, andBrent flashes a sinister grin. He hasn't moved on. He is still enjoying my pain.

"I told you she wouldn't listen to us." Sean's anger surprises me. "She's going to ruin everything. Just like her old man ruined it for our dads."

I know their fathers were laid off after the divorce, but I also know my dad offered them their jobs back as soon as he could, and he gave Brent and Sean jobs as well.

Brent shoots Sean a stare, and he backs down.

"Look, Emilia. We have a good thing going here. You don't want to ruin our careers over a misunderstanding from years ago, do you? Keith and Chad have families now." He plays to my conscience.

All four of them were horrible to me. They took their anger out on me. Brent was the leader of the group, and Sean was always too eager to be his next in command. Keith and Chad wouldn't have done what they did if those two hadn't pushed them—they always seemed like they just went along with everything Sean or Brent said, but they were still involved. Either of them could have stood up for me, but they didn't.

"I need to g-go." I point at the door, but before I can take my first step, Sean steps back and leans against the door, and Brent moves his body into my space.

"You're not going anywhere until I say what I have to say, Emilia. And don't worry; Rosie won't be able to interrupt us this time. She's out on a sales meeting. You're all alone." Brent's smile makes me want to vomit.

I am all alone.

"We've all been working really hard for this company since high school, and none of us are going to let you take that away from us." As Brent speaks, his hand moves up to touch my face, and I slap it away in disgust.

Another flash of anger crosses his face. This time, his hand shoots back out, and his cold fingers wrap around my throat as he pushes me into the files on the shelf. I can smell the fishy scent of his lunch on his breath as he stretches his face toward my own.

"You don't understand. We all know who signs our checks. And it's not you. We can make things very difficult for you here." As he spits out his words, he leans closer into my space. Sean laughs over his shoulder as Brent continues, "We were just boys back then. It was harmless fun. We're men now. You don't want to find out what we can do to you."

With his back to Sean, Brent lifts his free hand over my bra, pinching my nipple hard between his fingers. I squeal as I pry him off and push him back.

"Leave me alone."

His predatory eyes flash at my plea. Only the two of us know he just touched me. Sean is still laughing like an idiot, completely unaware of the threat Brent just made on his behalf, and I feel sick.

"Remember what I told you." Brent turns to Sean and motions for him to unlock the door. Then he shifts his eyes back to me. As Sean walks out, Brent offers a wink before his final words: "I will be seeing you around, Feelya."

My body deflates. I want to curl up into a ball on the floor and never get up again.

There is only one person here who can help me, and it isn't Rosie. Those four would ruin her career before she got the chance to report them.

I need to talk to Joshua and hope he isn't on their side. For once, I need to trust him.

The one person who I thought was out to get me is the only hope I have at ending this nightmare.

I lock up the personnel files, then I walk to Joshua's office as fast as I can, doing my best to smile at Faye as I enter the administration area.

"Is Joshua available? I need to speak with him n-now." She gives me a quick nod, and I push through his door and shut it quickly behind me.

"I'm sorry for b-bursting in. I need to talk to you about s-something." Now that I've started the conversation, I feel like I can finally solve some of my problems.

Joshua doesn't move. Standing in front of his full-length window overlooking the city below, he stays perfectly still for a whole minute, and my entire body trembles.

This is what I should have told my father years ago.

"J-Joshua. I said I n-need to talk to you."

Taking a deep breath, he turns to face me. I'm met with the same angry eyes I saw when I first stepped into this office to read my father's will. Something feels very wrong.

"Really? Tell me, Emilia. What lies have you come to tell me now?"

"**S**hall I drive around the block once more, sir?" my driver asks over his shoulder as we turn the corner for the sixth or seventh time.

"One last time. Thank you, Niko." I look out the window at the front doors to our building as we pass by.

I didn't feel like driving today, and now I'm thankful I chose not to. I haven't been able to focus on anything but my meeting with Emilia's instructors this morning, and each time I go over our conversation, my rage builds.

Emilia isn't working on a project right now, it must be for another class. Both instructors gave the same answer, and I clarified twice. There is no project. Emilia lied to me about needing time alone to catch up. I gave her all of the time she needed. I gave her space, and I was proud of her for working so hard.

She spent the last week in the file room and her evenings on her own. I was proud of her for nothing. She only wanted time away from me. It was part of my rule: eat dinner with me unless she was studying. She lied to get out of sharing a simple meal together.

I wanted this week to be different. I wanted to begin working on our new foundation, but it appears as though some of our old foundation still needs to be knocked down. By the time the car comes to a stop in front of the building—again—I'm more than willing to get to work.

As the elevator opens to my floor, I'm half tempted to burst into the filing room and have it out, but I decide against it. I need to remain in control, and having this discussion on her turf when I'm not composed is not beneficial to me. Instead, I stay on route to my office. I ask Faye to move my afternoon meetings, then send Emilia in as soon as she sees her.

As I sit at my desk, my mind wanders back to the first day she arrived here after Adam passed away. I could see it in her eyes. I know, deep down, she was ready to fire me on the spot. She had a hatred in her that set me off, and I felt the same. I couldn't wait to hear the caveat read out loud and watch her as she realized what it meant.

I thought we had grown since then. I was sure we were heading in a new direction. But nothing has changed. She's biding her time, and she's using lies to avoid me.

I walk to the window to look at the city. Problems seem small when you look at the big picture, but this one doesn't seem to feel any smaller. As the door opens, I stay still with my eyes focused on the horizon.

"I'm sorry for b-bursting in. I need to talk to you about s-something." There's a stutter in Emilia's voice. When we were younger, I figured out she would stutter every time she was telling a lie.

She probably found out I had her driver take me to her school and now she's caught in her lie. I'm almost entertained. I can't wait to see how she digs herself out of this one.

"J-Joshua. I said I n-need to talk to you." I'm done with her excuses. We're going to do this my way now.

As I turn to face her, her eyes go wide. She knows I'm not happy.

"Really? Tell me, Emilia. What lies have you come to tell me now?"

An immense satisfaction flows through me as she stops cold. I will not allow her to control any part of this conversation.

"S-something happened. I was—"

"Let me guess. You were going to tell me, right?" My voice is a little louder than I'd like, but it startles Emilia, and I don't think anyone can hear me through the heavy door, so I'm going to stick with it.

"Wh-what?" Her false ignorance is only earning her more punishment.

"You lied to me about your project, Emilia. I believed you. I fell for it the way Adam always used to fall for your lies. You would rather lie to me than put the work in to better yourself around here."

"That's not wh—"

"It's exactly what it looks like. You haven't changed, Emilia. I'm tired of your lies and your stories. I was tired then, and I'm tired now. You need to earn my trust. I've been too lenient with you."

As I speak, I move to the door and click the lock. As Emilia watches me lock us in, something flashes cross her face, but I'm too determined to right her wrong to entertain it.

I decide to stay in between her and the door, as she keeps glancing at it. She won't be leaving here until her slate is cleared.

"J-Joshua, I—"

"Go ahead, Emilia. Tell me another story. Tell me why you

lied to me. I can't wait to hear this one." I spit my last words out. I'm hurt. She hit me hard. I trusted her, and she took advantage of me.

I watch her try to form words, but her stutter is too much for her now. She knows she only has more lies to tell, and eventually she stops trying to speak and just waits.

"I'm disappointed in you, Emilia. All you had to do was follow my rules and do the work." I stand in silence for a long minute, watching her. She's gone stiff. There is nothing left to say, and she knows it. "Bend over the desk, Emilia."

"What?" she breathes out and takes another step into the room. She knows she can't move toward the door because I'm blocking her in.

"You heard me. Bend over the desk. Now, Emilia." My words are final. This won't be a pleasurable experience for her.

"I can't. P-please. Don't. I d-don't want to be t-touched." Her stuttering has increased, and her worry is now more like panic. Something feels out of place, and I'm not sure I've chosen the best option.

As I weigh other punishments, my attention falls on her hands. When she hugs herself away from me, I decide on a different route.

"Your mother's ring. Give it to me, Emilia."

"No, please. Don't." Tears well in her eyes, telling me this is the better punishment, so I double down.

"You've requested not to be punished in my office, where Faye may hear you." I remind her of my leniency. "I've chosen an alternative for you. Give me your mother's ring, just for now. You may have it back when you've earned it."

Emilia's eyes shift between her ring and the desk. Then she slowly removes it from her thin finger and holds it out. I take it from her and put it in my pocket.

She drops her head and walks past me. She's hoping to get off easy, but I have other plans.

"Emilia, you will not go out this week. I've instructed Niko to take you to school, then work, then home. I expect you seated at the dinner table every night."

She spins and tries to argue. "Rosie and I were going to get our dresses for the awards dinner."

"I don't care." My words are harsh, but I'm not willing to entertain any requests right now. "I will order you something to wear. I'll have someone come to the house tonight to fit you. This is nonnegotiable, Emilia."

She glares at me in defiance. I know she's plotting the day she is done here, and I know I have work to do to get her away from those thoughts, but I can't allow her disobedience to go unpunished.

Without a word, she turns and reaches for the lock on the door. The click echoes into the quiet room, and she leaves.

I once imagined I'd take a great deal of satisfaction in punishing her, but this has left me feeling drained.

The dining room feels larger when no one else is in it. Glancing around the table at empty seats, I remember a time when every chair had someone in it, and the laughter was so loud I couldn't help but smile along even though I was too young to understand what was being said.

The smile on my mother's face was infectious, and my dad was always the one sharing a joke or telling an interesting story.

Now I'm sitting here alone.

It took everything I had not to defy Joshua's request.

Request, I laugh to myself. Joshua doesn't request. He orders.

Regardless, it took everything I had to be on time. I was even a few minutes early. Now he is the one who is ten minutes late, and I'm sitting here staring at how alone I've become.

"Emilia?" Sylvia peeks through the door to the kitchen. "I've just heard from Joshua. He says he is running late tonight, and you are to eat on your own. I'll bring in your dinner." Her voice is soft, but it echoes into the almost empty room.

"That's okay, Sylvia. I'll take my food up to my room. I can grab it my—"

"Um, Mr. Darkly said to feed you in here or not at all, and I..." Her words trail off in a heartfelt plea, and I understand exactly what he told her.

"It's fine, Sylvia. Thank you," I answer. I don't want her getting in trouble for me.

Joshua is making it clear that I am to eat alone in this room tonight. Just like I left him to eat alone every night last week because of the school project I lied about.

I just needed some space to figure things out. None of this has been easy for me. I didn't ask for any of it. I worked so hard to put everything behind me, and now it's all catching up, and I can't process everything at once.

I know this hasn't been easy on him either. I saw how deeply he mourned my father's passing. But there is a big difference between our situations. He lost his mentor, but for him everything else is the same. He has his network of friends.

I was ripped out of my life. The last member of my family is gone. His mother is awful, but he still has her. I have nothing, and a look around the table confirms it. This isn't my life, and I don't belong here.

"Here we go, dear. I made a nice vegetable soup and fresh bread." Sylvia's motherly voice interrupts my thoughts.

"Thank you, Sylvia. Would you like to join me?" The expression on her face says sorry before she does, and I already know what she's going to say. Joshua has made it clear: I am to eat alone. I let her go. "It's okay. It smells delicious. Thank you." I pick up my spoon and grin to show her I'm fine, and she returns a smile as she leaves.

Dinner is a sobering event filled with nothing and no one but me. The only sound is my spoon as it clinks against the side of the bowl, and as my meal drags on, the loneliness I left Joshua with to begins to take its toll.

As I near the bottom of my bowl, the doorbell echoes through the house. I jump out of my seat, thankful to whoever has broken the silence. I bound across the hall and swing open the door, a little too happy to see the wide-eyed stranger staring back at me.

"Hello, I'm here for a Miss Emilia Connor?" The young girl glances down at her notepad, then back up at me.

"That's me. You are?"

"I'm Jessica. You can call me Jess. I was sent here for a fitting." As she speaks, she lifts a garment bag, and I step back to let her in. "Is there somewhere I can set up?"

Since I'm not sure when Joshua will be back, I opt for privacy. "Can we do this in my room?" Jessica nods, and I turn to lead her up the stairs.

Once in my room, I close the door, and she drops her bag and goes right to work. She unzips the garment bag, pulls out three dresses, then lays them on the bed.

"Don't worry about the fit. I can make anything your size. Just take a look and tell me which one you like the most."

The first dress is a bright red number, but it is a little too short for an awards gala. The second dress is stunning: a simple, full-length black sheath gown. I instantly love it. As I lift the third dress, I'm a little confused. It is form-fitting, short, and bright blue with a plunging neckline. I'm surprised Joshua would allow this option.

Sensing my apprehension, Jessica joins me at the bed and gasps.

"Oh, I am so sorry. I must have gotten this one mixed up with my last client's. I'll just run out to the car and get your third option."

I grab her arm before she leaves. "That's not necessary. I

like this dress." I reach over and lift the silky black dress. Jessica smiles.

"As soon as I saw you, I thought that would suit you the best." Jessica packs away the other two dresses, then turns and grabs her measuring tape and notepad. "Okay, I just need your measurements. Are you okay to get down to your bra and underwear?" Her question is all business, and I get the impression mine won't be the first body she's seen today.

I shrug, step out of my tights and top, and stand still, waiting for her.

"Arms out," she commands. As she moves the measuring tape around my body, jotting numbers in her book, I glance at the garment bag on my chair. A sliver of the bright blue dress sticks out, and my curiosity is piqued.

"What function is that beautiful blue dress going to?"

Jessica looks at me in confusion. I motion to the garment bag, and she looks over her shoulder. Then understanding registers, and she thinks for a moment before answering.

"It's going to Ravenous this weekend," is all she offers me, and I get the impression I should understand what that means.

"What is Ravenous?" Her hands stop working at my question, and she looks at me with her eyebrows knitted together, like I'm telling a joke, so I continue, "I'm new here." I shrug.

"Oh. It's a club for, um—adults."

"Oh. And they are having an event?" I try to sound casual, but I have no idea what I'm asking.

"You could call it that. The dress is for a woman who is—um, auctioning herself off."

Now it's my turn to freeze. "Like, selling herself? Does that really happen?" I've forgotten myself and dropped my arms. When I lift them back into place, Jessica keeps measuring.

"I'm not supposed to say anything, but yeah. I guess some

women just have no other options. Some men are willing to pay big money for some time with a beautiful woman. The club is really high-end—only the city's wealthiest are members. They have NDAs all over the place. I'm technically not supposed to say anything, so you didn't hear it from me."

"How much time and money are we talking about?" I skip over her warning and dig in. This is the most interesting thing I've heard in a long time.

"I think the time is negotiable, and I've heard some of the girls talking. It's enough to be set up for a long time." Jessica finishes talking, and my mind is so occupied that I fail to realize I'm standing stalk still with my mouth open, just gawking at her.

She lets out a little laugh, and I snap my lips closed and smile back as she steps to the dress and takes one last look at it.

"I think I have everything I need. I understand you need it before Friday. I will do my best to have it to you on Wednesday, but it won't be later than Thursday afternoon." She adds the black dress to the others and zips the bag up as I pull on my housecoat.

She looks around to make sure she didn't leave anything behind. Then she pulls a business card out of her bag and writes something on the back. "Here's my direct number if you have any questions."

I take the card then flip it over to see a raven with an intricate Celtic symbol. "That's a pretty design."

"Hm?" She looks up from the items in her hand. "Oh, that's a business card from the club. It is nice."

I keep the card in my hands, thinking it odd that there's no information other than the logo on it. There's no number or email.

Once we approach the front door, I reach out to shake her hand, and she offers me a prepaid receipt for the dress. As her car pulls onto the street, a new set of headlights pulls up our driveway.

That must be Joshua.

I run back to my room and close my door.

I drop my housecoat on the chair where the garment bag was, then I pull my pajamas on and climb into bed.

I'm not ready to talk to him again today.

"Is there anything else we need to discuss?" I check my watch as I ask. I have a conference call in twelve minutes, then two more meetings before I can call it a day, and it's already after four o'clock.

This whole week has been busy and stressful. Ever since I called Emilia out on her lies, I want to get the company dinner over with and take the weekend to organize myself.

"Nothing business-related, but—" I've barely had time to catch up with Noah, and I know he senses something is off.

"Okay then. Maybe we can catch up on everything else next week?" I attempt to cut him off and get on with my day.

"No, wait, Joshua. I know your schedule; you have a few minutes now. We need to talk. What happened?"

"What do you mean?" Acting oblivious is not my strong suit. I've always said what's on my mind, but the truth is, there are too many things on my mind right now to properly sort out.

"Don't play that with me. You know what I mean. Emilia barely looked up when I came in. She looks drained. You're not looking at me; it feels like you are both just going through the motions this week. What happened?"

I glance up, and he's right—I haven't been looking at him. I didn't even notice his tie was gray, and he's been sitting in front of me for the last forty-five minutes.

"I caught Emilia in a lie, and we had it out. She tried to lie her way out of it, and I punished her for it. She's been subdued ever since. Faye said she asked to do something that would keep her at her desk, so she's updating our electronic databases. I think she's processing her new reality."

"And you? You've been reclusive this week. What's your excuse?" He sits back, and I look at the time again. Eight minutes.

"I don't know. Her punishment isn't sitting right with me, but I'm too busy this week to deal with it. The dinner is tomorrow, and we're still getting some of the winner's names in from HR and finance. Once the gala is done, I'll have a couple of days to reassess everything. Did I tell you she met Alexandra?" Noah looks surprised, and I realize it has been a while since I've caught up with my closest friend. "They got along great. It turns out Adam told Emilia about her."

"Really? Does she know about the business then?"

I shake my head. "No. And she won't. She's a long way away from learning about that." I change the subject. "Any news on Kyle?"

"Last I checked, he's still gone. Emilia isn't on his radar anymore. What's going on upstairs? I went up yesterday, and everything is all over the place."

"I'm having the executive offices redesigned. Adam hired a company to reorganize the floor before he—well, and we couldn't cancel them, so I had some of the plans changed, and they are working through the week."

Noah sits back, and I sense the time ticking away. I have a

conference call in five minutes, and I'm beginning to feel the stress of managing the company without Adam. I need Emilia to be caught up today, not eleven months from now. I can't keep this pace up, and it is only going to get busier now that the shock of Adam's passing has worn off and things are returning to normal.

"Actually, there is one more thing, but it has to wait until next week. Until Emilia gets up to speed, I need your help with some stuff around here. Can I pull you off of assisting the buying teams and give you some temporary responsibilities?" Noah nods. I knew I could count on him. "Great. Let's talk about it on Monday."

I push my seat back to indicate the meeting is over. Noah rises, but he doesn't leave.

"Can I say one last thing—about Emilia?" I answer with a curt nod and wait for him to continue. "Look, I know I've said it before, but you may want to handle her carefully. She looks almost repressed right now. I don't know what happened between you two, but taking control can sometimes mean helping the other person navigate their ship through rough waters instead of steering it for them. She looks lost, and as your friend, I'm worried about both of you."

"I know. Thank you. It's been a tough time for her. She lost her father, and she has these rules to live by. I understand her situation. I support her, but I won't allow her to undermine my position. Now, I really need to cut this short. I have two minutes." I tap my watch, and Noah grabs his papers off my desk. I feel bad ushering him out so fast. I used to have more time to talk. "Look, we'll get together next week, outside of work, and talk about all of this."

As we near my office door, Noah's words become white noise as Emilia comes into view. Typing away at her computer, she doesn't bother to look up, and I realize her demeanor has changed this week. She's only focused on finishing her work and getting out of here. Her fire has been extinguished, and she is deflated. She looks like she used to when she'd try to get my attention and I'd ignore her.

This was never my intention. I need to correct this and bring back the person she was.

"I have all of the staff names for the awards, with their write-ups, and the Apex Group is on line one for your call, Mr. Darkly." Faye's voice catches my attention, and I acknowledge her with a smile.

"Have the printer add those names to the certificates, and make sure everything gets to the hotel for the presentations. Thank you, Faye." I step back into my office and close the door behind me.

There will be time to change things between us this weekend, I think to myself.

Friday morning at the office went by quickly. Since the awards dinner is tonight, everyone was given a half day to get ready as an added perk.

Things have changed a lot around the office in five years.

I found out at our team meeting this morning that award winners are given a paid vacation pretty much of their choice. They also get extra holiday time, among other things, and I can see why everyone is talking about the night.

I also learned that Joshua has asked Noah to work with him in management, and he has granted him many of the tasks I assumed I would be taking over. Not only that—he is having my father's office renovated. I've been excluded from all plans, so I feel like I am slowly being wedged out of my family's company.

Growing up, I never wanted to believe Joshua was like his mother, but more and more I feel like an outsider, both in my own home and in my own company. Just like old times, Joshua is excluding me from everything. I don't fit in with management, and I don't fit in with the rest of the staff. I just don't fit in at all.

I could feel my face turning red during the meeting. Tears threatened to spill all over my notebook, but I kept silent. Joshua had allowed me to get ready over at Rosie's, and I didn't want to lose the privilege because I asked too many questions or got upset in front of the team. So I sat silent, appeasing him so I could have this little luxury.

It was worth it.

Rosie and I laughed all afternoon. We filled up on junk food and had some wine as we dressed, and we did our hair and makeup to songs from our high school days.

"We're almost there. Wow. Look at the place. There's so much traffic." Rosie looks out her window as our driver takes the last turn before the hotel.

"I'll drop you off at the front, Ms. Connor. You have my number; let me know when you want to be picked up, and I'll meet you in the same place." Niko speaks over his shoulder as he pulls into the drop-off area. "You ladies have a wonderful time."

We say our thanks, hop out of the car, and make our way into the building quickly. The first face I recognize is Faye's.

"Oh, Emilia. You look stunning. You as well, Rosalyn." We smile and giggle together at her compliments, and she continues, "Everything is ready for you at your seat. The awards are ready to go, and I've included the names and their write-ups. When you are called up, just say thank you and start reading from top to bottom. Let each one get up, accept their award, and take pictures. That's it. I will see you later in the evening. You'll do great." She reaches over and squeezes my arm. Then someone catches her attention over my shoulder, and she's off. Rosie and I make our way up the grand staircase and into the banquet room.

The dining room is as lavish as I remember. My father brought me to a company gala a long time ago, and I couldn't stop staring at the beautiful men and women all dressed up. Looking down at my dress, I realize I'm now one of the beautiful people.

I just wish my dad was here to see.

The hum of conversation drifts around the room. Glasses clink together, and laughter flows from all sides. The music plays at a low level, but it will get louder as the night goes on. I do a quick scan for Joshua, but I can't see him anywhere. Then my stomach sinks as I do a second scan for Sean and Brent.

Sean is in the corner, talking with a group of guys. He hasn't seemed to notice me. It doesn't look like Brent is here yet. I take a deep breath to calm my nerves. Rosie won't let either of them get near me.

"Here's my table. Oh, good, I like these people," Rosie laughs as she looks at the name cards.

"You like everyone. Let's go find mine." I take Rosie's hand, and we walk around three more tables before I see Joshua's name on a card.

"Here's mine. There's the information I need for the awards later. Oh no..." I trail off in embarrassment. "I forgot to tell Faye to take off his name." I meet Rosie's confused stare. Then she sees the card with Kyle's name on it beside mine. It looks like I'll be sitting next to an empty seat tonight.

As if she's reading my mind, we both glance beside Joshua. My stomach lurches into my throat—Tawny's name is on the card next to his.

"Just a minute. Stay right there." Rosie spins on her heels and leaves me staring between two names I don't want to see at this dinner table.

In a few seconds, she's back by my side. She grabs Kyle's name off the place setting and replaces it with her own name card. Then she smiles at me. "See? All better. I'm your date. I didn't really like the people at my table anyway." She looks like she wants to laugh at her own joke, but she waits for me. Slowly, we start to smile together.

"Thanks, Rosie. I appreciate this. Thank you for always being here for me." Taking her hand, I lean in for more privacy. "I mean it. Things have been really hard lately. I know I don't talk about it a lot, but it means everything that we are still as close as we were." My face warms as I speak, and I know my eyes are a little watery. The look on Rosie's face tells me she sees it too.

"Hey. It's all good. We will always be besties. I know why you left; I know." She gives my hand a reassuring wiggle. Then she smiles, and I smile back, blinking a tear away. "Here, take a seat and get settled before you ruin your makeup. I'm going to say hi to a couple of people and get us a drink, okay?"

I nod, drop my clutch on the table, and pull out my seat. I'm half tempted to wedge Rosie between Joshua and me, but that would be awkward for her, so I sit in my designated chair.

I lift the water pitcher and pour myself a glass, then take a sip to settle my nerves as rustling to my right draws my attention.

Looking up, I find Tawny glaring at me. She's not quick enough to hide her disdain for me, but she attempts to downplay it. "Oh, hello, Miss...?" She lets her question linger, as though she doesn't know who I am.

I clench my teeth hard. "It's Emilia Connor. Hello, Ms. Davenfield," I answer as I look around for Joshua. I don't really want to see him right now, but I'd rather not deal with this woman on my own.

"Ah, yes. Joshua will be here shortly. He's just checking our coats and getting me a drink. He's such a gentleman."

I smile into my water as she settles into her chair. I'm happy it isn't the one right beside me. "Oh, I do hope this dinner doesn't go on too long. I'm looking forward to having Joshua all to myself later tonight."

Nausea rolls through me at her insinuation, and I swivel my head to try to locate Rosie in the crowd. I could really use that drink right now.

"You have big shoes to fill, you know." Tawny's statement confuses me.

"How so?"

"Everyone loved Adam. He was a great businessman and a fantastic speaker. I don't envy you getting up in front of your father's whole company and attempting to carry on his legacy. Now Joshua—that's a born leader. It just comes naturally to him." If her words were physical, they would have slapped me across the face.

One last glance tells me Rosie will still be a while. I stand on wobbly legs and excuse myself, then I glance around for the nearest exit. Just off to the side, I see balcony doors that are open a crack, and I walk straight for them.

The night air is cool—it's just what I need to calm my anxious stomach. I take a few deep breaths, then focus my attention on my surroundings. Numerous small balconies overlook the gardens, which are lit up beautifully by thousands of little lights. Each balcony has its own entrance, and I'm thankful I am not sharing this one with anyone right now.

The raucous din from inside fades as I look up to see faint stars trying to break through above the city lights. *I could see them better from Dad's cabin,* I think to myself. The moon hangs quietly in the tenebrous sky, and I wish for a moment I could fade away into the background and disappear.

But I can't.

I need to fill my father's shoes and get through this night, and I take a final breath to fortify myself. As I turn to rejoin the party, the blood drains from my face.

Two repugnant eyes stare at me as Brent stands silently at the door, blocking my exit once again.

"I missed you around the office this week—well, after our little thing on Monday." His words disgust me, and I can smell him from here. He started celebrating way too early.

"I need to get back to my table." I motion to the door, the same way I did in the file room, and he doesn't let me leave this time either.

"That dress looks amazing on you." His eyes have dropped; he's talking to my body now. I suddenly feel naked, dirty. "I told you I'd be seeing you around."

"B-Brent. Let me go." I try to get through the little space he left open, but his arm shoots out against the doorframe.

"I've been looking forward to tonight since I first saw you back here. Tonight, I get to watch you announce my name as a winner of one of the sales awards." As he speaks, my arms go numb.

How could I not have considered this possibility? I've been so busy that the thought never crossed my mind. And how does Brent know he's getting an award? As far as I understood, the winners only find out when their names are called, and the only ones with access to the information are HR, who approves the numbers from finance, and Joshua.

His wretched fingers move up my arm, catching my attention as he continues, "I cannot wait to hear you praise me in front of everyone. Everyone out there sees Emilia, but we both know who you really are. Don't we, Feelya?" He leans in, whispering in my ear. As his hands continue to touch my skin, I begin to shake. "I wonder if you'll stutter that sweet stutter I gave you."

Without giving him the satisfaction of hearing me stumble on my words, I grab his arms and push him hard to the side, wrestling my way into the hall. Before I can get far enough away, his muffled promise is loud and clear:

"I'll collect the rest of my award later tonight."

I never realized just how much went into planning these dinners, but celebrating our company's successes is important to everyone at Connor Realty. The meetings and preparations have taken their toll on me, and my patience is wearing incredibly thin.

The half-hour car ride to the awards dinner is the first time I've had to myself all week. I messaged Tawny earlier, then promptly turned off my phone. Since she is coming from across town, I made the excuse that I had some last-minute things to clear up at the office and suggested we meet in front of the hotel.

In truth, I would have loved to see Emilia in the dress she chose before we got to the dinner, but she had requested to spend some time with her friend. We've been walking on eggshells around each other this week, and I wanted her to feel relaxed when she got up to present the awards, so I allowed her the time.

I stop at the valet. A young boy jumps to my door and holds

out his hand for the keys, and I look up to see Tawny waiting on the steps in a deep red ball gown.

"Ms. Davenfield. You look beautiful. Thank you for meeting me here."

She wastes no time positioning herself at my side and hooking her arm through mine. "Thank you, Joshua. Please, call me Tawny. It is a party, after all." While I know she is happy to be here, her smile feels a little too sculpted.

"Of course. Shall we?" I gesture my free hand to the entrance, and we walk into the hotel to smiles and familiar faces.

Each time someone new walks up to say hello, Tawny tightens her grip on my arm. I've made it clear this is a business arrangement, but appearances are everything to her.

"Mr. Darkly. You look dashing." I recognize Faye's voice before I turn to see her.

"Faye. You look lovely this evening. You remember Ms. Davenfield? Tawny, this is Faye."

The two women share a smile and exchange pleasantries. I know only one of them is being sincere.

"I have a couple of last-minute items to address." Faye looks like I feel: frazzled.

"Tawny. This shouldn't take more than a few minutes. How about you go in, take a look around, and find our seats? I'll check our coats and get you a drink. White wine?" I ask, and she nods, then reluctantly releases her death grip on my arm.

"How can I help?" I ask.

Faye looks over my shoulder and waits for a few seconds. "Honestly, you just looked like you needed a break already." I laugh. There is no better assistant.

"Emilia is here already, and her notes are at her seat. Do you have your talking points on you?" I nod. "Good. The photographer is setting up, and I just came from the kitchen—

everything is on time. Try to relax. You've been working a lot this week. I'll check your coats for you." She reaches out and takes them from my hands. "I'm going to do one more sweep around, then I'll take my seat. My phone is on if you need anything." She smiles and doesn't wait for me to answer before she waves at someone at the front entrance and walks away.

I'm lucky to have someone as experienced as Faye. She's worked with Adam for as long as I can remember, and she knows these things like the back of her hand. Losing Adam was a huge blow to this company, but there are many great people here who have been keeping everything going.

It's time to put the stress of the week behind me and throw on the happy face everyone needs to see. The walk up the staircase takes a lot longer than it should, as colleagues stop me on each step to say hello. As I enter the ballroom, I glance toward our table. Tawny is seated at it, looking through her phone, so I make my way to the bar with the shortest line and order our drinks.

Tawny plasters her go-to smile back onto her face as I approach, and I notice a filled water glass at Emilia's seat.

"Has anyone from our table come by yet?" I ask nonchalantly as I hand her the glass of wine.

"Yes. That one who fills in for your secretary just left." She takes a sip, then tastes it for a moment before deciding it is acceptable, and I pull my chair out to take a seat. "I'm telling you, Joshua. You work too hard. You need better staff around you."

It's clear by her tone she is threatened, and I choose to defend the staff I need to keep me afloat.

"I'm lucky to have Faye on my team." I take a gulp of my drink. If more people don't sit down at this table soon, I'm going to need another one.

"Oh, she's okay. I'm talking about that Linda girl." My

mind goes blank for a moment before I realize who she's speaking about.

"You mean Emilia. Tawny, I told you, that's Adam's daughter," I respond, and she smirks.

"And she knows it too." I shoot her a curious expression, and she continues, "That one is riding her daddy's coattails. I bet she takes everything for granted. You look absolutely exhausted this week. Has she done anything to help you or her own father's company?"

"Emilia has been learning how everything works. It's unfair to expect her to hit the ground running. She just lost her—" I sense a rustle behind me, and my words cut off as Emilia catches my attention.

I open my mouth to say hello, but nothing comes out as the sight of her sinks in. She looks more than beautiful in her tasteful black dress. It's so simple it's ravishing, and I don't have the words to tell her how stunning she looks.

But something is off. Emilia drops her purse on the table and grabs the envelope Faye left for her. She tears it open with shaky hands, then shuffles through the pages. It looks as though she's found what she was looking for, and I watch her lips move as she quickly reads part of her speech.

Then she pauses. Her breathing is heavy as she spins and glares at me, then waves the pieces of paper in my face.

"I won't do this" is all she says to me, and I don't understand her hostility.

"What do you mean?" I try to remain calm, but my impatience flares up.

"I won't get up there and read this. I'm not doing the awards." As she declares, last minute, that she's bowing out, I stand slowly. Tawny huffs to my right, and I hate that she thinks she was right all along.

"Let's talk about this in private. Tawny, please excuse us." At my words, Tawny becomes merely an innocent bystander.

"Of course, Joshua." I hear her almost sing her answer, but I've already grabbed Emilia's upper arm, and I'm moving us toward the kitchen.

As we walk, Emilia tries to compose herself and wriggle her arm away, but she's not going anywhere. My fury rises with each step, and my grip on her arm tightens.

How can she pull this now? I've worked my ass off for this dinner, and all she has to do is stand up there and read from a piece of paper.

I push us through the kitchen doors. A few people in catering uniforms glance up, then go back to their work. I scan the area and find a small room just off to the side. The sounds in the kitchen are loud, and it's just what I need to muffle our voices.

Dragging her into the room, I close the door behind us and start in. "Emilia, you've known you were speaking tonight for a couple of weeks. This is unacceptable. All you have to do is get up there when you are called and say what is on that paper." My voice rises as I speak. I don't have time for this. I need to be out there with a smile on my face, and instead I'm stuck in here with Emilia as she throws a fit.

"I will not announce the winners. I won't, Joshua." Her demand grates into my eardrums.

I've had it with all of this back-and-forth. I've given her an easy ride since she's been back. She wants to file, I let her file. She wants to sit at her desk, I let her sit at her desk. She wants to get ready with her friend, I allow that too. As much as I hate to admit it, Tawny might be right. I've given Emilia a lot of leeway, and she still wants more.

"Enough." My voice is cold and detached, even to me. "Emilia, when they call your name, you will march yourself up to that podium and read out those names." She opens her mouth to speak, but I'm not done. "Your inheritance is riding on this."

"What?" The weight of my words sinks into her, and now I have her attention. It's clear we aren't understanding each other, and she still thinks she has some choices here.

"You heard me. You'll do what is required of you, and you'll do it with a fucking smile, or so help me, I will take everything away from you."

She gasps, and I wish I hadn't said those words.

In my anger, I went too far. The thought of taking everything from her—the business, the home, and even her father's cabin—never crossed my mind. But the threat just crossed my lips, and I won't pull it back now.

"I—" She falls silent, and she stares at me with tears welling up in her eyes, but I won't entertain her emotions now.

She's lost my sympathy for the time being.

"Do I make myself clear, Ms. Connor?" To drive my point home, I revert back to the title I used when we read her father's will, and she offers me only a nod. Then I turn and leave her standing by herself.

CHAPTER 48
EMILIA

As the catering staff clear the dessert plates, I look down at my slice of cheesecake. I took one bite and dropped my napkin over what was left. I don't think I ate more than a few bites of the whole meal. I mostly just cut the food and moved it around my plate.

Rosie kept leaning over to check on me, until Joshua told her I was fine in an attempt to quiet her. It worked.

Tawny held Joshua's attention. They talked through most of the meal. Every time they laughed together, she touched his arm, and I wished I was anywhere but here. It shouldn't have bothered me. But it did. He completely ignored me; he did everything possible to keep from looking in my direction. It felt like old times. It was old times.

He never changed.

My plate is taken away, and the open envelope underneath it stares back at me. I'm about to live my worst nightmare. Joshua is making me stand up in front of a roomful of my dad's friends and colleagues and honor the two boys who tormented me through high school.

He doesn't even want to know why I don't want to do it.

Maybe he already knows. My thought surprises me, but as I focus on it, it starts to make sense.

Maybe Joshua always knew. He signed off on their harassment issues; he probably got them jobs at dad's company, and now he's making me read out their names. Maybe this is how he pushes me out.

I'm a prisoner in my own home. I'm being treated like a child. I have rules, hoops to jump through. He's probably going to take everything no matter what. He's just holding my inheritance over my head, dangling it like a carrot.

And for what? Money. It's always about money. Nothing else matters to any of them. He's just like his gold-digging mother.

Joshua catches my attention as he stands and walks to the front of the room, and everyone claps. His feigned smile hides everything. As he opens his mouth to speak, I can't bring myself to listen to his voice. Everything is a lie.

"You okay?" I feel Rosie's hand cover mine under the table.

"I can't do this, Ro," I whisper.

"You've got this. I know you do. Just read it like you're reading a book report. Keep your eyes on me. I'll make funny faces for you like I used to in English class."

I meet her eyes, and she smiles and brushes a strand of hair off my face. I wish I had time to tell her everything that happened tonight, but I suddenly feel like it doesn't matter anymore.

Nothing matters anymore.

Joshua wraps up his speech to thunderous applause and shouts from the drunk tables in the back, and soon the host is back up at the mic, getting ready to introduce me. I take some deep breaths and try to center my thoughts, and when I hear my name through the speakers, I look up to see everyone smiling at me. Everyone but Joshua.

I stand slowly. I grab the envelope and my clutch and make my way to the front of the room. As I reach the podium, I notice the lights are bright enough that I can't see beyond the first few tables. But I can see Rosie, and that is all that matters. Her big smile is the only comfort I have here, and I look back down and open the envelope.

"Thank you. I—" My voice echoes through the speakers, and it sounds foreign to me.

Time freezes as I scan the paper and my eyes land on their two names. I really can't do this. Joshua will take everything away from me anyway. I can't be here anymore, but I have nothing.

I guess some women just have no other options. Jessica's words from when she was fitting my dress cross my mind, and I look up quickly to see a darkened room waiting in silence for me to continue.

Shuffling the paper to buy some time, I attempt to speak again. "I'm happy to b-be here t-tonight."

I hear a putrid laugh from one of the tables in the back. I know it is either Sean or Brent laughing at my stutter, and I don't want to speak again.

I shift my eyes back to Rosie; she is still trying to smile. She's trying to set me at ease, but two seats to her right sits Joshua, and the look on his face chills me to my bones.

She said an auction was happening this weekend. What was the name of the place?

When I remember, my fingers immediately go to my clutch. Joshua didn't let me go out this week, so I still have one week of my allowance on me in cash.

"I'm sorry. Forgive m-me." I whisper my words before I realize I've said them. I'm not apologizing to any of them—I'm apologizing to my dad. I'm not the daughter he deserved. I let him down, over and over again, and I'm about to let him down one more time.

I don't belong here. I never cared about our money. I was happier without it those five years away. Everything I cared about is gone, so why am I standing here fighting for things I don't want?

The answer to my question flips a switch in my brain, and everything around me dissolves. I've chosen this for myself. The lawyer said it the first day I got here; I am within my rights to forfeit. I can choose to walk away. I chose to place myself in this misery, and now I'm choosing to release myself from it.

But it is always about money. I'm going to need some to make a new start.

I drop the paper onto the podium and pick up my clutch.

"I congratulate all of our recipients tonight, but I can't read these names. I'd like to call Joshua Darkly up to do so." I clap to prompt the audience to do the same, and I watch Joshua stand with a forced smile. All eyes are now back on him. Without wasting another minute, I turn and head toward the exit to the kitchen.

I don't have much time. I have to get my things and leave, and I'll work out my plan while I'm moving. Grabbing the first server I see, I ask for staff directions to the front of the hotel and make my way down the narrow corridor and out the front exit.

I hail the first cab I see, give him directions to the house, and turn off my phone. With all the photos and presentations, Joshua will be up there for at least half an hour. Then he has his closing remarks, so I probably have no more than an hour until he can get back to his phone and start looking for me.

I owe him nothing, but I do owe Rosie something. I'll message her before I leave my phone at home. It's a company phone anyway, so I won't need it.

I've rebuilt before, and I will rebuild again.

By the time the taxi pulls up to the house, I have my whole plan set in motion, and I ask the driver to wait. I run up the stairs to my room in the dark, and I go through my next steps. I'll pack my essentials and some extra clothes. My old roommate gave me some of her more revealing outfits, so I will take those. I'll get to a hotel near the club, then I'll contact them to see if I can list myself in their auction. I just need enough to get a start.

Spending a short time with anyone is better than spending eleven months in this hell.

I chose to put myself here, and I'm choosing to leave. I recite my mantra again.

I pack the last of my things. I'm thankful Sylvia took the night off, but I'm sad I won't be able to say goodbye.

This is going to hurt more before it starts to get better, I tell myself as I grab the office phone and message Rosie.

Joshua has probably already realized that I am no longer there.

I drop the phone onto my bed and grab the backpack that contains my old phone. I'm thankful I haven't disconnected it yet as I run down the stairs, lock up, and get back into the cab.

"Do you know of a club called Ravenous?" I ask.

Two eyes size me up from the driver's seat. The driver looks to the roof of the car, as if searching his brain, before shaking his head.

A wave of panic hits me. I can't be here when Joshua gets back, but I can't have this guy driving all over the city, looking for a club and draining what little money I have left.

Then I remember: the seamstress left me her number.

I hold the card up to the dome light to read the numbers. That's when the driver notices the other side of it.

He points at the raven logo. "I do know that place. Most

people just tell me the address; I didn't know it was called Ravenous. It's just a building with a picture of that above the door. I thought it was some kind of secret club," he answers hesitantly, and I open my clutch and finger through the bills I have left.

"Take me to a hotel near there where I can stay for around a hundred a night."

It's been twelve hours since anyone has heard from or seen Emilia. After Rosalyn showed me her text last night, I had Faye and Noah cover for me. I made my excuses to Tawny and rushed home to confront her, only to be met with a dark silence.

Emilia had already been and gone. She left most of her things behind, including her work phone.

My anger peaked when I checked the house's security footage. I watched her get out of the taxi, then, twenty minutes later, she got back in with a suitcase and a backpack, and they drove off. Contacting the cab company was a dead end. I hung up on the kid after he recited his company's policy on client privacy for the fifth time.

I thought about texting all her contacts to see if anyone has heard from her, but the sad truth is, there is only Rosie and Sylvia, and I gave Sylvia the evening off.

"Any news?" Noah startles me out of my train of thought, and I look up to see him half-dressed in a pair of my pajama pants.

After the dinner, he came right over. He found me angry and raging at anything I could find. After I checked all of the places she could have gone—and it was a short list—I began to unravel. My anger over her extreme disobedience tangled with my worry over her well-being, and I was lost.

Noah began to put together a plan, and we worked through it in small parts, but everything led to dead ends.

I've been slowly sinking since then. Texting Rosalyn to get her ass over here wasn't the sanest plan I've ever had, but I feel like I'm running out of time.

"Nothing yet. I went through her things," I admit sheepishly. It was a shit thing to do, and I understand she needs some privacy, but she lost that privilege when she ran away and left her things behind. "She didn't leave anything important behind. Just clothes. Her laptop and the backpack she always carries are gone."

As I speak, I realize Emilia has become a ghost. Even before she left, she could always just disappear. She's become as transient as a leaf blowing in the wind, except for one thing: She needs money. Everyone needs money to survive, and hers should be running out.

She can't go to Kyle, and she has no family. She only has Rosalyn, so sooner or later she will need to get in touch with her friend.That's why I texted her.

A loud knock at the door surprises Noah, and he looks at me hopefully.

I know what he hopes, but it's not Emilia, and I shake my head. He leaves to answer the door, and less than a minute later Rosalyn joins me, followed by Noah, who is now wearing a shirt.

"Joshua." Rosie looks like she's barely slept, and I can tell by looking at her she hasn't heard from Emilia either.

"I put some coffee on; can I get you both a cup?" Noah

asks, and Rosalyn and I nod silently before he leaves. We stare at each other before she breaks the silence.

"And I quote: 'Get your ass over here when you wake up.'" Rosalyn crosses her arms in accusation.

"I know." She relaxes a bit. "I'm sorry." I don't offer apologies lightly, in my personal or professional life, and she knows this.

She pinches her lips together in a forced smile when Noah returns with three mugs, cream, and sugar on a platter. He serves both of us as Rosalyn takes a seat in a chair near me.

"Look. I was up all night. I couldn't figure out why she left so suddenly until you read the names." She glances at her purse, then back up as Noah quietly takes a seat off to the side. "Joshua, you were going to make her read out *their* names? Why?"

Her question resets me. I suddenly sense there is something I've forgotten, or something I don't know, and I answer honestly: "Because those are our award winners."

At my answer, Rosalyn sits upright and takes a long look at me. "Look, Joshua. My best friend is missing, and I don't have anyone else who can help me. I'm going out on a limb here, and I promised Emilia I wouldn't say anything, but I'm really getting worried now."

"Say anything about what?" My words are direct, and her wide eyes tell me she knows I'm not messing around.

"Before we get into that, I need to know, so I'm just going to ask. Did you know Sean and Brent used to torment Emilia in high school? Do you know what they called her?"

I take a quick glance at Noah. He shrugs and shakes his head.

I have no idea what Rosalyn is asking me. Emilia was a few grades behind me; I never cared enough to pay attention to her then. How would I know?

I shake my head. "No. What did they call her?"

Rosalyn shakes her head too. This is an answer I won't be getting from her. "Joshua, what matters is they bullied her, relentlessly, and you told her to stand up there and say all of those amazing things about them—which, quite frankly, aren't accurate."

I have to hand it to her: Rosalyn is a loyal friend. She's sitting in front of her boss, and she isn't wavering in her dedication.

"High school was a long time ago. Everyone has grown up. She couldn't get beyond a little school bullying to read from a piece of paper?" I'm not going to forgive her outburst this easily. "People change."

"That's the thing; they haven't changed. They are still—um —harassing women." Taking a deep breath, Rosalyn reaches into her purse and pulls out some papers. "And you're signing off on it."

"WHAT?" My anger flares at her accusation, and Rosie jolts.

"I have it here. Emilia found these in their files." Her hands are shaking as she holds the papers out. I grab them and scan the words on document, along with my signature. This is my signature, but I never would have signed something like this unless it was a dismissal.

As I flip through, Rosalyn continues, "She made me promise I wouldn't say anything the other day when I caught Brent intimidating her in the file room."

"WHAT?" I can't believe what I'm hearing. Noah has jumped out of his seat and is moving over to me to take a look at the papers. I hand everything over to him.

"I could tell he was trying to scare her. She was even stuttering; it was so bad." Rosalyn wrings the straps of her purse with her hands as she speaks.

"No. She stutters when she's lying. I figured that out years ago."

"No, she doesn't. She started stuttering in high school after —" She pauses. I know there is more to this story, but Rosalyn won't betray her friend. "She stutters when she has anxiety, and she's only ever stuttered when they've harassed her."

I sit back in my seat, staring at Rosalyn as my thoughts jump all over the place. She was stuttering on Monday when I called her out on lying about her school. But now that I think about it, she was stuttering before I even spoke. That morning, she was in school, then she had lunch, and then she was filing— in the room where Rosalyn said she saw Brent harassing her. After that, she requested to work at her desk for the remainder of the week.

"Was it last Monday that you caught Brent with her in the file room?" As I ask, Rosalyn thinks for a moment.

"No, it was the week before."

After Adam walked in on a member of his admin team having sex in the filing room, he had cameras installed in each room as a safety and security measure, just like they are throughout the building, except for, of course, the bathrooms. I'm thankful for his foresight.

I clear my throat to catch Noah's attention, and he looks up from the papers he's holding. "I need you to go to the office. Have security pull up footage of the file room Emilia was in on Monday. It's the new one my team uses. If she wasn't there, I need all cameras that picked her up since she got to work. She normally arrives around 12:10, then she has lunch. She spoke to me a little before two in the afternoon." As I speak, Noah nods, and I notice Rosalyn watching me. "I want full copies of Brent and Sean's files as well. Include everything. Expenses, sales, HR files—anything with their names on it. Also, pick a date on any of those harassment forms I apparently signed, then grab any footage of me signing papers on the date listed. I need to know how this happened."

"I'll get everything I can find, but Joshua? Have some patience. This will take a while." He turns to leave, and I stand.

"Forget it; I'm coming with you. We can find everything we need faster with two of us."

Noah looks surprised as I take a step to the door. "Okay, but clean yourself up first. You look like hot garbage. If there are any new guys in security, they'll never believe you own the company and I don't want to be an accomplice to aggravated assault on top of everything else."

Noah leaves the room, and Rosalyn looks a little more relieved than she did when she first got here.

My ire is flaring to life, and it's only heating up. I am ready to tear a lot of things apart, but for the first time in a long time, my anger isn't directed at Emilia, and it feels right. If Rosalyn is telling the truth, then people in our organization can't be trusted, and we need to stop it before we lose everything—and I lose Emilia—for good.

"You really didn't know, did you?" she asks solemnly.

"I have a feeling there is a lot you aren't telling me. But no, I didn't know. If you hear from Emilia, please let me know."

CHAPTER 50
EMILIA

"Housekeeping." A woman's voice outside the door wakes me up, and I automatically answer.

"I'm okay. Thanks."

Her shadow moves across the thin curtains as she goes to the next room.

Unfortunately, Ravenous is located in a nicer part of the city, and one hundred dollars doesn't buy much over here, but I'm okay with it. This place will provide more privacy, and it's clean enough.

My eyes land on the clock, and I can't believe it is almost eleven in the morning.

After I arrived last night, I put everything in a pile, and it's all still where I left it. The motel doesn't have a business center, so I had to use my own laptop, which was something I wanted to avoid. I want to make sure I can't be traced until I am on my way to wherever I'm going.

I kept my time online short—there's no way I'll check my email now. There are probably a dozen emails from Joshua telling me to fall in line, and I'm not mentally ready for that yet.

I found Ravenous rather easily, but navigating the website proved to be more difficult. They don't make it easy for just anyone to walk in and auction themselves off.

I had to provide a referral name and confirm I was over twenty-one before they would let me see the company contact information. It's clear they do not do business with minors. I ended up using Jessica's name; I hope it doesn't get her into trouble.

Just as I was about to send an email from an old account, I noticed a link near the bottom of the page titled "Auction Submissions." Clicking it took me where I needed to go, and I felt like I had wandered into a restricted area.

The form was lengthy. First up was an NDA. It asked for a pseudonym for privacy purposes but stated that I will need to show my real ID and sign a physical NDA under my real name once I am accepted and on the premises to protect everyone involved. Fair enough. I cropped a photo from my night out with Rosalyn when I first got back.

Next up was a list of sexual questions. It seemed like they were meant to weed out people who weren't really interested. I answered honestly and hit send.

I don't feel confident that I'll hear back. I refused to provide a phone number and only left my email address.

After that, I remember pacing and having a good cry. Then I woke up. Lifting the bedsheets to check, I confirm I'm still in my dress from last night, except now it is completely wrinkled.

I slept soundly though. For the first time in a long time, I slept without the weight of everything crushing me.

I drag myself off of the bed and over to my laptop, and I tap a key to bring it to life. While it starts, I take off the dress and lay it over the chair in front of the small wooden desk. Then I turn back to my email, and there it is in bold letters.

A response from Ravenous.

For a long moment, I can't breathe. This is my answer. This is my only plan right now, and it can't fall through. I only have enough money to stay here for two more nights, then I'd need to go back. That is not an option.

The first sentence fills my stomach with butterflies. I'm both relieved and terrified—I've been accepted.

A list of important details follows. There is no fee for those who are to be auctioned off, which is good, because I couldn't cover what it costs just to attend.

There is another form to fill out and send back, and it is more thorough. It includes a section where I'm to write out past sexual experiences, list my measurements, hair, eye color, and age, and what I won't allow during my time with the winning bidder. As I read a list of suggested limits, I'm thankful examples were included.

An itinerary of the evening is also included. I would be auction number four, but it doesn't list how many are after me. There is a list of dos and don'ts and a number to call if I cannot make it.

And that's it.

I close the laptop, and my naked reflection comes into view in the mirror over the desk. I had learned to love myself after high school, but Brent and Sean took that away from me all over again without even trying.

And here I am. A woman with no other options. I'm joining at least three other women—or maybe there are men there too. I have no idea. I have no idea how any of this works. Maybe that is for the best. I don't know enough to run away.

Tomorrow night, someone will hopefully pay enough for some time with me, and I will live the rest of my life by my own rules.

I wonder what it will be like. I listed my limits, and the

website had lots of information on consent and open communication.

My stomach flutters at the thought of selling myself. Turning myself into property and handing control over to someone else. It's what I always fantasized about—being controlled by someone who cares about me. But this is different. This is a transaction, plain and simple. No one is going there looking to buy love. They are buying obedience. They are buying a body.

They are buying a whore. The thought makes me want to cry, but there's something else. I want to cry because I feel shame. Shame because this has always been what I wanted.

I'm exhausted. I'm tired of being strong and keeping my mouth shut to appease the world around me. I'm tired of being reserved and pushing my own needs down deep. I'm tired of not understanding why I have these thoughts and urges. I want to give it all away. Just for once.

I wish I had someone to talk to about this.

Bending over my suitcase, I open it and pull out a couple of outfits my old roommate Kelly sent back from our dorm. The outfits were always too revealing for the old me to wear, but secretly I thought she looked amazing in them. I always wished I had her confidence.

I hold a couple of them up to the mirror. I go for a short, black, sequined sheath dress with a low-cut neckline and the black ankle-strap heels I wore last night. I hang my special outfit up to air out, place my heels on the floor under it, then dig out a comfortable pair of pants and an oversized sweater.

My stomach grumbles. It's been almost a day since I last ate something, when I was getting ready at Rosie's.

I remember seeing a deli beside the motel when we pulled in last night. I decide to take a quick shower before grabbing a bite to eat. Then I'll run the errand I need to run today.

My stomach rolls over itself at the thought of what I am about to attempt, but I've thought it through. Joshua is more than happy to dangle my inheritance over my head. He's giving Noah my managerial responsibilities, and he signed off on Brent and Sean's harassment complaints. When I was younger, I was pathetic to hope he wanted to spend time with me, and if I stay here, I will always be that stupid little girl. There is nothing left for me now. The only place for me is the one I'm going to create on my own. As soon as I am done with Ravenous, I will build my new home away from here.

There's only one thing left to do, and it has to be done today before the close of business. I need to see the company lawyers and sign away my inheritance. I need to cut myself loose and leave.

And I need to do it today. The papers will be officially accepted on Monday morning, and Joshua will be notified after that. By then it will be too late, and I'll be gone.

I chose to put myself here, and I'm choosing to leave.

CHAPTER 51
JOSHUA

The office runs on a skeleton crew on Saturdays. Most of the sales staff is out buying and selling, and the rest work a typical Monday-to-Friday workweek. The white noise is loud without the buzz of a full office.

When we first arrived, Noah went right to security to pull up our office footage. I made my way to the file room, thankful that Faye made me learn how everything is recorded and kept. After a few choice words and a wasted half an hour spent looking for keys to the cabinet I needed, I pulled everything I could find. I've been sitting in my office for the last three hours, going through years of signed documents, expense claims, sales information, and HR documents—all with either my or Adam's signature on them.

Adam couldn't have known about this either.

I was with him the day he chose to hire these two. As I review their files, more details come back to me. Their dads both worked for the company. They were laid off when Adam hit some hard times, but they were offered jobs again as soon as the business began to bounce back. A few kids from Emilia's graduating class were invited to apply. Adam always had a soft spot for Emilia's school.

I remember this time pretty clearly because Emilia was asked to attend along with Rosalyn, but she declined. At the time, I thought it was typical behavior for her, and I added it to the long list of things I could hold against her. Now it appears there was another reason she didn't apply, and I wonder if Adam ever knew the truth.

He couldn't have. He would never have hired Brent or Sean.

My phone buzzes on my desk. It's Noah again, reminding me to stay calm and continue searching with a level head. I'm starting to think he's found something on the video surveillance, but I keep going through my files, jotting notes and taking photocopies.

We'll have to meet with our lawyers. The list of infractions is long, and it is more serious than anything I've dealt with here. We have sexual harassment, forgery, intimidation, embezzlement, and fraud—and I'm sure there are other things I can't see right now.

It looks like Brent and Sean aren't the only ones in on this either. Most of this paperwork would have gone through either finance or human resources, and I click the mouse a few times to pull up our complete company hierarchy so I can try to link anyone else who had a hand in this.

As I narrow down the names, a knock at the door catches my attention, but I keep my eyes on the screen. Noah doesn't wait for an invite, he just pulls up a chair as close to the desk as he can get.

"Find anything?" Dropping my pen on the notepad, I lean back in my seat and rub my eyes.

"Okay. I know I said this before, with Kyle, but I need you to promise we will talk about what you are about to see."

"Are you fucking kidding me? Fine, I don't have time for this. I promise. Show me the video." Just knowing I am about to see something I don't want to see is making me angry.

"Okay. I sent it up to you from security. Let me get it here." Noah stands, reaches across to my mouse, and accesses a portal that I've always seen on my desktop but never used. A few passwords later, we're in.

He clicks the tagged footage and sits back in his seat. I blow the video up to full screen and wait.

"I can't hear anything." I tap at the volume control furiously as I see Emilia and another woman talking in the file room.

"There isn't any sound on the cameras. You won't need it."

Then Sean enters the room. As he says something, Emilia's smile fades.

Shortly after, Brent walks in. He smiles at the person with Emilia. Then she leaves, and my stomach knots as Sean locks the door behind her. Now it is just the three of them.

What I would give for sound right now. At first it looks like a regular conversation, except Emilia looks terrified. Slowly, Brent's demeanor changes. He turns and exchanges some words with Sean, then turns back and steps into Emilia's space, causing her to back up as far as she can. She's up against the files behind her as he continues to advance. Even without sound, he is clearly being aggressive.

I want to rip his arms off and beat him with them.

Sean looks like he's laughing as Brent continues to push himself on Emilia. She looks so scared and alone, and my anger rages as I remember this was happening as I sat, mad at her, in my office. I could have walked down the hall and stopped this.

"What the fuck?" I shout as Brent's hand comes up to Emilia's chest. He squeezes her so hard, her face contorts in pain.

I'm standing at my line right now. If this goes any further, Noah will be an accomplice today after all. Before I can plot Brent's death, both of them turn, unlock the door, and leave a visibly and understandably shaken Emilia alone. A moment later, she drops the files and runs out of the room. That's when she entered my office, stuttering and trying to ask for help.

I hate myself right now.

I look up to share an incredulous look of disgust with Noah, but he's staring at me with wide eyes. His hands cover the lower half of his face, and he looks pale.

Everything is spiraling around my head. Pinching the bridge of my nose between two fingers, I close my eyes for a long minute. I can't focus long enough to hold one thought in my head before another comes at me.

Brent assaulted Emilia moments before I called her a liar, and then I punished her by taking away her mother's ring. Emilia told me she wouldn't read their names, and I told her I would take away her inheritance. She uncovered these buried harassment complaints with my own signature on them.

"Hey, Josh." Confused, I open my eyes and see Noah staring back at me. "Hey, I'm not going to ask if you're okay, but we need to sort this out. Rosalyn will call if Emilia contacts her, and you said Sylvia will tell you if she comes home. She can't go far. You said she doesn't have more than a few hundred dollars on her. As the owner of this company, you need to call a meeting with the lawyers. You need to do this for her. I can get a representative from HR in here too." He pulls out his phone, and I nod my head.

"Wait. We can't involve HR. Not yet. This is bigger than just Brent and Sean. Everything we sign off on comes through—"

"HR or finance...shit." Noah finishes my sentence for me. "Do you know who it might be?"

I exit the program and open the chart I was looking at earlier. "I have my suspicions, but I want you to take a look and tell me what you see."

Noah leans in and scans over the names. It doesn't take him long to make the same connection I did. "Keith Wilkes and Chad McKay. They went to our school; they were a few years behind us. Is it them?"

"They graduated the same year as Emilia. They were also hired at the same time as their friends Brent and Sean," I confirm and Noah drops his mouth open in understanding.

Chad has worked his way up into a senior finance position, and Keith has been doing the same in human resources for the past three years. "I wonder if it is a coincidence that Sean and Brent have won the sales awards for the last three years—that's how long Chad has been overseeing the audit of sales numbers."

As I say the words, the severity of our situation sinks in.

"We need to get everything together tonight. I'll pull as many of the files as I can. Check back in with security; I want to see footage of who I signed papers for on the date of that harassment complaint. If it is Keith or Chad, pull up the days that match the dates on the written complaints and get them sent up. I also want them to find the incident last week Rosalyn told us about, where she walked in on Brent in the same file room."

Noah stands and pulls out his phone.

"Who are you calling?"

"I'm ordering food. I think it's going to be a long night." He puts the phone to his ear and turns his back as I remember the time.

I forgot about the time. Everything will close soon. I pick up the receiver and hit speed dial to our lawyers' office. We need an urgent meeting before Monday to sort out our next steps.

"Jim Mathers." The man on the other end of the line wastes no time on formalities.

"Jim, it's Joshua Darkly. I have an urgent matter to discuss with you, and it can't wait until Monday."

"I'll say. She just left here. You must be surprised."

"Surprised? Who just left?"

"Emilia Connor. She signed her forfeiture notice. Everything is yours."

"You sure this is the place? I'm not sure I feel comfortable dropping you off, even in this swanky neighborhood." The cab driver twists to speak, giving me another once-over as he does.

I could have walked from the motel, but one old cabbie's stare is better than a few blocks worth of harassment in this skimpy dress, even on a quiet Sunday afternoon.

"I'll be fine. I've been here before," I lie as I close the top of my jacket. Then I hold out one of my last twenties. "Keep it."

As if on cue, the door opens as soon as the taxi pulls away, and a tall, muscular man in a suit steps into the alley with me. He takes in my body from top to bottom, but the look he's giving me is different than the others I received since I stepped out of my motel room. Muffled music bumps from behind him, piquing my interest.

"Pseudonym?" a woman asks, surprising me, and I look up to see the guy staring back at me.

"I—um—Lily," I stammer, and papers shuffle behind the doorman's muscular frame.

"She's on the list."

The man's disposition instantly changes from security guard to host. He offers me a smile and takes my bags. Then he steps aside to escort me into the building, and I meet the woman who the voice belongs to.

"I'm Reva. I'll be handling you tonight. Anything you need, or if you have any questions, let me know. If you don't see me, just tell anyone who works here that you need to see Reva. Do you understand?" The woman smiles politely, but she's all business. I nod my head as she spins on her heels. She talks over her shoulder as she walks, and I catch up and fall in line beside her.

"I'm going to take you into the auction area, but we need to go through part of the club to get there. Keep your eyes on the back of my head, and follow me. Don't stop or speak to anyone, even if they speak to you first. They probably won't. We have strict rules for everyone tonight, but if they do, just keep moving. Andrew here will deal with them."

I look back to see the man from the alley walking behind us with my luggage as another man takes his place at the door. As we get farther from the exit, the music becomes louder, and there are some voices and other sounds I can't make out.

As we push through the doors, I realize the other sounds are moans and grunts, and they're coming from different areas in the large room. I try to keep my eyes on Reva, but my curiosity gets the better of me, and I steal glances out of the corner of my eye as I follow her.

The club is designed to suit many comforts, from tables and chairs to sofas and more comfortable seats. There is even a stage and a dance floor.

As I look around the room, I notice people looking back at me. I feel like I'm being assessed, and I wonder if anyone in here will be bidding on me tonight. Then I suddenly feel light-headed. Reality sinks in, and even though the room is warm, I feel cold.

Out of the corner of my eye, a naked woman stretches out across someone's lap. He raises his hand to spank her bottom, and another man caresses her hair. I'm reminded of Joshua, the way he punished me in the shower and how good it felt. It was a harsh act, but I felt cared for—which is now a ridiculous thought.

Nearing the next set of doors, Reva stops to pull a card out of her pocket. She swipes it through a reader off to the side, then the door opens, and we step through. Andrew makes sure the door is closed and locked behind us, and the sound from the club is muffled considerably.

Reva turns to look at me and smiles. "That is our main club area. All of our members have access to it, but it is separate from what we are doing this evening. This is our auction and special event area. It's completely secure. The people who are interested in bidding have paid the entrance fee, and they'll be arriving through a private entrance in a little while. The auction doesn't start for a couple of hours. We ask you to come early so we can have a proper meeting, answer any questions you have, and make this a great experience for you.

"I'm going to set you up in a room. It will be your room for the evening, and Andrew is assigned solely to you. He's here for anything you need, and he'll be just outside your room at all times, so you can leave your things in there. Shall we?" She stretches out her hand, and I turn to see door number four.

The room is about the size of my old bedroom. Soft lights caress along light gray walls, and the artwork is beautiful. There are no windows, but it feels comfortable. An oversized chaise sits in one corner, and it looks cozy enough to sleep on. As Reva speaks, I continue to look around.

"The room has everything you might need for the next

couple of hours. There's a remote on the table. You can watch TV, movies, or listen to music, and there are snacks in the mini fridge. If you would like anything more to eat, just let Andrew know, and he'll bring it. There is a bathroom through that door; it has a shower, bathtub, and a vanity so you can touch up. We also have a stylist who can assist you if you require. We do keep your phone and any other devices you may have on you—we had a social media incident a few years back. Until you sign the papers to accept your auction, you are within your rights to leave. We will not hold you against your will. Do you understand?" She pauses, and I tell her I do. "However, if you'd like to stay, Andrew will not allow you to leave this room until the auction. Some of our guests may arrive early, and we do not want you speaking to anyone before bidding. Remember to ask for me if you need anything that Andrew cannot help you with. Now, let's get you out of that coat and see what we're working with. But first, do you have any questions?"

"How many others are here tonight?" I feel shell-shocked; I honestly don't know what to ask.

"Normally there are five. Two canceled, which is unusual. We almost postponed, but you saved the auction. So, there are a total of four tonight." Reva isn't rushed or trying to get out of the room, so I feel a little more relaxed, and I ask another question.

"And those people in the club bid on us?"

"No. Most of our club members already have partners. They come here to relax and enjoy themselves, either in private or with an audience. The auction is open to our elite membership. These are men and women who value a higher level of privacy or who are looking for something specific." As Reva answers, she walks over to the table, sets down the papers she was holding, and pulls a pen out of her pocket. "These are for you to look over and sign. You have a couple of hours, so take your time. Before I leave you for a bit, I need some information from you."

She pulls out another pen and flips a little notebook to a blank page. "Let's start with your name."

"Right. It's Emilia Connor." I wait for her to write it down, but she just looks back up at me, and I suddenly become apprehensive. "Is everything okay?"

"Hm? Oh, sorry. I just remembered I forgot to do something. I apologize. Emilia—Connor?" she confirms, and I nod. "Thank you, Emilia. To verify, I need your mother and father's names, your date of birth, and this is a good time to get me that ID of yours." She smiles and starts writing as I pull out my wallet.

"Have you thought about your reserve price?" she asks, pocketing my identification. I pause for a moment, and she continues, "It's the lowest price you will accept. I assume you have an idea of how much money you require?"

I nod in understanding. "Yes, sorry. I was thinking no less than twenty-five thousand dollars?" It comes out as a question. I've never done this before. How do I know what the going rate for me is? "I was thinking, after the club's commission...I was thinking I need about twenty thousand to..."

As I ramble, she stops writing and looks up. Her eyes meet mine, and the hot sting of tears fills my eyes. I'm not sure if it's the fact I am utterly clueless, or that I just put a dollar amount on my worth, but I suddenly feel out of place, and I know it shows.

"Can I help you, Emilia?" she asks quietly. I nod, reaching across the table for a tissue to dab my eyes. "The people bidding tonight are paying five thousand dollars just to see you. Some of them won't even bid on anyone, as they are waiting for their perfect fit. If you happen to be that match for one of our members, they will pay much more than twenty-five thousand dollars. Setting a low price invites fence-sitters. Can I write down ninety thousand dollars with the term of one week? This way, the time you spend standing in front of everyone is shorter, and only those who are serious will bid. You are the last auction of the evening, so many will clear out of the room at your solid reserve. It might be less stressful for you."

I nod as I sniffle back my tears and try to clear my mind. "How do I know I'll be safe?" My stomach flutters as I realize I'm probably asking this question a little late in the game, and Reva pulls out one of the chairs at the table and motions for me to take a seat.

"It's okay. It's a valid question, Emilia. We vet each of our members carefully. Our regular members undergo a full background check each time their membership renews, so it's once a year. Our elite members are required to submit every six months. Their memberships are reviewed more frequently, to make sure they should retain their status. These are very important, high-ranking people. They have a lot at stake should they not adhere to our rules. The safety of everyone in our club is our top priority."

"When do we know each other's names?"

"They are bidding on you, your body, your face, and the answers you provided on the questionnaire. If you accept a bid, you will be offered a mutual agreement to sign—that is your contract. Once it's signed, they can give you their name if they choose, or they can have you call them by a title. They can ask your name if they wish to know it. Some don't want that information, and some may give you a name to go by during your time with them." She takes a long look at me when she's done talking.

"Okay. I think I'm good now. Thank you."

She smiles and stands up. "I'll leave you with these papers to sign. My last item is from the email we sent you—we have a staff nurse who will be in shortly to do some blood work and take a urine sample. Since we don't know ahead of time what the arrangements will be, we test everyone. I'll be back in a while. Please, help yourself to anything in the room." She walks to the door then turns back to face me. "I almost forgot—I'll need to take your phone and any other electronics you may have. They will be returned to you before you leave."

"Right." Reaching into my backpack, I quickly locate my phone and hand it over. "Thank you, Reva." She smiles at her name and knocks twice on the door before Andrew opens it. Then she leaves me alone with my thoughts.

"Thank you for seeing us on a Sunday, Jim. You remember Noah?" The two nod at each other as Jim and his team enter the office.

We've been sitting here for an hour already, waiting. They weren't late; we were early. I couldn't sit at home any longer when Emilia is still nowhere to be found.

"Sorry it couldn't be sooner, Mr. Darkly. It took a while to assemble everyone we need for this." He extends his hand to motion us through a door.

"Don't apologize. I feel terrible you are here during your daughter's wedding reception. This just couldn't wait."

As we enter the office, the men and women casually hang their coats over chairs. We continue into a conference room and take a seat while one of the guys walks over to the coffee maker and turns it on.

"I have to agree with you there, Joshua," Jim says with no hint of a smile. "You have a couple of serious issues that need solutions before tomorrow morning. Which one do you want to start with?" Everyone stops to look at me.

"Emilia Connor." At my answer, the lawyers around the table open their briefcases and shuffle to the information they need. Jim slides a piece of paper across the table to Noah and me.

"Greg, thank you. We will get our own coffee from here. I will let you know if we need anything." The guy at the coffee maker puts down the cups he's holding and quietly excuses himself while I take a look at the paper.

I see nothing on the page except her signature and a couple of initials at the bottom. My eyes trace the soft curves she made as she signed everything away.

"As everyone in this room knows, yesterday Emilia Connor visited me here at the offices and signed over her stake in Adam Connor's estate. This document states she is not willing to complete the requirements of the caveat, and she understands and agrees that she will hold no further standing as an heir to Adam Connor's estate." Noah sits quietly beside me, and my stomach sinks with each word as Jim continues, "This leaves you as the sole heir to his company and all personal assets. We were going to notify you on Monday morning, when the offices opened and we officially filed the paperwork. But your call yesterday leads me to believe you have some information pertaining to this."

I want to say a million things at once as my brain bounces around like a five-year-old on a sugar high. I need to stay focused, for Emilia's sake. I'll deal with her later. Right now, it is time to do business.

"Yes. I'm here to block this from happening."

Everyone around the table looks up from their notes, surprised.

I mean, really—who wouldn't want a fortune so vast that even their great-grandchildren couldn't burn through it all?

Me, that's who. I have more than enough money and a

company that challenges me. What I don't have is Emilia. And she belongs to me.

"Mr. Darkly." Jim speaks slowly, looking over his glasses at Noah and me. "She signed a legally binding document; this isn't something we can just ignore. We explained her rights—as a favor to Adam's memory, I explained them twice. She declined to have her own lawyer present, and she signed."

"I understand, but she was under duress and not of sound mind when she did so. And that is related to the second issue we will be discussing." Noah pats me on the back, and I realize I am properly maintaining control over myself and the situation.

Jim looks between Noah and me as he considers my words. Then he exchanges glances with the rest of his team.

"Fair enough. I'll table this part of the discussion until we handle the next issue. We will return to this before we leave today. I believe you have some information for us."

"My colleague Noah will fill you in, as he put these files together for presentation," I say as Noah stands and walks around the table, placing a blue file in front of each person.

The truth is, Noah did everything last night after I spoke to Jim and found out what Emilia did. Just like that, she signed everything away. Our communication has never been strong, and now it is costing her everything, and it is costing me her.

I couldn't focus. I missed her. She was here, in these offices, yesterday. If I had called sooner, I could have had Jim detain her or asked to speak with her. She's out there, alone, and she believes she's fully cut ties. It took everything in me to suppress the rage I felt.

"Good afternoon," Noah starts. Then he begins to speak about Sean and Brent's time with our company. Minutes turn into an hour as he goes through document after document, and we flip our pages in unison as we listen to him detail several counts of harassment, forgery, embezzlement, and cover-ups thanks to support from Keith and Chad.

It turns out they've been siphoning off the company by adding themselves as co-listers and buyers on their colleagues' accounts. It gained them thousands in commissions, and it got them the sales awards—which got them paid trips each year for the past three years. And all of it was approved by both finance and HR.

There was one incident of harassment that ended in a company payout. It involved a female employee who I thought had quit because she was moving to a new city. Finance and human resources were clearly involved, as the money was paid under a fraudulent company name, and human resources had to sign off on the termination and indicate they spoke to the employee and handed over the payment.

Every now and then, someone would mutter their shock under their breath as Noah touched on a new scheme and revealed more details.

As the hour came to a close, Noah sat back and asked if anyone had any questions. There were plenty, and Noah and I spent the next hour answering everything we could. Then Jim asked the million-dollar question:

"So how does this tie into Ms. Connor being under duress and not in the proper frame of mind to sign away her rights?" Jim holds up the forfeiture notice.

"She's the one who uncovered all of this. She has a history with all four of these men. It turns out they had caused her issues years ago," I answer.

"What kind of issues?" The name of the lawyer asking escapes me.

"They bullied her. This all just came to light yesterday. The point is, she found this hidden in their files. We—*I* trust our teams to do what we pay them to do. I don't go through individual files unless something is brought to my attention. This system failed us."

"And so she brought this to your attention?" Jim asks, confused.

"Not entirely. She was supposed to announce the award recipients. When she found out their names were on the list, she came to me and told me she couldn't do it. I misunderstood the entire situation. I told her I wouldn't hear it and she would be reading the names...." My voice trails off as my thoughts kick in, and I turn to Noah.

"Wait a minute. How did she know who was receiving the awards before she opened the envelope?"

Noah sits back in his seat, tapping his fingers as he thinks. "Both Chad and Keith knew their names were on the list because they put them there. Chances are, Brent and Sean already knew they would be on the list too," he answers, and a surge of excitement hits me.

"One of them must have spoken to her before she came back to the table and opened the file. That's why she was so visibly upset," I respond, and Noah nods his head.

"Gentlemen, can you enlighten the rest of us at the table?" Jim asks as we look back to everyone staring quietly at us.

"My apologies. Jim, I can't confirm this, but I have reason to believe that one of these men attempted to intimidate Ms. Connor on Friday night at the awards dinner. Other than her time here with you, she's been missing since then. I believe she is not of sound mind because she's been threatened and coerced to suppress this information, and she is leaving out of fear. Is that good enough for a stay on this paperwork?"

The men look at each other carefully. A couple of shrugs occur, and I'm not ready for their answer. "Jim, this is Emilia Connor we are talking about. Adam's daughter. I am technically now his sole heir, and I am telling you I do not believe she is thinking clearly. We all owe this to Adam. We all owe this to Emilia, who uncovered this fraudulent activity. We owe it to her to put a hold on the document until I can speak with her. Please, Jim."

Jim's eyes travel down to the large file in front of him. He has to know I'm right. This would have gone on for years had she not come back and simply looked in a file. I glance at Noah, and he nods. I've said my piece, and I've done the best I can for Emilia.

"I'll allow it. With Emilia's location currently unknown, you have one week to sort everything out. I will have Greg make an appointment one week from Monday regarding the documents she signed, and I expect you both in my office to sign—depending on your final decisions of course. Should neither of you attend, this version will be filed. Everyone?" Jim holds up the forfeiture agreement again and looks around the table as his team nods in agreement.

"Okay, our auditors will contact your office first thing on Monday. We need to do an initial assessment to confirm some things before we officially proceed. From what you have here, we are looking at multiple instances of embezzlement; I wouldn't be surprised if there were some felonies in here. We'll need a workspace for my staff and a contact." Jim looks at me to confirm that I will be the contact, but I shake my head.

"If it's all right with Noah, I'd like him to be the point person for this. I may be busy for some of the week as I try to locate Ms. Connor."

Noah nods, and Jim jots down some notes.

"You can use Emilia's desk," I say.

Noah stands and places a few of his business cards on the table, and I join him as the rest of the table rises along with us.

"Thank you for seeing us today, Jim. We'll let you get back

to your family. I appreciate your time." I reach out and shake his hand.

"I'll get back to them shortly. We'll set everything up for this week, and someone will report to you, Noah, tomorrow morning. If you need anything, you have our number. We'll keep in touch. For now, it is business as usual until we are ready to proceed."

I follow Noah into the reception area, where I grab my jacket and put it on. Then I check my phone for any new texts. Nothing.

I have so much to tell her, and now she's the one who has finally shut me out.

As we near my car, a vibration in my pocket makes my heart skip a beat. I hold my hand up to stop Noah, and I answer.

"Hi, Joshua. It's Alexandra. I need to talk to you." She speaks quickly, but I don't have time. I want to keep my line free in case Emilia decides to call.

"Lexa, I don't have time to—"

"Joshua. You need to come to the club right now. It's—"

"I'm sorry, I can't. Look, something's happened with Emilia, she's—"

"Joshua, Emilia is here. She's at Ravenous."

"What? What do you mean? How did she find you there?"

"That's what I'm trying to tell you. She didn't find me. She's here to sell herself tonight at the auction. You need to get here right now."

The only word I can use to describe this experience is "humiliating." Being asked about my sexual history, menstrual cycle, and hard limits is absolutely humbling.

The nurse was by earlier to draw my blood and pick up my urine sample. She was a woman of few words. The paperwork was straightforward, and I read through it quickly. It was basically a document saying I am here of my own free will, and I am.

I chose to put myself in this situation so I can be done with my other situation. I've turned myself into a possession. I understand that.

After the nurse left, I turned on some soft music and got ready. I like the dress I chose. It's revealing, but it hides enough that I don't feel uncomfortable. I did my hair and makeup. I'm not good with trying new things, so I just let my hair down naturally and kept my face simple.

I stand up from my chair as the door handle turns, and

Reva enters with Andrew behind her. While she walks to the table, he stays at the door.

"The auction has started. There are three in front of you, so I have some time to explain a few things." Butterflies begin to flutter in my stomach, and I walk over to the table and sit down with her as she continues, "Andrew is here so he hears what you hear, in case you have any questions and I'm not available. Each auction takes about five to ten minutes. You will enter the room and stand in the middle of the stage. The viewing area is dark, and the lights on you are bright. You can't see anyone in the audience, so don't try; you'll just look awkward. We communicate with our buyers digitally, so you will not hear anyone speak. Only the auction monitor will talk to you over a speaker, so it is very quiet in there. But if you hear a voice, do what they say, then stay on the stage and wait for your next instructions. Your reserve price will be sent to the buyers, and they have a couple of minutes to decide if they are interested and willing to meet it. Those who aren't interested can either leave or remain as a spectator only. Today's test results will be distributed only to the buyers who indicate interest. Then they'll have a couple of minutes with your results. All potential buyers already have your other information, like your hard limits, so they won't need much time to decide. Then the monitor will open bidding. You will not know what the amounts are until you come back here. We keep the numbers private for a few reasons, but know that if the monitor opens bidding, it means at least one buyer has accepted your reserve, and that is where it starts. Any questions?" She looks at me, but my brain is still playing catch-up.

"Probably. Um—what if I make a mistake or do something wrong?" My nerves go to work, twisting my stomach around.

"Just listen to the voice in the room. Andrew will be off to the side of the stage to help should you really need it. If all else fails, just stand up tall and look straight ahead with a relaxed smile." She checks her watch. "You have about five minutes. We can walk you to the stage now if you'd like."

"Um. Sure." Hesitantly, I stand. "Does this dress look okay?" I ask, and she turns to me, confused.

"It does, but you'll be going out there in only your panties," she says, and Andrew averts his eyes to the ground, offering me the chance to get undressed.

"Oh." I have no more words. Of course I'll be taking off my clothes. What did I expect? That someone would want to buy me so they could dress me up and take me to dinner? People need to see what they are buying. Of course I'll be naked.

I slip the dress off and place it on the back of the chair, then I step out of my heels.

"I'm ready." There is nothing else to say. I've signed everything away. I need to shut out the noise and just keep putting one foot in front of the other. This is my means to an end, and I will process everything another time. I need to focus on the next step, and then the next, until this is done and I'm free to leave.

My term was one week. Someone is about to own me for seven days. Then I'm done. I can do this.

Andrew opens the door, and I follow Reva into the main area with him trailing behind us. It is much quieter than before, and that makes it harder to block everything out. I focus on the back of Reva's head.

We walk into an area I haven't been before, then she comes to a stop outside of a door with a red light shining above it. She presses a button on the wall, and we wait another half a minute before the light turns green and we enter a dimly lit area. Reva turns to me and lowers her voice.

"I'm going to leave you here. When you hear the monitor call Auction Number Four, Andrew will show you where to go.

No matter what, stay on the stage until you hear, 'This ends the bidding. Thank you, Auction Number Four,' and Andrew joins you again on stage to lead you off." I nod, and she gives my arm a squeeze. Then she leaves, and Andrew and I stand in silence for a few minutes.

Each second pushes me further into compliance. This is what I've chosen for myself. I am now a product. I can't go back to any part of my old life. Most of it no longer feels authentic anyway. When I am done this week, I'll take the money start over.

I just want to live quietly. I don't want to owe anyone anything or feel the pressure of living up to a name. I would have given every last penny away just to have my dad back; now I'm giving it away so I can have my own life back.

Before I can sink too far, I hear the voice over the speaker:

"Auction Number Four."

"Follow me." Andrew steps in front of me. I take a deep breath and force my thoughts to stay behind as I follow him onto the brightly lit stage. He stops in the center and motions for me to stand beside him. Then he leans into me.

"Good luck. You'll be okay. I'm just over here." Somehow, knowing someone is here with me is comforting, even if it's a stranger.

Remembering Reva's words, I stand up straight and look forward.

The longest minute of my life goes by. Then the silence is finally broken by the anonymous female voice over the speaker:

"Auction Number Four, please turn to your left and face the side of the stage." Instantly, I turn. The voice has me turn to the back and then to the right before facing front, and I wait again.

This must be the time Reva talked about, when they can accept my reserve or not. There's some shuffling behind the glaring lights, and I can only assume some have chosen to leave. Then the room settles again, and another couple of minutes pass as I stand in silence, waiting for another instruction. With each passing second, I feel more awkward and out of place. I'm used to the feeling, but I still hate it.

"Auction Number Four, kneel with your hands clasped behind you."

I shut out the room. I pretend I am alone, and I do as I'm told without thinking about it. I'm probably not graceful as I bend over and get on my knees, but the audience isn't paying for a model. They are paying for obedience and submission, and that is all I have left now.

"Auction Number Four, keep your hands behind you, place your forehead on the floor, and keep your ass up." Again, I do as I'm told. Then I wait for the next instruction.

"Auction Number Four, stand in your original position." No sooner do I stand than the announcement I need to hear comes over the speaker.

The auction is starting. I stand still and face forward for what feels like five minutes, wondering what the length of time means. *Does the bidding process move slowly? Are there a lot of bids? Is no one bidding?* Different thoughts float through my head as the time passes, and just as I realize I've lost track of how long I've been standing—

"This ends the bidding. Thank you, Auction Number Four."

My stomach flips.

I've been bought.

I freeze at the thought, and my mind swirls with a host of new emotions. *Someone wants to own me,* kindles something deep inside of me, and shame prickles through my body as I realize this is filling me with something stronger than fear.

I have been bought. I'll be spending a week at someone

else's mercy, with only one obligation to them, and my world doesn't feel so heavy right now.

Andrew steps to my side and clears his throat. He points to a door opposite the one I entered through, and I walk off the stage to meet Reva standing in the hall. She spins on her heels, and I follow her back the way we came. I see one of the other numbered doors open, and out walks a sharply dressed gentleman holding a leash. I pause long enough to see that the leash is attached to the collar of a beautiful woman, who follows quietly behind him with her eyes on the floor. Then Andrew clears his throat again, ushering me into the room.

"Your buyer is preparing to complete the sale; we have a few minutes. I can tell you that your reserve was met—exceeded, actually. There were three main bidders, and two were serious. That is why your auction took longer than usual. I don't know your cut, but your final price was seven hundred and fifty thousand."

Reva stares at me as I gawk back. This is more than enough for me to start over, but at the same time, someone paying that much money for one week of my time completely astounds me.

"Wow," A commotion outside catches all our attention, and the door to my room opens.

In a fraction of a second, I go from excited to full of dread. I physically feel the blood drain from my face at the sight of Joshua staring back at me.

He looks like he wants to tear everything apart.

"Put your goddamn clothes on." He punches his pointer finger in my direction, and I immediately grab my dress and crawl back into it. I'm not sure if it is my compliance all evening or his tone, but I obey him quickly.

He turns to Reva and tries to speak to her, but Andrew steps in.

"Mr. Darkly, you shouldn't be here." His tone is respectful, and I find myself cutting into their conversation.

"Mr. Darkly? Do they know you, Joshua?" As I ask the question, everyone, including Joshua, freezes. His eyes burn right through me.

"You could say that, Emilia." His tone is condescending, and my anxiety rises. "I'm a private investor in this club."

"Of course you are. How could I not see it?" My anger builds. I finally have something good again, and here he is to burn it all down. It won't be enough for him when he finds out I've given him everything. He'll take this away from me too. "Of course you are," I shout, and everyone continues to stay still. "You controlling son of a bitch—literally!" I yell, and his nostrils flare. He knows I'm talking about his trash mother.

"Careful, Emilia," he warns.

"Or what? You'll spank me again, you sick fuck? Of course you own a place like this. You're so—you're so—"

"He doesn't own Ravenous, Emilia. I do."

I stop talking as an eerily familiar female voice speaks. I wait for Joshua to step out of the doorway, and my chest tightens as I realize it belongs to Alexandra. She's been standing behind him this whole time.

Her face is solemn. Everyone around her stands in silence, and it is clear she runs the place.

"Leave us," she says.

Andrew leaves immediately, and Reva walks over to the door and waits for a split second before Alexandra gives her a task. "Make sure the other girls and the auction guests are gone. Have Andrew stay outside the door until Emilia's buyer is announced."

Reva nods then exits, closing the door quickly behind her.

"You?" I suddenly feel a deeper level of shame. I hate

Joshua with everything I have, and I want to keep yelling, but anything I say to him now will be a slight against Alexandra.

"Yes, Emilia. This is my company. Joshua was one of my initial investors." I look over to him, standing by the wall. The anger on his face is barely contained. He looks like I feel.

The only thing is, I know he has nothing left to hold over me. But he won't find out until tomorrow that I cut myself loose from my hell and his guardianship is done.

"It doesn't matter. I'd like to be left alone now. I understand I have a buyer?" I ask for Joshua's benefit, and his jaw clenches as he continues to glare at me.

"You do. I'm here to discuss their contract," she answers. I know she's uncomfortable.

My father loved her, and now she knows this about me. I try to look her in the eyes, but I can't. I feel like I'm letting him down all over again.

"It's okay, Emilia." The uncomfortable tension is palpable, and as she speaks I realize how far I've fallen. I have nothing left.

"No. It's not okay. I'm selling myself to some stranger who is going to debase me and use me for a week. It's my choice, but it's not okay. I'm not okay, and no one is asking that."

I'm angry. I'm mad at myself, I'm mad at Joshua, and I'm mad at my father for dying and leaving me here like this. I can't hold it in anymore. My hurt flows with each word, and I expect this is the last time I'll ever see Joshua, so I have nothing to lose. I've already given it all away.

Tears run down my face, and Alexandra watches in horror as I fall apart.

"I tried. I wanted to try. But I can't. I'm not the daughter my father thought I was. I'm not a perfect person. He deserved better, and he's gone. Everything good is gone, and I don't want to try anymore. I never want to come back here. There's nothing left but pain, and I don't want to hurt anymore. This next week can't be any worse than what I've already been through. Please, just let me read my contract. Leave me alone. You're good at that, Mr. Darkly." I spit the formality out, and Alexandra stares between us.

I know she doesn't see the girl my father once described. It doesn't matter anymore anyway. Quietly, she places the piece of paper on the table and lays a pen on top of it. There are spaces at the bottom for my signature, my buyer's signature, and the company owner.

As I pick up the pen, Joshua steps forward. His tone is angry but contained, and he speaks slowly. "You sign that contract, and you'll find out how much worse it can be. Alexandra will explain it to you. She is going to tell you what it means to be owned, what your obligations will be. She is going to tell you what it means to sell yourself, to be someone's property, including but not limited to the many things your buyer can demand of you. You will fully understand that by signing this, you are saying this is what *you* want, Emilia. Listen to her. Do not sign that piece of paper if you don't completely understand and approve of what you will give your buyer, and make sure you understand the penalty for not fulfilling your side of the contract. Consider this carefully, Emilia. You sign that piece of paper, and all of your rules change."

"How did this happen?" I ask before the door to Alexandra's office is completely open, and Reva jumps out of her seat.

"Thank you, Reva. Keep me involved in this one." Lexa doesn't move. She offers her assistant a smile, and Reva excuses herself as I enter and take a seat with Noah trailing behind.

I haven't been able to get rid of him. I prefer to do these next few hours on my own, but he has refused to leave my side. I'm sure I'm not thinking rationally—having his voice of reason is probably good for me right now.

When Lexa said Emilia was going to sell herself, I lost my shit. No wonder she signed over the company. If Ravenous wasn't Lexa's, I would have never found her, and this deal would have been done tonight.

Then the one thought that overrides them all hits me: She has no right to sell what isn't hers. She has no right to sell what is mine.

"Joshua, when Reva took her name, she knew she sounded familiar. Then she confirmed Adam was her father, and she came straight to me. I verified her identity through our cameras, and I called you right away." She gently pats the desk, and I realize I shouldn't be so upset. Emilia is here now, and I finally have her back.

"Fine. Thank you, Alexandra. Where is she? I'd like to talk to her. I need to tell her..."

Lexa slowly swivels her head from left to right, and I stop to allow her to speak. "I can't do that. You know our auction rules. She's on her own until the bidding is over." I can tell she's trying to calm herself.

I know what the rules are—I helped her make them—but this is the last thing I want to hear.

"You can't let her do this, Lexa." I say her name in a challenging tone. Noah takes a step closer, but he remains silent, and they exchange a glance.

"You know I wanted to take some time off to mourn Adam. Reva has been filling in so I can train her to open our second club next year. She's never seen Emilia before; she didn't know who she was until it was too late, and we had to proceed. If I had seen her before she signed the papers, I might have been able to talk to her, but my hands are tied now. Emilia is an adult; she's been made aware of what will happen tonight. She knows she is selling herself, and she signed. I have a couple of buyers who have shown a particular interest in her already." I'm sure a blood vessel in my brain just burst with that little tidbit of information. "She is up last. Reva set a higher reserve for her, but I don't know if that will help. We have protocols, Joshua. The only way you will see her tonight is if you are the winning bidder. And, before you ask, I've added you to the auction list. The attendee price is five thousand tonight."

I sit back in my chair and steeple my fingers against my lips. I'm imploding. I've gone from concern to anger and back again. There is only one person in the world who can do this to me, and one way or another, we are going to work our shit out. Yelling at my two closest friends isn't going to accomplish anything.

Noah clears his throat. "You better add us both to the list. I'll pay the ten grand."

I roll my eyes at Alexandra. I know Noah won't let me go into a room alone with a bunch of strangers who are trying to buy what is mine.

Lexa taps her keyboard, then looks to the both of us. "Scan your IDs at the door. The first auction is ending soon. You can enter on the break."

I stand to leave, and Noah opens the door.

"Joshua?" Lexa calls out, and I turn. I'm not mad at her; I'm mad at myself, but I don't have the energy to smile. "I wasn't sure about you and Emilia when you first told me, but watching her through the cameras tonight and knowing what she's about to do, I really do think you need each other—on many levels. I wish you luck."

I don't need luck. I already know how this will end. I'm buying what is already mine. She will not leave here with anyone else.

The door opens for new guests just as we arrive, and security leads us to our seats. Noah has been uncharacteristically silent. He knows the rules. We've both been in here before. Not to bid, but to help Alexandra fill the audience in the beginning. She hasn't needed us in here for over a year, as these events draw high-end interest on their own now.

The second girl up for auction comes out. She looks almost like she's done this before. She walks ahead of her bouncer and stands right where she is supposed to. Her makeup is a little thick, but I know some of these guys will like it.

Her reserve is low, and a few bids roll in. Then she's off the stage and out the back door, almost a hundred thousand dollars richer.

I'm thankful Noah is here. The truth is, I miss Adam for these types of things. I could tell him almost anything. Except now I realize there was one thing I wouldn't let myself tell him, and that is how I felt about Emilia. I valued Adam's place in my life so deeply that I didn't want to risk my standing with him by telling him how I felt. If I had just explored my feelings for her earlier, we may not be here now.

The speaker calls out the third auction, and I don't realize she is standing on the stage until her information gets handed out.

I have one more to go until Emilia. My stomach knots tightly at the thought.

This woman looks more like a model. She's older than the last one, and the hairspray in her hair holds it like a sculpture. Her bright smile doesn't fade throughout the bidding. Someone will most likely buy her to violate, then use as arm candy.

My mind wanders to all of the things I want to do to Emilia.

I'm a lion right before he pounces. Watching, waiting, and trying not to give away too much. Crouching down, muscles tense and flexed, salivating with an intense hunger, just waiting for my prey to walk into my sights and stand a little too close to me.

Everything else fades away. Brent and the company, Kyle, Tawny, Adam's death, and Emilia's choices all become white noise when I hear the number I've been waiting for.

Number Four.

My prey.

Andrew is her security for the evening. Good; I like him. Not only is he one of Lexa's best, he is also a member of the club, so he has a deep understanding and respect for the people here.

He leads her onto the stage, and she follows obediently. I watch her bare breasts bounce as she moves, and I shift to adjust my cock as it tightens against my pants.

The feeling fades fast as I remember everyone else in the room sees her too. In a heartbeat, I go from wanting her bent over a table to wanting to run up on stage and drag her out of here. Then Noah taps my arm and points at the touchpad. I almost forgot to indicate I wanted to bid. What is she doing to me?

On stage, Andrew leans in and says something quietly to Emilia. She nods and watches him step away, and now she looks a little lost. Now I see what Lexa saw. She is nervous, but not afraid or disgusted. I'm not just drawn to her—my dominance needs her submission. She just doesn't understand this about herself yet.

Her reserve is set at ninety grand, and a couple of people stand to leave as others sit back in their seat and watch the show. Judging by the number of people still left in the room with me, I'm not going to be bidding alone.

Emilia's information is handed out: not pregnant, no STDs, only one previous sexual partner, and she is on birth control. Then the speaker asks her to move through a couple of positions, then kneel, and she obeys with an innocence that I know is going to drive up her price.

Everything about her is on point tonight, and it irritates me to no end. A naive, inexperienced submissive, willing to be molded. Her hair is naturally down, and her makeup is simple. Is she even wearing any? Fuck, this is so infuriating. I want to punch something, and Noah, sitting here with an amused look on his face, isn't helping at all.

"The fuck? Don't look at her." Incredulously, I whisper as low as I can. There's no way I'm getting kicked out of here now.

His soft chuckle grates along my nerves, but he does look down as the bidding starts. The room is quiet as the interested parties pick up the keypads sitting next to them. I leave mine by my side for now and look around the room. I can make out the other bodies, but their faces are obscured by the darkness.

I look over to my keypad. Her bidding is already up to two hundred thousand, and it's going up in increments of five to ten grand. I don't have time for this shit. I need to get my hands on her. I won't wait any longer.

I punch in four hundred thousand and wait. Bidding stalls. I know everyone just choked on the price difference. They now have one minute to place a higher bid or she's mine, and I feel victorious. Time ticks away until my screen flickers in the last ten seconds—someone is trying to outbid me by twenty-five grand.

I jump to half a million, and Noah clears his throat quietly. I shoot him a glare in the dark. Half a minute goes by before a bid for fifty grand more comes through.

My internal voice is screaming now. I want to stand up and threaten whoever is bidding for her, but I know my standing in the club would be on the line, investor or not. I don't waste any time; I enter seven hundred and fifty thousand. It's one of the highest amounts anyone has ever gone for, and a few bodies shuffle in the seats around us when I place my bid.

My lack of hesitation and the amounts I'm entering are sending a clear message to everyone in this room. It's as much of a threat I can manage before getting booted.

I'm telling everyone I won't be backing down.

The longest minute of my life ticks away. Then the silence is broken when the speaker thanks Emilia, and she walks off the stage. Buyers gather their things and prepare to leave as the lights flicker on. I'm the first one out the door. Alexandra is waiting on the other side, and she's ready for me.

"Mr. Darkly, please follow me." She looks between Noah and me like we don't know each other, and I walk behind her, barely containing myself.

She pauses before entering the back. "Our finance department is already preparing your agreements. I had Reva draw up a contract based on your member profile. Please look it over and make sure everything you need is here before she signs; the contract cannot be amended afterward."

She hands me the document, and I look for the things I require. A few things have been added, I assume based on the hard limits Emilia set, but none of my requirements have been removed. I check to make sure the items I really need are still in writing and hand it back to Lexa with a nod.

"I ask that my identity be kept confidential until she signs." I feel pushback in the looks Lexa and Noah give me, and I defend my request. "She is selling herself. I want to make sure she wants this. Who her buyer is is irrelevant. I want to know she wishes to be sold. Lexa, Emilia did something incredibly stupid this weekend. I cannot divulge specific details, but if this purchase doesn't go through, she'll have no money. She's lost everything."

Lexa's lips part; she looks sad. "Oh, Joshua." A long pause lingers as she composes herself. "Okay. Just keep her safe. You know we owe it to Adam, and to her. I really like her." Her brows draw together, and I know she is taking this hard.

"I give you my word; I will do what's best for her. It just won't seem like that in the beginning."

She nods in understanding. Sometimes these things don't happen easily. Sometimes the things worth having are worth going through hell for.

Alexandra grabs the handle to the back door, and I turn to

Noah, who has so far been acting as my counsel. "Noah, thank you. But go home. I'll have someone drive you to your car. See Faye in the morning; you'll be covering my work tomorrow while I settle us in. I'll let her know. I need to handle this part on my own. I know you're concerned, but I'm going in there to take what is mine. She's always been mine, but this isn't going to be easy on either of us."

He stares at me for a moment, then slowly nods and steps back. "Only if you agree to see me tomorrow evening. I need to make sure you are both doing well." I nod. "My phone is on," he says. Then he turns to walk out. Reva lifts her hand to the nearest security guard, and we proceed through the door.

Lexa stops in front of door number four. I know whose door this is, and everything sinks into my soul. My Emilia is in here. This isn't the road I wanted us to take, and certainly not so quickly, but she's placed herself at my mercy. The thought lights a fire in my veins, and I can't help the hungry smile that stretches across my lips.

Emilia doesn't know that I know she gave up everything. I have her now, and there is nothing she can do.

I am a lion.

Instead of eleven months, I have seven days. And instead of guiding her slowly, now I outright own her, and she is mine to do as I please.

And I will do as I please.

The contract sits on the table between us. As Joshua finishes ranting about what I'm signing away, I drop my gaze to the words on the paper. I signed off on the privacy agreements and most of the legal stuff earlier this afternoon. This is just the agreement between myself and my buyer.

Alexandra explained that nothing illegal is permitted, and all of my hard limits are laid out, along with what my buyer expects of me. It isn't as bad as my mind made it out to be earlier. I'm to obey my commands, be truthful, and do everything I'm told. My contract ends at this time next Sunday night.

Then I'm free.

When I look back up, Joshua is watching me with a look I've never seen before. Does he finally realize we are done here? That there is nothing left to control and everything my father worked for is his? He will probably be happy. He is finally getting everything his mother wanted years ago.

Even now, he speaks to me like I'm a child. I know,

compared to him and Alexandra, I'm inexperienced in many things, but I'm no child, and I'll prove it.

There was a time I looked up to him. I followed him around; I felt like I needed his attention. Maybe this week away with someone else will change all of that.

My senses are heightened. The ball of the pen glides across the paper as I sign my name. Then I look up to Alexandra's sad eyes, but I don't feel anything anymore. I steel myself and look over to Joshua one last time. This will be the last time I see him. I know I will never come back, and a broken part inside of me cries, but only for a moment.

The expression on Joshua's face has changed. My stomach winds tight—I've seen this look before. He wore it the day we read my father's will. His eyes are dark, and his lips are pinched together. He's containing himself, and the flash of a thought drifts in:

He looks like he knows something I don't.

"Mr. Darkly." Alexandra says his name, and for a moment I think she is going to ask him to leave.

Instead, he pushes himself off the wall, walks over to the table, picks up the pen, and signs the contract I just signed.

"What are you doing?" My voice rushes out, as the temperature in the room drops.

"I'm signing, Emilia," he answers flatly and without looking at me.

"But why? You don't own this company." As my head spins in confusion, he finally meets my eyes. The look on his face can only be described as triumphant.

"No, Emilia, I don't. But as of right now, I own you."

"No." The room floats around me, and I grab the back of the chair beside me to keep from falling over. "You manipulative—"

"Careful, Emilia," he warns a second time. I barely hear

him over the voice in my head screaming no over and over again. "I know this is new to you, so I will grant you this small mercy of information: I am within my right, as your owner, to punish you as I see fit and in front of whoever I wish."

I suck in a hard breath. My eyes shoot to Alexandra as she lifts the pen to sign.

"Wait. Please, wait. Um—don't sign that." I can't control my body as I shake from the inside out.

"Tsk, tsk, tsk. So demanding, Emilia. I see it will take some time to break you of the misguided idea that you have any say in your decisions."

Alexandra puts the pen down without signing, and I'm momentarily thankful. She steps back as Joshua moves into my space and speaks softly—though his words are anything but. "I will break you of that, Emilia. There will be moments over this next week when you'll wish you'd just put in the eleven months."

Joshua turns to Alexandra and nods. She steps back to the table, picks up the pen, and signs. The disappointment must be written all over my face, because she offers me an answer to a question I didn't ask. "The contract is binding once you two sign it. I am only a witness, but we have you on camera. My signature is only a formality. I'll leave you both to talk for a bit."

"Wait. I don't know if I can do this. What if I can't do this?"

Alexandra turns to answer me, but Joshua holds up his hand. She takes it as her sign to leave as he begins to speak.

"It's straightforward: the contract will be considered broken, and you won't get the money." Joshua places himself between me and the door. I hate being trapped. The walls feel like they are closing in on me. "I'll tell you what. You break this contract and come home with me right now. I'll pretend like your little escapade never happened, and we'll go back to work on Monday." There is a smug grin across his face, and I feel sick.

I can't go back to the way it was. That is no longer an option for me.

"I can't...." My voice sounds weak. My nerves and adrenaline have left me, and exhaustion has crept in.

"Oh, sure you can, Emilia. I mean, it's not like you just did something incredibly foolish and signed everything over to me."

My eyes slowly meet his as he mocks me, and my blood runs cold as I come face-to-face with my absolute darkest nightmare.

He knows.

He wasn't supposed to find out until tomorrow. I have no options left; I can't get out of here on my own. He knows he has my company, and now he has me.

"How?"

"I spoke to Mr. Mathers this weekend. I had some business to discuss, and he had your little bombshell to tell me. I can't begin to tell you how disappointed I am in you, but I will show you when I get you home." Pausing, he leans in with a sneer. "I guess I should say when I get you to *my* home."

"So then what? You'll abuse me for a week? You don't want to do this. You don't want me. You have everything. Just let me go. I don't want all of the money; I'll take the amount you offered to Kyle." I have nothing left to offer. He doesn't even have to give me what he bid. I'm sure he can break the contract now and make me leave, penniless.

"Never say that name again. Do you understand?" he growls through gritted teeth. Sniffling, I nod, and it relaxes him.

"I will do what I wish. It's of no concern to you. Do you understand your place under this contract?" He holds up the piece of paper, and I nod again.

"Good. Now, there's just one more thing we need to get

straight before we leave. Stand up." While my mind obeys because it knows I need to, my body obeys a little too willingly. "Drop your dress, Emilia. You'll show me what you showed everyone on stage tonight."

My breath stops in the middle of my throat. There's no one else around now. My duty is to Joshua.

Everything has changed between us. He's no longer the boy who ignored me, but now I wish he was. I thought he would always push me away, not buy me. But I've agreed to this, and I do agree to this.

Maybe this final week is what we both need before I leave for good.

I don't notice my hands shaking until I reach up to the straps on my shoulders. I look up at Joshua, hoping he's changed his mind, but he stands frozen in place, waiting for me. As I drop the dress, his eyes roam down my body, and he takes a bold step in front of me, lifting his hand to brush some hair off my face. His touch feels tender.

His hand doesn't stop as he trails his fingers down the length of my neck, along my clavicle, and over my sternum toward my breasts. The cool air hits me, and my nipple prickles into a pert bud just as his palms glides over it, and my breath is shallow.

"Do you want me to fuck you, Emilia?" His words coax goosebumps to form across my skin.

"No." I try to sound confident.

"I'll remind you, you are under contract. Your answers must be truthful. Now." Leaning in, he kisses my shoulder delicately, and my heart gently floats away. "I'll ask again. Do you want me to fuck you, Emilia?"

This is a trap, I know it is. He's toying with me now, and I'm being led to some form of slaughter, but I have no way out, and I can't break this agreement. I close my eyes and listen to the sound of his lips kiss against my skin. I answer honestly: "I —I don't know."

As my eyelids close, a tear pushes through and rolls down my cheek. He's going to take a lot more than my body this week.

Breaking away, he scans my face, and I can't tell what is going through his mind. Then he takes half a step away from me. "It's time to take you home. Turn around and face the wall."

I leave my dress on the floor where it fell and do as I'm told. Joshua's suit presses against my bare back as something drops in front of my face and onto my neck. A moment of panic sets in, and I reach my hands up to find out what is happening.

"There are many lessons you need to learn this week, Emilia. Trust is one of them. This is your collar. I am locking it on you, and it can only be unlocked with a key I hold. I'll take it off when our contract ends or when you break it. Until then, I will work with you. I will guide you, and I will teach you. You will be rewarded and you will be punished, and none of it will be easy." He grabs my bottom as he speaks, reminding me of the spankings he gave me, and I audibly gulp down my nervous tension.

He turns me back to face him, then sucks in a breath as he stares at my new collar. I don't know yet what it looks like, and as I reach up to touch it, I think I see him mouth the word, *Beautiful.*

"Put your dress on and gather your things. It's time to go. Avert your eyes to the ground; do not speak unless I allow it. Show me you can obey, and I will delay your punishment until we are alone—this time."

No sooner do I pull on my clothes than the door opens again, and Alexandra walks in to take the signed contract from

Joshua. My eyes briefly meet hers, then I quickly drop them down and stand quietly as Joshua says our goodbyes.

Conflicting emotions clash in my heart, and my mind is all over the place, but the one thing I focus on is getting out of here without being punished in front of Alexandra.

"I'd like to visit with you and Emilia later in the week, if that's possible," she says. I think she is looking at me, but I refuse to look up.

"I will text you in a few days," Joshua replies. Then a tug on my chain has me following him out of the room.

Before we are entirely out of the room, he stops. I almost run into him, but I manage to still myself. "And, Lexa, thank you." His voice is low, and I don't hear a response. Then there's another tug, and we are on our way again.

I've made my own choices up until this point, and nothing has worked out.

Maybe you need to leave the choices up to someone else for once.

The thought ignites a fire that burns deep into my core.

My body trembles at his promises; my mind swirls with worry and shame at his threats. I know I can get through the next seven days. As much as I want to run away, there is a deep darkness in me that needs to do this. I want to know what it feels like to be owned, and I feel a carnal rush knowing my owner is Joshua Darkly.

Emilia was obedient and quiet during the drive home. She looked out the window as we drove through our old neighborhood. Her situation is sinking in, and she's slowly shutting herself down, turning off her emotions, in an effort to get through this week.

I won't allow it, but I will tolerate it for the drive. It gives me time to think.

If I'm being honest with myself, we could have done this differently, but this is what I want. I don't want to sit around for eleven more months, waiting for a good time to introduce certain aspects of my life to her. She sought this out, and I am more than willing to accommodate her. The downside is, I only have one week. But I will use every minute of it to break her of the idea that she doesn't belong to me.

I could have told her what I knew the moment I saw her, and maybe it was manipulative to allow her to sign herself over to me, but then she would have thought that running away and defying me would get her what she wanted.

I made a promise to Adam the day he told me about his mentor idea. I told him I would do everything I could to help her get what belongs to her. I remember feeling an incredible rush at the passing thought of owning her, even if it was under more professional terms.

The moment I touched her tonight set everything in motion. It solidified my place. Hearing her admit her uncertainty charged me. She will ask for many things from me this week, but first I need to sort out some issues between us.

She has no idea what I have planned for her, and it's going to be a long night.

I park the car in front of the house and look to my right at her sitting quietly. It's now I realize she isn't actually looking outside. She's lost inside her head, and she hasn't realized we have arrived.

I tangle with my own mixed feelings. I could tell her about the investigation and ask for her help, but that could prompt her to shut down, and I need information from her. So instead, I open my door without a word and walk around to her side, opening the door and taking the leash to lead her into my domain. I won't allow her to walk into this house without being led in. She needs to start this week knowing her place.

To my surprise and satisfaction, she follows without a word. Stealing a glance over my shoulder, I can't help but smile. Her head is down, and she's walking respectfully behind me.

The lights click on in the house we've both called home at different times, and the place feels different.

"You can look up now, Emilia." It's the first thing I've said to her since we left Ravenous. Her eyes stay on the floor, but her breathing deepens. Her hesitation can mean many things, but I have a hunch I know what it is. "You grew up here. This is the only home you ever knew. Your mother and father loved you here. This house holds your dreams, your innocence, your heart. For a time, it was your safe haven. When you ran away on Friday night, you thought you would never see it again. And now here we are. I'm going to make you face a lot of things, Emilia. Now look up."

She steadies her breathing as she lifts her eyes to meet mine, and I know she isn't ready to look around yet. I drop her bag and backpack, then take my own coat off and lay it across them before meeting her eyes again.

"Where did you stay this weekend?"

"At a motel near the club," she answers quickly.

"Do you have anything there you need to pick up?"

She shakes her head.

"How did you hear about Ravenous?" I ask.

She pauses for a moment. "The woman who fitted my dress mentioned something." A small flash of worry crosses her face. I'm learning to read Emilia; she doesn't want anyone else getting in trouble for her actions.

In truth, the mistake was mine. I asked Alexandra to send someone over for a fitting. I didn't give her much information, and she innocently sent her own staff.

I have too much on my plate already, so I decide to let this go.

"Did you eat at Ravenous?"

"Um, no. I was too—nervous." Her face flushes, and I think she's mistaking nervousness for excitement. I watched her closely on that stage; she was curious.

She's holding on to a tether. It ties her shame to her, and she allows it to weigh her down and hold her back. I'll hold on to this bit of information until later.

"When did you last eat?" I lower my voice.

"This morning. I had a muffin in the motel lounge. I ate

half of it; it was a bit stale. And I had a sandwich yesterday before I saw the lawyer." She offers more information than I asked for, and I'm pleased with her willingness to cooperate.

"Good girl. Remove your shoes." I don't know if she understands why I'm pleased. She briefly looks away, but not quickly enough to hide the small lift of her lips.

My praise affects her.

I wait for her to take off her heels, then I continue, "I asked Sylvia to leave some food in the fridge. Don't worry; she isn't here. Come, we need to eat first." I unhook the leash from her collar and walk into the dining room.

Her bare feet pad softly behind me, and she instinctively walks to her chair.

"You won't be sitting at the table tonight."

She pulls back and looks at me as though I caught her with her hand in the cookie jar. "You'll kneel—here." I point to the floor beside her father's old chair, and her shoulders droop.

Her exhaustion shines through as she scuffles into position. When she lowers herself to her knees, I can't help myself. I reach out and brush my fingers through her hair. She is my good girl. Her head dips against my hand before she recovers and holds it up high.

"I'll be one minute. Don't move."

I make my way down the short hall and into the kitchen. The food is where Sylvia said it would be. I asked for something light, and there are small sandwiches and fruit cut up on a plate. I grab a bottle of water and return to the dining room—she hasn't moved a muscle, and I smile again as I stand behind her.

Sliding out the chair at the head of the table, I take a long breath and sit down in Adam's seat. Both of us know what this means. I'm the head of this family, and she kneels in honor of this. I watch her body for signs of internal conflict. There are none. She isn't fidgeting; she isn't moving at all. I know she's tired. She'll eventually get her rest, and then she'll push back, but I decide to reward her for her good behavior now.

I allow her to take the water bottle and drink on her own. Her fingers brush over mine, and my nerve endings feel sensitive to her touch. I watch her gulp the water down, then return the cap and lift it back up to me.

I scan the plate of food. It's clear Sylvia was hoping Emilia would return. Her favorite sandwiches are here, along with a couple of mine. I lift a chicken sandwich and lean toward Emilia. She lifts her hand to take it from me, but I pull back.

"Hands on your lap. You'll eat as I feed you." Her lips part as I speak, and her eyes travel from mine down to the food I'm holding in front of her.

The silence around us is arousing. Her soft breath is hypnotizing. Licking her lips, she twists to meet me and takes a bite. Her sultry eyes stare back at me, and the anticipation is intoxicating.

I feed her a few more times until I notice her hesitance. Dropping the sandwich onto the plate, I lift the largest strawberry to her lips, and I watch them part as she takes it into her mouth and bites down. A trickle of juice runs over her chin, but she doesn't move her hands. I abandon the strawberry on the plate and go in search of the drop that is about to fall.

I hold the trickle of juice on the tip of my finger for a long moment as she swallows and waits for my lead. Meticulously, I draw my finger closer to her mouth, which is now stained red by the strawberry, and she parts her full lips once more, allowing my finger entrance.

Her lips close around my finger, running the buds on her moist tongue along my skin. The connection sends a surge of sensation through me, and I grow hard. The uninhibited groan she makes as my finger leaves her mouth almost unravels me.

We will continue this another time.

"Stand, Emilia." I prompt her to move to the middle of the room, about eight feet away, and face me. She moves slowly. I know she's tired. I am as well, but there are a few things left to do before she falls asleep. "I told you at Ravenous your rules would change. Remove your dress."

She sighs out her hesitation, and I lift a brow, challenging her to defy me. Her fingers pull the straps off her shoulders, just like earlier, and she stands in front of me in only her panties. I take a few bites of a sandwich and a couple pieces of fruit, and I wash it down with some water while she stands still, watching me. Then I push the plate away, stand to pour myself a drink, and return to my seat at the head of the table.

"You will spend the next seven days here with me. I may need to leave at some point, and if I do, I will give you a task to complete. You are not to make any contact with anyone. I will speak to your instructors on Monday; you will be away for the week. Your only commitment is to me. You will not leave the house this week unless I allow it. You will refer to me as Mr. Darkly—you will earn the right to use my first name again. You will get up when I say, go to sleep when I say, bathe when I say, and you will obey me at all times. Do you understand me?"

There is no mistaking the void look on her face: resignation. She's too tired to test me now, and she's capitulated to my demands.

She nods her head, and there is something I've wanted to hear her say.

"You may speak, Emilia. I want to hear you say you understand and accept my rules."

She clears her throat. "I understand and accept your rules—Mr. Darkly."

My cheek twitches with a smile.

I take a long, satisfied sip of my drink. Then I set it down and lean back in my chair as I take in her naked form.

"Good. Now tell me why you defied me in front of the whole company when you refused to read the awards on Friday night."

CHAPTER 58
EMILIA

When I ran away on Friday night, I set in motion a series of events that cut me loose, and I left my world behind.

And now here I am. Tired, exhausted, and out of options. And Joshua is dragging me right back to that podium.

The events of today are beginning to wear me down, and a bit of delirium comes on as Joshua asks me about the awards on Friday night. I remember the bright lights heating up my face. My throat was dry, and my stomach rumbled, probably because I couldn't eat during the dinner.

Joshua handed me a complete ultimatum: get my ass on the stage and praise the hard work and good character of two men who tormented me like the puppet he wanted me to be, or he'll take everything away from me. And guess what? I didn't do it, and now I have nothing.

My freedom depends on telling the truth and answering his questions. But how can I? If I expose Sean and Brent, Joshua will know I know he signed off on everything. If I don't, I break my contract and leave here with nothing.

"I don't agree with two names on the list." I already know in my bones my answer won't be good enough. He's not messing around now.

His eyes burn a hole deep into my head, until finally he stands and walks out of the room, telling me only to stay put. A few uneventful minutes later, he returns and steps in front of me.

"Eyes on mine," he says, and I snap my attention to his eyes while he bows his head. He brushes against my breasts, then he rubs my nipple between his fingers. The sensation feels nice, but it fades as a piercing pinch sends shock waves to my brain, and I cry out.

"Deep breaths, Emilia. Eyes on mine." I don't dare look down. I start to take deeper breaths to try to even out the pain when Joshua does the same thing to my other nipple. "You may look."

He steps back to his seat, grabs his glass, and takes another sip before sitting back down. "Do you know what those are?"

Shit. Of course I know what these are, but I didn't think they would hurt so much. Aren't sex toys supposed to be fun? That's why they're called toys. I release a long, drawn-out whimper as I try to compose myself long enough to answer out loud.

"They're n-nipple clamps."

"And do you have any experience with these? Have you used these before?" he asks in a serious tone.

"N-no. Why do they h-h-h-hurt so much?" My voice is almost gone. I'm basically just breathing out my words.

Then he smiles. He sits back in his seat and smiles, abandoning the facade that he isn't enjoying himself immensely.

"You're very sensitive. Keep breathing, and the pain will dull. Why are you wearing nipple clamps, Emilia?"

I know the answer immediately. It's because I'm wasting his time. He's telling me he will no longer tolerate anything but complete openness. "Because I'm holding information back from you, and you're impatient." The throbbing in my nipples is causing my own snark to show.

He chuckles at my answer, but I'm sure he'll use my attitude as fuel for something else. "Very good. Now, these are little weights." He holds up some metal, teardrop-shaped objects, and my eardrums vibrate with my heartbeat as he explains, "Every time you don't tell me what I want to know, I will clip one onto the clamps, and you will feel the pain all over again. Do you understand?"

"Yes, Mr. Darkly."

He adjusts his groin at my answer, and I realize he is getting hard.

"Good. Which two names on the list?"

"Brent Davis and Sean Garner, Mr. Darkly."

"The awards are based on sales. Why don't you agree?"

"I—" I pause for a second too long, and Joshua stands. Without a word, he walks over to me and places the first weight on the chain hanging between my breasts. The tug is sharp.

"You knew their names were on the list before you tore open the envelope and yelled at me. How?" My eyes well with tears as he asks his question. How do I just say it?

"Brent cornered me on one of the balconies. He told me he couldn't wait to hear me say his name."

Joshua clenches his teeth at my answer. "What else did he tell you?"

"He said he would collect the rest of his award later that evening."

I can't read him anymore. He slides his drink closer to him and takes a gulp of the amber liquid, but he doesn't take his eyes off me.

"Why would he say that? Do you and Brent have a history?" My brows knit together at his question.

He had to have known. I was the dirty little secret of my class. Brent told me everyone knew, that they whispered about me behind my back.

The sudden pull on my nipples snaps me out of my thoughts as Joshua adds another weight to my chain, and I decide I don't want any more.

"He and Sean used to bully me in school. You know this. Brent told me you knew all about it and didn't care." I fist and release my hands by my side. How can Joshua humiliate me like this? I'm not crying, but tears are rolling down my face as he sits in front of me, just staring.

"What did they call you?"

The ringing in my ears overpowers my other senses.

This is what Joshua wants. He wants me to humiliate myself in front of him and live out the nightmare I tried to run away from. This is my punishment.

If it means I'm free from this place in one week, I'll do it. I won't let him intimidate me.

"F-Feelya," I answer, and he takes another sip then clears his throat.

"Why?" His eyes look angry as he swirls his drink, then places the glass on the table and clenches his hand into a fist.

"The first time they caught me was out by the football field after school. They dragged me into the boys' changing room, and they told me my dad was the reason their fathers were unemployed. It was right after the layoffs, when your mom took most of his money." He looks like he wants to challenge me on that point, but I won't let him deny it. "Times were hard, and they said it was our fault and I was going to pay for it. They made me lift up my shirt, and they touched me. I'd just turned sixteen. Brent and Sean told the other two to wait outside and keep a lookout, and they'd make sure I didn't tell. Brent pushed me down on the ground, and he pulled up my skirt, and they took turns touching me. They said if I told, it would hurt my dad."

I take a deep breath. A big part of me feels good that I've confronted this. I told my story. I won't let Joshua hide from it.

He takes a long look at me, and he seems to stumble on his next question. "Uh, you said that was the first time. There were others?"

I nod. "It went on until my senior year. It wasn't often. I always tried to be around people, and I stopped going out after school."

"When is the last time Brent laid a hand on you?"

My head feels heavy, and I'm not sure if it's the memory of that slimeball's hands on me or just the long day. I know my answer is going to surprise Joshua. "Last Monday. He touched me in the file room."

I wait for his eyes to widen in shock, but they don't.

He doesn't look surprised at all.

"I know, Emilia." His confession rattles me to my core.

"You did know. I knew it. How—" Joshua raises his hand as I prepare to start yelling, and I suddenly remember my agreement.

"It was brought to my attention yesterday. Your determined and very loyal friend trusted me with some information, and I verified it using the cameras in the file room," he says, rubbing his face.

"There are cameras in the file room?" I ask.

"Apparently, you aren't the only one who didn't know that. You tried to tell me, didn't you? When I took away your mother's ring?" His question catches me off guard, and I rub the finger the ring once wrapped around.

I blink rapidly a few times. What does this information mean?

"I...yes." My words trickle into the room, and Joshua sighs audibly before standing and taking the last gulp from his glass.

"That is a discussion for another time, and it is not why we are here right now. Go to the table and bend over it. Place your hands on the surface." Joshua rolls up his sleeves as he speaks. "We are here right now because you chose what you thought was the easy way out, and I'm here to show you it will be the hardest path you'll walk yet.

"When I sat at the table on Friday and watched you step up to the stage, I was fixated on you. You carry yourself with your father's grace, and you are beautiful. You disappointed me when you left, and you disrespected me in front of *my* entire company. You let me down, Emilia."

He's right. I never considered him then, but now that I look at it from his perspective, I showed extreme contempt for him—publicly. My heart sinks deep into my stomach.

"I never meant to—" I try to plead my case, and his hand lands carefully on my lower back, settling me in place. I stop moving, but the weights clipped to my nipple clamps continue to sway. I feel new sensations with each swing, and my brain swirls pain and pleasure together until I can't tell which I feel.

"Shh. You need to atone for your indiscretion, Emilia." Leaning over my bare back, he whispers in my ear as his fingers travel down my spine and over the curve of my ass. "You need to ask for your punishment." He punctuates his sentence with a kiss on my neck, and a whimper escapes my lips.

He's right. I don't know how he's right, but I need to create balance. "I—I'm sorry."

"I know you are, Emilia." His tone sounds sympathetic. "Ask for this. Show me how sorry you are." His voice is so soft, I could almost fall asleep to it. Each kiss ignites little sensations between my legs, and my head whirls around.

Another kiss draws me to him. I'm nothing but an object stuck in his orbit, slowly being pulled closer with every word, every touch. I'm drifting aimlessly toward him, and craving the inevitability of our collision.

"Please—I need you to punish me, Mr. Darkly," I plead, and I mean it. I need him to punish me. I need to give this to him as much as I need it for myself.

"That's my good girl." He squeezes my bottom gently as he leaves one last kiss on my neck.

Reaching across the table, he pulls another toy toward us, and my eyes widen. I thought he would be using his hand.

"What's that?" I forget my place and ask.

He moves his face in front of mine. I can only assume he's trying to memorize my reaction.

"It's a paddle." And before I can ask if it's going to hurt, his eyes squint into a smile of their own as he shows me his other hand. He's holding a long, thin item. "And this is a vibrator."

CHAPTER 59
JOSHUA

The smallest whimper from her brings me dangerously close to utter insanity.

Since the second her eyes widened at Ravenous when she learned she belonged to me, I've been waiting to get Emilia back here so I can show her how she has been holding herself back. I crave to teach her that denying who she is and what she needs will only hurt her. Yet here I am, learning those same lessons about myself.

We've both silenced our predilections for too long. We've pushed each other away, and for years we went round and round in circles.

I won't let her ignore this any longer. Neither of us will place ourselves second again.

My anger teeters on the edge of out of control. Sitting still and listening to Emilia relive her time at the hands of those four in high school set me off. I sat, completely contained, in front of her as she bravely spoke, and now I have so much energy, I feel like I could power a small town. I want to run and punch and not stop until I pass out.

Those four will pay for everything they've done, but they aren't my focus now. For once, I'm not thinking about myself; I'm thinking about Emilia. I can burn this energy off in a more pleasurable way for the both of us.

When Emilia saw the paddle, she didn't back away. Her eyes danced to mine, and she didn't object.

The vibrator was a different story.

I sense Emilia can take her punishments. She even understands the need for balance. Her hesitation is in taking pleasure from me, or possibly enjoying pleasure at all.

"You'll keep your palms on the table and stay bent over, just like this, until I tell you I am done." I don't ask for her understanding, but she nods softly anyway. "You'll close your eyes for the entire punishment. If you open them, I'll add more."

I want her to shut out everything around us and place herself in my hands. This will help her to concentrate. She takes one long look at me, searching my face, and I keep my expressionless mask on. Then she closes her eyes and parts her lips to breathe deeper.

Standing tall, I square myself and rub the fleshiest part of her ass to warm her up while she continues to breathe at a steady rate.

The first smack is light, but it's enough that the shock causes her to jump. She settles herself quickly, but the weights keep swaying, pulling her nipples taut. I imagine the ache in her breasts is becoming less painful and more enjoyable, and my lips twitch at the thought.

Which reminds me...

Placing the paddle on the table, I turn the vibrator on to its lowest setting and reach my fingers down to her entrance. She's already coated with her slick arousal, and she faintly moans as I slide my fingers effortlessly along her labia and around her entrance.

Then I realize the moan is coming from me.

She bears down on her hips as the vibrator slides in easily until it sits on its own inside of her. I wrap my arm around her stomach from the front and hold her loosely in place with my free hand while I pick the paddle back up to continue her punishment. The vibration hums slow and low, and I know it isn't enough to grant her an orgasm.

The second smack from the paddle is more forceful than the first, and each of the next ten smacks increase over the last. I'm beginning to enjoy myself, and I lose count after a few more until she finally says she is sorry.

"What are you sorry for?" I stop momentarily to let her speak, and I look at her face. Her eyes are still closed.

"I was disrespectful and I left on Friday."

"Hm." I hit her even harder with the paddle and the vibrator hums along. "While I thank you for that, you may think you're sorry, but you don't believe you are—yet."

I paddle her again, and her fists clench in frustration. The punishment is beginning to get to her, but it isn't effective yet. She's only saying sorry to keep from facing her actions; I'll continue to punish her until she is truly sorry.

"Did you know there were other people in the audience who bid on you? One was quite determined. Have you thought about where else you could possibly be right now?"

"Wh-what?" Her response tells me her hurt never allowed her to see the danger she put herself in.

"There is so much you didn't list on your hard limits. Have you considered what might have happened to you if Ravenous were owned by someone else? If I hadn't been told where you were?"

Her silence is my answer.

"I asked you, that night in the shower, who you belonged to. What was your answer?" I paddle her again, and she chokes out her answer.

"You." Her lips pinch together. What I need is coming. It's building inside of her, I can tell by how tightly she fists her hands on the table.

"That's right, Emilia. You"—*smack*—"belong"—*smack*—"to me." *Smack*. "You ran off with what is mine, and you tried to sell it." *Smack*. "The next time you say you're sorry, you better mean it."

Smack.

She sucks in a deep breath as I watch her face. Her eyes are still closed, and she is fighting hard to hold everything in. I raise my hand to deliver another when her deep sob catches my attention.

"I'm sorry!" she blurts, and somehow I know the anger in her tone isn't meant for me. She feels her guilt now, and her tears escape through shut eyes as her face turns a deep red.

"What are you sorry for?" I ask again.

"I ran away. I got scared, and I was alone, and I ran away from you. I am scared. I don't understand what is happening, but I put myself in danger. I tried to sell myself, and it wasn't my decision to make. I'm sorry." Her last syllable drags on with her sobs, and I have what I need.

I place the paddle down beside her and rub her heated ass. She drops her forehead and sobs on the table. I instruct her to keep her eyes shut, and I allow her tears for a couple of minutes before I stand her up and remove the vibrator. She whimpers at its loss. Then I turn it off and place it near the paddle.

Stepping back, I guide her with me and sit in her father's old chair at the head of the table. I part her legs with my knee and bring her forward to straddle my thigh as I lightly draw my fingers up her torso.

She braces her palms on my shoulders, waiting for my lead.

Her obedience is overwhelming. Her eyes remain closed, and she breathes heavily. My touch is faint, but I know she feels me in her very soul. All of her senses are heightened. Her tears roll down her neck and over her chest, and I swirl my fingers through the trail of her guilt.

"Keep your eyes closed, Emilia. Just feel everything and react. It's just the two of us now." I cup my palm over one breast and squeeze softly. Then I stretch my neck out and lick the tip of her nipple, and she whimpers through her lips. She groans out her gratitude, and I release her first clip as I continue to taste the saltiness of her tears on her pert bud.

She hisses in a deep breath before moaning at the sting of the clamp's release, and I kiss her softly. I know the low vibration between her legs from before and these soft licks and touches are unraveling her. Her head sways, following the spikes of pain and pleasure as I remove the second clamp before dropping it on the floor at my feet.

"Look at me, Emilia."

A flood of tears escapes as she opens her eyes and blinks a few times before settling her attention on me.

I place my hand palm up on my thigh between her spread legs. She inhales a deep breath as I lift a finger toward her entrance and graze along her wet lips, barely touching her. Her hips jerk back, but I guide her forward with my free hand on her hip.

"I gave you the chance to return to the way things were; you chose this path. This means I have a short amount of time to show you who you are. You'll see what I see, and you'll ache for what I will provide soon enough. Keep your eyes open and watch."

"Um..."

"You may speak."

"Are you—are we—uh—going to—um—"

"Are you trying to ask if I'm going to fuck you, Emilia?"

"Yes."

The time she spent with anyone before me was wasted time. She wasted herself on people who never appreciated her. Her naivety is alluring. Her raw honesty, intoxicating. Her submission, absolutely enthralling.

"No," I answer, and the soft gyration in her hips slows down.

"Are you going to make me beg for it?" She almost sounds disappointed.

"No. That needs to be earned, and you haven't earned it yet. Neither of us have," I answer solemnly.

"How do I earn it?" she asks. I increase the pressure in my touch, and her hips move again.

"You will start by accepting yourself without shame. You won't understand your place, or my ownership of you, unless you accept who you are. It's okay to want this, Emilia." I know there are parts of her still conflicted. "No more questions. Keep your eyes open and fuck yourself on my hand until you come."

I've been building her toward an orgasm since I placed the first nipple clamp on her, so she isn't going to last long. Her arousal coats my fingers as I run them along the length of her labia. Then I position two fingers at her entrance and wait for her to show me what she wants.

Placing her hands on my shirt, she gathers the fabric into her fists as she lowers herself onto my fingers and grinds her clit against my palm. As she lifts herself off then returns a second time, I wrap one hand around her and cup her red ass, reminding her of where she belongs.

I squeeze hard each time she drives her body down, and her walls clench tight around my fingers. She keeps her eyes open and set on mine as we both lose ourselves in the rhythm she is slowly increasing. Her breasts bounce freely in front of me. I lean in, sucking one into my mouth, biting her nipple between my teeth before releasing it, and her face loses all composure.

Her apprehension is gone. Her cadenced thrusts become a carnal taking as her grip tightens and she wantonly rides my hand, chasing her orgasm.

She enjoys the pain I've given her. This is something she needs to learn about herself. I begin to spank her bare ass, and a long, guttural groan flows out of her as her bouncing increases.

"Tell me how it feels to be mine," I order as I continue to slap her, and she doesn't slow down. She's too close to stop now.

"J-Josh—"

"Ah, ah, ah. You address me properly or I stop—"

"Mr. Darkly," she screams in a panic. "It feels so good, M-Mr. Darkly. Please don't stop."

My next spanks land harder on her ass, and she arches her back as her thrusting becomes erratic.

"Are you going to come like this, Emilia? Needy and rutting yourself on my leg while I spank your bare ass?"

The realization of her own deviance hits her as hard as her orgasm does. She screams, "Yes, Mr. Darkly!" As she drives herself down and grinds her clit onto my hand, her body convulses around my fingers. I reach up to grab the hair at the base of her skull and force her attention onto my face.

She will watch me as she surrenders herself to her orgasm; she'll know it was me who gave it to her. The person she ran away from. Her eyes go wide as she continues to wriggle on my thigh as aftershocks leave her, and the evidence of her need soaks into my pants.

Her head feels heavy in my hand. It's late, and she has no energy left tonight, which is just as well. Neither do I.

She whimpers as I slide my hand out of her. "You're my good girl, Emilia. This is who you are, and you are mine." For effect, I lift my fingers up between us so she can see what she's done, and she stares silently.

Her mouth drops open as I taste her, and I take advantage. I remove my fingers from my mouth and push them into hers. Her tongue is soft and warm, and my own moan escapes me before I regain control over myself.

"Stand," I order, and she instantly obeys, but her body is sluggish. "Sit." She takes a cautious seat on my lap, wincing at the pain from the paddle. I'm not sure if she realizes she is still holding on to my shirt for dear life. "Lay your head down." I pull her toward me and wrap my arms around her, and she snuggles her head into my neck.

We sit silent like this for almost ten minutes. I draw soft lines along her body and wait for any signs that she wishes to speak, but no indication comes. Eventually her breathing slows, and her body becomes heavy.

She's fallen asleep.

After I open my eyes, it takes a few seconds to remember where I am. My body sits heavily on the soft mattress, like it could swallow me whole and I would be okay with that.

Squinting against the early morning rays, I look through the window and recognize this place; it's the old spare room in our house.

Joshua's bedroom.

Reminders of last night register like a slideshow skipping through my mind, and I bolt upright at the sudden memories. Simultaneously, the deep throbbing on my butt cheeks causes me to wince as I hit the end of my rope—literally.

Reaching to the pull at my throat, my fingers search along my collar until they find the leash, and I grip it tight as my eyes follow the chain all the way over to the headboard.

I've been clipped to the bed.

I pull myself onto my knees and crawl up the mattress to inspect my tether. It is a simple clip. Anyone can unfasten it, even me.

But I don't.

This is Joshua's way of showing me that it is my choice to be here. I release the chain and run my fingers over my bare skin. He left me naked last night, and somehow I think I would have been disappointed if I had woken up with clothes on.

I pinch my nipple between my thumb and forefinger, a reminder of the heady pain. I came hard looking into Joshua's eyes and riding his fingers. I let go to him, and he carried me to the most intense release I've ever had. Then he carried me to his bed.

Did he sleep with me, or did I sleep alone?

I'm lost in my thoughts, and I fail to react when the door opens. Then I look up to catch a slow grin spreading across Joshua's face. Reality hits as I look down: I'm kneeling on the bed, naked and playing with my breasts, and my face heats up with embarrassment.

"Good morning, Emilia."

"Good morning, Mr. Darkly." At least I haven't forgotten his rule.

"I gathered some fruit and water for you to nibble on while you get ready. I imagine you are hungry after the events of this weekend. There isn't much here; I have more downstairs. You were very good for me last night." He places the plate and bottle of water on the nightstand, and the bed bows as he takes a seat and picks up where my hand left off—at my nipple. "Did you like this pain?" he asks, pinching.

"I—think I did." His questions make me feel vulnerable, and I don't hate it. I just need to get used to exposing myself to him.

He smiles at my answer. "I've decided to allow you to shower on your own, as a reward for not unclipping yourself. It pleases me that you are open to accepting your place here."

I smile back. I'm not smiling because I get to shower myself, although I can't wait to get under that water. I'm smiling because I've pleased him.

He instructs me to meet him in the dining room for the rest of our breakfast when I am done. He tells me I am to appear naked, and butterflies flutter restlessly around my stomach.

"Relax, Emilia. Sylvia has the week off, paid. I told her this house is off-limits while she is away, and she is to contact me if she has to enter for any reason. No other staff is here. It is only you and me. I want you to feel safe while you explore yourself."

And that is exactly what I did over the next ten minutes in the shower. My hands sought out all of the places Joshua touched me last night, and I rediscovered myself with a new understanding. My own hands rubbed over the curve of my ass, reliving the pleasure wrapped in pain that Joshua doled out when he paddled me.

What I once considered a darkness was only misconception, shadowed and pushed down in fear. In this big house, all alone with Joshua, I finally feel safe enough to entertain the thoughts I never understood.

After drying off and braiding my hair loosely over my shoulder, I find myself almost skipping down the stairs to see Joshua, and my little voice stops me. I still feel nervous that letting myself go completely will only make it hurt more when this ends. I've wanted Joshua's attention for so long. What happens when he decides to take it away from me again?

The question of where to sit is answered immediately. A plate sits on the floor beside Joshua's chair, and he watches stoically as I accept my place and sit down beside him.

"Good girl. You've made this easier on yourself by obeying me. You may choose your own breakfast and feed yourself today."

I gather my plate and stand, and as I scan the tray of muffins and rolls, I feel a little sad that he won't be feeding me.

What is happening to me?

As we settle into eating, he watches and waits until I take a big bite, then he asks me a question.

"Why didn't you tell your father about what happened to you in high school?"

I chew my food as I consider my answer. "I didn't want him to feel responsible, and I know it would have hurt him. I always planned on telling him when I was older and I'd put it behind me. But then—"

I look up at him, and he nods. He's granting me mercy, so I don't need to continue talking about my dad's death, but I can't stop. "He'd be so ashamed of me now." The muffin suddenly feels too big in my throat, and I gulp to try to get it down as my eyes begin to sting.

"Emilia, Adam was a good man. The greatest I ever knew. He would never be ashamed of you."

I don't agree, and I drop my eyes to the ground. The knife Joshua was holding clinks onto the plate and his seat creaks along the floor as he leans over, then he lifts a finger to my chin to return my eyes to his own. "Adam knew all about me and my need for control. He helped me manage and focus myself, and I'm going to do the same for you. Adam wasn't just my boss, Emilia. He was my mentor. In business and in my—personal interests." He raises his brow, as if to insinuate he is talking about what is happening between us.

"No. I don't believe that. My father wouldn't give this his blessing."

Joshua looks at me hard for a moment. "He would if he knew this is what you want." His voice is soft, and I appreciate his kindness, but I shake my head in disbelief.

He straightens in his seat and reaches for some papers on the table. "I've been going through some of Adam's things. In addition to Connor Realty, there are some investments and other businesses that will need to have decisions made about them soon. Here is one investment I thought you should see." He holds the paper out in front of me and waits while I take them and look over the top page.

It's an investment agreement, and I look further down the page for the entity. "He invested in Ravenous?"

Joshua nods. "Adam met Lexa through an acquaintance with mutual interests. She was looking for solid investors within the lifestyle so she could get her business up and running. She wanted everything done aboveboard with the well-being of the club's members at the forefront. Adam liked her instantly. He is the reason I invested in Ravenous as well. Over time, everyone was paid back. Adam invested the most money, but he insisted she clear the slate with everyone else first. This investment is outstanding." He takes the paper as he finishes speaking.

I feel numb.

I always thought I was the one who knew my father the best. but I only knew him differently than Joshua did. Of course my dad couldn't confide in me about this. What parent would tell their absent daughter their darkest secrets? But Joshua knows them all, and this is something I need time to deal with.

In an instant, my guard goes up.

"I'm surprised." Already I know my words are meant to be a wall. I don't want to continue this conversation right now, so I'm grasping at straws to change the subject. "With how much you've talked to my father, he really never mentioned how badly your mother drained him in the divorce."

It's not until his face drops that I realize I've hit a sore spot. "I told you, Emilia. You are misinformed. My mother barely got anything in the divorce. Your dad's company went through rough times around the same time. It was a dip in the market. It was only a coincidence." His answer sounds like the skipping of a broken record.

"I'm not wrong, Jo—Mr. Darkly."

"Then you're lying, and you know I won't tolerate anything but the truth," he warns.

"That's the thing," I challenge. "I know what I will lose for not telling the truth. You can rip up this agreement, and I get nothing. I'm not lying. Your mother took almost everything we had. Why won't you believe me?"

His anger is growing, but I can't help myself. He won't let me bring this up again, and I'll say my piece before he takes everything else from me.

He rubs his hands over his face, pulling his features long. "It's your word against my mother's, Emilia. Adam is the only one who can settle this and—"

"No. He's not. Are you telling me that you really haven't realized that you, as the owner of this company, can at any time ask to see the financial records? You can call up the lawyer's office and obtain the written settlement; it lists the company's financial losses as a result." I'm beside myself. He can answer this with a few phone calls.

His ire is replaced by something I can't read.

Abruptly, he stands and clears his throat. "I have some business in the office to deal with. I will be gone for a few hours. While I am away, you are to clean up breakfast. Then go into my room. Open only the top drawer of my dresser. There are various instruments and toys inside. Pull out those you have never used on yourself and place them on the bed in two piles. The first, at the foot of the bed, are the items you want to try. The second pile, at the top of the bed, are the ones that scare you or make you nervous. In two hours, you will kneel at the front door and wait there until I return. You will not answer the door or make contact with anyone. Do you understand?"

My brain scrambles to keep up, and I nod as he turns and leaves me in a cloud of confusion.

A wave of uncertainty hits me. I don't feel like our morning was supposed to end this way.

I don't stand up until I hear the door close. The faint rattle of his keys tells me he's locked me in.

I suddenly regret my decision to challenge him, and I jump to my feet to clear everything away quickly. I'm still tired from last night, and if I can do my chores quickly, I might have enough time to take a nap before I need to kneel and wait for him at the front door.

When I arrived at the office, two people occupied Emilia's desk, and Noah was running between my desk and hers, dropping off papers and answering questions. Faye was typing away, and when her eyes met mine, she looked more serious than I had ever seen her.

I canceled all of my nonurgent meetings for the week, and I assigned Noah as my proxy for the ones that needed to happen. I spent the first hour compiling everything he would need. Luckily, there were only three meetings and calls that could not be postponed, and his involvement in two of them was minimal.

My next hour was spent catching up with Noah. A third member of the legal team, the intern from our meeting on Sunday, was also around the office, but he was mostly holed away in the file room, gathering files and photocopying.

Noah sent urgent and confidential requests to our head of security to pull video for all of the dates and locations in the reports.

After two hours in the office, Noah told me to attend to my

personal matters. Apparently, I'm no fun to be around when I'm impatient.

I've been hesitating for the last two hours. There is something I need to do, and I'm delaying.

Just considering Emilia's words makes me feel like I'm betraying my own family.

How did it never cross my mind to look into our company losses when I took over the business? Or maybe it did, and subconsciously I didn't want to know the answer.

Cordelia would never win Mother of the Year, but could she be capable of something like this? If she got more than she indicated, why lie to me about it? I've made my own way since I turned eighteen. I sent her my commissions and bonuses to keep her afloat.

If I'm being honest with myself, I don't know which version I hope is the truth.

I pull into the driveway, park the car, and make my way to the front door. Anticipation builds with each step. Just the thought of her waiting obediently makes me walk a little faster.

The door opens to a quiet house, and it takes me half a second to register that she is not where I instructed her to be. Glancing to the dining room, I notice everything has been cleared as I asked, but there is no other sign of her.

Has she decided to run away from me again? The thought rings through my ears, and my chest feels tight. I take the steps two at a time. Checking each room on the top floor, my heart beats faster as I find each one empty and cold.

She ran away to college; she ran away from the dinner. I can't take this again.

By the time I get to my own room, my world stops. She did as I requested. My drawer is open, and there are two piles on the bed. The one at the foot of the bed is smaller than the one at the top. She's nervous about a lot of things.

I grin. *Good.*

But the piles aren't what has captured my breath. Lying between them is my Emilia, and she is sleeping peacefully. Quietly, I remove each toy at the foot of the bed and place them back in my drawer. Those will be used another time.

Trailing my fingers over the toys that make my little Emilia nervous sends jolts of excitement through me. I can't wait to show her the pain and pleasure each one of these will bring to the both of us.

I make every effort not to wake her as I pull the chain from the headboard to her collar. I clip her in place, then I choose a toy and position myself beside her on the bed.

A soft moan escapes her in her sleep as my fingers make their way between her closed legs. It doesn't take long for her eyes to flutter open as I rub along her slick lips. I place a hand on her throat, telling her to stay put as I continue to work my hand between her thighs.

"Open for me, Emilia," I order in a whisper. Sleepily, she grants me more access as her legs part.

I love this look on her. As she watches me with wide, innocent eyes, her breathing deepens, and little moans escape her when I hit a sensitive spot.

"Close your eyes, Emilia," I order a little louder, and she lays her head against the bed and allows me to lead her where I want her. A wolfish grin takes over my face as I lift her leg and dip my head to her core. I'm heady with lust. I need a taste of her almost more than I need my next breath.

I remove my hands, and my senses coil together as my tongue runs along her labia. She groans, mirroring my own desire. Locking my lips around her sex, I suck her in hard, tasting her now-swollen nub.

She's entirely vulnerable to me. Lying here with her eyes

closed, she offers herself to me. I almost decide not to finish what I started.

Almost.

WHACK.

Emilia registers the pain a fraction of a second after the crop hits her engorged clit, and her eyes shoot open.

I allow her to attempt to sit up, knowing the leash will hold her in place, and she squeals as she chokes on her collar.

The instant she realizes she can't get up, she instinctively tries to close her legs. I allow her attempt as tears fill her eyes. I don't allow her to move up the bed and away from me though. Clamping my hand over her hips, I pin her to the mattress and give her half a minute to process.

"Spread your legs and be still. Why are you being punished, Emilia?" I wait for her to figure it out.

"Oh no! I—"

WHACK. She hasn't opened her legs yet, so I shift her to the side and take a swipe at her red ass from last night. Pain on top of previous pain always hurts more.

"Owww!" As she cries out, I pull my hand back to land a second hard whip on her ass. Then she chooses the lesser of the two evils and opens her legs for me.

I" wasn't kneeling by the door. I—I fell asleep."

WHACK.

The thing I like about the crop is I don't need to exert a lot of energy to get the desired effect. Especially since Emilia has already told me it makes her nervous. I'm pretty sure she's never had a crop used on her, and I would even bet she's never had her pussy slapped, which makes this extremely enjoyable for me.

Another smack, and her face flushes as she watches me, doe-eyed. I won't hide my satisfaction. Out of the corner of my eye, her hands clutch the bedsheets at her sides. She's not objecting to her punishment; she's bracing for more.

Steadying her breaths through gritted teeth, she takes each additional whip of the crop in stride. Eventually, a stray tear escapes over her blushed cheek.

"Rules, Emilia. You belong to me now, and you have rules. They aren't optional. I demand you serve my needs before your own this week. Do you understand me?" I land an aggressive hit squarely on her pussy, and she chokes out her answer.

"I understand. I'm sorry, Mr. Darkly."

WHACK. Her eyes go wide at her continued punishment.

"Ow. Stop!" she cries out, but she keeps herself open, and I can't help myself.

"That's not good enough. You will atone for your transgression. You've been handled with kid gloves your entire adult life, and it's taught you nothing. You will learn your place, and you will earn it." I feel spit cover my lips as my anger builds.

WHACK.

My thoughts race to all of the times I could have helped her if she would have only spoken up. And the one time she did try to speak up, I was too far gone to listen. I'm mad at both of us.

"Please, Jo—Mr. Darkly. Please. I'm sorry. It won't happen again. I promise." Her cries snap me out of my daze.

I've gone too far. I've lost myself to my own anger. I can't let that happen again. Emilia needs to understand our dynamic, but this is a bit too much too soon, and I freeze. She raises one shaky hand to me and pleads silently with wide eyes.

She's afraid of me.

My knuckles have gone white around the handle of the crop. I drop it onto the bed, then I slowly rub her pussy, from the sensitive spot on her clit down to the wetness that is gathering at her entrance, and she whimpers.

I crawl up alongside her and cradle her in my arms. She fell asleep so quickly last night, and I worry that my aftercare wasn't sufficient. Hesitantly, she reaches for me and pulls me to her as she cries softly into my chest. Just as I settle in beside her to soothe her and explain, the doorbell rings.

Shit. It's close to dinner time; it's probably Noah, checking up on everything. I just punished Emilia harder than I ever have, and I don't have the chance to take care of her in the aftermath.

This is the state he gets to see her in. He couldn't have come at a worse time.

"Get dressed. We have company," Joshua says coolly, leaving an empty space around me when he stands and walks out of the room.

My entire body is still trembling from my punishment, and foreign feelings are making me anxious. These are things I've never felt before, and I don't understand them, and he just left. And now I have to entertain someone?

How does he turn these things off and on so easily? The question leaves me wondering if he's done this before, if he's owned someone.

I wince as I get off the bed. New pain mixes with old, and I look around Joshua's room for these clothes he spoke of. My eyes land on the door that separates his room from my own.

He just told me to get dressed, he didn't say in what.

I open the adjoining door and step into my old room. It's just as I left it Friday night; my things are still all over the place. I couldn't carry everything I wanted at the time, so there are a lot of clothes to choose from.

I unzip the bag I left behind and fish out my tights and a

stretchy long-sleeved shirt. It's what I wore for all-night study sessions in my old life.

My old life. Is that how I categorize it now? My old life where I felt alone, and my new life where I am alone. The paths to my freedom seem to be crumbling away with every choice I make.

I catch a glimpse of myself in the mirror above the dresser, and I barely recognize the person gawking at me. My face is flushed, and shame surrounds me. I'm a person with rules; I'm owned. For someone who vowed to reject money, I slapped a price tag on myself and sold myself to the highest bidder.

And every time Joshua is near me, I react viscerally. Those punishments hurt, and I found myself becoming aroused with each jolt of pain.

What is wrong with me? The twisted look of disgust staring back at me shocks me out of my thoughts. I can't want these things. This is so different than what I used to want.

Isn't it?

Voices from downstairs remind me I have rules. Smoothing out my shirt, I erase my scowl and wander out of my room and down the stairs.

I know who it is before he turns around. Does Noah know I've been bought, or am I to pretend everything is as it was? My eyes jump between Noah and Joshua as I ponder my question.

"Hey, Sweets." Noah's use of my nickname is welcome, but I'm still met with a tinge of sadness. It reminds me of a time when my ignorance truly was blissful.

Joshua glances at Noah, but he chooses to allow the pet name. I have a feeling Noah is probably the only one who would get away with calling me that. Their friendship must be very strong.

"Let's sit in the lounge. Noah, I will be present for this,"

Joshua says. Noah nods and walks through our hall like he's been here before.

"Present for what?" I whisper, but Joshua isn't entertaining any questions from me. He just reaches his arm out to show me where I'm supposed to go.

Noah makes himself comfortable, and Joshua pours two drinks. He hands his friend one, then turns to me. "Emilia, would you like a glass of water?"

I shake my head. It's not lost on me that I'm not being treated like a friend. That isn't what I sold myself as.

As both of the men settle into their seats, I look to Joshua for direction, and panic settles in. I must look out of place just standing between them, and I don't want another punishment for disobeying.

"Emilia, you may sit on the couch beside Noah." I flush as I take my seat quickly, and Noah watches me with a gentle smile on his face.

Joshua swirls his drink in his glass, then takes a long sip and leans back in his seat. Speaking carefully, he continues, "Noah is here to talk to you."

"Oh?" I answer cautiously. This feels like a trap, and anxiety builds inside of me. Joshua has instructed me to tell the truth. What if I'm not ready to talk about something?

"I was with Joshua last night at Ravenous, Emilia." His words hit me hard. So he doesn't just know. He saw me degrade myself on stage.

"Oh." My voice lowers, and I drop my gaze to my lap as my skin prickles with embarrassment.

"We're both concerned for you." I fidget with my sweaty palms as Noah speaks. "I truly hoped you would give this year and Joshua a chance." I watch from under hooded eyes as he exchanges a glance with Joshua, who gives him a curt shake of his head. It's a silent conversation among friends.

"Do you understand what you've done?" His tone is unassuming.

"Yes. I sold myself, and Joshua bought me."

Noah winces. "I prefer you to say he bought ownership of you, Emilia." Noah's wording confuses me, and Joshua clears his throat, drawing my attention to him.

"Noah and I disagree slightly on definitions. I say I bought you; Noah has more of a hippie view on things. It's irrelevant. You belong to me—entirely."

"So you approve of this...this..." I don't have the words to describe what this is. I'm hoping Noah will fill in the blanks.

"Has Joshua hurt you?" Now it is Joshua's turn to cringe. He knows what he's done, and I suddenly feel a little more confident.

"Yes. Last night, he spanked me, and today, he, uh—he, um—did the same thing, but somewhere else." My eyes must be as big as saucers, and my face burns hot as Noah slowly nods his head.

"I see. And, um, did you deserve those—spankings?"

I straighten at his question, then I slump back down. I lower my eyes to my hands, which are clasped together on my lap. I can't lie. I told Joshua I won't lie, and if I start now, he'll question everything I've said.

"I—I—yes," I whisper as I steal a glance at Joshua. He almost looks proud of me.

"And what did you do?" Noah asks in the same tone.

"I disobeyed Mr. Darkly," I answer.

Noah raises his eyebrows at my use of his formal name. "How did that make you feel?"

"You mean that I got caught?" I ask, and Noah laughs at my question.

"No. How did it make you feel when you disappointed him?" Two sets of eyes watch me, and I feel exposed. Both of these men understand whatever this is more than I do, and I feel like I'm being led into something.

I shrug. "I don't know."

Joshua clears his throat at my answer. I do know. And he knows I know. And so does Noah.

"I think you do know, Emilia. Do you know why I gave my blessing when Joshua bought you?"

I shake my head.

"That night at the bar. When you saw Joshua, you couldn't hide it. Not from me. You were dancing in my arms, and you were as stiff as a board. The moment you saw Joshua, your body relaxed; you looked relieved. There was no fear.

"You never feared him, Emilia. For as long as I can remember, you sought Joshua out. When I would come over after class and we'd hang out, you were always nearby. It was innocent at first. You were young, and you wanted his attention. But then you grew up, and I caught you looking at him more times than I could count. That night in the bar, you had that same look. I don't believe you fear him. I believe you desire him, and it is your need you fear, and you fight it. Emilia, I think you fear yourself. No matter how far you run, you never really get away, do you?"

I risk looking up at Joshua. Am I so easy to read that everyone knows how I feel but me? I don't know what to say. Every thought in my head at this moment feels like a lie.

"You scared me today," I whisper, and Joshua clenches his lips into a thin line. It's written all over his face, and he knows it.

Today was the first time I felt afraid of Joshua. It put everything else into perspective. His eyes were wild.

"What do you mean, Emilia?" Noah sits forward in his seat, concern replacing his relaxed demeanor.

"I—" I forgot we weren't alone. As I look over at Joshua for a clue on how I should proceed, I begin to stutter, and the color drains from Joshua's face.

He raises his hand to silence me and puts his glass on the table beside him. "I'd like to answer that." Noah nods his head, and Joshua begins.

"I was punishing Emilia for an incomplete task. I pushed both of us to our limit." Turning to focus on me, he continues, "You don't yet know what it means to be mine. You gave yourself to me long before I bought you, and a flash of fear got into my head as I was delivering your penance. I almost lost you, Emilia. But then I realized, we've spent most of our lives almost losing each other, and one of these times will really be the last if we aren't careful. You're too valuable to me, and I won't lose you. I won't force you to stay, and I only have six days left to show you who you are. I'm not perfect, but I'm not a monster. I'm not Brent or Sean. You are not doing anything here you haven't chosen for yourself. When your time with me is done, I will let you go if that is what you want.

"The moment I saw fear in your eyes today was the moment I dropped the crop. You are my guide as much as I am yours. I didn't get a chance to comfort you and tell you this after, well, because—" He tilts his head to Noah, and I finish his sentence.

"Because Noah showed up." My voice is quiet as I process his explanation. I know he didn't need to give it to me. He could have just explained to Noah and left me in the dark.

"Ah, great. My timing is stellar then." Noah attempts to break the tension. "Emilia, I'm going to be honest. Joshua was just as worried about you as I was. I wasn't just coming over tonight to see how things are. Joshua asked me to come over and help him decide if he made the right decision."

"What?" My eyes bounce between both men.

"He put your well-being before his own needs. He wanted

to know if he should buy you out and let you go, or if he should keep you for the week and try to get through to you. You should know, in addition to the money, he was willing to sign over your father's cottage and everything you wanted from the house, and your time here would be done, effective immediately.

"On the flip side, you also need to know he is opposing your signature on the forfeiture notice. He is currently fighting for you to retain what is yours because he wants you to want to stay and try. He trusts my judgment, and he has unwavering confidence that staying is what is best for you. So, tell me, should he let you go for good?"

Should he let you go for good?

Noah's question hangs in the air like a ticking time bomb ready to detonate and take everything I treasure with it.

I watch Emilia. She shifts her focus between the both of us before she sets her sights on something just out of her reach. The weight of Noah's words seems to settle into her.

I stay still, watching her as she internally wrestles with everything she now knows. It feels as though time inside this room has stopped while the rest of the world goes on without us.

Noah laid everything out for her. I'm willing to give her the amount she sold herself for and the cabin she loves so much. All she has to do is tell me she doesn't want us.

What have I done? The thought sends chills down my arms as I sit here waiting for her answer.

One year with her turned into one week, and now it's down to one question.

I'm out of time.

"I'd like you to leave, Noah."

It takes me half a minute of silence to process her words. It seems Noah is doing the same; we're both sitting here gawking at her.

"Respectfully, Noah, this is between Mr. Darkly and me. I'd like you to leave us alone—under one condition." She shifts her attention from Noah to me, and my heart pounds into my chest. "For the rest of tonight, I want to talk with you. You said it yourself: There is no one else here. I can explore myself freely. I think we owe it to ourselves and each other to say everything and anything. The good and the bad. Do you agree, Mr. Darkly?"

The English language is abundantly filled with words, yet I can't find even one to describe how I feel right now. Pride, joy, determination all flow together. And so I nod.

As he places his empty glass on the table and reaches for his jacket, I notice Noah trying hard to keep his own emotions in check. But I can tell he has a smile in there, waiting to come out. I feel it myself.

She's chosen to stay. She wants to try.

Noah offers his goodbyes and quickly leaves us standing in a room that suddenly feels a little too small.

"Joshua," I offer, and Emilia raises her eyebrows in confusion. "Please, call me Joshua. I've missed it. I like hearing you say my name." Even the smallest of truths makes me feel uneasy. This is going to be harder than I thought.

Her lips curve into a warm smile as I reach out my hand, gesturing for her to sit on the couch. I sit across from her. We've caused each other a lifetime of pain and suffering because neither of us could admit anything—to ourselves or each other.

"What is that?" Emilia's question breaks the silence, and I follow her gaze to the table.

My attention stops dead on the pink glittery glue peeking through the cracks in my old picture frame.

"It's my picture of my father and I."

"I know what it is. Where did you get it? I haven't seen that since—" Her eyes search the ceiling as she tries to remember.

"Since your thirteenth birthday. I found it in your old fort a couple of weeks ago."

"Right." She keeps her focus on the frame, and I see the sadness in her eyes. She must be remembering how I ditched her on her first teen birthday.

"I hurt you, Emilia." My voice is soft. I don't even want to admit that ugly truth to myself, let alone out loud to her. "Over and over. I hurt you because I was hurting. And as we grew older, I hurt you because it was easier to hurt you than love you."

"Wh-what?" Her mouth drops open.

"When Adam told me you were leaving for college, it hit me hard. We can only run away from our truth for so long before we need to stop for a rest. And that's the thing about the truth—it doesn't need to rest until it is realized, and sooner or later, we need to face it. But I never did, and look where it got us."

Emilia's eyes grow wider with each sentence I say, and I feel lighter with each word.

"I ran away," she answers.

"Pardon?"

"You were right. I ran away to college. I could have gone here, but I told myself I left because I wanted to prove to everyone I could do it on my own, and that was partly true. But I could have done it on my own here. I could have stood up for myself with Brent and Sean, and I could have been just as independent here. I ran away from seeing you. I thought if I could just be on my own that this stupid infatuation I had with you would fade, that I would grow to hate you as much as I pretended to, then I would be free from my pain."

This is the most honest we've ever been with each other.

"What do you have nightmares about, Emilia? I overheard you and Sylvia talking. Is it about Brent and Sean?"

Her face pinches into apprehension. I get the feeling this is a topic she wishes to avoid.

"I started getting nightmares in high school. At the start of my senior year. Brent and Sean are a part of them, but mostly I dream I am trying to talk to you and tell you what happened, and you shut me down. You yell at me and tell my dad and everyone calls me a liar."

"Your nightmares are about me?" The strength of her truth mentally knocks me over.

"You have to understand, Brent and Sean told me you knew about everything and didn't care. By then, you and I weren't talking to each other anymore. I had no reason to believe they were lying. Every time I tried to talk to you, you would shut me down or tell me I was a spoiled brat. I was embarrassed about what they did to me, and I felt so much shame that you knew, and that my dirty secret haunted this house. I guess it all came out in my dreams."

"I didn't know at all. I don't think anyone other than those four knows your secret, Emilia. Someone would have said something to Noah or me. I'm sure of it. They preyed on you. They shamed you into keeping their secret. You have my word: they will pay for everything." My anger gets the better of me, and my words come out a little more forceful than I'd intended.

My anger pushes me in all of the wrong ways—Emilia has made me understand this about myself. I crave control, yet all of this time, I allowed my anger to control me.

Emilia isn't the only one here who needs to grow. If I'm being honest with myself, she isn't the one who needs to grow the most. I've allowed fear and anger to dictate my actions. I

can't continue down this path, or I will lose Emilia for good—
and I will deserve it.

Emilia needs someone as strong as she is, and I need to do better.

"I guess we both have a lot to learn about each other." Her eyes glisten as she speaks softly, and my heart breaks at the sadness in her tone.

Shifting from my chair to the couch beside her, I do something that should shock her, but instead she responds naturally: I slide my arms around her shoulders, and she leans into my chest for a hug.

A long minute passes. I'm about to pull away when her body heaves in my embrace. When I move her away to take a look at her face, something soaks into my shirt at my chest.

She's been crying.

Her tears tell me everything I need to know. She's chosen to make herself vulnerable to me, and I can't fuck this up.

"I know you've felt alone, and I've done nothing to make you feel differently. I don't know how to come back from all of this." I say my second sentence to myself, but Emilia answers me anyway.

"We start here."

Those three little words, spoken from her soft lips with her tears trailing over them, are all I need to hear tonight. This is everything I've ever wanted. Her. All of her.

In an instant, my anger is gone. I've pushed it away like it is nothing. It *is* nothing compared to how precious she is.

I move my palms to either side of her face, and we take each other in. I examine her flushed cheeks, watery eyes, and the smallest beauty mark near her eye I never noticed before. She's finally given me all of her, and I know I'll never have enough.

The only thing left unresolved between us tonight is this

ache I feel in my bones. I'm not close enough to her. I want more.

Her lips are the only thing I see, and when one tear strays too close to her mouth, I can't help but chase after it.

Before my lips find hers, her hands fist my shirt as she pulls me in. Soft moans escape her, and I swallow them whole. We stop only to breathe, and our eyes find each other at the same time.

A faint sound escapes her before she catches herself and smiles, and I return her grin with one of my own.

"That's a nice start." She touches her lips with her fingers, and I shift back to give her a little space. But I keep my hand on her to show her I'm not going anywhere.

"It is. I'll be honest. The first step isn't the one I am worried about—it's all of the others. Emilia, I can't promise I won't stumble, but I do promise I will always hold your hand, and I won't let you fall."

"I'd like that. I don't understand a lot about—um—all of this." As she gestures between us, it isn't lost on me that she's avoiding eye contact.

"Do you mean my ownership of you?" I feel myself settle at the change in topic as she nods her head. "While you may not be knowledgeable—yet—I do believe you have an inherent understanding, Emilia."

"What makes you think that?"

"Your curiosity, for one. You're asking questions. You want to know why you are the way you are, like it's something you caught and not something that has always been a part of you. You ran away to bury that part of you, and because you subconsciously realized I'm the one who brings it out in you. I'm the one who makes you want those things."

"You're giving me a lot to think about."

"Well, here's a little more: I'm confident I can give you

what you need. You have a deep desire for things you may think aren't acceptable, but I want to show you how wonderful those things are. And I will make you want those things, Emilia. I won't let you leave here until I've shown you just how deep and beautiful your darkness is."

I scan her face for signs of disagreement, and I'm not surprised there are none. "I want all of you, Emilia. Set everything aside for the rest of the week and give me every part of you. It won't always be a painless process; the act of growing beyond who you think you are isn't always easy, but it is worth it. Will you do that for me?"

"How do you feel about these last two days, Emilia?" Joshua lifts a fork of chicken from my plate, and I lean forward to take a mouthful.

Chewing my food offers me time to consider his question. These last two days have been carefree. That's the best word I can use to describe it. We've had many talks about our past and how we feel now.

He listened as I spoke about my time away at school, and I learned about his work at the company and his personal life. I spent the last two days naked and learning about some of the items in Joshua's dresser drawer. I had no idea some of them can bring both pleasure and pain, and if I'm being honest with myself, I'm not sure which I like more.

Joshua asked me about my last few years of high school, and he offered up information about himself freely.

We spoke honestly about how we felt about each other, including our hatred. At first it was hard to hear and say, but as we delved into deeper, darker parts of our souls, it became freeing to let go. There were tears—mostly mine, but I wasn't entirely alone. I learned to read Joshua better, and I saw a new emotion emerge on his beautiful face: regret.

All of this time, I wasn't suffering and struggling alone. We both pushed away the one thing we needed. The lives we lived always worked against us, and alone, we crumbled. Without the support of the other, we both fell into our own hells. We realized that I may have run away physically, but he ran away emotionally.

We stayed away from a few topics—his mother being one of them. I could sense him guide the conversation elsewhere when it got close. I'm in no hurry to talk about her; I don't know if we are strong enough to weather that potential storm yet. I sense he is struggling with his own demons where she is concerned, and I've decided not to attack her anymore. She is his mother, and she will always be a part of him. That is all in the past, and I want to start looking toward our future.

"I feel good about them, Joshua. I never thought we would be at this place. I still think I'm imagining it sometimes."

Chuckling at my answer, he scoops up some potatoes and reaches across again. Before I take the bite, I say, "I never knew you were such a good cook. Don't tell Sylvia, but this is the best roast chicken I've ever had."

His eyes light up at my compliment. "Thank you. Actually, it was Adam and Sylvia who taught me how to cook. A few years ago, I asked them to teach me a few things."

Asking for help is not a strength of Joshua's. It never has been. I'm happy he had a strong relationship with my dad.

The potatoes feel like they are expanding in my mouth, and my eyes fill with tears at the thought of my missed time with both of them. I struggle to swallow.

"Are you okay?" Concern replaces Joshua's smile.

"I'm fine. Thank you. Just remembering my dad." I lift the napkin to my lips, then drop it onto the plate to indicate I am full. I try to change the subject. "Um, Joshua? I'm not complaining, but why do I have clothes on?"

He pauses for a moment, then chuckles, and my lips pull into a smile at the sound of his laughter.

"You are so precious. I'll make a mental note about your naked preference." He adds a wink to his words. "You have a visitor coming by tonight for a visit."

"Is it Rosie?" I can't contain the hope in my tone as I reach for my glass of water.

"Not this time—you are still to have no contact until my time with you is over. However, I will let you know I've spoken to her, and I've told her you are fine and we are working a few things out. I've asked her to refrain from speaking with you this week."

"And she was okay with that?" I ask, a little too doubtfully, and his smile grows.

"She said she is looking forward to speaking with you at eight o'clock on Monday morning or she'll be—and I quote—*so far up in my grill*." His impression of her makes me smile again. "You have a really good friend in her, Emilia."

I nod in agreement, but before I can attempt a second guess, the doorbell rings. Joshua leaves the room, and I stay seated. We've already been over his expectations about following or staying, and he made no motion for me to join him, so I'll gladly stay where I am.

I know who it is instantly when I hear her engaging lilt from the hall, and I'm both excited and nervous to speak with her. The last time I saw Alexandra, I wasn't in a good place.

The thought of being bought by anyone other than Joshua sends chills down my spine.

Alexandra has a way of lightening a room just by entering it. She smiles warmly when she sees me seated at the table, and I can't help but smile in return.

"Emilia, I've invited Lexa over for a visit. She wanted to see how you were doing here—with everything." As Joshua speaks, Alexandra crosses the room to stand beside me. I rise to greet her, unsure of what to do and thankful as I see her reach out for a hug.

Her embrace is warm, loving. "I hope you don't mind." Her eyes scan my face as she speaks.

"Not at all. I'm happy to see you. Can you join us?" I gesture to the seat across from me, and she removes her scarf as she walks over to it.

"Actually, it will just be the two of you tonight." Joshua pauses, and I notice the confused look on Alexandra's face. He must notice it too, because he offers an explanation: "Noah texted earlier, asking if we could meet for drinks to discuss some things. I thought you would both appreciate time alone to talk and get to know each other."

I meet Alexandra's eyes, and her smile is huge. She looks like I feel. I'd love to get to know her better. Having someone in this lifestyle who is not Joshua or Noah is making me feel more comfortable already.

We've both come so far in just a couple of days—Joshua would never have allowed me to speak with Alexandra alone on Sunday night, and I don't blame him.

He needed to take charge of me that night. I had no control of my own left, and I was sinking into nothing. That's all he's ever done when he's watched me stumble. The only thing we were missing was an open line of communication and trust in each other. And he's giving it to me now.

"I'd love that. Thank you, Joshua," I answer, and I stand to clear our plates before he raises his hand.

"I'll take those. This was my dinner for you, remember? Can I get you each a glass of wine?" he asks, catching me off guard.

I've become accustomed to our dynamic. Taking comfort in obeying Joshua has given me a peace I haven't had in a long time. A hint of panic sets in at the thought of returning to our old ways, and I look up to Joshua for some guidance. Meeting my eyes, he pauses, and his face falls for a fraction of a second before it quickly returns.

"Make no mistake, Emilia: You are still under my ownership. You can have two glasses of wine with Alexandra. Have a glass of water after each one. You may talk about anything you'd like, but you may not talk to anyone else. I expect you in bed no later than ten, and you are to remove your clothes after she leaves. And make sure the door is locked behind her. Do you understand?"

My cheeks warm at my instructions. I'm not embarrassed by them. I'm centered, and I nod my understanding and thank him as he turns his attention to Alexandra. "Emilia does not have her phone on her. If you need me while I am out, please text. Otherwise, I will assume you two are enjoying yourselves. If there is nothing else, I will get you that wine and clear these plates. Have a good night, ladies."

Alexandra nods, and Joshua wastes no time taking our plates into the kitchen and returning to fill our glasses. Without lingering further, he gives me a secret smile and a wink and leaves the room. Seconds later, the front door opens and closes, and he's gone.

The aroma from the wine tickles my nose as I take my first sip. This is a reward of sorts—the visit with Alexandra and the wine. I know it is. Since I asked Noah to leave a couple of nights ago, we've spent our time putting in as much effort as we can to understand ourselves and each other. Joshua was right: it hasn't been easy on either of us, but the light at the end of our tunnel shines brighter with every step.

"How are you doing with your arrangement, Emilia?" Alexandra sips her wine and leans forward in her chair.

"It's been an interesting few days, but I think I am doing well. I am better than I was on Sunday night, if that helps." I lean back in my chair to get comfortable.

"It does." Her eyes drop to her glass for a moment, and when she looks back up, her face has fallen into concern. "You should know I was the one who told Joshua you were at Ravenous. It is against procedure, but I was really worried for you. Can you forgive me for betraying your trust like that?" Her eyes are wide with worry, and it takes me a few seconds before I find the words to respond.

"Being mad at you never crossed my mind. You need to understand: I wasn't in a good place when I walked through your doors. I was scared, and I felt alone. When I saw you, I was embarrassed. I felt ashamed, but I wasn't mad at you. I was mad at myself and Joshua, but things have changed. I guess I'm thankful that you looked out for me. Things would be very different for me right now if you hadn't told Joshua where I was."

Alexandra's eyes roam around the table, then back up to meet my own as she shifts in her seat. "That can't be easy to admit, Emilia. I have to say, I'm impressed with your self-awareness and your openness to discuss yourself like this."

"It isn't easy, but we promised each other we would try."

"Because of your agreement?" she challenges.

"Because Joshua and I owe it to each other and ourselves. Because burying what tears us down only hinders our growth." My answer surprises both of us.

All of this time, I considered Joshua my worst enemy when it was always me. I hurt myself. I ran away, a few times. I pushed Joshua away. I shut my doors, and I was hell-bent on never opening them again. I locked out my own happiness because I was so afraid of letting in some pain as well.

"I couldn't have said that better myself. I won't pry. How you both are exploring your arrangement is your own business. But I will say, I see a stronger part of you emerging, and I love it. Don't get me wrong, I thought you were amazing to begin with, but this new growth is inspirational. I must admit, you are bringing out a different side to Joshua as well. It's more of a maturity—that's not the right word. It's a deeper understanding of himself in his role. I've never met anyone yet who has been able to move him beyond where he was." Her words make me blush. "I know your father is proud of you, Emilia."

I feel a sadness wash over me. "How do you know? I feel like I messed so many things up. I should have talked to him more."

As I speak, Alexandra moves into my father's old chair and reaches out for my hand. "I know because he said it all of the time. He told me you reminded him of your mother. He said you were a force, just like her. He loved your mom with everything in his heart, and you were their greatest creation."

As she speaks, I can't hold back the tears, but I smile through them. I miss my parents so much, but somehow, hearing this is bringing me peace.

"I guess I know that. I was more worried about my connection with Joshua and some of these new things." I hope my words infer I am talking about the types of things Joshua is teaching me.

Alexandra takes a long look at me. I get the sense she is wrestling with something as she opens her mouth to speak, then closes it again. I raise my eyebrows, silently asking her to tell me.

"Your father once told me that the wrong Connor met the wrong Darkly."

I scramble to decode her words, and she takes another approach.

"As difficult as Adam's marriage to Cordelia was, he was always grateful it brought Joshua into your lives. It tore him apart that you two fought so much, but he saw something. He loved Joshua like a son, and he knew everything about him. Everything. Adam asked Joshua to be your guardian because he truly felt you were what was best for each other."

"You knew about the will?"

Alexandra nods. "Your father and I shared everything, but it is none of my business where you and Joshua are concerned. My only concern is that you are happy, and you are safe."

She pauses to take a sip of her drink. Then, nodding to herself as though she's made a personal decision, she puts her drink on the table and continues, "Your father was the love of my life, Emilia. I'd never known what it meant to lose a piece of myself until the day Joshua called to tell me he was gone. And all of this brought me to you. Every bit of praise, every wonderful thing he told me about you is true. When I look at you, I see his love, his kindness, and sometimes his stubbornness." We share a smile. "I know you are exploring some new things about yourself, and I just want to say I hope we can be friends, close friends."

She lets my hand go and takes another sip of her wine, swallowing it hard as she blinks rapidly. I know what she's doing—I'm doing it too. But neither of us can keep the tears in, and my own eyes start to tear.

"I want that." It's too late for me to do the blink trick. On my first attempt, fat tears fall out of my eyes and down my cheeks, and I reach for a napkin. "I'm sorry."

"Don't be. But now you did it." I look up to see her own tears rolling down her face, and we both exchange a soft laugh.

I feel like my life is filling back up. I always had Sylvia and

Rosie, but now Joshua and Alexandra are here, and what had become a family of one is expanding again.

As our emotions settle, I decide to change the subject and do what Joshua suggested we do: get to know each other.

"Alexandra, can you tell me more about Ravenous? I'd like us to get to know each other better." I raise my glass, and she clinks hers against mine in celebration of our newfound friendship.

"I would love to. But first: please, call me Lexa."

"How is Emilia?" The words are out of Noah's mouth right after his greeting.

"Can't a guy get his jacket off and order a drink first?" I try to buy some time and raise my hand, catching the waiter's attention.

Noah leans back into his seat, easing off for now. The waiter approaches, and I make it easy on him by ordering a couple of beers and telling him that's it for the night.

Noah and I have many things to discuss. I don't need to waste any of this waiter's time, and I sure don't need him wasting mine.

"Look, I actually want to talk about Emilia for a change, but it has to wait. Tell me what's happening at work."

Noah looks over his shoulder to make sure we're alone. "We have a meeting tomorrow morning at the office you need to be present for. It turns out Keith caught wind we were pulling files from HR, and he asked for a meeting with me today. He knew exactly what we were looking for, and he doesn't want any part of it. He wants out, and he wants to talk."

"What did you say?" I ask. Noah opens his mouth as the waiter comes back with our beers. Thinking better of it, he thanks the waiter and waits to answer until we are alone at our table.

"I told him the conversation needs to be on record. He didn't want to at first, but I told him our investigation would continue with or without him. He knows he's in deep. He doesn't want to keep sinking. He agreed, and we set the meeting for tomorrow morning. I told him you and our lawyers would be present; I've already contacted them. I told Jim to bring anything he would like to add." Noah takes a gulp of his beer as I let everything sink in.

I'm mid-thought when my phone vibrates in my pocket, and I check it in case it is Lexa. It isn't, and I decline the call and place the phone down.

"Do you need me to do anything before the meeting?"

"Between the lawyers, myself, and all of the hard work that Faye has been doing, we pretty much have everything we need. I had to tell Faye what was going on. I thought she should know in case anyone started asking her who the new people in the office were. She asked if it had to do with Emilia running off on Friday night. I told her it was partially related. Faye has a soft spot for Emilia. As soon as she heard that, she was all hands on deck." Noah chuckles, and I'm happy Emilia has more people in her corner than she realizes. "All you need to do is show up. I've scheduled him for nine thirty. We meet with the lawyers at nine."

"Okay. Thank you for managing all of this. I can't tell you how much I appreciate it." My phone vibrates on the table a second time, disrupting my train of thought.

"Do you need to get that? Is it Emilia?"

I lift the phone once more to check who it is, but a nagging thought at the back of my mind tells me I already know, and

I'm right. I can ignore one call, but if I don't answer the second, it might escalate, and this is one person I don't want showing up at my home when Emilia is there and I'm not.

I glare at the screen, then fire off a quick text saying I'm in an important work meeting and I will call as soon as I can. Then I drop the phone back onto the table.

My mood suddenly sours.

"It's my mother. I froze our joint account today; she must have found out." I take another gulp of my beer, hoping to get rid of the bad taste in my mouth.

"Does that mean you got the financial information you were looking for?"

"Actually, I haven't gotten anything back yet. This time, I decided to listen to my little voice and trust Emilia. I haven't said anything to her yet; I've been trying to avoid the topic of Cordelia because I know it upsets her. And I'm trying to square my thoughts on the whole thing. Is it odd that a big part of me knows that Emilia was telling the truth all along and my own mother has been lying to me? I mean, she lied and took all of my bonus money from me for years. I think the thing that surprises me most about all of this is how, now, I'm not surprised. Once the walls that kept me from trusting Emilia started coming down and I gave her truth the weight it deserved, I see everything in complete clarity. I already know what I'm going to find out about my mother, and it won't surprise me one bit. You call that crazy, right?"

"I call that an epiphany, maybe. Definitely growth. Emilia is good for you. I'm happy you both have been able to set aside your perceptions of each other. Speaking of which." Noah allows his words to linger, a silent suggestion that now is a good time to start talking.

"Speaking of which," I say mockingly. "We are doing well. Better than well—we are in a good place right now."

"*Good?* I'd say it's better than that. Your sub put herself in her place and threw me out of your house on my ass. That had to have felt pretty damn nice." He finishes his beer and catches the waiter's attention.

"That part was fantastic, actually." I snicker as Noah laughs and orders water for us.

"And how are you?" A serious undertone returns to his words.

I know what he's trying to get at. I've been wrestling with the inevitable end of our contract.

I've lost count of the number of times I've had to silence my demons over the last forty-eight hours. Our time is coming to an end, and I need to stay focused. I can't allow my fear of losing Emilia to take over my actions. Learning to release myself to trust in Emilia has been a huge milestone, and I can't let go of that.

"I won't lie; It's taking everything I have to live in the moment. I was so focused on owning her that I lost sight of earning her and deserving her."

Noah stares, dumbfounded, at my response. He's completely unaware of the waiter dropping off our drinks. After a long silence passes, he says, "Who are you, and what have you done with Joshua?"

"Jackass."

"Ah, there you are." He chuckles. "But seriously. Wow. I like this Joshua a lot. But don't tell the other Joshua, because he'll kick my ass."

"This one might too."

Time flew by too quickly once I started talking about Emilia. What used to be a rushed conversation flowed easily. I love talking about her, and I find myself more open to Noah's advice where she is concerned.

My mother texted me twice more, reminding me to return her call, and in the end, I didn't have it in me to deal with her tonight. Sending one last text, I told her it was too late, and I would call her tomorrow.

By the time I reach my room, it is almost eleven, and the house is quiet. Emilia has cleared away the plates and washed everything in the kitchen.

The bedroom door opens without a sound, and my eyes immediately focus on the bed. One thin sheet barely covers Emilia's lower body, and a jolt runs through me at the sight of her naked form.

I have yet to bury myself deep inside her, giving us both what has been building between us, but the time we've spent growing together over this week has been worth it.

Still, my cock stirs and my balls ache at the sight of her nipples forming the smallest bumps.

It's only a matter of time.

Slowly, I step around the bed to give her a kiss on the forehead, and that's when I notice it.

The metal chain that connects to the bed has been fastened to the loop on her collar. I didn't ask her to do this. She chose to bind herself to our bed, and I feel my cheeks stretch wide in a ridiculous smile.

The more I let go of her and trust her to find herself, the more she looks to me for guidance and gives herself to me.

This is a lesson that took way too long for me to learn.

CHAPTER 66
EMILIA

I woke up this morning feeling more secure than I have in a long time. After Lexa left last night, I removed my clothes as Joshua instructed and rushed through the cleanup in the kitchen. I worked faster than I needed to, and I found myself upstairs in Joshua's room almost an hour before he told me to be there.

Butterflies swirled in my stomach when my eyes landed on the chain he used to bind me to the bed. As I traced the metal links, I felt his pull deep in my belly.

The more freedom Joshua gives me, the more I don't want it. It doesn't compare to the liberation I experience when I am his.

I was in bed a half an hour before it was required of me, but I couldn't sleep. My thoughts kept running wild over the events of last week and Joshua not being at home. In a desperate attempt to stifle my brain and get some rest, I reached for the chain and clipped it onto my collar, testing its connection with a satisfying tug. I don't remember anything after that, I must have finally drifted off, and I didn't wake up until Joshua's alarm went off this morning.

"I need to go into the office this morning," he said. "Some things have happened this week, and one of Brent's friends, a coworker, has asked to meet with us. He wants to come clean about his part in what has been happening at the office."

His words hit me with a flurry of emotion. Could he really be willing to speak out? Or is he being sent in there to try to cover things up for his buddies?

Joshua asked if I wanted to be present for the conversation. I asked his opinion, as I'm not sure I would be ready if it didn't go the way I want it to. He must have sensed my apprehension, and he responded by saying he supports any decision I make. But he suggested I sit this one out, as they are still gathering information, and it might go better if I wasn't there. I agreed, and that is why I'm now sitting here naked, on the floor of the study, in a position Joshua taught me.

I'm not supposed to get into position for another half an hour, but I began to feel anxious about their meeting, and this helped calm my nerves.

It helps me feel close to Joshua when he isn't here.

My mind drifts to an alternate future. What would have happened if I hadn't run off during the awards dinner? Would Brent still be terrorizing me? Joshua and I wouldn't be where we are now; we would still be working against each other. I would still feel defeated and alone, and I would still be pushing down an important side of me. I wouldn't know this deeper level of love and trust.

Love.

Do I love Joshua? Have I always?

Is this what I've fought so hard, what I've run away from?

And what happens after this week is done?

Sooner or later, I need to step back into the real world that is still going on outside of this house. Joshua and I have come a long way, but is our foundation strong enough to weather what may come?

In truth, if nothing had changed, I would still be fighting my guardianship under Joshua, and I would despise him for it. But now everything is different. I don't see his ownership as something that holds me back. His authority gives me a clarity I've never known.

"What the hell is going on?" I'm jolted out of my thoughts by Cordelia's shrill voice echoing off the walls of the study.

Disoriented, I freeze as my brain struggles to catch up. Standing in the doorway to the study is Joshua's mother, and the disgusted look on her face ignites my shame.

"Cordelia, what are you—" My words drop off as I try to stand. Then realize I was just kneeling naked, waiting for Joshua, and I try to cover myself with trembling hands.

"Is this what you've been doing? Trying to turn Joshua against me by whoring yourself out? You just wait until I tell Tawny what you've been doing." Shrieking her disdain at me, I suddenly realize she isn't coming into the room, and I have no way of escape. She's blocking my only way out.

"P-please—I..." I glance around and run toward the window, wrapping myself in one of the heavy curtains as panic sets in.

I know I locked the door today. Right after Joshua left. I remember locking it.

Did Joshua let her in?

I discard the question as soon as it enters my head. He wouldn't. She must have a key.

"All this time, you played the poor, innocent victim. What's the matter? Joshua still doesn't believe you? Do you think spreading your legs will change his mind?" I've never heard

Cordelia cackle before, but then again, I haven't been alone with her since the divorce.

"It's not what it looks like. Please leave and let me get to my room." My voice sounds meeker than I'd like it to, and she stays where she is, placing her hands on her hips.

"So you're the reason then?" Her sneer leaves her face, replaced by a cold glare.

"I don't understand." As I clutch the fabric around my body, the room suddenly feels cold.

"What did you say to Joshua about me, you slut?"

Something has happened between Joshua and Cordelia. I don't know what it is, but judging by her rage, she feels like it's my fault.

"I didn't say anything to him. I—" I push my body against the window behind me as she takes a few steps into the room, but I still can't get past her.

"Save it. He didn't believe your lies then, and he won't believe them now. I'm his mother. Who do you think he's going to listen to?" She grabs at the fabric near her neck in a feigned attempt at playing the victim.

"I don't know what you're talking about. Please leave." I'm just shy of pleading now.

"Why should I? It's only a matter of time before Joshua tires of your *lies*."

"I never lied." My patience is gone. I know I told myself I would bury my hatred for Cordelia for Joshua's sake, but this is different. I still need to stand up for myself.

"No. That's right, you didn't," she almost sings, catching me off guard. "But he will never believe you. It'll always be your word against mine, his own mother's. You're nothing more than a spoiled little brat. He'll grow tired of you constantly lying about me, and he will cut you loose. You'll lose this company just like your father should have all of those years ago, and all of his money will eventually become mine."

"Is that so?" Joshua stands in the doorway, blocking both of us in, and I watch the color drain from Cordelia's cheeks before she plasters a smile back onto her face.

"Joshua. I didn't hear you come in. I caught Emilia in here—like this. Joshua, she's got no clothes on." Her disbelief and my current naked state make me drop my head. I'm humiliated, ashamed—and in front of Cordelia, no less. I hold the curtains tighter around me.

"Then she's doing what I told her to. What are you doing here?" He draws her attention away from me and onto him. He's challenging her to share her disgust with him instead, and she backs down.

"When you didn't return my calls, I thought I would drop by to talk. What do you mean you told her to?"

"Emilia is none of your concern. Mother, you live three hours away. You didn't just happen to be in the neighborhood."

"Well, no. But our account is frozen; I couldn't take anything out yesterday."

Now that the conversation is about money, I may as well be a ghost. Cordelia is only interested in me when it serves her.

"I froze the account. You won't be needing any more of my money. You never actually needed it, did you?"

"How much of our conversation did you hear?" she asks cautiously before digging herself in deeper.

"Enough," he answers flatly, waiting for her response.

"Joshua. You know Emilia has a history of lying to you about me." My anger boils into my face, heating up my cheeks, and I'm about to defend myself when Joshua speaks.

"I said ENOUGH. As in, I've had enough of your lies, Cordelia. You are disrespecting Emilia in her own home, and I won't allow it." The ire he aims at his mother shocks us both, and Cordelia stumbles over her words.

"B-but, Joshua—"

His hand shoots up between them, demanding silence. "That is enough. How did you get in?"

"You gave me a spare set of keys. Um..." She pulls out her key ring and fumbles to show him the one she used. "Do you want it back?"

"No. That's not necessary. I'll be calling a locksmith to replace all of the locks on the property as soon as you leave—which is right about now." He doesn't leave anything open for discussion, just crosses his arms across his chest and steps to the side so she can excuse herself.

As she takes a step toward the door, he places himself in front of her, and hope returns to her face.

"You owe Emilia an apology."

"What? What for?" I know Cordelia. She cannot utter any kind words to me. This is more than a punishment for her. This is just shy of a death sentence.

"What for? Let's start with you lying all of this time. Throwing her—a child at the time—under the bus to cover up your infidelities. Constantly turning me against her with nothing but more lies. But you know what? I came home today only to see Emilia, and I don't want you here any longer than you need to be. So I'll settle with you apologizing for the disrespect you've shown her in her own house. She is not in the wrong here—you are. Apologize. Now."

When Cordelia's face returns to mine, she is a shell of the person she was only a few moments earlier. In the frenzy of emotion, I almost forgot I was standing here naked and clutching the curtains for modesty.

She will never like me. The lies she told run deep into her

soul, and she truly believes it is me who destroyed her life. Her own choices still have nothing to do with it for her.

"I apologize for bursting into your home and disrespecting you like this." It isn't lost on me that she hasn't said my name, nor has she actually looked into my eyes. She's staring somewhere over my left shoulder, probably out the window behind me.

"Th-thank you," I mutter as I meet Joshua's gaze.

He's angry, but it feels different this time. He isn't angry at me. He's protecting me.

Cordelia turns back around. Humbled, she lowers her gaze to the floor and slinks past Joshua. Before she can reach the front door, Joshua spins to look at her.

"One last thing. Going forward, when you speak to or about Emilia, you speak to or about me. I'll take any disrespect toward her personally. Do you understand?"

I don't hear her response from the other room, but I know Joshua is satisfied by it. The door closes, and I feel as though, somehow, Cordelia has taken that chapter of my life with her.

Joshua steps into the study and sets his attention back on me with a mischievous smile.

"Hiding what is mine, Emilia?"

My body reacts to his words. My head drops shyly to my shoulder, and I step out from my hiding place, leaving the cover of the curtains behind. Then I shuffle to the spot on the floor he wanted me in when he got home, and I kneel down, resting my palms on my thighs. I straighten my back just like he taught me and look him in the eye.

He told me our eye contact is the most important thing to him.

Stepping in front of me, he crouches down and brushes his fingers around my breast. Then he pinches my nipple while keeping his eyes on mine, and I stay still, staring back. The memory of his mother's visit is a distant thought. We are here alone together, and that is all that matters.

"I love you like this, Emilia. Never be ashamed. You belong to me, and I will always protect you." I can't help the muscles stretching my face into a wide smile. "I apologize for that intrusion. I did not know she would come here. It does raise the issue of your safety, but I will deal with that."

Joshua straightens and sits down on the couch, patting the empty space beside him. It's a silent invite to join him by his side. "You may speak freely."

"You found out about your mother?" I feel like I'm built out of questions now.

"Not in the way you think. When I began to trust what you were saying was true, many other things made sense. I requested those files, but I haven't gotten them back yet. In the back of my mind, I just knew you were right. I cut her off yesterday. Listening to her today made me sick. I am so sorry for all of our lost time."

"I feel the same way, but our lost time is because of me. I think we need to forgive ourselves as much as we need to forgive each other."

"In many ways, I know I don't deserve you, Emilia. But I will."

I'm in no mood to allow Cordelia to ruin our day, so I ask a new question. "What happened at the office today?"

Joshua eyes me, then a small smile creeps across his face. "It's the beginning of the end. Keith caught wind of what we were looking for, and he sat down with us to tell us what he knows in exchange for us not pressing charges against him. He also talked Chad into talking. The lawyers were there, too. We have everything we need to proceed with Brent and Sean."

As he speaks, he pulls me in and combs his fingers through my hair. "It turns out that Brent and Sean were blackmailing them into helping increase their sales numbers. They held what they did to you over their heads and got them to falsify some reports. They said they would take them down as well if they were ever caught. I was there for the first part of the meeting, but Noah stayed behind with the lawyers to video their confessions and list their offenses. Our meeting with Sean and Brent is tomorrow afternoon. We told them to bring legal representation. This is it."

"You've had a busy day," is all I manage to answer. My head is spinning, and I feel overwhelmed.

"We both have. I need to ask, Emilia. Do you want to be there when we speak to Brent and Sean?"

Less than a month is all it took to turn my whole world upside down, and I have Emilia to thank for that.

In that time, I've found my place as much as she's found hers. We still have a lot to explore and learn, but now, because of her, I am a better version of myself. Because of her, I've learned the awful truth about Cordelia, and because of her, we are sitting on a mountain of evidence against two people who have been defrauding our company for years.

No one has said a thing to each other since our initial greeting. The lawyers are seated together, reviewing paperwork, no doubt going over everything we need for when Sean and Brent get here. Noah is seated off to the side with his own pile of papers and a notepad, and two security guards are seated by the door.

I have a notepad in front of me, and I've leaned forward to write a couple of things down, but my mind is elsewhere. Stealing yet another glance off to my side, I watch Emilia out of the corner of my eye.

She didn't hesitate last night when I asked her if she

wanted to be present. Her confidence in our dynamic soared when she watched me deal with my mother in front of her, and I couldn't be happier. Except, as the minutes tick by, I sense an unease settle into her.

Her slender fingers keep reaching for the neck of her sweater. I worry the collar that's hidden under the turtleneck is too much for her today, so I keep watching her.

Closing her eyes, she sucks in a deep breath and runs her fingers over the fabric where her collar is. She sighs, and a hint of a smile covers her lips.

It's not too much for her. This situation is too much; her collar is calming her.

We've already spoken at great length about today. She doesn't have to say anything if she doesn't wish to, and if she is spoken to and doesn't want to respond, all she has to do is remain silent, and I will take over the conversation for her. I've already told her how strong she is, not just for this, but for everything.

"Security just called; Mr. Garner and Mr. Davis are on their way up." Faye looks around the room, and the men stir at her announcement.

"Thank you, Faye. Show them in, then take a seat in the back corner."

Faye nods then closes the door. I've already asked her to be present and record her own notes in case we miss anything.

Leaning into Emilia's space, I whisper, "How are you?"

She startles a little, showing her nerves, but she settles quickly. "I think I'm okay, actually. A bit nervous, but I think it's just the waiting," she whispers back, subconsciously touching the fabric over her collar again. I smile, alerting her to what she is doing, and she smiles back.

Our little secret.

"Just remember, any time you want to leave, just stand up and walk out. We are all here for you."

Her eyes roam around the room at the team we've assembled, and she smiles again. "We've got this." She includes me. It isn't her. It isn't me. It's us—it is *we*.

"Yes, *we* do," I answer as the door opens, and in walk Brent and Sean.

I notice a stark difference between the two as soon as I see them. Sean's eyes are wide, and he immediately scans our team of lawyers and the security on either side of the door. He knows what he's done.

But not Brent. His eyes thin into slits, and his gaze immediately settles on Emilia as though he's ready to pounce and devour her alive.

Standing, I rein in my desire to jump across the room and choke Brent until he passes out.

"Gentlemen, thank you for meeting with us today. Have your lawyers reviewed everything we've sent over?" The lawyers exchange nodding glances with each other, but I need to hear it from Brent and Sean.

"Yes." Sean looks like he wants to vomit, and Brent only nods. He reminds me of a poker player. Holding his emotions close to his chest until he hears what we have to say.

"Great. Take a seat." I motion to the chairs we've set up, and the sound of papers shuffling fills the room. Everyone prepares their notes, except for Brent and Emilia. His eyes rake over her, and a possessive urge rises inside of me. I know he has no claim over her—my anger is building because his lecherous leers have caused her to look down, and I can't wait for this meeting to be done so I can check in with her.

I start by introducing the lawyers, then Jim takes over, officially covering the list of infractions we've uncovered. Sean's eyes drift to the ground. I've purposely asked Jim to leave a few things out at the beginning, to see how deep they will dig to try to get free, and it looks like Sean is ready to accept his fate.

As the conversation continues, I take a moment to remember these two in high school. Sean was always more of a follower. It was no secret that his dad started drinking after he was laid off from Connor Realty, and he was verbally abusive toward his son. I wonder if he ever felt his father's fist during those times. I was a few years older, so I don't know much more about them.

If his home life deteriorated, I could see him clinging to his friendship with Brent. But Brent is another story. His family didn't suffer during the layoffs. His mother owned a successful business, so his parents just became partners after the layoff and decided to expand.

Brent's reasons for "making Emilia pay" had nothing to do with layoffs or money or hardship. Judging by his disgusting stare, his interest was solely about her, and it always has been. He used the layoffs as justification for his abuse.

There is no justification.

As our lawyer continues laying out our case, almost everyone in the room has their heads down. Most are taking notes. Sean can't look anyone in the eye, and Brent is still staring Emilia down. Knowing what I know now, this is as close as he will get to violating her again. The tension in his glare is making me sick.

I have to hand it to Adam: He hired the best law firm. Jim and his team have covered almost everything we need, and Emilia and I haven't had to say a thing. I glanced over to Faye a couple of times as she feverishly took notes, and I saw her mouth drop open in shock once. That look said it all.

Brent and Sean sit quietly while they are notified of their immediate termination. Their lawyers hand over their credentials and access cards, and Noah promptly takes them.

When the legal ramifications come up, Sean becomes agitated.

"What do you mean, legal action?" Sean asks his lawyer in a shaky voice, and Jim steps in to clarify the severity of their situation.

"Mr. Garner, this isn't a simple termination. You weren't just consistently late; I just spent fifteen minutes outlining your blatant abuse of this company. You and Mr. Davis have forged reports and committed benefits and payroll fraud. There are instances of asset misappropriation, bribery, and harassment. You will be brought up on charges, and you will both see the inside of a courtroom. This isn't over. Your termination is only the start."

The color drains from Sean's face as Jim spells out his dire future for him.

As Jim prepares to wrap up, Brent speaks for the first time, but it isn't aimed at any of us. It's all for Emilia.

"You can't prove anything. It's your word against ours. You drop the harassment charges, or I'll personally take you to court for damages, Fee—Ms. Connor." His disdain for her is palpable, and the men in the room stare dumbfounded at his outburst. It isn't lost on me that he almost used the name he calls her.

There are so many things I would like to do to Brent right now. My top option involves drawing blood from his face, but I can't let him derail our focus. I won't let him make Emilia feel like she is alone, nor will I give him any chance to claim the role of victim here.

Leaning forward, I tap a couple of keys before pointing at the big screen hanging in the room.

Sean looks embarrassed as he realizes the filing room had cameras; Brent looks livid.

Even without sound, Brent grabbing Emilia causes everyone in the room to gasp. Everyone looks visibly disturbed except Brent as he watches himself violate Emilia. Faye gasps, but Emilia stays stone still. I had already asked for her permission to play the video if it was necessary, and she agreed.

Sean leans hard to his left, trying to place some distance between himself and Brent. I think he's realized that anchoring himself to his friend will only take him down deeper.

Stopping the footage, I don't say a word. Instead, I let my silence speak for itself for a change. I'm leering at Brent with the same intensity he had for Emilia, and he finally slinks back into his chair. I'm almost proud of my actions when I notice Emilia in my peripheral vision. She's staring him down herself, and she isn't looking away.

There's the Emilia I remember. She's strong. She's taken back her own control, and she isn't backing down.

For the first time, Brent breaks his glare and looks to his lawyer for backup.

"Gentlemen." His lawyer stands, and Brent stands along with him. "The termination portion of this meeting is complete. Jim, send me the final papers; we will sign them later today. We'll talk later about everything else. I need some time to speak with my client."

Surprisingly, Sean remains seated. I notice his lawyer has placed a hand on his arm, advising him not to join Brent. The two don't exchange any looks as our first security guard leads the way, and Brent follows his lawyer out, not daring to look back at Emilia.

As soon as they leave, Sean's lawyer stands and nods to our legal team. "Gentlemen, Ms. Connor, at this time, I will be advising my client to seek separate charges. Jim, I'll be in touch." He doesn't hesitate in vacating the office, followed closely by a somber Sean, who won't look anyone in the eye.

The muscles in my face have wound so tight that I need to take a deep breath to release some of the tension. I look around the silent room. I nod briefly to Faye, letting her know she can excuse herself, and she and Emilia exchange a kind glance.

I've asked Noah to oversee the acting positions in HR and finance until we can get back on track, and I excuse him so he can begin the official process of termination.

"Jim, I can't thank you enough for everything." I stand and attempt to move along everyone's exit. I want nothing more than to be alone with Emilia.

"It was all thanks to your staff. Noah and Faye were invaluable." He reaches out to shake my hand, and his attention moves to Emilia. "Ms. Connor. It is a pleasure to see you here. Have you and Mr. Darkly come to an arrangement I should know about?"

Emilia's eyes go wide, and I feel giddy at her innocence. She thinks he's talking about our private relationship, and I answer for her before she says anything she isn't ready to.

"Yes. We are working on that. Emilia and I will see you in your office on Monday morning, as you requested, to discuss the future of Connor Realty." Realization calms her features as she meets my gaze.

"Wonderful. I will wait until then. In light of his history of harassment against Ms. Connor, I would like to suggest adding a temporary restraining order against Mr. Davis." Jim's legal team waits for the decision, and I find myself pausing when Emilia answers.

"I think it is a good idea, Jim. Thank you." Graceful yet loaded with power, Emilia reaches her hand out to Jim, commanding the end of the conversation. I couldn't be prouder.

As everyone files out of the room, I notice Emilia crumple a bit as she turns to me with a big smile and a deep sigh.

"We did it."

"Yes, we did, but I need to say this: I couldn't have done this without you, Emilia. I'm so proud of you." My need to physically connect with her is intense. I take a step toward her, placing my hand on her shoulder, and she sinks into me, wrapping her arms around my midsection and burying her face into my chest.

As she steps out of our embrace, I pull a little box out of my pocket and hold it out to her. I know she knows what it is by the look on her face.

"Oh, Joshua. Thank you." She wastes no time opening it and hugging her mother's ring close to her heart.

"I wanted to give it to you this morning, but with everything going on, I forgot. You touched your collar earlier, and it reminded me. I should never have taken this from you, and I never will again." Her eyes glisten as she smiles. "How do you feel, Emilia?"

"I think I'm okay. I'm suddenly exhausted. It's not even noon yet, and I could take a long nap."

"That's understandable." I run my fingers through her hair, trying to catch a whiff of her scent. "I need to do a little bit of work here, then I have a surprise for you. But you need to be rested. I'll send you home with our driver. Set your alarm for five this evening, then take a shower. Sylvia is still away, so... you know the rule."

"Clothes off," she says, almost too eagerly.

"Clothes off. I'll see you downstairs for dinner at six. You are not to come down before then, no matter what you hear. Understood?"

"I understand."

"Good girl. Gather your things. I'll walk you to the car in case anyone is lingering downstairs. And, Emilia?" She turns to face me with wide-eyed interest.

"Get some sleep. You won't want to be tired tonight."

I remember locking the front door behind me. I watched the handle jiggle as Niko checked it from his side before driving himself back to the office. After that, exhaustion took over. My climb up the stairs to the bed was a bit hazy.

I slept soundly for four hours. Then the alarm buzzed, and as I sat up, I heard a faint rustling downstairs. Joshua was already home and busy doing something. My curiosity was definitely piqued, but I decided against sneaking down to see what it was. He gave me my instructions, and I gladly followed them.

Since I didn't have to waste any time picking out my clothes, I'm ready a whole ten minutes before he said I could go down. The anticipation is killing me. I traded pacing around the bedroom for sitting quietly at the top of the stairs as my mind wanders to all of the creative things he might be doing down there.

"I know you're there, Emilia. You can come down now." There's humor in his voice.

"I was being quiet. How did you know I was here?" I stay put.

"I can see your toes sticking out on the steps. Are you going to join me, or are you going to make me tell you again?" Behind the playfulness in his voice lies the hint of a threat, and I'm not sure I'm ready to test his patience yet.

A hungry smile inches across his face as I pull myself out of my hiding spot and descend the stairs toward him. As he reaches out his hand to take my own, my heart thuds into my chest.

His eyes dance over my body, and I am no longer shy in front of him. His inspection makes me giddy. Goosebumps appear on my arms, and a chill tickles up my spine as I step off the last step.

"Are you curious, Emilia?" His flirtatious tone makes my cheeks warm up.

"Yes, Joshua."

"I'm proud of you for staying upstairs. I have to admit, I thought you'd be trying to sneak around to see what I was doing." He runs his fingers through my hair, and I automatically lean into his touch. I'm surprised I haven't started moaning, it feels so good.

"Thank you. It wasn't easy." Considering my lack of experience in this lifestyle, I'm curious about everything.

"I imagine it wasn't. Before we start our evening, I need you to do one thing for me." He ends his sentence with a kiss on my head, and his fingers gently brush over my breast.

"Yes, Joshua?"

"I need you to go upstairs and get your pajamas on."

"Of course, Joshua. I—wait. What?" Snatched out of my lustful anticipation, I don't think I heard him right. But judging by the smug look on his face, I heard him crystal clear.

"I need you to go back upstairs and put on your pajamas.

Get into your coziest ones. I like the purple pants you wear with the stripes, and a tank top if you are comfortable."

"I don't understand. You said you wanted to see me naked."

He smiles at my confusion. "I always want to see you naked, Emilia. And I thank you for that." He gives me a sultry, slow wink. "But tonight, I want something else from you, and I want to give you something I should have long ago."

"And what is that?"

"My time." His tone turns a little somber. "We've both had an intense week, and our time is nearly up. Normally, this would make me freak out and look for a way to keep you."

"And now?"

"And now I realize how valuable every moment with you is. When we were younger, I pushed you away so many times. I don't blame you for not asking me to do things. A lifetime will never be enough time with you. It got me thinking about the times you wanted to see a movie and Rosie couldn't go, and you asked if you could tag along with Noah and me. I had no idea you didn't want to go on your own in case you ran into Brent or Sean, but that was why, wasn't it?"

I nod my head because it's partly true. I was so afraid of running into them that I gave up going out. But I also asked him because I wanted some time with him, and he never agreed.

Well, tonight, I decided what I want from you."

"What is it?"

"All I want is your presence. I cleaned out the theater room in the basement and bought as many movie channels and streaming packages as I could. I have pizza, soda, chips, and candy down there. I want to sink into that oversized couch with you and block out everything else. And if you get into your pajamas and make it back here before I do, you'll get to pick all of the movies we watch tonight. How does that sound?" He twirls my hair between his fingers then lets go, waiting for my response.

"That sounds—" I spin and take the steps two at a time, and I'm halfway up before he's realized I just stole a head start.

His feet thunder up the stairs behind me, and the rush of the chase burns through my veins.

"Oh, Ms. Connor, you know I'm always looking for a reason to punish you." A giggle flies out of my mouth at his threat, and I can't contain my laughter as I run down the hall and into his bedroom, closing, then locking, his door behind me.

He hits the door hard. I hear him mutter under his breath, and I run through the side door into my own room, where I begin tearing into my drawer as snickers and laughter flow freely.

The door to my room flies open, and he looks a little unhinged. I freeze in place and watch him take in the situation. Then his eyes focus on the pants in my hand.

My purple stripy pants.

Deciding against taking his precious time with me, he runs through the side door into his own room. My cheeks stretch into a ridiculous smile as I fumble with the waistband and pull the pants on.

Through my laughter and heavy breathing, I hear him running around his room. I'm overloaded with excitement as I start pulling tops from the drawer and showering them around the room as I look for the one I want when—BINGO!

I find the soft tank top I'm looking for and frantically run to my door as I pull it on over my head. Joshua's heavy footsteps approach as I run back down the hall, and he mutter profanities as I cackle my absolute delight—he's forgotten that the door is still locked from the inside, and I hit the top of the stairs as he unlocks it and pulls it open.

I glance over my shoulder; his smile is indescribable. He's

triumphant even though he's about to lose this race. But more than that, he looks elated.

I beat him to the bottom by four steps. He picks me up when he reaches me and spins us around. His chest booms with his own laughter, and my stomach hurts from laughing so hard. I have happy tears in my eyes.

"This, Emilia. This is everything I want."

I couldn't have said it better myself. I feel lost in a flood of emotion, and I can't think of one thing to say back when his arms tighten around me, and his lips find mine with a hunger that radiates.

As if the final piece of our puzzle has been set into place, my mouth opens, begging him to devour me whole. He lifts me just high enough that I can wrap my legs around his torso and link my arms around his neck.

My eyes close, and a moan escapes me as he moves me out of the room. I don't care where we're going as long as I'm with him.

I get the impression this isn't part of his plans for our evening, but this need has been building for years. I won't hold myself back any longer, and I pray his restraint is gone as well as he takes me into the darker depths of the house and turns on the light. My eyes scramble to recall the room we've ended up in.

It's been a long time since I was last down here, and it looks just as I remember it. Every Saturday night was family movie night. Mom started the tradition when I was just a kid, and we watched together every weekend until she passed away. After that, our hearts weren't into watching without her.

This time, my memories don't crush me like they used to. Now, with Joshua, I'm looking forward to new memories and new experiences with him.

I release my legs, dropping myself to the floor. Then I reach for his T-shirt and begin pulling it off him.

His eyes search mine. I know he's trying to decide if this is a good idea, and I'm so tired of appearances. If we only have this time left, then this is what I want. It's what I've always wanted. All of Joshua, with me and inside of me.

I've fantasized about him over and over again. As far and fast as I run, I can't escape my truth, and my truth is that this is the man I need.

"Please, just don't...stop." Desperate to keep our connection, I plead with him, and he doesn't hesitate.

He pulls my top off, spins me around, and pulls my back into his chest. Then he grips my neck while his free hand dives below my waistband, and I spread my legs for him.

He's holding me in place like a doll. I moan and gyrate against his fingers, feeling my slick need on his hands and no shame at all. When I arch my back to coax him deeper inside of me, his hard length pushes into my ass, and determination sinks in.

My need to please him grabs hold, and grind my hips back against his erection, coaxing a deep groan from him.

"Joshua, please," I beg again.

"Say that again," his husky voice growls into my ear.

"Please, Joshua. I want you to fuck me." As if entirely possessed by my need, I open my mouth and let my heart speak. "I need you." And it's the truest thing I've ever confessed.

After a flurry of spinning and the quick removal of pants, he pushes me deep into the couch and climbs on top of me. There was no planning for this; there were no preparations. I am his, and he is taking what he wants—we both are.

"This is your place, Emilia. You are mine. All of you." He centers himself at my entrance, and my impatience takes hold.

"Yes." Clawing my hands along his backside, I pull him into me. We moan in unison, and he pulls out easily before thrusting himself all the way in. I let out a cry, but I'm not in pain. My wail is the realization of my world coming together. This is my place, my home, and he is my owner—and I've never felt so secure or free.

Finding an intense rhythm, he pistons into me without effort. My wetness coats us both, and I open myself up to him. With each push, he hits a sensitive spot along my clit, and I arch and buck along with him.

He lifts himself off my chest, returns his hand to my throat, and wraps his fingers around my neck. As he continues to fuck into me, I crumble under his control.

A wolfish grin crosses his features as he watches me whimper underneath him. He knows who I am. He understands my needs, and he's the only one who can grant me this. I'm entirely vulnerable to him now, and the thought sparks a growing burn inside of me that I know I won't be able to control.

"I-I'm going to—holy shhhh..." My body is no longer my own. Joshua has complete authority over me now, and I tremble with the realization I am completely his. I always have been.

"Come, Emilia. I want to feel you come on my cock. I want to hear you."

After his words, everything fades away as my orgasm hits me, and I cry out his name. His length pulses deep inside of me, and he groans out his own release as his weight pushes us both into the couch.

I pant as we both struggle to steady our breathing, and our hearts beat in unison as we sink into each other.

I'd forgotten how comfortable this couch is.

Still sensitive, the aftershocks leave me in waves as his body shifts off of mine. He scans my face, and the expression on his own is unreadable.

"You are beautiful, Emilia." He sits up, pulls me onto his lap, and gently brushes his fingers along my body. "While I have no regrets, this wasn't my intention."

"I know. But I think it's something that's been lingering for a long time." He kisses the top of my head as his fingers trail through my hair. I decide to lighten the mood.

"Now I'm glad I took a nap." My head bumps on his chest against the force of his laughter. "And I don't know about you, but I'm suddenly starving."

I meet his gaze, and his smile brightens all of his features. "Well, it's a good thing I have pizza. I'll tell you what, we'll get dressed, and I'll set up the food while you pick out the first movie—although I'm still not sure if you won, considering you cheated."

"Ha. I didn't cheat."

"Really? What do you call it then?"

"Hmmm, outsmarting you, maybe." I wink, taunting him, as I pull on my pajama bottoms.

"Careful. I can't tell you how much I love the sound you make when I punish you. Now, pick out a movie and get comfortable."

CHAPTER 69
JOSHUA

"You're slouching," I observe as I take a bite of my salad.

"Sorry, Joshua." As Emilia straightens in her seat, her gaze returns to her plate. She's quickly learned to read me, and I smile.

"It's harder to hide these things when you're naked. I love looking at you. All of you." I fork another bite into my mouth and keep my eyes on her, enjoying the way she flushes.

In truth, her posture is fine. It doesn't matter to me one bit, but I've come to realize that Emilia enjoys correction when we are alone. It's a reminder of her place, it's a reminder that I care, and it arouses her to no end.

Her chest rises and falls, and each breath is a little deeper than the last. She shifts in her seat. I have no doubt she's wriggling her hips to ease the anticipation building inside of her.

She senses her own vulnerability. Her nipples have hardened, and I wonder what thoughts are playing out in her head.

"It's our last night together under the contract. I have twenty-four hours left with you, and I will spend them playing with you. I want to show you some things about yourself that you'll never be able to deny. There are some truths inside of you that need to be told before you decide your future. I will allow you to make one decision about what happens tonight." I stop and take another bite, chewing slowly to give her enough time to find the courage to ask her question.

"What decision, Joshua?" Solid eye contact. My fingers practically vibrate at the sight of her appetency.

"Is there anywhere in this house you do not wish to be subjugated in?"

Her mouth drops open at my question, but she quickly recovers, swallowing hard. "N-no. I'm good."

I smile at her response. Mostly because it is something a beginner would say. Her nerves must be getting the better of her; she doesn't understand what I'm asking.

"I'm going to help you out this one time, because you are new to your station and because I want you to enjoy this as much as I know I will. I want to expose you. I'll show you how depraved and intensely beautiful your desires are, and you'll beg for many things tonight. Is there anywhere in this house you would prefer I didn't do that? Your father's bedroom, maybe?"

She sucks in a deep breath as her eyes pop out, confirming my hunch that she thought it would only be happening right here. "Oh—right. I'm sorry, Joshua. I wasn't thinking. No, not in my father's room." She reaches for her glass of water, no doubt for her throat, which sounds like it's gone dry.

"Anywhere else?" I challenge, and she now takes a minute to consider it.

"No. The other rooms are fine. I'm okay." Her innocent smile is like a siren's song.

"Very well. I notice you picking at your plate. Are you full?"

She nods.

"Excuse yourself and kneel for me in your bedroom. Face your bed, and don't move until I tell you to. I'll be with you shortly." I take a gulp of my own water and watch her slowly rise. Bowing her head, she excuses herself and makes her way to the door.

"Emilia." She turns and waits. "I mean *your* bedroom. The one you had before you left for school."

The one where the nightmares happened.

She hesitates for a half a second too long. Since moving into her other room beside mine, I know she's tried hard to put that one out of her thoughts.

I've seen that room.

Adam didn't change a thing when she left. She put some blankets over her dresser, probably trying to forget those memories, but I've put everything back just the way she remembers it.

"Yes, Joshua." Stoically, she lifts her head and leaves the room. I imagine she is preparing herself for the onslaught of memories both good and bad, and that is where I will have her.

I wait until I no longer hear her footsteps. Then I make my way up to my own room and over to my dresser, pulling out my top drawer and tracing my fingers over the items I'm thinking about using.

I decide against the blindfold—that's for another time. She will watch every moment; she'll be a witness to and an accomplice in her submission.

I won't let her leave here without knowing who she is on a deep level. I'll ingrain her nature so profoundly into her soul, and it will happen in the room where she thought I had abandoned her.

In the end, I leave everything in the drawer. I remove all of my clothes and make my way to where she sits. After everything I had imagined using on her, I am empty-handed and wearing only a predatory grin.

This will all happen by my own hand and with items in her own room. Her surrender, her pain, and her pleasure will come entirely from me tonight. I won't even restrain her—I'll make her restrain herself. She'll have an active role in giving herself to me.

She doesn't flinch when I step into the room; her shoulders rise and fall steadily. She's relaxed, and her posture holds a confident trust.

A wooden hairbrush sits on her dresser, and I cross the room and lift it, tapping it against the palm of my hand to test its sturdiness.

I know I'm in Emilia's peripheral vision. She can see all of me, and I don't bother to hide my erection. There's no shame here.

Her head is bowed toward the floor, but as I turn around, I notice her pupils shift forward. I move to stand still behind her before leaning over and snaking my arm around to her front.

"Don't slouch." I pinch her nipple—not too hard, but enough to get her attention. I want to warm her up before I really start with her, but this needs to be addressed.

"Ahhh." She whimpers and bows forward even more, and I increase my compression.

"I will let go when you sit up properly," I whisper in her ear. I'm fully aware that I'm not making this easy for her.

Straightening and further jutting out her breasts is counterintuitive for her now, so as she attempts to arch her back I loosen my grip, and she returns to the position I want her in.

"You're my good girl, Emilia." I release my grip and massage her nipple between my fingers.

"Thank you, Joshua."

I return to standing behind her and run my fingers through her hair. She starts to slouch forward but quickly corrects herself. Instead, she drops her head back and closes her eyes.

"Keep your feet together, and spread your knees open. If anything becomes too much for you at any time, just say stop."

She nods and complies, proudly displaying herself for me, and I brush her hair.

A moan escapes her as her face relaxes and her eyes soften. She's mine to mold, and I continue to draw her in deeper with each soft comb through her hair. Her head lulls and moves with my movements, following my lead.

Crouching down behind her, I wrap my own body around hers. Then I trail the bristles over the mounds of her breasts, teasing her nipples as I slide my free hand down over her abdomen, and her thighs involuntarily spread wider.

The start of a sigh escapes her. Then she quickly closes her lips with a low hum, and her hips buck ever so slightly as I push into her folds, my fingers gliding effortlessly along her slick lips. Keeping the pressure low, I continue to draw her along.

"Stand up." She shifts to get up, and I rise with her, keeping my hand and the brush on her. "Go to the end of the bed." She pads the few steps forward. I bend her at the waist, and her hands come down onto her duvet. "Stay."

She steadies herself with deep breaths, and I allow her a few before I start to tap the brush gently over her ass and upper thighs. She adjusts her stance but remains quiet as her backside blushes.

Dropping the brush to the bed, I run my hand over the curve of her ass. She is warm. I pull my fingers out from the heat of her core and place them over her mound, near her clit. With my other hand, I knead her bottom and wait for her to fall into a rhythm with me. It isn't long before she rocks in place, urging for more, and I pull my hand back and land a firm spank on the fleshiest spot on her ass.

At my contact, she arches her back and drives herself forward, inadvertently pushing her clit onto my fingers. She groans at the conflicting sensations. Pushing herself off my hand, she presents her ass to me for another, and my dominance rises to meet her needs.

When I land another, harder hit to her ass, she slides herself forward again, humping herself onto my fingers, then back to wait for another.

Blow after blow lands on her now-reddening ass; each one is subtly harder than the last, but she continues to push back for more, and her breathing has become ragged and harsh.

"Do you want me to stop, Emilia?" My first words stun her out of her head.

"No." Her answer is a plea in itself.

"Then say it. Use that pretty little mouth of yours and beg me not to stop spanking you," I growl into her ear.

"Please, don't stop, Joshua."

"Why?" I land another hit on her cheek, and she drives herself forward in a frenzy.

"I need this. I need to feel this. Please, I need you to punish me."

"Why?" Her hips rock back, and I connect my palm before she's even in place.

She begins to whimper. "I love this. It feels so good. I need this. I need you to do this to me. Please."

"What do you want, Emilia?"

"I want you."

"I already know that, baby. Open your eyes."

She sucks in a deep breath. As she opens her eyes to the sight of me punishing her in her old bedroom, she loses the last bit of her composure.

Swiftly moving my hand into her hair at the base of her skull, I fist the strands and lift her to standing. Then I walk her over to the mirror on her dresser, positioning her face so she can look at herself. Her eyes focus on the sight before her as she braces her palms against the wood.

"Keep your eyes on yourself." I spank her again. This time, she sees the utter delight on her face as she slides her clit into my fingers, and I ask again, "What do you want?" I punctuate each word with a strike of my palm as she watches herself carnally reduce to her base self.

"I want you to fuck me, Joshua. I don't want to run away. I belong to you, and I want you to make me feel it."

Gripping her throat, I hold her head to the mirror and lift her leg onto the dresser. Then I slide my fingers into her folds and along her labia until I find her clit. Before her moan finishes, I'm inside of her in one push, and she gasps, reaching her hands out to brace herself on the dresser.

"Eyes open. Watch yourself become my good girl, Emilia."

She whispers "yes" as I begin to thrust into her, jerking her body forward. I become temporarily fixated on her round tits bouncing, and when I look back to her, her eyes are searching her reflection.

"Who do you belong to?" My skin heats up at the pace I am maintaining.

"I belong to you."

"Who?"

"I belong to you, Joshua."

"Who?" I demand.

"You, Joshua. I'm your good girl. I'm your whore. This is what I need. I need to be yours."

She grips tight around my length as her realization sinks in, and her confession lights me up. I continue my onslaught behind her, and her arms go limp as she moans.

"You are mine. And as long as you choose to be mine, I will never let you go." I plant a smack on her ass as I continue to pound into her, and she surrenders herself to my hold and slides her leg further onto the dresser, opening herself to me fully.

A fire lights in my belly as her hand slowly lifts to her breast and she touches herself, pinching her nipple between her thumb and forefinger.

"Harder," I order. "Pinch yourself harder." Her fingers tighten their grip, and she pulls and twists.

"Other hand. Touch yourself. Make yourself come. Show me how dirty my girl is."

Sliding her hand over her mound, her fingers search for her most sensitive spots, and I watch intently as I fuck into her from behind. Words dribble out of her mouth as her body jerks and rocks along with mine, and I follow her building cries to the edge of our orgasm.

She spasms in my grasp, and I hold her firm as we both fly into the abyss. She screams my name, and it's followed by a deep, releasing growl of my own. I hold myself deep inside of her as she catches her breath.

She lifts her hand, coated in her release, and stretches her fingers out toward the mirror as if reaching out to touch her reflection. She looks lost in her thoughts.

Gently, I pull her back from the mirror and onto her bed, shifting to place myself beside her.

Her body still shows signs of aftershocks as she trembles. I trail my fingers along her torso, careful to avoid any sensitive areas. Her eyes are open, staring quietly at the ceiling.

Before I can ask how she is doing, she breaks the silence.

"I'm breaking our contract, Joshua."

It feels as though my heart has stopped.

"What?"

"Our contract. I want out of it, and I release you from it."

Her words cut into me. For once, I'm at a loss as to what to say. I took a chance. I gave as much of myself as I took from her, and she wants out.

She must notice my concern, because she quickly continues, "Oh, no. You misunderstand me. I'm asking to be yours." She shakes her head softly and tries again. "I'm probably not doing this right."

Propping herself up on one elbow, she turns on her side, lifting her leg over mine. "I don't know how to tell you that I don't want the money from the contract, Joshua. I just want to explore more—together. I don't want you to own me because I sold myself to you. I want you to own me because I give myself to you. I want to rescind my forfeiture notice and continue on with you."

My heart feels lighter than it ever has. "If you're sure. Emilia, all of our times together aren't going to be like this. There will be punishments that you won't like, and there will be sessions where you'll beg me to stop making you come. I want to make sure you know—there are deeper levels."

"What I know is I want to explore all of them with you. Is that good enough for now? Can we end the contract?" She stays still, waiting for my reply.

"We can end it. I'll get the key."

Her neck cranes to look at me better. "Key?"

"To your collar."

"Oh." Her fingers reach up for her collar, the physical source of her strength over the last few days. "I didn't know you had to take it off."

"There's a chip in the collar. To protect both parties. It has a tracking function, and it alerts Ravenous that a contract has ended once it's unlocked," I say, and she lies on her back in thought. "Give me a minute to get the key, and I'll let you go."

It's been five hours since I released Emilia from our contract. No longer owned through a purchase, she cried a little once the collar was freed from her neck. After sitting with her and talking to make sure she was okay, I walked her back to the room attached to my own so she could take the night to consider everything without me hanging over her.

It was a mistake I regretted instantly.

I've been sitting on my bed in the dark ever since.

I'm not going to get any sleep without her here, safe beside me in my bed. I settle on the decision to get up and go get her when a faint knocking on my door stops me.

"Come in."

The door opens, and Emilia treads softly into the room. "Um, I can't sleep." Her voice is filled with a combination of exhaustion and frustration. "Without you."

I pull the covers down and pat the bed beside me, and she hops right in, sliding herself as close to me as possible.

Nestling her head into my chest, she takes a deep breath as I wrap my arms around her and pull her into me.

"Do you think maybe we can get a different collar for me to wear?" Her tone is low.

I smile against her soft strands as kiss her head, but I leave her question without an answer for now.

A couple of minutes pass, and her breathing becomes heavy as she drifts off.

Tomorrow is a new day, the start of our new life. Together.

She doesn't know it yet, but I've already started making the last collar she will ever wear.

RUN WILDE IS NEXT IN RAVENOUS

FROM THE MOMENT HE SAW HER, HE WANTED HER…SO DID SOMEONE ELSE.

NOAH WILDE

Wearing a tray full of spilled coffee isn't how I imagined I'd ever run into someone like Hazel and now, she's all I think about. She has a quick wit and an innocent heart and I'm instantly intrigued.

She thinks I'm playing around but I'm going for keeps and I'm not the only one. Something isn't right and every step we take forward is met with a step back.

Someone is trying to sabotage our connection and I need to get to the bottom of it before I lose her forever.

HAZEL MASTERS

After high school, my life went on without me while I lost almost everything I held dear.

Now, I'm working hard to get back on track when I bump into a mysterious stranger—literally. Our first meeting is a disaster and he ends up leaving me with more questions than answers when he only offers me his first initial—*N*.

I should focus on my classes. I should search for stability. I can't afford to play games with my second shot at having a life. The lessons of my past are screaming at me to walk away.

So why can't I?

** Run Wilde is the second book in the RAVENOUS series. Each book can be read as a standalone.*

ACKNOWLEDGMENTS

I wrote Step Darkly live each week on a reading app called Radish Fiction. Dedicating myself to publicly publishing a new post each week lit the fire I needed to continue on with this story even when I felt I couldn't.

I want to thank Radish and, more importantly, all of the great people who found me through the app and sent messages of encouragement. Your interest kept me going.

I want to thank everyone who helped me bring this book to life:

Cover design: Kirsty Still (Pretty Little Design Co.)
Editor: Caroline Knecht
Photographer: Wander Aguiar
Cover Model: Kaio Queiroz

Also and as always, I want to thank you for reading this story. I write because I love to but knowing you enjoy reading my stories is the icing on the cake.

Until next time... XOXO

ABOUT LUNA

Luna Kayne is a multi-genre romance author located in Canada. She writes dark, explicit, romantic suspense with a hint of humor and angst. Her men are dominant and often stubborn, and her women are usually underestimated. As for tropes and sub-genres, nothing is off the table.

In 2021, she won an IPPY (Independent Publisher Book Awards) award with her novel, *Step Darkly* which earned a bronze medal.

Visit LunaKayne.taplink.ws for
updated links and info.